Passion's Stolen Moment

A piercing air-raid siren sliced through both the sky and the interior of her head. A moment of silence followed, then a tremendous explosion, and flames illuminated the street as he grabbed her and towed her through a doorway. He pushed her flat against a cold, stone wall and covered her with his body.

Frances could hear his breathing and her own, could feel the condensation forming in the space between them as the air from their lungs blended. She reached out blindly and pressed her mouth to his. She felt like some primal beast, freed at last from all convention. "Touch me!" she urged. "Touch me!" Her fingers wound tightly into his hair. The stone wall was suddenly warm; she'd taken flame. She clung to him as he wrapped her in his arms and moved beneath her. "I love you, love you," she chanted softly. "I love you."

CHARLOTTE VALE ALLEN

Matters of the Heart

BERKLEY BOOKS, NEW YORK

This novel contains events and characters that were cut
from the whole cloth of the author's imagination. Any
resemblance that might be perceived to actual people,
living or dead, is strictly coincidental.

MATTERS OF THE HEART

A Berkley Book / published by arrangement with
the author

PRINTING HISTORY
Berkley edition / March 1986

ISBN: 0-425-08659-3

Acknowledgements

I am grateful beyond measure to my beloved Lola, Norman, and Guinea Pig for their willingness to spend long hours sharing their recollections of the Midlands in 1940-41 and of the bombings of Coventry and Birmingham. I am greatly indebted to Evelyn Lawrence for her courage and truthfulness in the course of months of conversation that, in large part, inspired the basis of this novel. I thank the staff of the Darien library for their assistance in the research. No one could be more fortunate than I in having two such exceptionally interested, helpful, and loving associates as Meg Blackstone and Linda McKnight. To Cousin Judy who supplied all the information regarding medications, thank you. And finally, as always, my gratitude to Walt and Kimmie for their tolerance while, once again, I turned the household upside down.

PROLOGUE

Connecticut, 1962

The situation was frustrating and fatiguing, worrisome and distracting. Frances could hear all that Hadleigh was saying and found herself, surprisingly, in agreement with much of what her daughter had to say; but she simply couldn't respond. There was a segment of her brain that wanted very much to engage itself at long last in this dialogue. She'd waited years for a confrontation that didn't seem now as if it would take place after all. Not only could she not respond, she was also exhausted. She just hadn't enough energy to deal with Hadleigh. Which was, really, a great pity.

Another surprise: She enjoyed the sound of Hadleigh's voice, and found it rather like an anchor, grounding her to this time and this place, giving her a clearly defined point to which she could return. The disadvantage, however, lay in the distraction factor. The more closely she listened to what her daughter was saying, the more difficult it became for her to fix on her focus. Impossibly, she wanted to be able to do both: to respond to and deal with, finally, Hadleigh's lifetime accumulation of unanswered questions; she also wanted to think of the past. This duality of purpose was exhausting her further.

Mercifully, a time of silence arrived, and Frances was able to review Hadleigh's words, finding in them undeniable elements of truth and, more significantly, evidence of Hadleigh's emergence as a person in her own right. It had been a long time happening and Frances was in no small way responsible

for the retardation of the process. She'd long since acknowledged her culpability, but hadn't ever made any sort of
declaration to Hadleigh. She'd been unable. After a lifetime
of refusing either to explain or to apologize—at least in any
direct fashion—it appeared she might never have an opportunity to do either. It *was* a pity. Their time together would
have been far more successful, their relationship would have
been infinitely more compatible, had Frances been able to step
out from behind the barricade of her carefully calculated
defenses in order to make herself visible and comprehensible
to her daughter. Certainly over the years she'd found all sorts
of justification for why this had never occurred, but she could
readily see now that no amount of justification could ever
recompense Hadleigh. How could one possibly say to one's
child, "I couldn't, simply couldn't tell you"? It was worse
than no explanation at all.

There were fragmented memories, recollections that made
Frances wince with distaste, particularly in view of that sense
of eminent justification she'd felt for so long in a mode of
behavior that could only be described as off-center, even mad.
Madness, yes, was unquestionably what she'd indulged in
when, faced with the options, she'd discovered herself unable
to pursue safely any other course. And even after the madness
had passed, she'd dragged it out upon occasion—like a well-
worn, comfortable disguise—to shield herself from the need to
deal with situations that rarely evolved as she'd have wished.

A pathetic excuse, really, but she had been mad for a time;
quite mad. Hopelessly, helplessly mad. And the crime lay not
in her madness but rather in her refusal ever afterwards to
make good in tangible fashion some portion of the damage
she'd done—especially to Hadleigh. The truth would, at last,
be made clear to Hadleigh very soon now, but she doubted the
skeletal facts would offer sufficient release. No. What Frances
most wanted was for Hadleigh to experience an infusion of
understanding that would bring with it all the basic elements
of forgiveness. It grieved her now to think that her actions,
whatever the cause, had impaired Hadleigh to such an extent
that she'd never be able to live fully; that she'd blinded
Hadleigh to the truth of Hadleigh's own strengths.

Never complain, never explain! Really! What sort of credo
was that for a life, for a mother? Viewed from this point, it
had been nothing more than a frightful cover for her inability

to confront matters head-on. Yet there were things she couldn't explain, things that defied rational explanation. And she gave up the right to complain when, one dismal afternoon, she decided to resurrect a love that she now knew hadn't ever existed, except within the confines of her own distorted imaginings.

Much of the past was rain-drenched, its boundaries and details smeared beneath a permanent downpour. But she could remember with alarming clarity even the slightest detail of that afternoon when, in the course of a telephone conversation, she'd made the decision to abandon everything for the sake of a self-indulgent fantasy. That telephone conversation had been the embarkation point for her journey into madness. No one and nothing else was responsible. It was extraordinary to recognize now how little it had taken to send her on her way. It was as if all her life up to that moment had been nothing more than a pastel prelude to everything that followed. She'd assembled her emotional baggage, and off she'd gone, allowing her nerve-endings rather than her intelligence to lead her.

Hadleigh was speaking again, and Frances listened. Her listening was a kind of counterpoint; she italicized certain of her daughter's remarks, underscored others. She was saddened, rendered regretful by the words, yet made increasingly optimistic. Hadleigh was gaining her own sources of courage; she was locating her strength, perhaps even drawing it right from Frances's rapidly diminishing supply. Good! she thought. It was a slim gift, but a gift nonetheless. Perhaps this is how it ends, she thought, with my feeding you directly from my cells as I once fed you from my breast. She had loved the infant; she'd even, briefly, loved the process by which she'd provided that inchoate nourishment. They'd been part of one another in a primal, never-to-be-duplicated fashion, at a point in her history when nurturing had been well within Frances's capabilities. It had been a brief period, but one, perhaps, that had seen the formation of an enduring bond between them. The bond did exist; it always had.

Hadleigh was—and how Frances wished she could tell her this!—an infinitely more lovable person than the woman who'd carried her to completion and then heaved her into the daylight. Hadleigh's determination to love and be loved by so impossible a mother was nothing short of remarkable in

Frances's eyes. That Hadleigh could still care for her, that she could go on demonstrating her caring, was almost more than Frances could bear. It would have been infinitely more appropriate if Hadleigh had separated herself once and for all. It was what Frances had always expected, but Hadleigh obviously had her own form of selective vision, and obviously chose to see qualities in her mother Frances had spent a lifetime trying to conceal.

Her thoughts were interrupted by a sudden image of Arthur that brought with it fully her undiminished loneliness for him. His features filled the screen of her mind and she studied them for several long moments, remarking upon the quality of the light that surrounded him. Chagrined at her own actions, she feared she was becoming one of those dreadful aging women who drifted off into vague recollections that rendered them unbearably dewy and nostalgic. Nevertheless, the sight of Arthur chewed at her, making her impatient with the limitations of her body. Without the body, she might have travelled anywhere in time; she might have been young again, but with finer insights and the skill to replay events to a more satisfactory conclusion. She was sliding toward self-pity and refused adamantly to fall into the cloying trap. Yes, all right, she did love, had cared—for Arthur, and for Hadleigh. And, yes, it might be too late to make restitution to Hadleigh, but there was Bonita; still a final answer to be found. Go on! Frances mutely urged. It's coming closer. We'll have all we need to know very soon now. And then, when it's ended at last, perhaps I'll rest for a bit.

Matters Of The Heart

PART ONE

England, 1940

One

Despite the war, or perhaps because of it, there was an element of repressed gaiety, even of anticipation, in the air. Frances couldn't help but be aware of it; it seemed to swell in the darkness like some actively growing organism. She recognized that it was frivolous of her to be on her way to a New Year's Eve party, and probably even indiscreet. But with Arthur sequestered somewhere within the confines of the ministry, and for heaven only knew how long, and the children safely ensconced with her mother in Leamington, she had no reason to feel guilty for accepting Mandy's invitation. In fact, this evening's festivities had been the focal point of her days since Mandy's telephone call.

"Edwin's back from America," Mandy had told her a fortnight earlier. "Isn't that super? The party's to be at his flat. There'll be masses of people. We've been on to everyone we ever knew—rather a combined reunion/new year celebration. What fun!"

"I thought he'd moved permanently to New York," Frances had said, trying not to reveal either her surprise or the sudden excitement she felt at the prospect of seeing Edwin again after so long.

"I expect he thought he had," Mandy had said, "but all too evidently it hasn't worked out that way. Everyone *told* him Elsa was simply too American for it to work, and never mind all her pots of money. That marriage was doomed from the outset. *Anyway*"—Mandy had pounced explosively on the word—"he's still got that marvellous flat. You remember, don't you, Fanny? That extraordinary place off Kensington Church Street?"

"I remember," Frances acknowledged.

"Come any time after nine. And don't be shy about contributing. A bottle of something or other, if you can manage it, or any sort of food. We're really scavenging, I'm afraid."

"I'll see what I can find," Frances had promised, eager to be done with the conversation. She wanted to sit down quietly somewhere and consider the implications of Edwin's divorce and what, if anything, this might mean to her.

Now, making her way up Kensington Church Street—she'd elected to come by bus and underground in order to have additional time to think—with a bottle of gin in her handbag, she told herself she was too old to be thinking and feeling the way she was. Duty stated clearly that she should be with her mother and her children, instead of hurrying over the shiny wet pavement, buoyant with curiosity at the prospect of seeing Edwin Raines-Baker again after close to fifteen years. She felt a surging expectancy so physically overwhelming it caused her flesh to shrink.

What she'd scarcely dared admit to herself until this time was her immense desire to do something that might seem to others to be utterly out of character, but which would, in truth, be totally in keeping with the person she privately knew herself to be. She yearned for a state of total vulnerability wherein all possible sensations, both physical and emotional, would become known to her; she wanted something she believed only Edwin capable of providing: she wished to experience the full impact, a complete knowledge, of passion. Since Mandy's call, she'd been unable to think of anything or anyone else but Edwin. It didn't seem to her odd or unusual that she was readily able to reconstruct his image in her mind. She knew he wouldn't have changed all that much. He'd still be tall, with a tendency toward overweight; he'd still have that wonderfully racy sense of humor and cascading laugh; he'd still dress with extravagant good taste; he'd still have an appetite for rich foods and fine French wines. No, all that would have changed was his status.

She'd never known him as a single man. He'd married Elsa two years before Mandy had introduced Frances to Edwin in the foyer of the Haymarket theatre between acts of a play she could no longer remember. Of course she'd met Elsa then, too, and remembered her now mainly as a woman of startling bluntness given to expressing herself, without thought, in a harshly grating New York accent. Elsa had had execrable taste in clothes, and not even her wealth had been sufficient to keep her from the arena of constant criticism. She was a woman who'd always been determined to be at the forefront of whatever was going on, yet who had absolutely no flair for adapting to the latest fads. The result was that her bobbed hair had accentuated the sharpness of her features rather than softening them, and the formless dresses heavy with hand-done beading gave her an amorphous appearance, as if she'd either finished growing too early or had yet to complete the process. Frances had never been able to make sense of the marriage. Edwin and Elsa hadn't visibly had anything in common except, perhaps, money. They had operated, as far as Frances had been able to see, on completely separate planes, and not at all in tandem. It came as no surprise, really, that they'd finally divorced. What was surprising was that the marriage had lasted as long as it had. Frances gave all the credit for this to Edwin. He was the sort of person who'd have driven himself half mad trying to make things come right—despite the obvious impossibility—before ultimately conceding failure.

Frances had fallen in love with him at their first meeting. Since he was married, she'd felt fairly safe within the perimeters of her secret state of loving. There had been only a few occasions—some long minutes in conversation together at dinner parties, sharing taxi cabs on several evenings—when she'd been so overcome both by her awareness of his inaccessibility and of her own terrible attraction to him that she'd been rendered almost incoherent, and had literally suffered a kind of anguish until she'd found herself once more at a reasonable distance from him. She was quite certain she'd never allowed him to see her accurately; she'd been less sure, less honest in her dealings with him, because she'd been so desperately afraid of finding herself involved in a sordid affair with a married man. Her great fear of operating beyond the bounds of social acceptability had prompted her to marry Arthur the year after Edwin and Elsa had departed to take up life in America.

Her fearful adherence to convention seemed ludicrous to

her now in view of the war that was going on, and the stilted
narrowness of the path of her marriage to Arthur. She had
married him because she wasn't as defiant as she'd have liked
to be, and she'd grown weary of answering the less than
discreet questions about her future that her mother's family
seemed to take a special delight in asking. There were, too, her
own friends who, having married and settled in Surbiton or
Kent or Twickenham, had begun to urge her to follow their
lead, reciting the benefits of married life and motherhood.

It was most ironic that the chief of the instigators, the
unquestioned champion of marriage and life in the suburbs,
had been none other than Mandy Adams, who turned out to
be the first of the group to grow fashionably fatigued and
seek a divorce. It was Mandy who'd moved back into London,
bought herself a trim flat in Portman Square, and returned to
her job as secretary in the firm of barristers and solicitors Edwin's grandfather had founded. Everyone was carefully informed that the job was simply to save her from boredom.
Certainly Mandy had never had a need to work; she had
several inheritances providing her a substantial annual income. "One must," she'd forever declared, "display one's independence." The secretarial job was the flag of her particular
country and she flew it with dauntless bravado. It was at Mandy's insistence that Frances was on her way to the party,
despite her initial misgivings.

"My dear," she had drawled with typical ennui, "it's all
so frightfully do or die, what with this war business and the
wretched rationing. There's not an excuse in the world I'll accept, Fan. Leave the children with your mother—How is your
mother? Is she well? Do give her my love—and put yourself on
the train. I'll collect you at Paddington, if you're feeling frail
and have a need to be met. I'll even put you up at my flat, if
you've suddenly got the collywobbles about staying on your
own. Surely, Arthur wouldn't object to your having a bit of
fun."

"I'm not concerned with what he would or wouldn't
mind," Frances had declared recklessly. "And I'll be fine on
my own in the flat."

She'd stopped by the dusty, airless Chelsea flat to deposit
her overnight case in the bedroom. It was clear Arthur hadn't
been home in weeks. Neither had the char been round. The
only evidence of Arthur's having been there was an unwashed

teacup perched on the side of the kitchen sink, and one silvery-blond strand of hair coiled into the identation on his pillow. He'd napped on top of the bedclothes; the impression of his body's weight still remained. Impatiently, she'd tidied the bed before unpacking her bag.

In a shockingly low-cut black jersey dress with heavily padded shoulders, her hair especially golden from recent lemon rinses and framing her face in meticulously sculpted rolls, Mandy greeted Frances at the door, deftly plucked the bottle of gin from her hand, left a kiss hovering in the air near Frances's left cheek, then pushed out of sight back into the crowd, leaving Frances on her own in the foyer.

Frances didn't mind. She took off her coat, gratified to see that the flat was almost precisely as she'd remembered it. The main room—one certainly couldn't call an expanse perhaps forty feet wide by sixty feet long a lounge—was more than half filled with people, and the noise level was high. She stood with her coat folded over her arm, taking in the details of the place: the immense windows at the far end—covered by heavy blackout curtains—that started some five feet above the floor and rose to the ceiling fifteen feet above; the three-foot-deep "sill" of the window, beneath which were storage cabinets; the tiny kitchen, like a child's building block, to the left of the room; and the bathroom/lavatory on the right. At the entry, where Frances stood, the space had been divided to create a small foyer and, to the right as one entered, a good-sized bedroom whose windows gave onto the street.

Edwin's father had been posted for some time in India, and the furnishings of this flat were from that bachelor era. A heavy wood screen of six large, carved panels was positioned to hide the kitchen. Between the screen and the main portion of the room stood a massive refectory table and eight straight-backed, hand-carved chairs. Here and there were chests of varying sizes with elaborately carved tops which depicted acts of a decidedly sexual nature. A number of brass pots and trays were placed on the mantel-piece and window sill, and three outsized, brilliantly colored Indian carpets were arranged on the floor to minimize the vastness of the space by creating oasis-like areas—by the refectory table, by the fireplace, and to one side of the front door where there was a comfortable arrangement of large floor pillows and low-slung leather chairs.

In younger days, when she'd come here, Frances had felt slightly disreputable, as if this were not a place where someone actually lived, but rather a theatrical stage-setting contrived initially by Edwin's father in order to enhance his image and, then, passed down to his son in order to perpetuate some rather nonsensical male legacy having to do with masculinity and sexual license. The impression she'd always had was that neither Edwin nor his father had thought it enough to be a successful barrister. That would have been too dreary for words, especially after those thrilling years spent in "the colonies." Edwin, almost inadvertently, managed to give the impression that he wanted people to realize that, despite the prosaic aspects of his daytime life, he was someone whose true tastes—in matters overtly sexual and faintly bizarre—had in no way diminished, either with marriage or with time; he was someone of character and unpredictability; he could ride on the crest of an impulse as well as any art student or theatre type.

Frances had believed then and still did that depictions of bared breasts and erotic acts had no place on display in one's lounge. Nonetheless, as she'd done since her first visit here with Mandy eighteen years before, she assumed a tolerant attitude. She was, after all, forty years old; she was married and had twice given birth. In the overall scheme of things it hardly had significance that a forty-two-year-old man still had a fondness for the trappings of his youth. If anything, she found it touching to note how completely unchanged were the furnishings of the flat. It was as if an entire era had somehow been preserved here, and she thought, whimsically, that if she listened very closely, she might even hear an echo of that rowdy American prohibition-era jazz Elsa used to play day and night on her Gramophone.

Coats were piled haphazardly on the bed. Frances added hers, paused to check her image in the dressing table mirror—the bedroom furniture was very ordinary, almost disappointingly so—then moved, smiling, out into the main room. Her reunion with Edwin was going to be momentous, she knew. Her sense of this had been so strong that in order to calm herself, she'd spent a number of hours during the previous week committing her thoughts about him to paper. She planned she would one day present these letter-type documents to him. She had, throughout the time writing, pictured him in the act of reading her words. The image had stirred her to frame her thoughts most precisely in order that he might appreciate not only her sentiments but her skill with language. She was, belatedly, going to reveal herself completely, and he would be deeply moved and more than a little impressed. He would see how very well suited they were to one another.

It had occurred to her, while in the midst of writing these letters, that she was allowing her imagination to run unchecked. Edwin might be involved with some new woman; he might be about to remarry; he might be entirely altered, and not someone she'd find in the least attractive. Not so, she'd argued. Edwin would be even more Edwin. She had long suspected that he was someone who would become more and more himself until he'd succeeded in creating a prototype. She knew she was not mistaken in her impression of him as a man determined to create himself entirely in his own image. But on the offchance that her intuition might have been impaired in any way—by marriage, by child-bearing, by the stresses of the war—she'd placed a telephone call to him at his office. He'd come on the line at once, exclaiming, "Frances! This is a splendid surprise! How are you? Are you in town? If you're in town, I insist we dine together straightaway!"

She'd laughed, greatly reassured by his enthusiasm. "Mandy rang me about the party and I simply wanted to say hello and welcome you home from the land of the twang."

"My timing rather leaves something to be desired," he laughed. "Twang, indeed! When will I see you? And where are you?"

She reasoned that he couldn't possibly display so keen an interest in her were he involved with another woman. This was such a comforting piece of logic that she was able to relax, answering, "I plan to be at the party. It's just that I was so delighted to hear you'd come back, I thought I'd tell you so directly."

"That's my Fan!" he laughed happily. "Well, if I'm not to see you before then, I want your promise right now that you'll dine with me after the party."

"I'd adore it!" she'd told him.

"Perfect!"

They'd talked another minute or two and then rung off.

Heartened, she'd commenced the second of the "letters" that now reposed, discreetly hidden beneath a box of unopened stationery, in her desk. Putting her thoughts and feelings on paper seemed to her almost, and perhaps more, significant an act than delivering a child out of her body. It was exquisitely painful, undeniably real, and alarmingly final. One could no more wish the child into non-existence than one could will away the caring one felt for certain people. At moments she felt terrifyingly helpless in the face of her love for a man other than her husband.

The reality of the reunion was bound to be a letdown. She'd over-rehearsed it in her mind. She told herself it simply wasn't possible for anything or anyone to live up to the floridly embellished dreams she'd concocted.

Edwin did appear very pleased to see her and placed a chaste little kiss on her lips. It had been absurd of her to expect him to draw her into a fevered embrace, especially when, as they began to talk, she realized that as far as Edwin was concerned she was safely married to Arthur. How could she have forgotten to apprise him of the truth? No matter. It would only take a moment or two to make it clear to Edwin that she was neither safe nor married in any true sense of the word.

"Let's find somewhere to sit," he suggested, his hand on her arm propelling her toward the window. They sat together on the deep sill, taking a moment to look closely at each other.

"You haven't changed in the least," she lied, finding him more corpulent and somehow, oddly, less direct than she'd recalled. His features were smaller, his mouth more cautious in the shaping of words than she'd remembered. The prudence he exercised in speaking belied the seeming spontaneity of what he actually said. How strange, she thought, to be seeing all this!

He laughed and looked down at himself, placing one large hand over his midriff. "I'm two stone heavier." He shook his head. "Lack of exercise, among other things. You now, Fan, look exactly as you did, precisely as I remember you."

His complimentary tone, and his admitting to memories of her seemed confirmation of her intuitive powers. There *was* something between them. All it required, on both their parts, was acknowledgement.

"Bring me up to date," she said eagerly. "I want to hear all about America, and why you've come home, and what you plan. Everything."

"We need drinks. Is it still gin?"

He really did remember her, even to her preference in drinks.

"Gin would go down beautifully," she said. "A light anaesthetic mildly diluted with bitters."

With a laugh, he moved off toward the makeshift bar set up at one end of the refectory table. While he was gone, she opened her bag, found a cigarette and got it lit, somewhat surprised by the faint tremor in her hands. She inhaled the smoke gratefully. It was something she didn't dare do within her mother's viewing. Whatever pleasure she derived from an occasional cigarette simply wasn't worth the lecture the sight of one would inspire her mother to give. They were filthy things, props for film actresses, tarts; they certainly weren't fit to be found in the hands of a self-respecting matron, a mother of two, wife of a well-placed government employee.

"Mandy tells me you've left town for the duration," Edwin said, giving her her drink.

"Not entirely." She took a welcome swallow, then explained. "I come in at least once a week to collect the post and to make sure nothing's gone amiss in the flat. It's really for the children . . . I'd be more than happy to stay and take my chances, but one can't take risks with the children . . ." She lifted her shoulders to express her powerlessness as well as her disdain for the possible dangers of London. "As for Arthur, we scarcely see him now. It's to be expected, I suppose, in view of his position in the ministry." Her smile was deprecating, intended to indicate her boredom both with Arthur and his not-to-be-discussed work.

"I suppose," Edwin agreed, not sure how to interpret her gestures and facial expressions. Were the messages mixed, or was he well on the way to being squiffy?

"Enough of that." She tossed her head impatiently. "I want to hear all about you, Edwin. Are you back for good now?" Perhaps he'd be leaving again in the near future. She'd be willing to go with him, anywhere.

"That's been taken out of my hands for the present," he answered before taking a swallow of scotch. He found it truly amazing how little she'd altered with time. It was also surprising and highly flattering to rediscover her intensity and to be on the receiving end of it. He'd forgotten this aspect of her, and wondered how he could have failed to recall so integral an aspect of her nature. Frances's appeal had always been compounded and heightened by her intensity, if she cared to make one the subject of her attention. Conversely, she was capable of making one wretchedly uncomfortable if she chose to show one her dislike. Her wit under those circumstances, he reminded himself, could be lethal.

From an entirely superficial viewpoint, she was an undeniably handsome woman. Handsome, he mentally chided himself, wasn't quite the right choice of words. She wasn't beautiful in any classic sense, although her lifelong thinness—no doubt a direct result of that almost simmering intensity—gave her clothes a highly stylish look so that she invariably appeared elegant. She had interesting cool gray eyes, slightly slanted; arching cheekbones; and fine, pale skin. Tonight she was wearing a deep blue velvet frock, very simply cut, with long sleeves and a bit of a flare to the skirt. He glanced approvingly at her carefully crossed knees and slim calves.

"You do look wonderfully well, Fan," he gave voice to his approval.

"And you," she replied, more truthfully now. He was growing increasingly familiar to her, thereby validating her thoughts of their potential as a couple. As she watched his mouth shaping additional, careful words, it occurred to her, with a near-violent inner shiver, that she wanted to be alone and naked with this man. It had been one thing to daydream, using recollections and intuition; it was something else altogether to be side by side with the living embodiment of all her expectations, and realize the extent of her longings. "Sorry," she said. "I missed what you were saying. The lowing cattle" —she cast her hand in the direction of the other guests—"set up rather a din."

He leaned slightly closer to repeat himself and she had to concentrate on the sounds in order not to succumb to the temptation to touch with her open hand the appealing curve of his boyishly round cheek.

"I was asking how is Arthur."

Hadn't they already dispensed with Arthur as a topic of conversation? Possibly she'd only done it in her own thoughts. "He's been all but invisible for months, since the start of it all, really." She spoke quickly, as if the speed of her words would hasten the end of Arthur's impedimentary status as her husband. "I've no idea when he'll next be allowed home."

"I expect you and the children must miss him," Edwin said politely.

"Actually," she answered, slowing her speech, "I don't. The children do, of course. He's a wonderful father." For the first time, she experienced a pang of guilt at her disloyalty. In truth, Arthur was not only a fair and demonstrably loving father, he'd always been a kind and tolerant husband. The problem lay in her inability to love him passionately. "I'm afraid," she went on, "I don't miss him a bit."

Edwin's eyebrows lifted. "How wicked of you, Fanny!" He smiled admiringly, as if wickedness, in all its degrees, was a quality he especially deemed valuable in a woman.

"I suppose it is," she agreed. "I didn't used to be wicked, did I?"

"I don't think so. But then we've all changed. It's the times."

"No. I do believe I have grown wicked. It hasn't anything to do with the war." Again he smiled, and she felt his approval almost as a caress. "And what of you? What have you become, Edwin?"

His smile dimmed. "Oh," he sighed. "I've become middle-aged, two stone heavier, and frightfully weary, I'm afraid."

"You're none of those things," she contradicted. "It must be peculiar, though, living on your own again after so long with the uncontested queen of the Prohibition era."

He didn't laugh as she'd hoped, but seriously assured her, "It's delightful, actually. It became very sticky toward the end. Elsa and I did battle endlessly. It was most unpleasant, even rather sordid."

"How long has it been since the divorce?"

"Almost two years now. It took quite some time to sort things through. You know, who had the right to what, that sort of thing. In the end, I said to hell with it and let her take whatever she wished. Except, of course, for this flat. She had the effrontery to try to claim it, if you can imagine. Put paid to that in short order, I can promise you."

"You don't mean it!" Frances was appalled. "She wanted this place?"

"Bloody unbelievable, isn't it?" He was patently pleased to find her in agreement with him.

"It is a bit. I am sorry you've had such a frightful time of it," she sympathized, her hand on his arm. "I would say, though, that the timing couldn't be more perfect. I always could cheer you up, and I'll do it again."

"What a good sort you are!" Once again his features held surprise. "I was always very fond of you, Fan."

"And I you," she responded, confident now of the reunion's outcome. The two of them would make love, if not tonight, then in the very near future. Edwin would come to recognize the power she had to make positive changes in both their lives, and he'd fall in love with her—if he hadn't already done. The details were unimportant; they'd take care of themselves. She'd made the decision to allow this to happen, and she hadn't been mistaken. Now she'd assist him as Edwin caught up to her thinking.

Never had she felt anything remotely comparable to her present confidence. Once she made known her feelings, this man would love her. Her sense of precognition was extraordinarily potent. Slipping her arm through his, she inched closer to him, gazing upward through her lashes to say, "I realized this past fortnight that I know quite a good deal about you, Edwin."

"Oh?"

"Not historical fact," she reassured him, certain he had any number of fascinating skeletons hidden away in locked closets. She laughed softly and withdrew her arm from his to light another cigarette. "What I mean to say is I realized that I know you, know the sort of person you are, the things you like and dislike. Does the idea of that disturb you?"

"You have my complete attention." He struck her now as a rather large-sized, mischievous boy, eager to hear and, possibly, challenge her claims to knowledge. "I'm the first to admit the joy of being the primary and sole topic of any conversation."

She found this remark vain, and would have bridled at it at another time, but she was too eager to proceed to pay overmuch attention just then.

"But I'm keeping you from your guests," she said suddenly, looking around, hoping he'd say he preferred to remain sequestered with her.

"Not at all," he said gratifyingly. "We'll get to everything in time." He drank more of his scotch, then looked at her mouth. She did have a lovely mouth. He didn't think he'd ever noticed before, but now that he studied her, she seemed far more aggressively female than he'd recalled. Not her actions or words, but her sheer physical presence—that almost palpable intensity—was most compelling. He could picture himself bending her to his need; heady images of a wildly compliant Frances, nakedly open. He was going to have to proceed with cautious discretion. Frances was the sort of woman who might be dangerous simply because of her capacity for purposeful single-mindedness. Since he no longer knew clearly what he wanted, either immediately or for the future, he would have to take care not to allow either his own physical interest or her evident willingness to direct events. Still, he reasoned, there was no need to go overboard. It was a new year, and it was splendid to be home again, here with old friends at the outset of a new decade, with the second half of his life yet to be lived.

He glanced appreciatively at the neckline of her frock, rather stirred by the gentle swell of her breasts. He drank more of his scotch, at the same time redirecting his eyes to the crowd.

At his side, Frances commented, "You could, you know, part them like the Red Sea."

He laughed loudly, as ever tickled by her irreverence.

Two

To Frances it seemed as if the party took place without them. She was so caught up in revealing to Edwin all she believed she knew about him—his overt preferences, what disappointed or elated him, which general events had impressed and shaped him to his present form—and he was so intrigued by her low voice and her attitude of unshakable conviction as she delivered a number of assessments of his character that were fairly frightening in their accuracy, that neither of them was aware of the passage of time until the others erupted into excited noisy cheers.

"It's the new year," she said.

"So it is." He confirmed this by a glance at his pocket watch, then returned his eyes to her. She really did have a beautiful mouth, the thought, taking advantage of this sanctioned opportunity to kiss her. He'd intended merely to touch mouths, but she responded with such abandon that he momentarily forgot everything but the novelty of having a woman so plainly desirous of his attentions offer herself so wholeheartedly. When they separated at last, he studied her for several long moments, working to amend his previous concept of her. His hand had come to rest in the invitingly small curve of her waist and he felt beneath his palm the tremulous substance of her. He'd always been intrigued by the fragility of women, the apparent insubstantiality of their construction versus the actuality of their strength. The contradictory aspects of women had become so perplexing to him that he'd

16

recently promised himself never again to become involved in any committed fashion with one. It might be lonelier and less interesting to live on one's own, but it was infinitely less traumatic and frustrating; infinitely less expensive emotionally and in every other way. He'd learned, during the final years of his marriage to Elsa, that the reward for loyalty was anger. Things could not be compelled to come right merely because one was prepared to make an extra effort and to put in additional time. It required the combined efforts of both parties, and while he'd known that the two of them had had nothing left to build on, still he'd had to make the effort to preserve the marriage. It had all had to do with his sense of honor, and his instincts toward integrity. The price he'd paid had been in the area of trust. He believed Elsa had abused it time and again. Now, he refused to allow himself to trust any woman.

Since the divorce, women had made themselves available to him in staggering numbers. He wouldn't have thought he was sufficiently appealing to attract so many women, or that there was such a shortage of men that, by attrition, he'd become endowed with appeal. At the start, fresh from the wars with Elsa, he'd been wildly flattered to be the subject of so much attention. He discovered, though, in very short order, that there were hooks hidden in nearly all the invitations, especially those sexual ones that seemed so spontaneously offered.

He told himself he might, at some far-off future date, feel sufficiently restored to risk a second marriage, or some permanent sort of arrangement, but for the present he wanted to continue to enjoy his relatively new freedom. He still felt as if he'd been violently flayed by the divorce, and that strips of his flesh hadn't properly healed. He'd come to believe, finally, that women were unknowable and treacherous, that they operated with only self-gratification in mind, and that even the most seemingly affable females who declared themselves intent only upon friendship all harbored secret goals centering on possession. He wanted to enjoy life, to do only those things that offered pleasure and diversion; he wanted no part of any situation that would place demands of any kind upon him.

Yet here was Frances, whom he'd known forever it seemed, displaying a knowledge of his present instincts and his private views that was startlingly accurate. While it was unquestionably comforting not to have to explain himself, to be so readily understood, he was nevertheless unsure what it all meant, or how he was supposed to react.

He'd always found her most likeable, very fine-looking; and looks were of considerable importance to him. Her company had never been tiresome; she had that clever way with words and, in a fashion, seemed refreshingly unaware of herself, especially when compared to someone, say, like good old Mandy who, if anything, was so archly aware of everything about herself that, in the end, her knowingness became endearing. Mandy was his only long-standing female friend. Fan wasn't in the least like her. If the truth were to be known, he was forced to admit he had little, if any, real idea what Fan was all about. He knew only that he was surprised by her, and decidedly intrigued.

"You have grown wicked, Fan," he commented with a smile, feeling the situation threatening to slide beyond his control. He was terribly attracted to her, but he no longer had any appreciable faith in his sexual instincts. Desiring a woman was too often misinterpreted to mean more. Yet right at this moment, he did desire this woman and, allowing his impulse to rule him, he succumbed to his instinct to kiss her once more. Parting reluctantly from the potent softness of her mouth, he asked, "Have you broken with Arthur?"

"Not actually," she answered after a moment, dragging her attention away from the churning action of her interior. "I expect I'm simply looking for an excuse, something to force the issue."

"I don't think I follow," he lied, greatly alarmed by the notion that she was seeking someone to play correspondent in her divorce.

"It's of no consequence," she said, sensing his alarm, and puzzled by it. "You've had a dreadful time, haven't you?" she commiserated. "I *am* sorry." She turned to look at the others who'd linked arms and were singing "Auld Lang Syne." She reached to take hold of Edwin's hand as something very like grief squeezed her throat. She was close to weeping, and couldn't allow herself to give in to tears, but her grief was very real. It had to do with years of disappointment, and the optimism with which she'd come to this reunion; it had to do with her fear that nothing would ever materialize in quite the fashion she hoped. She felt she'd never exercised any real measure of control over her own life; it had fallen into the unheeding hands of others, and now she might not be able to reclaim it. Here she was, inches away from someone she wanted desperately, someone who she knew shared many of her sentiments, and still she feared her ability to make him see how well-suited to one another they were. She yearned for him to place a claim on her, to declare her the woman he should, by rights, have married; she wanted him to pierce her flesh with his own and bring her the fulfillment she knew he could provide. Just then, she despised Arthur for keeping her hovering on the verge of important physical knowledge for fourteen years. She'd come to loathe those moments when he gave out the clues to his desire, those moments when he expected her to acquiesce in wifely duty to a pastime that contained nothing for her but immense irritation. She'd long-since guessed that the opposite side of that irritation was a sublime pleasure, and she wanted to experience it with Edwin. She wanted it so excessively that she didn't know what she'd do if he failed to desire her.

"Would you like me to stay?" she asked, striving for a casual tone.

"Stay?" He smiled pleasantly, confused.

"After the others have gone."

"Oh!" He thought at first she meant to help him with the clearing up, but then he understood she was offering to stop the night with him. Giving her hand a squeeze, and still smiling, he said, "I'd adore you to stay. But I know myself, and it wouldn't be a good idea at the moment. It simply wouldn't work just now. Aside from that, I think it's going to get to be a very late do." He was taking pains to be gracious. After all, he was fond of her and had no desire to be hurtful. He also wanted her and, from moment to moment, was too readily able to visualize himself engaging in violent intercourse with her. When it was done, she'd be there with vansful of expectations he had no wish to know about. It just couldn't be done.

"I haven't any other plans," she said complaisantly. "I'm not expected home until tomorrow evening."

"Let's pick a day and time this very moment for when next we'll meet." He put all the energy and enthusiasm he could muster into this invitation, hoping she'd be reasonable. He despaired of scenes, and of women who created them.

He didn't want her to stay. Her letdown was so instantly acute she felt physically ill. Clearly he wanted her. It wasn't possible to confuse the urgency of those kisses. Perhaps she'd failed to make herself understood. She shifted forward to kiss him again, then sat back expectantly.

"It truly isn't the right time, Fan," he said with a kind of gentle despair. "It would be a disservice to both of us."

"I do see," she said falsely, swallowing back some of the pain. He wasn't rejecting her out of hand, and she knew too well the vagaries and significance of timing. She had no choice but to accept his rationale. And he was, after all, keeping the door open. "Will you ring me?" she asked. "We'll set a date."

"Of course I will," he promised. "Tomorrow, first thing."

"I'll write down both numbers, the flat and my mother's number in Leamington."

She did this quickly, on a piece of paper she found in her bag. As she wrote, she silently beseeched him, Please don't break my heart; please don't do that. She gave him the paper and, in return, he found for her one of his calling cards, saying, "Make a note of the number here, why don't you. It's quite impossible to talk at the office."

It was all highly symbolic: They were exchanging numbers and promises; they were laying the foundation for a future together. She tucked his card into her bag and was feeling quite secure when, moments later, he excused himself to wish his other friends a happy new year. Watching him move through the crowd, she enjoyed the satisfaction of knowing they'd be together very soon. She'd go with him to that bed upon which several dozen coats now reposed, and they would make a physical commitment. The prospect made her very happy. He was going to love her and she, in turn, would restore his faith and trust. She would demonstrate love beyond his imaginings, and for the rest of his life he would wonder aloud at how he'd ever managed to survive as long as he had without her. She would display for him the bounties of love, and her reward would be an intimate knowledge of what lay just beyond her present sexual horizon. She'd be allowed to view an entire panorama of which, thus far, she'd been given only glimpses. She would be pushed beyond herself into a realm of exorbitant stimulation. It was Arthur's failure to recognize her need for a little more time, a little more attention, that had filled her slowly, year after year, with contempt for him. Despite his career successes, and his admitted talent as a father; despite his unfailing charm and evenness of mood;

despite his continuing applause of even Frances's most minor accomplishments, he'd never acknowledged her capacity for passion. He was, she believed, one of those men who saw sexuality in a woman as unseemly, and in the early stages of their marriage he'd appeared to be discomfited by her ardour, hastily concluding their congress before withdrawing from the arena of their lovemaking. Her interest in his anatomy, and her own, had shocked him.

She had despaired of her naivete and ignorance, wishing she'd known more so that she might more explicitly have stated her case. Then they might have managed to put down some very real foundation for their marriage, because she did, after all, find him appealing in any number of ways. As it was, she'd been shamed out of her curiosity and into her night-dress. Her ongoing state of ignorance was about to come to an end, she thought now, tracking Edwin's progress through the room. The man she'd always loved had come home from America, and they were going to be together. Perhaps he didn't cut as fine a figure as Arthur did, but she wanted him. It was even possible he'd change his mind and invite her to stay the night after all, especially in view of the frequency with which their eyes met over the heads of the others as the evening progressed.

He'd said he'd ring first thing, and she fully expected to speak with him before she left for the station. As she bathed and dressed, she listened for the sound of the telephone; she paused at the door before leaving the flat to gaze at the silent instrument. Undoubtedly the party had gone on—as he'd predicted—into the very early hours of the morning, and he was sleeping late.

She stared through the train window at the rain flooding the countryside, tired but buoyed by the certain knowledge that Edwin would very shortly be contacting her to arrange their next meeting.

"Was it a smashing party?" Ben asked at tea as he reached for the margarine and began attempting to spread it on his bread.

"Let me do that for you," Frances offered indulgently, taking his plate. "It was very nice," she told him. "It didn't at all feel as if there's a war on. Everyone was in such high spirits."

"Were there lots of super things to eat?" Hadleigh wanted

to know. Since the outbreak of war, her primary interest in life had become food. It annoyed Frances and she'd been growing increasingly short-tempered with her daughter. To compensate for her irritation, she often gave drawn-out, overblown answers to Hadleigh's questions, as if words might defeat some nebulous, but negative quality flourishing in the ten-year-old and prevent it from arriving at full flower. There really was something about the girl that drove Frances half mad. She was unable to define specifically the quality; she only knew it was infuriating, and her instinct suggested that barrages of words might form the only suitable defense against it. The results were negligible. Hadleigh was inquisitive, but utterly obedient, a compulsive eater and asker of questions.

"Actually," Frances went on, "it was as if everyone brought something that'd been in the back of the pantry for ages." She smiled over at her mother. "You know the sort of thing I mean: like that bottle of *marrons glacés* that's been on the shelf for as long as I can remember."

Hadleigh, having also noted the abandoned jar, had, only days earlier, smuggled the sickly sweet confection to the bottom of the garden where, with a spoon, she'd quickly gobbled the contents. She now ducked her head and paid close attention to applying fish paste to her bread.

"Oh dear," Deirdre sympathized. "It must have been most peculiar."

"It was a bit. Ben, do leave a bit of jam for the rest of us. We may not be able to get more. It really wouldn't do to finish the lot in one sitting."

Chastised, Ben proceeded to scrape some of the thick layer of strawberry preserves from his bread back into the glass bowl on the table, mumbling an apology under his breath.

"You're such a greedy little pig!" Hadleigh accused, then looked for approval first at her mother and then, failing to receive it, at her grandmother who smiled in her forgiving way and said, "He's just six, dear. Go easy on him. You were every bit as greedy at six."

"Was I, Nana?"

"Every bit."

Hadleigh laughed happily, then reached to tug at Ben's jumper, saying, "I didn't mean it really."

" 'S all right," Ben said.

"That's right," Deirdre approved. "We mustn't squabble."

Frances drank two cups of tea, one after the other, and did her best to ignore her mother and her children. She wanted to think about Edwin, and summoned up the pressure of his mouth on hers, the greedy probing of his tongue. At once she felt again the delicious slippery eel of pleasure swimming along her veins. He'd ring her this evening, and they'd plan the coming weekend in London.

"You seem rather distracted, Frances," her mother observed.

"I'm just tired. It was a very late night, then I hurried to catch the train."

In truth, she'd been unable to sleep. It had been a long, exhausting day, capped by the party. Yet as soon as she'd lowered her head to the pillow, she'd started drafting reveries about herself and Edwin. In the course of a few nighttime hours she was able to map out the better part of their future life together: She'd manufactured new decor for the West Kensington flat; she'd taken them off on trips abroad, and on leisurely peace-time tours of the inland waterways; she'd fed them sumptuous meals she'd painstakingly prepared after hours of scrutinizing cookery books; she'd slept and awakened a thousand times, first having danced in manic, unashamed frenzy beneath his cleverly resourceful thinned-down body. She didn't in the least feel guilty for her failure to include her actual family anywhere in these dreams. After all, she hadn't taken complete leave of her senses. She knew she was spinning daydreams out of air, and that she had very real responsibilities. But she'd been unable to sleep, and at last she'd turned on the bedside lamp and smoked a cigarette, wishing that Edwin would give in to a whim and ring her.

He didn't. The cigarette gave her a sore throat; and she finally abandoned the idea of sleep. She remade the bed, tidied the flat, bathed, dressed, collected the post, and rode the underground to Paddington where she'd had a cup of powerful tea in the station buffet while waiting for the train.

At this moment she wanted the day to be over so that she might sleep deeply and awaken refreshed for Edwin. She put off going to bed for as long as possible, first overseeing the children's preparations for bed, and listening less than attentively to their prayers. Then she sat with her mother in the lounge for a time, hearing the nine o'clock news on the BBC

Home Service, absorbing without interest information on the rationing of meat, bacon, cheese, fats, sugar, and preserves; the details about the enrichment of bread and margarine by the chemical addition of certain vitamins and minerals; comments on the increased consumption of milk, potatoes, cheese, and green vegetables. It sounded as if the war had solely to do with food, and little else. Throughout, she watched her mother, who listened closely, her knitting forgotten in her lap, as if these messages were being directed specifically to her.

"What do you make of all that?" Frances asked her, curious.

"We'll have to go carefully, Fan," Deirdre replied with utmost seriousness. "If we're not very careful, we might find ourselves without food. They'll try to starve us into defeat. We are an island, after all."

Frances stared at this woman, unable to make the connection between these sensible comments and the lifelong frivolity of the woman who'd made them. Deirdre Chapman's parties were still spoken of in awed tones, as were her ballgowns and lavish buffets. It had been long ago, of course, before the Depression; before the Chapmans' liquid assets had all but evaporated, leaving them in greatly reduced circumstances. After her husband's death of a heart attack in 1934, Deirdre had sold off the small house in Mayfair, along with most of the furnishings, and had returned to Leamington where she'd lived as a girl, to buy the present house on Kenilworth Road. Exercising her previously unsuspected financial acumen, she'd arranged to reinvest the funds left to her in conservative, income-producing stocks. She'd resumed old friendships and she and her friends had, until the outbreak of war, met regularly to regale each other with half-forgotten tales of their daring youthful exploits. They laughed, flushing, over glasses of noxiously sweet sherry, at being reminded of the time naughty Dee had been presented at court minus one shoe, or the occasion when, having had just a bit too much champagne, she'd awakened to find herself on the boat-train to Calais with her best friend's husband. Luckily, no serious improprieties had taken place, but all this and more comprised table-talk over weekly bridge games.

"When did you become so involved, Mother?" Frances asked.

It was Deirdre's turn to stare. "Good God! Perhaps you'd

best go to bed. You're so fatigued you're not thinking clearly.''

"No, I am thinking quite clearly," Frances persisted. "Tell me."

"Frances," said her mother patiently, "this country is at war. Our food is being rationed. The Germans are sinking our ships and bombing our cities. We're *all* involved, whether or not we wish to be. I do think you should go to bed, dear. Obviously your night in the city's tired you out thoroughly. You never have had very much stamina."

Deirdre had been fond, throughout Frances's entire life, of making sad little statements having to do with Frances's short stock of energy. For years, Frances had energetically argued in her own defense and had, in her early twenties, stayed up for days and nights on end to prove her stamina was equal to anyone's. She'd given up taking exception some five years earlier when it had occurred to her that her mother was never going to surrender her right to sing this particular theme. This evening, however, Frances briefly forgot her former resolve and, bridling, said, "I have as much as I need." Then, reconsidering, she relented. "Perhaps you're right. I am terribly tired."

"A good night's sleep will do you a world of good." Deirdre picked up her knitting, her eyes still on Frances. Over the last few months Frances had been undergoing subtle changes that revealed themselves in her moods and temperament. It was Deirdre's belief that Frances might very well be experiencing some sort of premature menopause, a belief that was confirmed from time to time when Frances seemed to be lit by interior fires, her face flushed and glowing as if from the heat.

Lowering her eyes at last, she got on with her knitting. She, along with half the civilian population—or so it seemed—had taken to their needles to knit blankets, sweaters, and socks which the Red Cross received most gratefully. Deirdre knitted squares. When she'd done enough of them, she sewed them together to make blankets. Since the declaration of war, she'd completed three of these misshapen, quite hideous constructions.

"You go along now, Frances," she said, her needles clicking. "I'll see you in the morning."

Frances bade her goodnight, and went off upstairs.

For a second night, she was unable to sleep. She lay on her

half of the bed—habit and an ingrained reluctance to collide in
sleep with Arthur keeping her squarely within her self-allotted
territory—turning from one side to the other, flirting with the
near edge of sleep but unable to slip beneath it. She badly
wanted and needed the tonic of nocturnal dreams to restore
her energy and her equilibrium, but it was no good. She simply
couldn't unwind. First she was overheated, then she shivered
with the cold. She threw off the bedclothes, then dragged them
back over herself. Finally, she switched on the bedside light,
got up, and found Edwin's card in her bag. Edgy with boldness, she gave the operator his London number. He answered
almost at once and she was so relieved she could scarcely
speak.

"It's Frances, Edwin."

"Oh, dear," he said guiltily. "I was to ring you, wasn't I?
I'm afraid it's been an impossible day, on top of which it
seems I've misplaced your number. I'm so sorry, Fanny. Did
you get home without mishap? You weren't driving, I hope.
It's positively nightmarish, what with these absurd air raid
precautions."

"They are absurd, aren't they?" she agreed. "It's all I can
do not to howl when I see everyone here trotting about with
little cardboard boxes, fixed with bits of string, slung over
their shoulders; going everywhere with their gas masks. But
isn't it extraordinary!" she hurried on. "I had the feeling you
might have mislaid that slip of paper. I thought that when
I gave it to you. That's why I'm ringing now, to say what a
lovely party it was, and how very happy I am you've come
home. Did it go on and on forever? Are you simply done in?"

"I am rather," he laughed. His laughter seemed to her an
incredibly intimate sound. How could they be close enough to
speak to one another in lowered tones, yet be unable actually
to touch? "The last of the lot went reeling out of here at eight
this morning. It did go on rather too long, but it was a smashing do, wasn't it? And you had a good time, you say?"

"A lovely time," she confirmed, comforted and encouraged
by the easy manner in which they were conversing. "I simply
can't tell you how wonderful it is to be back in touch again,
after all these years."

Listening, he recalled her mouth, and the kisses they'd
shared; he thought of her small breasts and narrow waist and
the heat of her embrace, and he was grateful she wasn't nearby

because he wanted, again, to make love to her. And that was something that would complicate his life horribly. Yet he was very tempted. "It is wonderful," he concurred. "We really must make plans to meet when next you come into town."

"I'm quite free, really. It's entirely up to you. You choose the time and I'll make the necessary arrangements. I can be on the train at very short notice. I'd so like it if we could have a chance to talk quietly together, without masses of people pressing in on all sides."

"That would be good, wouldn't it?" he said, not anywhere near as taken with the idea as she so evidently was. "Let me have a look at my diary, and I'll ring you tomorrow. How would that be?"

"That would be perfect. You do know, don't you, that I understand *completely*. I *know* how you feel, and it's perfectly legitimate under the circumstances. I'm very good at friendships, you know, Edwin. I'll be able to help you."

He wasn't sure what she was talking about, although the faintly panicky reaction he had to her words was working to erase the pleasant recollections he'd had of her welcoming mouth and fascinating figure. He wished she wouldn't say quite so much as she did. She seemed, in each of their conversations, to go just that tiny bit too far, so that he was left on edge without really knowing why.

"You've always been a good friend," he said, feeling his way to neutral territory. "I'll look at my book and let you know what might suit."

She knew she should leave it at that, but she was reluctant to have the conversation end. She also wanted, somehow, to impress upon him how special was her ability to comprehend the twists and turns of his thinking.

"I've put a few thoughts on paper," she said hesitantly. "Perhaps we'll have an opportunity to discuss them."

"Thoughts?"

"Along the lines of last night's conversation."

"Oh, I see." He was suddenly perspiring, uncomfortable with her attempt to reconstruct last night's scenario. "Well, it's good of you to ring, Frances, and I will get back to you tomorrow." Gently, he said goodbye and put down the receiver, then searched for his handkerchief to blot his damp forehead.

She returned to bed and fell at once into a wonderfully deep sleep from which she abruptly and very completely awakened less than three hours later, and into which she could not return, even after her consumption of a large glass of hot milk and two aspirin tablets.

She got through the following morning with the aid of several cups of strong tea and was able to nap for an hour in the afternoon when her mother volunteered to take the children for a walk to the shops down the road. She kept herself alert, and within close range of the telephone so as not to miss Edwin's call when it came.

By four-thirty, as she was preparing scones for tea, she began to review her evening with Edwin, searching for anything she might have said or done then, or in the course of the previous night's telephone conversation, to put him off. She didn't think she'd offended him, although it was possible that he didn't reciprocate her interest and had merely been being polite. She refused to accept that their exchange of kisses had been nothing more than the end product of good manners. He'd responded most positively to her. So why, then, had he failed, for the second day in a row, to ring as promised? In all likelihood he'd had a full day at the office and hadn't had an opportunity to get to the telephone. Undoubtedly, he'd ring during the evening once he'd returned home, had a meal, and settled in. Unless he'd made plans to spend the evening with friends. No, he'd be unlikely to have two late nights in one week. He'd be in for the evening, and he'd ring her. She nodded confirmingly as she slid the tray into the oven and glanced at the clock to note when the scones would have to be removed.

She stepped through the kitchen door and into the garden where she lit a cigarette with trembling hands. She told herself it was a reaction to the cold out of doors, and tucked her free hand into her armpit as she smoked and looked at the ruin winter had made of her mother's garden.

The telephone rang and she threw down the cigarette to go flying into the kitchen and through to the hall to lift the receiver.

It was Arthur, and she felt a sudden inrushing of something very like rage. For all she knew, Edwin might, at this very moment, be trying to get through, and here was bloody Arthur keeping the line engaged.

"How is everything?" she asked him, scarcely able to contain her angry impatience.

"Are you all right, Frances? You sound rather off."

"I'm perfectly well, thank you. I was in the garden and had to come rushing in to answer the telephone."

"Oh! How are the children, and Deirdre?"

"We're all very well, Arthur. How are things at the infamous, untitled Ministry?"

"That's indiscreet," he chided. "I've a spot of good news, actually."

"Oh?"

"I'm to have the weekend free. I'll be arriving on the five forty-five train Friday. I thought you might collect me, if there's enough petrol. I know it's difficult, driving with those covers on the headlamps, but if you'd be good enough to meet the train, I'll see to navigating our way home. There is enough petrol, isn't there? You haven't been driving wastefully, have you, Fan?"

"I haven't been driving at all," she said curtly, thoroughly depressed by the abysmal prospect of having to spend an entire weekend with her husband.

'Sorry," he apologized. "That was uncalled for on my part."

"Quite!"

"Are you sure there's nothing amiss?" he asked anxiously. "You don't sound yourself at all. You're not ill, are you, Fan?"

"I am perfectly well. I'll fetch you from the train," she assured him, then cried, "Oh, bloody hell! I must ring off! The scones are burning!" She threw down the receiver and raced to the kitchen where, without thinking, she snatched the tray of scones from the oven with her bare hand. It took a moment for the pain to register, then she thrust her hand beneath the cold water faucet and stood, furiously weeping, as the frigid flow turned her hand numb. Her plans were ruined. She fervently wished a bomb would fall on the Ministry and kill the lot of them, most especially Arthur.

It only made sense to ring Edwin that evening to explain that Arthur would be coming up for the weekend. She detected a certain nuance to Edwin's tone, but was unable to decipher its meaning.

"I thought it best to let you know straightaway," she told him.

"It's very good of you, Fan. I hadn't decided on the weekend," he said with intentional vagueness. He really was rather irked. He'd said he'd ring her and before he'd had a chance to make good on his word, here she was ringing him for the second evening in a row. It was as if she considered the two of them an established pair and was obliged to keep him abreast of the daily developments in her life. That she might be thinking in these terms disturbed and offended him, but he wasn't clear how to discourage her without alienating her altogether. He truly was fond of her, but her persistence and her assumptions really were becoming off-putting.

"I was so looking forward to coming into town," she said plaintively, hoping he'd express regret at being unable to see her.

"I'm sure it must be dreadful for you in dreary old Royal Leam."

"Unutterably." She laughed, elated by his comprehension of her plight. "We'll have to rearrange our plans, I'm afraid."

What plans? he wondered. Had he made a promise and forgotten it? "Did we make plans to meet, Frances?" he asked, keeping his voice light.

"Not definitely, no. I did think we'd meet at the weekend . . ." Her words tapered off. "I mean to say, I thought . . . I really did so want to be with you . . ."

She was sounding altogether too lovelorn, even besotted. Her voice, her words were setting off small sirens in his brain. "Look, Frances," he said quickly. "Why don't I ring you midweek, and we'll see where we are at that point?" At that moment, he had absolutely no intention of ringing her, but he knew it was what she wanted to hear, and that it would suffice to put an end to the call. "I'll do that, shall I? You have a good weekend with Arthur, and we'll talk again midweek. Give everyone my best, won't you?" He rang off, then stood breathing heavily, as if he'd just barely escaped something immensely menacing.

Frances held the receiver in her hand for some time after the connection had been broken, the weight of the instrument fully commensurate with that of her mounting anger. Damn Arthur! Once again he was going to deprive her of something she craved.

She was so visibly angry that the children backed away after tea and went upstairs to play with the dollhouse in Hadleigh's room, the two children tacitly united in the face of their mother's incomprehensible behavior.

"I say," Ben whispered, "Mummy's ever so cross, isn't she? Why, do you suppose?" He examined a miniature Chippendale desk, considering where best to place it in the dollhouse's sitting room.

"I *hate* her!" Hadleigh hissed fervently. "She's wicked, wicked, wicked. I hope she *dies*!"

Ben was so shocked and frightened that he burst into tears. Frightened herself, and guilty, Hadleigh had to promise him her sweets for the next three days in order to quiet him. She was terrified her mother would hear his loud sobs and come to investigate. Since Ben was an impossibly inept liar, he'd blurt out the truth, and then heaven only knew what dreadful punishment Hadleigh might receive for having wished her mother dead. It was worth three days' loss of sweets to guarantee Ben's silence.

Unable to imagine what had so upset Frances, Deirdre decided it was best not to inquire, and retired to the lounge with her knitting, leaving Frances to do the washing-up alone. Ordinarily, Deirdre would have stayed to dry. They'd been sharing the work since the housekeeper had left to take a high-paying factory job, but if Frances was going to be so damnably unpleasant, then she could jolly well clear up on her own. Deirdre settled into her chair and got to work, glancing every so often over at the kitchen doorway, beyond which she could hear Frances slamming pots and crockery and breathing in audible gusts that sounded almost asthmatic.

Frances tried to calm herself, ashamed at having displayed her rage to her mother and children. They'd done nothing. It was all Arthur's doing. He'd ruined her weekend with Edwin, a weekend when they might have gone to the cinema, perhaps to see one of the new American films. And, afterwards, there'd have been a late supper, or she might have prepared something for them to eat in that odd little kitchen at his flat. Later, secured in the darkness beyond the blackout curtains, they'd have removed their clothing prior to embarking upon a lengthy, voluptuous voyage culminating in a release so violently fulfilling it might literally snap her spine or entirely dissolve her bones. Because of Arthur, none of it would happen.

She leaned against the cooker, watching the small steady

flame of the pilot light, bewildered by the savagery of her emotions. She felt as if she could kill someone. The feeling was so strong that her hands curled in on themselves in flexed anticipation. She had momentary visions of guns and knives, of blood gushing from ragged wounds; she saw eyes fixed into permanency bearing a glaze of disbelief; she saw herself bringing about the termination of another's life and witnessed it with a sense of wonder, even of satisfaction. "My God!" she whispered aloud. "What's happening to me?" The ferocity of her imaginings badly frightened her. She pushed away from the cooker and went into the lounge.

"I'm sorry," she told her mother. "I was simply filthy to you and the children. I can't explain it. It's just that . . . I'm so tired." She ended on a lamenting note her mother at once latched onto.

"You do look worn out," Deirdre agreed. "Why not try to get to sleep early tonight?"

"I can't sleep," Frances complained. "And when I do manage to fall off, I'm wide awake again after two or three hours."

"Perhaps you should stop over to the surgery and have a word with Dr. Connors. He'll prescribe something to help you sleep."

"I think I might do that," Frances concurred distractedly.

After a long soak in a very hot bath, and having taken a dose of the sedative powder Dr. Connors had prescribed, she lay in bed hearing the children and her mother settling in for the night. She gazed into the darkness waiting for the weight of weariness to close her eyes, and was unaware of drifting into sleep until she came awake three hours later. She wanted only to go back to sleep, but it seemed as if the enormity of her wanting it worked against her. She was so tired that tears streamed from her eyes, her nose ran, and she yawned repeatedly. For more than an hour she remained unmoving, eyes closed, certain she could get back to sleep. In a state slightly beyond waking, she let her thoughts move to Edwin. An error. At once, she was entirely awake, her heartbeat accelerating.

Nothing like this had ever happened to her. It was most alarming. She pulled on her dressing gown and went downstairs to the drinks cabinet in the lounge. Something alcoholic might relax her. Listening to the night, she sat at the far end of the sofa, sipping neat scotch—Edwin's preferred drink; it made her feel closer to him—and smoking a cigarette. Her mother would come down in the morning, sniff the air, and sail into accusations. Frances really didn't care. Whatever she had to do to get some rest was justified, even to invading Arthur's precious cache of scotch.

The drink and the cigarette long-since finished, she sat on until she felt thoroughly chilled in the unheated room. The coal fire had burnt itself out many hours before and it would have been too much of a waste, not to mention too much of an effort, to light another. Stiffly, she got up and carried the glass and the ashtray to the kitchen, then went slowly back up to the bedroom. It was after five and the sky looked as if it was beginning to come loose at its distant edge, fraying to reveal a pale interior. She stood at the window for a time watching the shades of gray gradually alter. All this would be ended soon. She'd make her break with Arthur—and damn the consequences—and she and Edwin would be free to construct a marvellous new life together. Then, she'd sleep a newborn's sleep for nights without end.

Three

It had been so long since she'd actually seen Arthur that the sight of him came as something of a shock. She'd painted her mental portrait of him in such dreary, ineffectual colors that his appearance in person, emerging from the train to step onto the platform, was jarring. She watched him as she might have a stranger, fascinated by his handsomeness and obvious good health. Despite his, to her mind, character flaws, he was undeniably good-looking—so good-looking, in fact, that she was softened in some vital way merely by his appearance. She had to wonder why, simply because it felt as if she'd come to the end of her fondness for him, she'd sought to alter his physical reality. If she'd stopped to think about it, if she'd simply studied closely the faces of their children, she'd have seen that no one as ugly as the Arthur of her imaginings could have fathered two such undeniably beautiful beings.

Now she felt guilty, and even angrier than before. People would think her mad to give up so handsome a man for one who physically had only style and a certain jauntiness to recommend him. She hated herself for being someone who'd think in this fashion, for being someone who bothered to consider what other people might or might not think of her actions. More than anything else she wished she were a woman—like Mandy, for instance—who heeded her instincts, without fear of possible repercussions.

After an unexpectedly warm embrace to which, to her consternation, her body responded eagerly, Arthur held her at arms' length, asking, "Are you unwell, Frances? You look terribly tired."

Unable to meet his eyes, and chafed by his concern, she said, "I've had some difficulty sleeping, but I've been to the surgery and Dr. Connors has prescribed a sedative. It hasn't been particularly effective, but this will pass, I'm sure." She handed him the key to the two-seater standard Swallow, then walked along at his side, bewildered by his fair-haired, blue-eyed presence. His color was amazingly good for someone who claimed not to have seen the light of day for months, who had been, as he claimed, breathing in stale air and eating unpalatable food.

"I am sorry, Frances. I thought you sounded rather down when we spoke. Perhaps you'd best go directly to bed when we get home."

"I'll be fine," she said dismissingly.

Doubtfully, he glanced over at her, then returned his attention to the hazardous activity of driving with almost no light to assist him. Once safely out of the station, however, he had to look again at her—not really able to see her—asking, "Are you quite sure nothing's amiss?" his concerned hand on her arm. "I've never seen you quite so . . ."

"Oh, for God's sake, Arthur! I'm simply tired. Please don't try to attach dramatic innuendo to it!" She kept her eyes averted, knowing that, had she been able to make out his features, she'd have seen them creased with hurt. He was a man who disliked raised voices, arguments, even the mildest degree of dissension. The children's spats had, on occasion, driven him almost to tears, and he'd literally begged them to try to be kinder and more tolerant of each other. Amazingly, she thought, they inevitably responded positively to their father's imploring. His great decency was inescapable. She wished he were less than he was; it would have made everything so much easier for her.

"It really is frightful," he said after several moments, "driving in these blackouts. It's nothing short of astonishing there haven't been more serious accidents. One would expect to see collisions on all sides." He smiled over at her, the underside of his features barely illuminated from the faint glow of the instrument panel. "I suppose," he wound down, "people must be exercising a high degree of caution. It's impressive, all in all."

She murmured her assent, temporarily lulled by both the darkness and the motion. Being driven about had always had a soothing effect upon her, and Arthur drove well, considerate of his passengers. She wondered what sort of driver Edwin might be. She suspected he'd be the type who'd affect recklessness in order to enhance his image of himself as an unconventional man. She smiled to herself, fondly amused. The man would likely be most distressed were he to know how thoroughly she'd penetrated into his motives.

From habit, she got out to open the gate across the driveway, then waited as Arthur maneuvered the car into position on the paved area in front of the garage where the Rover was stored. With the petrol rationing, it was impractical to use the large sedan unless absolutely necessary. Periodically, Frances started it up, then sat behind the wheel having an illicit cigarette while the engine sent quite pleasant vibrations through her.

The children came shrieking out from the lounge the moment Arthur opened the front door. Frances stood apart to watch the reunion. Deirdre smiled benevolently from the lounge doorway, for all the world like someone queuing for her ration of Arthur's affection.

His suitcase hastily set to one side, he dropped to his knees to embrace both children at once, laughing as he replied to their overlapping questions: Ben wanting to know if Dad had managed to find the Royal Horse Guards model needed to complete his set; Hadleigh asking whether or not Daddy had brought any sweets.

"The answer to all questions is yes," Arthur declared, inspiring another round of shrieks.

Wincing at the noise, Frances sidestepped the quartet to hang away her coat in the cloakroom under the stairs before heading into the kitchen to put on the kettle. As she prepared a light meal—the children had foregone their tea in order to sit down at the table with their father—she listened to Ben's surprisingly well-informed questions about the latest happenings in the war, which Arthur made an effort to answer despite Hadleigh's repeated interruptions. She really was the most infuriating child, Frances thought, as she adjusted the flame under the soup she'd made earlier in the day. If Hadleigh wasn't going on and on about food in one form or another, she was sure to launch into an unanswerable series of questions about how one felt about this color or that, or about a particular flower, or animal, or tree. The girl seemed endlessly fascinated with the details of subjects most children wouldn't deem worthy of notice. She'd driven Frances nearly round the bend when, at age four, she'd insisted on knowing her mother's feelings about grass, of all things. Did Mummy think it was pretty? Did Mummy think it was good? Did Mummy like to walk or sit upon it? Did Mummy think cows really, truly, liked to eat it, or did they eat it just because farmers wouldn't give them anything else? It had gone on and on, one answer provoking another question, until, exasperated, Frances had broken short their outing in Regents Park—that landscape having inspired the relentless questioning—and taken Hadleigh directly home in a taxi, thereby breaking her promise of afternoon tea at Brown's Hotel. Hadleigh had borne up well enough in the taxi, but had burst into heart-broken sobs the moment they were through the door of the Cheyne Walk flat, and had fled to her room. Her refusal to come out for tea further maddened Frances who, newly pregnant and ill with it, told the red-faced, sobbing four-year-old she could "stay in there until hell freezes over!" With the door closed between them, Hadleigh had gone suddenly silent, undone by her mother's imprecation. Just as Frances had been about to turn away, she'd heard murmuring and, tiptoeing near to the door, had listened to her little girl fervently declaring, "I hate you hate you hate you!" Frances had straightened and looked wide-eyed at the closed door, fully satisfied at that moment, first because she respected Hadleigh's courage in making this declaration and, second, because it did very much feel as if the two of them hated each other, and Hadleigh had just confirmed it.

In time, Frances came to recall that afternoon with a gritty sense of shame. The memory was of the two of them at their worst and, although she'd have liked to blame her deplorable behavior on her pregnancy, she knew there'd been a great deal of truth in the occasion. They seemed destined to fail in their roles as mother and daughter, a fact heightened by the easy love Frances felt for Ben. The discomfort she and Hadleigh experienced with each other proved to Frances that maternal love was not a natural instinct, that parents didn't simply, arbitrarily love their children. It didn't please her to discover this but it did seem to justify the distance she and Hadleigh maintained.

On her way to the dining room to lay the table, Frances stopped briefly to glance into the lounge where, with his suitcase open on the sofa, Arthur was revealing the gifts he'd brought for Deirdre and the children. He happened to look up and, smiling, said to Frances, "Are you going to come collect your gift?"

"In a moment," she answered, continuing on to the dining room, her head aching from the avid shrillness of the children's cries.

"Oh, Daddy!" Hadleigh crowed. "Thank you! You've brought all my favorites, even pontefract cakes. Look, Nana!"

"You're a very lucky girl," Deirdre stated. "A very lucky girl indeed. You'll want to save your sweets now, won't you? Mummy's just getting the tea."

Ben kicked Hadleigh lightly on the shin, whispering, "Remember!" and Hadleigh was crestfallen. She owed a portion of her sweets to Ben and had forgotten all about it. Never mind, she told herself. She had tons, more than enough to share.

By the time Frances had finished laying the table, the volume in the lounge had abated and there were only the low tones of Arthur's and her mother's voices as they commented on the day's newspaper headlines. Frances paused just outside the lounge, for a moment overcome by desire to have things the way they were before Mandy's announcement that Edwin had returned from America. Life had had a comfortable predictability, and, before the evacuation, some pleasurable moments in London. Arthur adored the theatre and films, and the two of them had gone frequently, with and without the children. There'd been dinners out with friends, and quite a lot of entertaining at home. While, at times, it had felt very much as if some game without specific guidelines were being played, and that she and Arthur were the star turns, there had been very little free time for her to dwell upon what might be missing in her life. There'd have been no problems now at all if Arthur could have recognized her need for closeness, for an intense intimacy. She might even have been able to love him if he'd only been capable of putting aside what she viewed as his sexual squeamishness; if he could have taken hold of her in one electrifying moment of realization and devoted himself to an impassioned exploration of her body she might never have located the ground in which to plant the seeds of her dissatisfaction. Even now, she realized, she'd be willing to capitulate to a display of desire. It wasn't yet too late.

"Do come along, Frances!" Arthur beckoned.

Feeling brittle and rather ill from lack of sleep, she stood blinking at her husband and her mother, who looked over at her with smiling faces. Arthur got up from the sofa and came toward her.

"I managed to get out for an hour to do a bit of shopping," he said, one hand opening to reveal an oblong jeweller's box. "I know you've been having rather a rough go of it," he said in a lowered voice, pressing the box into her hand. "I thought you might like this."

"Thank you." Her mouth was parched. All her joints seemed to have gone dry as well, so that bending her head to look at the maroon velvet box took quite some effort.

"Open it, do!" he urged, his expression one of doting fondness that caused her to wonder how and why he could possibly care for her as he so visibly did.

"Open it, Mummy!" chimed Ben, looking up from the game of checkers he was losing to his sister.

Frances looked from one to the other of their expectant faces. The impact of their combined attention was very like a dark blanket they'd wrapped around her. She wanted to turn and walk out the front door, flee her cumbersome responsibilities to these people. Breathing in the coal-smoke-scented air and the exhalations from these other lungs was like absorbing into her system the essence of her obligations. Forcing herself to be calm and to remain where she stood, she got the box open to see the heavy gold link bracelet Arthur had purchased.

"It's exquisite," she said, dazzled anew by the opulence of this man's generosity. His gifts came infrequently and not, perhaps, when she would have liked to receive them, but they were always lavish and in perfect taste. "Thank you," she added, trying to moisten her lips. "Thank you very much, Arthur." She kissed his cheek, then stepped away. "I'll just see to the food." She all but flew to the kitchen, the box enclosed in her fist.

She was tempted, as she stirred the bubbling soup, to drop the gold bracelet into the pot. She could almost see the maroon velvet of the box disappearing beneath the surface, could imagine her mother's exclamation as she lifted her soup spoon to find the bracelet dangling from the end of it. How perfect! she thought, lifting the lid from the tureen. The telephone rang and she jumped, the tureen lid nearly falling from her hand as she turned to stare at the doorway. It was bound to be Edwin. Arthur would answer, hear an unfamiliar male voice asking to speak to his wife, and he'd come in demanding explanations. Dear God! she thought. What should she do? She wasn't geared up for a confrontation. In all her projections of the future, Arthur somehow knew that it was ended, that their marriage was over. She'd never anticipated the actual telling. The ringing stopped, and she listened, hearing Arthur's voice, then a pause.

"Telephone for you, darling!" he called.

"For me?" Her voice was unnaturally high with nervousness. She prayed it wasn't Edwin. She was too exhausted to offer Arthur anything like a reasonable explanation. Wiping her hands down the sides of her apron, she hurried into the hallway to give Arthur a wobbly smile as she accepted the telephone from him and said hello into the mouthpiece.

"Fanny, darling!" Mandy cooed. "I've been meaning to ring you since the party but simply haven't had a chance. Is this an inopportune moment?"

"I'm afraid it is," Frances told her, shaky with relief. "Could I ring you back? We're just about to sit down to a meal. Arthur's managed to get away for the weekend."

"Be sure that you do," Mandy said. "We really must talk. I'm simply dying to know what's going on."

"Whatever do you mean?"

"Oh, darling!" she laughed. "*Everyone saw* the two of you! Now promise you'll ring me first chance?"

"Monday." Frances looked around guiltily, as if Mandy's voice could be heard throughout the house. *Everyone saw the two of you!* She'd given no thought to that, either. Matters were getting badly out of hand.

"Don't forget!" Mandy said, and rang off.

Returning to the kitchen, she decided she was going to have to take Mandy into her confidence. There was nothing else for it. She managed to get the soup into the tureen without mishap, as her mind raced over the details of what she'd tell Mandy. She wanted to weep. Calling to the others as she went, she carried the tureen through to the dining room.

Arthur was so considerate, so tentative and grateful, she could barely feel him. His hands, his mouth, his body where it was joined to hers, might all have been parts of a ghost. He required pathetically little, she thought, trying not to think of how she must look with her naked limbs enclosing Arthur's pale, bobbing body. Dangerous words collected in her mouth, defying her need to speak: one-word commands that would startle, possibly even horrify, this man who, despite his activities, seemed scarcely aware of her. Arthur relieved himself within her; he used her, she thought, as a private convenience, not unlike the public conveniences he used for certain other aspects of relief. From moment to moment there were hints, twinges, signals of possible pleasure, but he never stayed, never showed any awareness that the way he'd moved just then, his shifting, had caused an involuntary surging within her. She wanted to scream as he shuddered in satisfied silence then slipped quietly away to pull on his dressing gown and go padding off to the bathroom. His opening and closing of the bedroom door allowed a balloon of cold air to enter. It threw itself upon her heated body, almost more potent than the man who'd inadvertently created this brief draft.

Habit called for her to don her nightdress and cover herself with the bedclothes, but she was too enervated to move. She wondered drowsily if Arthur nurtured secret dreams of his own, if he was, perhaps, abandoned and lusty in those dreams. Was it possible he was as bored with her passivity as she was in pretending it?

Arthur closed the door quietly, seeing she'd fallen asleep just as he'd left her. He stood by the side of the bed, gazing down, entranced by the lean length of her body, positively thrilled by the glistening dampness of her upper thighs. What would happen, he wondered, if he were to investigate closely the provocative region of her groin with his fingertips, his tongue? He imagined her recoiling in disgust, thrusting him away, repelled. He dared do nothing that might upset her, but he did think often of making love to her in ways depicted on smuggled foreign postcards. It was possible, he reasoned, she might welcome the novelty. It was also possible she'd be permanently alienated, and he couldn't risk that.

Carefully, he drew the bedclothes over them both, then lay at her side, sighing deeply. He felt very fortunate, all in all. He had an exceptional wife, two fine children, even a mother-in-law he actually cared deeply for. Once this war was out of the way, they'd go for a holiday, all of them, take a motor trip through France, or even go to Canada to visit his cousins there. He hadn't seen them in years, since the twenties when they'd gone off to Canada for what was intended to be a two-year stay but what had ended as permanent residency. He very much wanted to see Canada, and America, too; always had. The immediate future, however, didn't look rosy. Once Chamberlain was out of the way and Churchill was in place, they'd soon put a stop to the German offensive.

Sighing again, he turned, aligning himself against Frances, tucking his knees into the back of hers as he ran his hand lightly down the silken length of her flank. He shouldn't have done it. At once he was aroused, and didn't have the heart to wake her. He wouldn't have, in any case. They hadn't made love twice in one go since their honeymoon when, jubilant at having won her, he'd been unable to maintain his distance and had buried himself deeply inside her three and four times daily, until she'd protested, making him aware that she'd grown sore from the frequency of his attentions. He smiled, remembering how wonderfully naive she'd been, and how uncertain.

She opened her eyes in the darkness and prayed it was morning, but she'd been asleep only four hours. It was three in the morning. She'd go back to sleep, she told herself, curling inward only to realize with a jolt that she was naked. Arthur had done no more than pull up the blankets. At any other time he'd have awakened her with a gentle reminder having to do with the prospect of one or the other of the children coming in to find her without clothes. While she was not at all bothered by the prospect of being seen unclothed by her children, the idea did seem to bother Arthur. She found sad this additional proof of his morbidity regarding matters of the flesh. Yet wasn't it odd that he chose always to make love with a light on? Could that be some small proof of his secret dreams? She shifted to look at him but he was turned away; she couldn't see his face. He was well over on his side of the bed, taking up very little room.

From the outset of their marriage they'd stayed faithful to the boundaries, each remaining within their half of the bed. Edwin now, she thought, would likely be a restless sleeper; he'd push his substantial weight to wherever his need dictated. She might be forced to take refuge on one of the Indian carpets in the lounge, atop those large pillows. She could see herself creeping from the bedroom, leaving behind a happily sated Edwin. Upon awakening in the morning, he'd emerge to find her cocooned in blankets and pillows on the floor in front of the fireplace. He'd rouse her with an amused laugh, or he might join her there, exclaiming over the delirium into which her body forced him.

She wasn't going to be able to sleep. It was pointless even to try. She put on her nightgown and robe then went round to the far side of the bed where, on her knees, she peered closely at Arthur's face. She could distinguish only outlines and, in frustrated sadness, sat back on her heels with her arms wrapped around herself for warmth, wishing the weekend was ended and Arthur was away from here and back within the bowels of the ministry.

As on the night before, she poured herself a measure of scotch, lit a cigarette, and went to sit on the edge of the sofa in the unlit room. Wind whistled in the chimney. Beyond the windows night sat like an old woman awaiting an end. The whiskey cauterized her throat, scalded her empty stomach; the cigarette scorched her lungs. She derived a terrible satisfaction from this tangible evidence of her suffering. If it hadn't been so ungodly an hour she'd have rung Edwin just to have his voice fill some of the emptiness. But they'd talk come Monday, and make plans to be together. Only a matter of days and she'd be allowed, finally, to imprint herself indelibly on Edwin's heart and mind. He'd be altered irrevocably by the gifts she'd give, and the ultimate revealing of herself to herself would be his gift to her. Then, once these first concrete steps had been taken together, burrowing deep into the cushions and warmly secure, she would sleep.

Four

"I really don't know what you're implying," Frances prevaricated, gripping the telephone tightly, her palms damp.

"Oh, darling!" Mandy laughed knowingly. "You needn't be coy with me. I was your staunchest supporter, fobbing everyone off with tales of the great reunion. The two of you were quite adorable together. I'm simply dying to know what sort of progress you're making."

There was no progress that Frances could see. Edwin consistently promised to be in touch, then failed to do it. Frances wished there were some way she could force his hand, push him to see the importance of keeping his promises to her. "You do go on!" she admonished Amanda, her eyes drawn to Arthur's antique duelling pistols displayed behind the glass of the curio cabinet in the dining room. "There's no 'progress' to tell about, nor will there be any. You're reading far more into it than there actually is . . . was."

Mandy drew an audible breath, and in a less giddy more conspiratorial tone said, "Someone's nearby, is that it? Of course, that's it. Look! Are you coming into the city? I'm longing to see you. We must talk."

"I expect I'll be in at the end of the week to fetch the post, see what sort of condition the flat's in. I'd adore to see you, too, but I promise you there's not a thing to talk about, at least not where Edwin's concerned."

Mandy laughed again. "You're too, too dear! Keeping

45

everything strictly on the q.t. Edwin's no better. I haven't been able to dredge a thing out of him. If I didn't know better, I might believe I'd imagined the whole thing."

"Neither of us has anything to tell," Frances insisted. "Simply because two people meet again after many years and spend a few hours catching up doesn't mean they've embarked on anything more significant than conversation. You do tend to let your imagination run wild."

"Now, be truthful!" Amanda pushed. "I did *see* the two of you. And you know perfectly well what I mean. In all the years you've been married to Arthur, I've never seen the two of you get up to anything remotely as passionate as those fevered goings-on between you and Edwin. It actually looked as if the two of you might strip off and go to it right on the spot, in front of the whole crowd."

Frances forced a laugh. "I congratulate you! You have what is undoubtedly the severest case of deluded vision I've ever encountered. Of course we kissed. Everyone did, as you'll recall. It's accepted custom at the new year."

When next she spoke, Mandy's voice had undergone a complete transformation. The bantering had ended. "Frances," she said quietly, "we really have to talk. Since it's all too clear you're of no mind to volunteer yourself, it's only fair to tell you that anyone with half a brain and failing eyesight could see you're mad about Edwin. I thought all that ended ages ago, when you married Arthur. Obviously, it's anything but ended. The thing of it is, darling, I'm not sure you're aware just what you're letting yourself in for. Edwin's not the same as he was. Surely you can see that for yourself. And there are other things you should know. I owe you that much, at the very least. You're going to have to trust someone, you know, and I've always been totally above-board with you."

"I know that," Frances agreed.

"Then meet with me. If you're going to fling yourself headlong into an affair, or at least try to, then it behooves you to be aware of just what sort of morass you're about to find yourself in."

"Morass?"

"All right," Mandy relented. "A poor choice of words, but not so terribly far off the mark. When will you be in? What day? I'll fetch you from the station. We'll have lunch, at the Cumberland, say, and we'll *talk*."

"Has he some illness?" Frances asked worriedly, dropping her guard. "Is that what you're trying to tell me?" Was he going to die? she wondered despairingly. That would be too cruel, too unfair. He couldn't die when she'd only just found him again, before they'd had any sort of chance to be together.

"He's not ill, at least not physically. Tell me the day and which train."

In the end, Frances told her, then rang off to pace the hallway for ten minutes before going back to the telephone to put in a call to Edwin at his office.

"How was your weekend, Fan?" he asked politely.

"Faintly tolerable," she answered, thinking for a moment of how she'd knelt at the side of the bed studying Arthur's sleeping features. Why was she thinking of that now? Arthur had no part in this. "I wanted to let you know I'll be coming into the city Friday. I could stay the weekend."

He was rendered speechless for a few seconds, aghast at the idea that she might think she would spend the weekend with him. Dismissing this as being well beyond the realm of her probable thinking, he swallowed, then said, "You'll be in on Friday, you say?" It really was too much, he thought, reaching across the desk for his diary. He'd have to have a word with his secretary about screening future calls. Frances's ringing him at home in the evenings was allowable, to a degree, but he just couldn't have her breaking in during business hours. What *could* she be thinking of? He was starting to feel very pressured. "You'll be at the flat?"

"Yes."

"Good." He pushed unfelt energy into his words. "I'll ring you there, and we'll plan an evening together. Let me just note it in my book."

She could hear him turning pages, and the suspension of his breath—the picture of a diligent schoolboy slotted into her brain, and she smiled—before he exhaled, almost sighing, to say, "There! It's noted. I could," he said, forgetting himself, "try for theatre tickets. Or we could take our chances queuing for a film. It might actually be possible to see one in its entirety without the sirens interrupting." What on earth was he doing? he wondered. He was encouraging her when it wasn't what he wanted to do, not when it was becoming very clear that she was bent on considerably more than friendship. This was confirmed when she responded, "We could just have a quiet meal together. We're nowhere near caught up on all we've got to talk about. And I had hoped to show you some of what I've put down on paper."

"There is rather a lot of ground, isn't there?" he said, his breathing suddenly sounding labored. Why, why couldn't he come straight out with it and say, Look, I'm really not up to this? Why the bloody hell couldn't he do that, instead of inadvertently encouraging her by dint of his refusal to be impolite?

Rashly, she said, "I've thought of you constantly since the party, Edwin. There are things we must discuss. It was so lovely to see you, to be together again after so long."

"It was indeed," he answered, recalling the avidity of her kisses. Again forgetting himself, held in recollection of other moments, he said, "You do have a marvellous mouth."

The remark caused her lungs to flutter, as if she'd been plunged into a vacuum. "I'm prepared," she said meaningfully, "to make changes, if needed."

"Oh," he said, misunderstanding, "you needn't on my behalf."

"How sweet you are!" she told him, pleased.

This was entirely out of hand. "Darling Fanny," he said, his attention caught by the sight of his secretary standing patiently in the doorway with dictation equipment in hand, "I'm many things, but surely not that. I'm afraid . . ."

"But you are," she insisted, cutting him off. "Very sweet. Oh, I know it's the sort of thing men loathe hearing about themselves, but it does apply. You know, I could come to your flat, prepare a meal. You're not one of those alarming types with a talent for cookery, are you?"

"Good God, no!" He waved away his secretary, appalled by her possibly overhearing any part of this conversation. "One opens tins and deposits the contents on toast, that sort of thing. Of course, there's always the club." That would be the ideal place to take her: neutral territory, with any number of friends about. He'd be able to maintain his distance and deal with her more successfully. He wouldn't be tempted by her physical charms.

"I'll feed you. I'm not brilliant, but I do manage a passable meal from which anyone has yet to expire."

"Blast! I must ring off. I'm due in a meeting. Look, Fan.

I've put it down in the book. I'll be in touch at the weekend and we'll plan from there. Good of you to ring me." He put down the receiver with harried haste even though she was still speaking. It was horrendously ill-mannered of him, but she did instigate this sort of reaction with these repeated calls. It might be best to meet for a meal at the club, have a quiet chat with her about all this frightfully urgent communication. He was starting to feel under siege, and he couldn't imagine what had caused her to alter so radically. She'd always been so appealingly remote, so wonderfully languid. Now here she was, pushing close without invitation. It put him in mind of Elsa, although the two were quite different. It was the implicit demand that unnerved him, and the unavoidable concept that here was yet another woman who wanted something of him, without allowing him a reasonable opportunity to decide for himself what, if anything, he was willing to give. He was angry with Frances, and angry with himself for being unable to cope. He was being forced into untruths, half-truths, dishonesty, and he hated it. Rattled, he summoned his secretary, then groped among the papers on his desk, searching for a letter to which he meant to reply.

Frances wandered into the kitchen to put on the kettle. The children and her mother would soon be back from their daily pilgrimage to the shops with their ration booklets. God, but she'd be glad when school resumed! Hadleigh at the Kingsley School and Ben at Arnold Lodge, Deirdre off to visit her friends on the odd afternoon. Having everyone underfoot day in and day out was a very real hardship just now. Once the children were back at school she'd try again to find another housekeeper. She disliked bedmaking and laundry and the never-ending need to cook meals. The bloody war had made a shambles of everything. She yawned hugely, her thoughts turning to sleep and her mounting need for it. Dark pouches were forming beneath her eyes, and her facial skin was developing a dry, papery feel. Altogether, she felt desiccated and brittle, as if she might crumble upon being moved without warning. It had been well over a week since she'd rested properly, and Dr. Connors' powders had done little if any good. At least the weekend was over and Arthur was back in London. He'd kissed her on the platform with infuriating fullness, holding her too close, as if he were one of the men in khaki returning to base. For a second or two, before he'd released

her, she'd experienced a dreadful craving to be free of his embrace. It had seemed he was suffocating her, squeezing the air
from her lungs. She'd had to restrain herself from heaving her
way out of his grasp. Finally, he'd broken away, snatched up
his valise, and climbed aboard. Dutifully, she'd waved until
the train was well past the station, then she'd surrendered her
platform ticket to the attendant and walked stiffly out to the
Swallow.

That night she spent hours writing down her thoughts and
feelings about Edwin. She didn't date or address the pages.
When the right moment came, she'd note that day's date and
an appropriate salutation. For now, it was enough simply to
shape each word lovingly in its turn. It drew her closer to him,
and gave tangible definition to her feelings.

It was past midnight when she was ready for her nightly
quest for sleep. The bed, without Arthur, seemed immense
and somehow terrible. Beds were such voluptuous places, potent in their limitless connotations. She spread her limbs experimentally, relishing the possibilities of the space. Every
part of her hummed with an awareness of the activities that
could occur on this expanse of white linen. And, suddenly, she
was afire, the bedding merely a wall to contain her heat. Edwin came to mind and her extended arms and legs grew taut.
She began to melt inside; evidence of this flameless combus-
tion seeped onto her thighs. Her nightdress was a weighty im-
pediment, and she dragged it off over her head, then stretched
wide her arms and legs to the cool reaches of the bed. She kept
her eyes tightly closed, to preserve the purity of the heat. Her
hips lunged gently upward and all at once, entirely alone,
goaded by her longings, she was at the brink of that abysmal
pleasure that had haunted the perimeters of her life for far too
long. What did it take? she wondered, venturing to place her
hands over her breasts. Where was the source of this fire that
threatened to immolate her? God! What if one of the children
should awaken and come seeking comfort from some bad
dream? She looked to confirm that the door was securely
closed.

She was the only one who'd know of this breach of behavior, this violation of her mother's admonitions to her as a
child never, ever to touch herself again in that shocking fash-

ion. She was all of a piece. Why was it necessary to segregate the parts of herself in order to conform to parental rule, a rule long-since ended?

Forty years old and untouched. It was wrong, fundamentally wrong. Initially, in the course of their first, fumbling unions, Arthur had only inadvertently touched against her in his efforts to penetrate her previously unused body. He'd taken aim and kept on with it—amid many murmured apologies—until he'd located the place where he'd wanted to be. It was so damnably simple for men! They needed to do nothing more than gain entry and rub themselves into quick, groaning pleasure. Why was it so much more complex a matter for women? Why couldn't a woman be satisfied as readily? Mandy had, any number of times over the years, intimated a first-hand knowledge of sublime sexual pleasure. Perhaps that was why she dared wear such outrageously low-cut dresses that revealed her plump, smooth breasts, and why she wore, upon occasion, a certain smile that told of privileged information.

Forty years old, she'd twice heaved her way into motherhood, rending herself in the process. Strangers knew her more intimately than her own husband: the midwife and Dr. Connors had, across her bloodstained thighs and belly, reached to congratulate her on the success of her deliveries. To Arthur, for several days each month, she was a pariah. He seemed distressed by the paraphernalia of her womanhood. Perhaps he was distressed by her altogether. She had no idea. She no longer cared. It was her right to know if she, too, could travel beyond herself into a state of comprehension. She would know.

She tended to the fire with previously unsuspected skill, awed by the rapid-banking flames that climbed upward, consuming everything in their path. A brilliant golden light glowed beyond her welded eyelids and she gazed sightlessly, straining toward the very core of the fire, her dissolved interior flowing from the charred ruins. Ultimately, there came a moment when she couldn't exhale from her swollen lungs; she was a galvanized effigy of her former self gaping blindly at the flickering penumbra beyond the light. Then, the air rocketed from her mouth as seismic tremors shattered the foundations upon which she'd always stood. Collapsing downward through the debris, her joints oiled beyond capacity, she crumpled and fell, to sleep a sleep like death.

Gray light lay against the bedroom windows like a film upon the glass. She'd actually slept for six hours—the longest time since New Year's Eve. She'd slept. So why did she feel so drained? And why, when she sat up to pull on her nightdress, did her limbs feel bruised and rubbery? Her eyebrows drew together as recollection of her nocturnal activities came to her. Mortified, she pressed her cold hands to her cheeks and forehead, recoiling in the light of day from what she'd caused her body to do beneath the concealment of night. How *could* she have done that? She'd wanted it to be Edwin who initiated her into the rites of pleasure. Now it might all be ruined. No, no. She'd be more confident now. That was it. She'd have no need to explain or apologize for her ignorance. No need. Dear God! What a squalid enterprise! It wasn't meant to be done alone, but in tandem. She couldn't think.

All that had seemed justified and necessary at midnight appeared bizarre, even demented at daybreak. While preparing breakfast she alternated between self-congratulation and chagrin. Each time she thought her feelings had fixed, that she'd settled her emotions, she swung to the opposite pole. By the time her mother and the children came into the kitchen and seated themselves at the table, she felt as if she were soldered to live wires. Currents travelled under her skin, short-circuiting at her brain. The cup of tea she hurriedly drank was no help. She needed something stronger, something to shut down the subcutaneous electricity.

While the others ate the dry cereal and toast she'd fixed, she went to the drinks cabinet in the lounge, uncapped the whiskey bottle and held it to her mouth. Two long swallows and the bottle was back in the cabinet, and the electricity had been replaced by a conflagration in her stomach. She gasped, then shook her head and forced herself to take long, deep breaths. The blaze within subsided to a tolerable warmth and she returned to the kitchen for a second cup of tea while she stood by the stove, watching with distaste as Hadleigh wolfed down two rounds of toast in half a dozen bites.

"No one's about to take your food from you!" she rebuked the girl. "Do try to eat like something human! I've seen dogs in kennels with better table manners.''

Hadleigh looked over, instantly upset. ''Sorry, Mummy,'' she choked out, then gulped audibly before dropping her eyes.

''Take your time, dear,'' Deirdre said placatingly, patting her granddaughter's hand. ''You do eat far too quickly. You don't want to give yourself a stomach ache.''

Contempt for her mother and her daughter wrinkled Frances's face. The two of them sickened her at times, with their little games. This particular game presently being played had to do with Deirdre undermining Frances's authority with her children. In spite of the fact that she'd merely paraphrased what Frances had said, her tone said volumes; her tone said: Do it for Nana, darling. Pay no mind to grumpy Mummy.

''*Please* don't *do* that, Mother!'' Frances snapped. ''She has the table manners of a Sherpa on expedition. What we're concerned with here hasn't to do with stomach aches. It has to do with the fact that Hadleigh's an inordinately greedy little swine and is going to end up rather a matronly looking girl if she doesn't learn to curb her appetite and to consider others before pushing every last bit of available food into her ravenous little maw.''

''Are you still having difficulty sleeping, dear?'' Deirdre asked, a surreptitious comforting hand placed out of sight on Hadleigh's knee.

Hadleigh's head was bent almost to her plate, and she gazed at the crumbs on the tablecloth, wishing God would come right through the ceiling and kill her mother.

''My sleep habits have nothing to do with this!'' Frances ranted on. ''You spoil her terribly, and I'd be most grateful if you'd allow me to reprimand my children without interfering.''

''I wouldn't *dream* of interfering,'' Deirdre replied, her expression one of affronted innocence. ''But they're only children, Frances, and children do have healthy appetites. No harm's been done. I know you're frightfully tired, but you are rather overboard. This is a most unpleasant way to begin a day. Perhaps it would be best if you went back and tried to get a bit more sleep.''

In the silence following this suggestion, Frances was able to hear a replay of all that had just been said. The tone of her own voice, the viciousness of her words, were hateful. Her mother was right. She was very far overboard. "I'm sorry," she said. "You're quite right. That was a bit much." Her inner voice dictated she should apologize to Hadleigh. She looked at the girl's bent head, and at that moment, Hadleigh fixed her liquid brown eyes on her mother. I am utterly reprehensible, Frances thought, lacerated by her daughter's visible pain. "I think I'll take a bath," she announced, and fled from the kitchen, overhearing as she went, Deirdre softly consoling Hadleigh.

"We mustn't take it to heart, my dear ones. Mummy's not herself just now."

If Mummy isn't herself, who is she? Frances mused, climbing the stairs. Who is Mummy, if she isn't herself?

She continued to ponder this question as water ran into the tub and steam slowly coated the mirror. The electric fire over the door threw down heat as she stripped. The steam in the air had a metallic taste and she licked her lips thirstily. As usual, the tub was taking ages to fill. She looked at the slow-rising water, all at once aware again of her body. The door was locked, the shade in place over the window. Mist shrouded the ceiling light fixture. Her vision seemed clouded as she thought of what she'd done to herself in the night. If she pressed her thighs tightly together she could feel a throbbing, and a wonderfully abraded sensation in her loins.

If Edwin were there, he'd be bound to respond to the sight of her, to be greatly aroused by the feel of her skin. His hands would travel this way over her breasts and down her belly, across her hips. Her flesh would shrivel in precisely this manner, each cell contracting—a million microscopic spasms.

It happened more quickly this time, and she fell collapsing against the tile wall, her chest heaving, her body shuddering in the moist air. "Edwin," she gasped, fearing she might faint. The whispered invoking of his name was a plea, a prayer. She *had* to share this. She didn't think she could live if he didn't take her to his bed and make good their unspoken vows.

Her body rapidly cooling, she saw herself performing acts she'd never before dared imagine: she knelt before his naked form and abased herself in honor of her boundless love for him; she explored his body with talented hands and mouth, astonishing them both with her rapacity. She devoured him; she forced the length of his engorged flesh deep within her and was blissfully riven by what she alone could contain.

Scene after scene played itself out before her: They were perfect, maddening. She insisted it be Edwin, but partway through every act, Edwin's form began to alter, until it was Arthur who joined with her in progressively more tumultuous congress.

Five

Having discovered her sexuality, she couldn't stop herself from repeatedly seeking to reaffirm its existence. Once or twice in the days that followed, and nightly without fail, she investigated the boundaries of her stunning capacity, both increasingly disturbed and elated by her ability, in mere minutes, to push her body into convulsive jolts of pleasure.

She felt remorseful and constantly on edge, fearful that somehow these terribly private actions might have some visible effect upon her. All her thoughts were of this and of her soon-to-be meeting with Edwin. Everything else was an intolerable disruption. By Friday morning, as she was preparing to leave for the station, it was most apparent that both the children and her mother were looking forward to having time to themselves, without her. This compounded her guilt, yet it was further substantiation of how little she'd be missed when she'd made her break from them.

Once she and Edwin had come through the unpleasantness and the legalities of divorce and were settled into a routine of sorts, she would likely have the children to visit on weekends and school holidays. The arrangement would suit her mother down to the ground. She'd be free to fuss over Hadleigh and Ben, and to spoil them thoroughly. Ben would always be a decent boy, but Hadleigh would show the full unfurling of her colors and demonstrate her limitless curiosity and insatiable appetite. Fine. Deirdre would be able to play out her role as martyred mother/grandmother to the hilt. As for Arthur, she had no idea what he might do. If the war continued, he'd be free only on the rare weekend, and it wasn't as if he came home each evening from a regular career. The love of his life, if he had one, was the strictly hush-hush goings-on in the Ministry of Defense, and none of their friends even knew of his affiliation with the ministry. It was generally believed he held some position of minor significance in the Ministry of Education. His beloved Ministry would sustain him. And Deirdre would dote upon the abandoned husband/father. The four of them would knit together into a tight little group, in no small part held secure by their common hatred of her. Good. She didn't care to have anyone tagging after her, pulling at her skirt and insisting on his or her fair share of her caring. She wanted Edwin. Edwin wanted her. They were going to have each other. She refused categorically to become emotional about the breaking of old ties.

"You've taken complete leave of your senses!" Mandy declared. "I mean to say, I know you've always had a bit of a thing for Edwin, and quite possibly he's had one for you, as well. But you can't throw over Arthur and walk away from your children. Well, I suppose you can. But honestly, Frances, don't you think you're being just the slightest bit hasty?"

"I'm not expecting it'll all happen in the next fortnight," Frances said reasonably. "I'm speaking of eventualities."

"I had no idea . . ." Mandy lit a cigarette and inhaled deeply, trying to marshal her thoughts. "I honestly don't know where to begin," she said. "How much has he told you?"

"Edwin? About what?"

"About himself, about his life before, during, and after the break with Elsa."

"I know what sort of life he's had."

"Has he actually spoken of it?"

"Not in so many words, no." Frances looked at this woman, her childhood friend seated opposite, and wondered why they were having this conversation. Who was Amanda anyway? Had they ever really known one another, beyond recognition of their facades? Naturally she knew the oval face with its uptilting blue eyes and short, pointed nose, the rather pouty mouth with its fullish lower lip. She could see silver strands here and there in Mandy's blond hair, and wondered idly whether the lemon rinses Mandy applied frequently affected these first signs of her aging. Or did Mandy care that parenthetical lines were taking form around her mouth and at the corners of her eyes? Mandy had a lifelong tendency toward plumpness, but she dressed to accentuate her best features, her full breasts and long, rather thin legs. For a moment, Frances's eyes rested on Mandy's breasts as she attempted to visualize what her friend might look like without her smartly cut black pinstripe suit and white silk blouse with jabot. "Have you been with him?" she asked. "Is that what you're trying to get to here?"

Mandy laughed, waving away the cloud of smoke between them. "Not in recent times," she admitted. "Years and years ago, before he ever met Elsa, we had the briefest of affairs."

"What was he like?" Frances asked eagerly, causing Mandy to laugh again, so that Frances at once regretted her impetuosity.

Her head tilted appraisingly to one side, Mandy said, "It hasn't gone that far yet with you, thank heavens. I might possibly save you some bother."

"This is becoming a bore," Frances threatened. "If you've something to say, say it. I despise all this hinting about and innuendo."

"This isn't you!" Mandy stated, taken aback. "This cannot be the Frances I've known all my life."

"We don't know each other, Amanda," Frances said flatly. "We're simply familiar with each other's faces and certain details of past history. What do you think you know about me, really?"

"Patently not as much as I'd thought." She paused, then said, "Are you aware that women would queue up to get Arthur?"

"They're welcome to him."

"You can't be serious! He's always been considered *the* catch. I realize one can't know about a marriage, even if one sleeps under a couple's bed, but still! You do surprise me!"

"I surprise myself," Frances admitted without warmth. "Do tell me whatever it is you're so anxious to get off your exceptional chest."

Mandy emitted a bark of laughter. "Thank God! I thought for a moment I was sitting here with a complete stranger. I'd like a fresh drink," she said, beckoning to the waitress. "Will you have another, Frances?"

"I think I will."

"Again, if you would," Mandy told the waitress, then turned to face Frances once more. She took the time to extinguish her cigarette, rubbed her small, meticulously manicured hands together, then folded her arms on the table. "Whether you care to believe it or not," she said seriously, "I believe I do know you. I also know Edwin. Rather too well."

"Oh, surely not too well!"

Somewhat impressed by Frances's defiance, Mandy conceded her acceptance of the terms of this encounter with a nod. "Since you insist, I'll be blunt. Edwin has a multitude of problems, always has had. Much of the blame can be safely laid at Elsa's feet, but the majority of his problems existed long before he ever met her. And for all the railing he does, and the grievances he has against her, I do believe Elsa managed to keep him all of a piece for a good, long time. The truth is: Edwin simply has no idea who or what he is."

"Be more specific," Frances asked, growing faintly alarmed. Whether she was speaking the truth or not, Mandy obviously believed every word she was saying. Her posture now, and the furrowing of her features, graphically displayed her concern.

Mandy moistened her lips, then lit a fresh cigarette, becoming more and more ill at ease. Why had Frances taken it into her head to be so suddenly difficult? "Look, darling," she began. "You've been infatuated with Edwin forever. All right. Fine. Have a fling, if you must; get it out of your system. But please don't make any major decisions until you've tasted the wine, so to speak. That's really all I'm trying to say. Edwin's the first to admit he's not good for the long haul. He's simply not interested in committing himself to anything long-term or permanent at this juncture. To avoid even the faintest whiff of it, he'll lie, he'll stall, he'll do anything he has to to maintain his freedom. His only real interest now is in 'fun.' It's all he's talked about since his return from America. Fun. If it isn't 'fun' he doesn't want to know about it. If it smacks in any way, shape, or form of obligation, responsibility, or attachment, Edwin will do absolutely anything to avoid it. So, darling, if you think you're simply going to switch over from Arthur to Edwin, you're more mistaken than I can possibly tell you. It just isn't going to happen."

"Why are you saying all this? Are you trying intentionally to upset me?"

The waitress set down the drinks, then moved away. Mandy watched as Frances lifted her glass and drank thirstily. "I would never," she said softly, "intentionally upset anyone, least of all you. Frances, I slept with the man half a dozen times. It's an enormous amount of work."

Frances blinked, slowly setting down her glass. "I thought you *adored* sex, that you found it highly delectable. You told me you divorced Lionel to be free to do *what* you wanted, *with whom* you wanted. You were determined to hear the siren song of sex, you said, Amanda. You were the emancipated woman of our generation; you told us so yourself."

"All true. But that's not what I'm on about here. My God! Even Lionel was less work than Edwin. In fact, he was a positive *joy* after Edwin. Frances, Frances! Edwin himself admits he isn't sure if he prefers to sleep with women or men. Now do you understand?"

"No, I don't," Frances said stubbornly.

"He's been to bed with both sexes—regularly. There!" Mandy made a face. "I can't put it more bluntly than that. No. I can. I will. You're important to me. We've been friends for almost thirty years. I refuse to stand by and watch you throw yourself at the head of someone who's in no position to catch you, and wouldn't anyway, given a choice. Edwin and I made love as if I were a *boy*." She looked around furtively, to be sure she wasn't being overheard. "Do you even know what that means?" she demanded angrily. "It's loathsome admitting to this, but I'll bear it if it'll prevent you doing something not only foolhardy but possibly even dangerous." She leaned closer, her voice dropping to a whisper. "I truly don't believe you understand what I'm confiding to you, Frances. So I'll *make* you understand. The truth is I've never been completely successful in ridding myself of the sick-making feeling that for a period of weeks, some years ago, I played an active part in what was, to all intents and purposes, a homosexual romance. I got down on my hands and knees for him. I *never saw* his *face*. Everything we did together were things two men could and would have done and, in fact, do. Edwin has since confirmed that. Most apologetically, I might add. I went along with it at the time because it was an experimental era for me and I thought I might fancy something a bit *risqué*. I hated it, Fanny. It was painful and degrading. And it wasn't that I mightn't perhaps have enjoyed doing those same things with another man but rather that, in Edwin's case, there was such anger and confusion that both of us were damaged by the experience. Public schools are *not* the lofty institutions people would have us believe. He didn't confide a great deal, but he did tell me enough to give me a very clear picture of the sort of things some of those boys got up to. It's affected his entire life. Now!'' She took a deep breath and sat back. ''Are you still going to tell me you're willing to throw away all you have to risk pain of one sort or another with Edwin? Talk of not knowing people! You haven't the faintest notion who he is. And what's worse, neither does he! He's managed to convince himself that the lies he tells, and the promises he breaks, and his constant dishonesty, all spring from his basic good manners. Rather than be rude and risk upsetting anyone by giving direct answers and stating his true preferences, he avoids and avoids and avoids. Oh, he knows he does it, all right. But he pushes it all neatly under the umbrella alibi of 'one's need to behave decorously.' '' Having spoken her piece, she swallowed half her drink in one go, all the while keeping close watch on Frances.

Mandy's words seemed to fall like solid objects into her brain, clogging her skull cavity. She had to sit in silence for several minutes, pushing among the words, trying to find the ones she wanted to deal with. In spite of Mandy's argument, Frances's immediate reaction to her depiction of Edwin's and her aberration was one of sexual excitement. It was in terribly poor taste for Mandy to have been quite so revealing about their amatory acts, and Frances could only feel a strong dislike of her for having been so indiscreet. She also now believed that Mandy was not the sexual adventuress she'd hinted she was. Hadn't she just admitted to disliking the act? I wouldn't have disliked it! she thought fiercely. Edwin could do anything conceivable to her and it would only send her into more of her magnificent convulsions. Mandy hadn't been woman enough to deal with him. I am, she thought, grateful now for her delirious experimentation. She mightn't have been up to the task, had she not taken matters in hand. Literally. God! She flushed at her new boldness. The thought of getting on her hands and knees to have Edwin make love to her was wildly exciting. Just the thought of it created an ache in her lower belly.

"You think I'm exaggerating," Mandy said, "or that I've revealed myself to be deficient in some way. I can almost read what you're thinking on your face." Mandy gave a shocked bark of laughter. "I think," she said slowly, "you just may have lost your senses, after all, Frances. You haven't actually heard what I've told you. You're sitting there processing my words, filtering out the parts you don't wish to know about."

"I'm doing nothing of the sort," Frances lied, still actively engaged in doing precisely that. "You admit yourself all this happened ages ago. You don't know that he's the same way now."

"I *do* know! That's what I'm saying. Edwin's told me that himself. We're close friends, Frances. Edwin and I see one another regularly, socially. We're friends, and we talk. What we talk about often has to do with his deep fears regarding his sexual preferences. It could be unspeakably damaging to him, were it to become known he's had dealings with other men."

"I'm certainly not about to repeat this tale to anyone!" Frances declared haughtily.

"No," Mandy said. "You won't, because you've refused to hear it. Will you do just one thing for me? Please?"

"What?"

"Do whatever it is you think you have to do, but in the name of everything sacred, please, don't say anything yet to Arthur, or do anything drastic, until you've met and talked with Edwin. He did mention there was the possibility of his seeing you this weekend."

"That's right," Frances said proprietarily. "We do plan to be together."

Mandy saw the smugness on Frances's face, and sighed. "I need another drink. I'll get pied, but I don't think I'm up to going back to the office this afternoon anyway. Not after this." She turned to signal the waitress, then asked, "Would you care to get pied with me?"

"I'll just finish this one," Frances demurred, disdain for Mandy easing the clogged feeling in her head. The woman drank too much, smoked too much, said far too much. The qualities she'd admired for so long in Mandy now seemed nothing more than an illusion.

The two sat, nurturing their private thoughts, until Mandy's fresh drink was delivered. "I know," Mandy said softly, sadly, "you think I've the morals of an alley cat. You've always looked down your nose at me because I've been indelicate enough to refer to some of my encounters with men. But I'll tell you this, Frances: I've never in my life been irresponsible. I've never knowingly harmed another living soul. You're about to harm absolutely everyone, but you will not listen. I don't know what it is, but something's happened to change you. It's very frightening. The odd thing is I'm somehow more afraid for Edwin than I am for you. You've got the strength of your convictions, however misguided they might be. You've also got the madness of a sexually repressed woman and you think you're going to solve all your problems by fixing on the last man on earth who's in any way equipped to deal with you. Frances, go home. Take the next train back to Leamington, and wait this thing out somehow. Perhaps you could confront Arthur with your needs. The man adores you. He always has. I'll wager anything you've never indicated your dissatisfaction to him. Have you?"

"It's too late in the day for talking to Arthur. And in any event, naked bodies tend to embarrass him."

"Poor Arthur. And poor you. I'd like to believe that this will come right, but I know it won't."

"Could it be that you're envious?" Frances asked, genuinely curious.

"Would that it were so simple." Mandy stared into her gin and tonic. "I'd be delighted to find you worthy of my envy, Fan. In this instance, anyway. Lord! This is hateful. I've never had to stand by and watch someone so determined to create havoc. It's an unpleasant position to find oneself in."

"Oh, surely no more unpleasant than getting down on your hands and knees."

"That was heartless, and horribly cruel!" Mandy protested. "I told you what I did in confidence, and because I wanted to help. You'd like it, wouldn't you, if I damned you to hell and stormed away. I'm not going to do that, Frances. I'm going to finish my gin, and then I'll have the beef, I think. After that, quite possibly, I'll have one last drink before I walk home. I'll walk very slowly and while I do, I'll think about you. I'm going to hope that when worse does come to worst, you'll remember that I warned you. I may even be willing to help, if

I'm able; if you haven't damaged absolutely everything. You have a lovely husband, and two very nice children. Hadleigh especially. If I'd had a daughter like her, I'd never have left Lionel. I'm not able to have children. There's something else you didn't know. It's one of the reasons why I've felt free to indulge my appetites. You don't have that sort of freedom, do you, Frances? You produce your seeds and bleed them away, month after month. You'll count on Edwin to protect you, won't you?" She laughed softly. "You've thought of none of the practical aspects, have you, Frances? It's been endless fantasy, with no grounding anywhere in reality. Until a few minutes ago, I considered you my oldest and dearest friend. I never dreamed you were capable of such bitchery. I think you should go now, Frances. We have nothing more to say to one another."

Frances stared at her for a moment, then got up and left.

Frances stopped to buy basic foodstuffs, then carried them home to the flat. No sign of Arthur. Her bag was where she'd left it that morning, just inside the bedroom door. The two drinks she'd had were roiling angrily in her empty stomach and she went to the kitchen to put away the milk before making a pot of tea and some toast.

She ate standing, looking with dismay at the accumulating dust on every surface. It irked her to think that the char had quit without so much as a word of warning. The place was badly in need of cleaning, and she decided she might just as well do it. It would help work off some of her residual anger with Amanda.

She knew she was tipsy but she hadn't had so much to drink that her senses had been thoroughly dulled. She had to speak to Edwin, to caution him about his dealings with Frances. After leaving the restaurant, Mandy stepped into the nearest call box and dialed the office number. It was only just gone three. He wouldn't have left yet for the day.

"Oh, Mrs. Adams, I'm afraid he's with someone."

"Damn!" Mandy swore under her breath.

"Beg pardon?"

"Sorry. I won't be back this afternoon. Would you be good enough to ask him to ring me at home? It's important that I speak with him. A matter of some urgency has arisen."

"I'll certainly give him the message, but I've no idea how long he'll be."

"I'll be in all evening. Ask him please to ring me."

Upon arriving home, she sat down in the lounge near the telephone, with the slow passage of the afternoon becoming more and more agitated. It was vital to talk with Edwin. She couldn't rid herself of the sensation that something dreadful was going to happen, and if she could talk to Edwin she might help prevent any unpleasantness. She sat distractedly enjoying a rare bit of January sunshine as it pierced the leaves of the pot plants aligned on the window ledge. Her thoughts circled repeatedly around Frances and the singularly nasty hour they'd spent together. Frances was most definitely having some sort of breakdown. Perhaps she was one of those women for whom turning forty represented attaining the darker side of life. She herself had had a smashing time on her fortieth the previous year, inviting all her friends to a party she gave. They'd all had far too much to drink, and had danced until four the next morning. Someone had stopped the night with her. Who? She couldn't remember. All she had was the distinct impression of frenzied love-making on the bedroom floor. She smiled, thinking of the dress she'd had made for the occasion, of black taffeta with a deeply scooped neckline and full, billowing sleeves, and a skirt that had seemed to catch air currents and lift as she'd danced. What a marvellous time that had been! Frances hadn't come; she'd telephoned her apologies, reciting what had sounded like a prepared speech having to do with Arthur's being detained at the ministry, and Ben down with a cold.

She glanced at her watch. Coming on five and Edwin hadn't yet rung her. She got up and for a second time telephoned the office.

"Mrs. Adams, I did give him your message," Sarah told her. "But he was in a frightful hurry and dashed off without dealing with any of his messages. I did tell him, though."

"Thank you. Have a pleasant weekend, Sarah."

Where had Edwin been dashing off to? she wondered. It was quite possible he was hurrying back to his flat to freshen up for an evening with Frances. That being the case, it would take the better part of an hour for him to get from the City to West Kensington. Then, allowing another hour for bathing and changing, if she tried to reach him at the flat at seven, she just might catch him before he went out. Pausing to turn on the table lamp, she resumed her seat on the sofa. The light beyond the window had gone. She'd get up in a minute or two to draw the blackout curtains, but for the moment, with the glass reflecting the lamplight, it was almost possible to forget about the war, and the ARPs, and the voices from below that were certain to begin bellowing, "LIGHTS!" in response to the well-lit windows of her flat.

Why didn't he ring? Frances stopped regularly to turn in the direction of the lounge, listening. Nothing. She spent more than an hour shaving her legs and underarms, then massaged cream into every reachable area of her skin, rubbing gently, appreciating the softness beneath her hands. When the last vestiges of the scented cream had been absorbed into her receptive flesh, she walked defiantly nude—as if daring Arthur to arrive home and find her in the midst of her preparations to sleep with another man—into the bedroom to dress, conscious, with each item of clothing she donned, of how she'd appear to Edwin as he removed it.

She'd unearthed her bridal lingerie that had lain, untouched, along with her wedding and reception gowns, in a large carton in the box room. The cream-colored silk undergarments felt coolly perfect, slithering against her as she drew on her stockings then stood, half-turned, before the mirror to ascertain that her seams were perfectly aligned. She placed with a fingertip dots of perfume at the base of her throat, behind each ear, and in the bend of her elbows. Then, clad in her silks and a pair of black high heels she'd worn only twice before on special occasions, she went into the bathroom, where the light was good, to apply her makeup.

As she brushed her dark brown hair, she debated the wisdom of putting it up. If she left it down, there'd be no troublesome pins to fuss over. Yet she did think she looked better with her hair backswept, accentuating the lines of her cheekbones and jaw. She experimented, listening all the while for the telephone.

Dressed and ready, finally, she stood before the table holding the telephone, willing it to ring. It was coming on for seven. What to do? They'd talked of theatre tickets, or a film, but she'd volunteered to prepare him a meal. She'd made that offer but hadn't bothered to buy ingredients, and now it was too late. The shops were closed, and she hadn't any rations left. She rushed to the kitchen to review her purchases. Nothing suitable for an evening meal, just bread and cheese, milk and two eggs. She was being silly. Edwin would have laid in everything necessary. He was expecting her, and she'd wasted precious time awaiting his confirmation.

She collected her coat, bag and keys, snapped off the lights and ran out to try to find a taxi.

Six

Arthur was far enough distant to require a second or two to ascertain that the figure who came flying out onto the pavement from the block of flats was, indeed, Frances. He raised his hand and called out, but he was too removed to be heard. He ran forward, thinking to catch her up. She was moving at quite a clip, and scanning the road, undoubtedly for a taxi. He came to a halt as she reached the corner and turned out of sight.

Each time she heard a car approaching she looked around hoping it might be a cab. But by the time she'd reached the entrance to the underground she'd already decided it would be faster to go by tube and bus. She couldn't afford to waste time, and clattered down the entrance stairs, almost falling in the very high heels. Steadying herself with the handrail, her nose wrinkled at the thought of the countless unclean hands that had travelled this same territory, and of the families that were bound to be installed below ground for the night. Going by underground after dark had become singularly unpleasant. One had to step over and around seemingly endless bodies both upon entering and leaving trains. And the air down here was simply foul! She held a perfumed handkerchief discreetly to her nose, promising herself she'd wash her hands at Edwin's before so much as touching the food.

A train had just pulled in. She ran to board, found a seat, and sat catching her breath. What if she'd left it too late?

What if Edwin had decided she wasn't coming after all? He might at that very moment be opening a tin of beans or spaghetti while bread toasted under the grill. Oh, but he couldn't have forgotten! He'd made a note in his diary. Had she got it wrong? Was she supposed to have rung him? She just couldn't remember the details.

As the train hurtled along its subterranean course she reviewed their most recent conversation, trying to find some point where she might have omitted to pick up on something he'd said, some arrangement she'd failed to observe. She couldn't think. The long-term effects of her sleepless state were undeniable. If she didn't soon rest she might cease to function altogether. Like some overused piece of machinery, her component parts might break down, causing the machine as a whole to quit. Edwin was the key. But what if she'd got it wrong and he wasn't there?

He had to be home, had to be. She so badly needed to be with him, to have him declare his love for her. He would be there; he would.

Out of the underground and racing along Kensington Church Street, her side was beginning to ache; but she kept up her pace. The stitch in her side evolved into pain, and she was forced to slow somewhat, startled upon nearly colliding in the darkness with a bulky figure. Damn this war! she thought, her heart racketing wildly in the aftermath of the near-collision. People were forced to live like bloody moles, groping about in the dark, trying to find their way. As if all the enforced precautions were going to make a bit of difference! The Germans dropped their bombs regardless; air raid precautions were certainly no deterrent.

She came round the corner into Edwin's street and slowed her pace further. It wouldn't do to appear at his door winded and disheveled. He was a man to whom appearances mattered greatly. She'd always known that, and had admired him for his standards. It was vital to maintain her composure, for both their sakes. Had there been sufficient light, she'd have stopped to check her makeup, but that was out of the question. She had to be content with running a shaky hand over her upswept hair as she lifted the door knocker, praying he'd waited for her.

He was home. Hearing his footsteps, she began to smile.

"I do hope I'm not too terribly late," she told him, wondering why he looked so bemused as she glided past him into the foyer. "I simply couldn't find a taxi and had to come by underground. One should avoid tube stations at all costs these days." She laughed softly, elated by her safe arrival. "It's rather like travelling steerage class."

He pushed closed the door, watching as she entered and went directly through to stand by the fire, warming herself. "Frances," he said, "forgive me." He took several steps toward her. "Did we make specific plans to meet?" He was positive they'd done no such thing, and was flabbergasted by her unannounced arrival. She hadn't even bothered with a preliminary telephone call. He glanced around the room, then looked back at her. "I'm sure I . . . Didn't we leave it that I'd ring you?"

"I couldn't recall." Her smile holding, she turned so that her back was to the fire. Why was he staying so far away? And why hadn't he complimented her on how she looked, or offered to take her coat? "Isn't it ridiculous? I knew we'd planned to dine together, but I could not, for the life of me, remember what arrangements we'd made."

"As I recall," he said evenly, keeping hold of his temper, "you said you'd be at Cheyne Walk, and it was my intention to ring you tomorrow." How incredibly presumptuous this was of her! "This is rather inconvenient actually . . . You see, I do have other plans for the evening."

Why was it, she wondered, that in person he invariably failed in so many ways to live up to her thoughts of him? He wasn't anywhere near as attractive as her mental pictures of him, nor was he as warmly welcoming as she'd expected. She had her work cut out for her here, all right, but she was up to it. The first step was to dismiss these irrelevant criticisms from her mind. "I'm not usually so hare-brained." She willed him to respond to the smile that was starting to make her cheeks ache. "Not only could I not recall what plans we'd made, but I forgot altogether to shop for our meal. I was to lunch with Mandy, and we did meet, but I'm afraid it didn't come off quite as planned. I do hope you remembered."

"Hope I remembered?" What *was* she going on about? Couldn't she hear what he was telling her? Was it possible she had a hearing problem? Could something so elemental be responsible for all this nonsense? "What was I to remember, Frances?"

"Not to worry," she intoned cheerily coming away slightly from the heat of the fire. "We'll go to your club, as you suggested." She wanted to embrace him, looked at his mouth, and felt a preliminary twinge of pleasure. "If you did remember to shop, I'll be happy to fix something." She wasn't hungry, but food did seem to be a part of the agenda.

"I am sorry," he said again, puzzling over why this slim, almost frail, woman should strike him as quite so fearsome. He was actually rather afraid of her, and understood all at once what it was Mandy had been trying to tell him. "There's been something of a misunderstanding, Fan," he began, then stopped. This was nightmarish! Why was she here? They hadn't made definite plans, yet she was going on as if they had, as if he'd made all sorts of promises. He'd done nothing more than state enthusiasm at having seen her again at the party. She'd opted to interpret this as something else altogether. Did this mean he was going, in future, to have to curb his every spontaneous impulse? Was he meant to act other than naturally in order to protect himself from scenes such as this? She was removing her coat, plainly intent on staying, and he despised himself for his inability to stop her with a few well-chosen remarks. She was bound to become emotional if he displayed anything other than courtesy. Bloody, bloody hell!

"We'll have a drink, shall we?" he offered. He'd give her a drink, clarify the situation with as little pain as possible, then see her on her way.

"Lovely!"

Groaning inwardly, he went to fetch her a drink. He hated his dependence on good manners, and there were times, such as this one, when the very concept of being "civilized" was anathema. What a damned nuisance! he cursed mutely, purposely dallying over fixing the drinks. He wished without any real hope that when he returned she'd have come to her senses and be gone. This was nowhere near over. God only knew what else she had in mind! She did remind him of Elsa, with her dogged persistence and her refusal to hear anything but her own words. Why couldn't women listen? Why did they insist upon directing events? The quality he liked least in women was their determination to be in charge of others. Frances hadn't been this way, years ago. Now here she was, bent not only on control, but on scandal. Wasn't her husband in some ministry or other? Dear God! All this heated indiscretion! The last thing on earth he wanted was to find himself an unwitting correspondent in a filthy divorce action. He was beginning to feel decidedly queasy. He'd give her a drink and then, as politely as possible, get rid of her.

She watched him go into the kitchen, realizing she was going to have to take definitive action. He seemed not to sense the significance or depth of her feelings for him. All too likely he was aware, but feared misinterpreting. Men were like that. She'd have to make a graphic display he couldn't fail to understand. He'd see her nude, before the fire, and confess his feelings for her. He required delicate prodding, but that wasn't unreasonable in view of how dreadfully Elsa had wounded him. She, Frances, would make atonement for all previous sins committed against him. It was one test of her love; she could meet the challenge. Yet her fingers fumbled, and she couldn't go beyond removing her dress. She lacked courage, she thought lamentingly. Was she doomed forever to fail at bringing her dreams forward into reality? At best, in recent times, she'd only been able to create outlines that lacked color and shading.

Arranging herself by the fire, clad in her silk bridal teddy, her back to the room, she waited, feeling the cold collecting against her exposed skin while the heat of the coal-fire scorched her legs. What was taking him so long? How long did it take to pour liquor into two glasses? She wished he'd hurry.

At first glance, he thought she must be wearing some sort of ludicrously abbreviated frock. Drawing closer, he saw she'd taken off her dress, and he almost dropped the drinks. Instantly bathed in perspiration, he was mortally ashamed for her. She'd gone mad, and he was going to have to deal with her. Once he'd sent her on her way, he'd never again leave himself open to such a distressing situation. Damn it all to bloody hell! Why did this have to happen to him? He was a peaceable man. All he wanted from life was a bit of pleasure, some fun. He didn't go about mixing it up, made no demands of people, yet it seemed everyone had demands of some sort to make on him. The unfairness of it was positively galling!

"Frances!" he exclaimed. "What *are* you doing?" He spoke sharply, his temper finally breaking. "You're going to embarrass both of us with this." He set the drinks down on the mantel and retrieved her dress from the floor. "Please, put this back on!" He held the garment out to her.

"You don't mean it, Edwin." She slid her arms beneath his to embrace him, her head coming to rest on his shoulder. "I do realize that, for form's sake, you feel obligated to make some protest. But it's truly not necessary."

For the briefest moment, he wasn't sure he did mean it. The pressure of her body was seductive, and he was swayed. That was the problem, though. He was constantly tempted, one way and another. "I'm afraid that I do mean it," he said more quietly, seeking to extricate himself. She seemed glued to him. "This is most awkward," he went on, hoping they'd be able, both of them, to salvage some measure of their dignity. "I'm indeed most flattered you'd feel this way, but I'm simply not able to reciprocate at this moment."

"What are you saying, Edwin?" She lifted her head to look at him. He'd stop fussing soon, and they'd make love. The teddy was growing damp from the heat of their bodies.

"Please," he begged, trying to return the dress to her. "Do put this on. We'll have our drinks and talk calmly."

"I'm perfectly calm, extraordinarily calm. I know precisely what I'm doing." Her hands swept over his broad back. "We're going to make love. I've thought of nothing else for weeks. I adore you. You know that. I always have."

"Frances," his voice sounded as if he were strangling, "you can't be serious about this. We've seen each other precisely once in fifteen years."

"Feelings remain constant," she said placidly, despite the inner agitation she was starting to feel.

"I haven't *shared* those feelings, Frances. I've been entirely unaware you thought of me as anything more than an old friend."

"You know you're going to give in," she said, trying to kiss him. He shoved her away, again pushing the dress at her. When she made no move to take it but simply stood gazing at him, his anger exploded its careful containment.

"*I want you to put this on at once!*" he ordered, his face growing dark. "Put it on, and then leave! You must leave, before this goes any farther and real damage is done."

"What damage? What are you saying? We talked of being together. You want me . . . The things I've done for you . . . so many things . . . And I haven't slept, haven't been able to sleep night after night. We planned to be together."

"We did nothing of the sort!" he argued. "And whatever

you claim to've done for me has been inspired solely by your own imaginings. I've *said* nothing, *done* nothing, to encourage you."

"But you have! Promising to ring me day after day . . ."

He was shaking his head. "No! You've chosen to interpret matters to suit yourself. I've done *nothing.*"

"Edwin!" she cried, losing control. "I *love* you! I have done for such a long time."

He was continuing to shake his head, denying her. "It's rubbish!" he insisted. "Absolute rubbish! I don't know what's got into you, but this is pure and utter nonsense!" He turned his back to reach for her coat.

"Why won't you *listen*?" she implored.

He wouldn't look at her, wouldn't listen. He'd inspired her to give up everything, and now he claimed not to want her. Suddenly, she despised him, despised the sight of his overweight figure as he bent to pick up her coat. Her body vibrated with the intensity of her sudden hatred for him as her hand shot out and closed around the poker leaning to one side of the fireplace. The poker rose into the air and, as he was straightening, caught him on the side of the head with a thick, muffled thud. He half turned, his eyes wide with disbelief, then he staggered, her coat falling from his hands as he lifted one hand toward his face. He went down on the floor before the gesture was complete.

Quivering with rage, she stood waiting for him to get up. When he failed to move, she struck him again, then allowed the poker to slip from her hand. His hair was darkly wet; blood sheeted down the side of his face. It didn't look quite real; the red was so hotly vivid, like freshly applied paint. She touched the toe of her shoe to his arm. Nothing. He was dead. She'd killed him. Had she? Was he actually *dead*? "God!" she gasped, suddenly aware of noises outside. They'd been there for some time, but she wasn't sure if they were real or merely inside her own head, where her thoughts seemed to have acquired density and substance and fell crashing against each other loudly. A shrieking whine sundered the air. Shivering, she listened. Her mouth was open and a thin wail was coming from somewhere within her to blend with the ceaseless screaming of the sirens. She looked down to see the blood oozing still, coating Edwin's cheek, forming a widening puddle on the carpet. Her knees wanted to give way; her body seemed to want to fall into fragments. She held her hands to her ears to block out the noise. What had she done? She hadn't meant to do this, but he refused to listen. Why couldn't he have listened?

"Why wouldn't you?" she asked hoarsely, quaking, startled by the sound of her own voice into taking action. She snatched up her dress, coat, and bag, and fled. Arriving in the street, as mysteriously as it had come to her, her momentum was gone. Panting, her possessions pressed tight to her breast, she turned to look back at the door through which she'd passed. What to do? Where to go? Think! She couldn't think.

"Quickly!" a man's voice directed, an authoritative hand taking firm hold of her upper arm. "Come with me!"

The hand propelled her forward at a run along the street. Supplied now with a direction, she ran, instinctively ducking her head as a piercing whistle sliced through both the sky and the interior of her head. A moment of sudden silence was followed by a tremendous explosion. The resulting burst of flames illuminated the street, bleaching it of color. Objects hurtled through the air. Something rammed against her back with such force she went down on one knee. The hand on her arm yanked her upright, and they ran on.

"We'll never make it to the tube station!" his voice shouted above the din of falling debris. "In here!" He towed her through a doorway and pushed her flat against a cold, stone wall where they stood very close together in the lull.

She could hear his breathing and her own, could feel the condensation forming in the space between them as the air from their lungs blended; she could almost grasp the commingling air. Allowing everything to fall, she reached out blindly, clamped her mouth to his, and clutched his arms frantically. The mouth against hers opened to speak and she broke the fevered kiss only long enough to whisper a warning to keep silent. While she grappled with his trousers, she shrugged the straps of the teddy from her shoulders. Two seconds and she was naked but for her garter belt and stockings. A few seconds more, and with her direction, they'd managed to join. She was being rhythmically driven against the wall. She felt like some primal beast, freed at last from all convention. Exquisite, brutal satisfaction. "Touch me!" she urged, finding his hand

and inserting it between their bodies. "*Touch me!*" He obeyed, and, at once, she was close to attaining a pleasure bound to decimate her. Edwin at last. Her fingers wound tightly into his hair, she bent one leg around the back of his to ensure the continuation of his beating presence within her. The stone wall was warm suddenly; she'd taken flame. Her body rigid, a long shallow scream ripped from her throat. Her body jerked about, out of control. She clung, pinioned, to the still-thrusting force. Then he sighed shudderingly and fell limply forward against her. "I love you, love you," she chanted softly. "I love you."

Beyond their place of concealment, the last of the wreckage had settled in the road. The sirens wound down to a growl. Silence. Her hands groped over his body, pressing, seeking, examining his moist softness. She was so deeply moved, engulfed in love for him. Beneath her hands he was responding. Proof. This was her proof. "Once more," she crooned. "Again, please."

"Not now," he answered in a normal tone that made her wince with its loudness. "We must get you home, Frances."

"Just once more, darling." She stroked him insistently.

He stood apart from her, depriving her of warmth. At once she began shivering violently. She was glad to pull on the dress, and then the coat, as he gave each to her. How good he was to take such care of her!

"Are you ready? Come!" He took her hand.

"Wait! My bag." Her searching hand came into contact with a slimy, clinging mass and she cried out in disgust before realizing it was her abandoned teddy. She located her bag and got to her feet.

The street was lit by blazing rubble. She gazed unblinking at the destruction as they headed toward Kensington Church Street, picking their way over broken glass, shattered pieces of furniture, huge slabs of masonry, mounds of brick. Coming abreast of a small group working to clear the debris, she suddenly realized Edwin's building had been reduced to a smoking heap of bricks and timbers.

"Edwin!" His name was an involuntary whisper as she came to a halt, trying to think. She'd struck him. He hadn't moved, and she'd struck him again. But they'd just made love; she'd touched him more meaningfully than she'd ever dreamed possible. He was seeing her safely home. But, no. How could he be? Dear God! If it wasn't Edwin who had hold of her hand, who was it? She was terrified to turn and see who was standing at her side. It simply had to be Edwin. But that couldn't be. Was this real? Could she have dreamed all this? Would she awaken now to find herself in bed in Leamington?

A scream was collecting strength in her lungs. Terror was a tangible constriction around her heart, a knot in her belly. She wet her lips and turned very slowly, her insides drawing themselves into small, tight coils. It was Arthur who was seeing her home. *Arthur*. Not Edwin. Edwin was somewhere over there, beneath that cairn created by German bombs. She'd killed him and the Germans had buried him. Her breathing had turned ragged; she began to weep. With a slight tug on her hand, Arthur drew her away. Frances craned around, looking back over her shoulder, at the small group working to clear the debris, searching for survivors in the wreckage. They'd find him, then they'd come for her.

Her terror was undiminished. Things were exceedingly confused; she could find no order to her thoughts. Desolate, she was powerless to resist Arthur's ministrations. He got her undressed and into the tub; he even bathed her.

"You're badly bruised," he said sorrowfully, gingerly touching the large, darkly discolored area of her back where she'd been struck by a flying brick. "Poor darling." He soaped and rinsed her with the greatest care, pausing to kiss the torn flesh of her knee.

The soothing motions did ease a measure of her fear. Temporarily calmed, she stood obediently while he dried her, but was seized again by terror when he stroked her shoulder. His mouth on her breast revived for her the hated sensations of nursing; recent pleasures battled with past recollections. A third emotion nudged aside the others, making room for itself: direct fear of Arthur. He had to know what she'd done. Why else had he been there?

"Come lie down, Fan. I'll fetch some liniment."

"I don't want any."

"Just lie back." The heel of his hand easily brought her down. "It'll help, I promise."

"Really," she protested weakly. "I don't need it."

He loomed over her with new and alarming authority. "You must let me, Frances. Otherwise, you won't be able to move by morning."

"Wait!" She grabbed hold of his hand, desperate to learn how much he knew. "You must wait."

"Certainly." Smiling, he sat down beside her on the bed. He looked different, altered. Was it because of what they'd done together? Or was it what he now knew about her?

"I don't understand," she started uncertainly. "What I mean to say is . . ."

"How did I come to be there? Is that it?"

"Yes," she said thickly.

"As chance would have it, I had the evening free and was just arriving back here when you came out. I was curious, so I tagged along after you. Actually"—he laughed—"I couldn't imagine why you were in such a tearing hurry." He shrugged. "I was on the pavement, deliberating, and when the sirens sounded I was about to come in after you when you came out. Lucky thing I decided to follow, wouldn't you say?"

"But what . . . I mean . . ."

"I don't think we need discuss that tonight, do you, Frances?"

Through parched lips, she answered, "No. I shouldn't think so."

"Good girl. I'll just bathe. Won't be more than a minute or two."

Her eyes followed him as he crossed the room. Surely he knew. Why else had he pursued her? Perhaps Mandy had told him. Or even Edwin himself. She lay waiting, wondering if he planned to exact payment of some kind in exchange for his silence. She hadn't the strength to care. He could kill her, for all it mattered. Nothing mattered now.

Her exhaustion was so complete she thought it might be possible to die of it. Yet her fear was such that it might keep her awake forever. When she tried experimentally to close her eyes all she could see was Edwin sprawled on the floor, and the slow-dripping blood flowing from the wound in his head.

"Are you asleep?" Arthur's low voice jarred her.

"No." Again she wet her lips. "I'm not asleep."

"Roll over and let me do this for you." He uncapped the

bottle of liniment. At once its unpleasantly strong odor nipped at her nostrils.

She obeyed and for long minutes he rubbed the liquid into her skin. Again, she was lulled into semi-awareness.

"There we go," he said, recapping the bottle. "That should do the trick."

He went off, saying something about washing his hands. She must have dozed because when next she was aware of him his body lay along the length of hers and her thighs, of their own volition, were parting to enclose him. She looked into his eyes thinking that if she hadn't already gone mad, very likely she soon would be. She felt very near to the portal of some dark and dreadful place; her entry would be as effortless as Arthur's slow glide forward into her.

Seven

She waited for Arthur to make some statement of his knowledge, but he said nothing. After kissing her sweetly, he left to return to the ministry with his promise to ring as soon as he possibly could.

Stiff in spite of the liniment, Frances rose and got ready to return to Leamington. Throughout her every action—stripping the bed linens which she'd take with her to launder, pouring a cup of tea in the kitchen, bathing, dressing—she expected the arrival at the door of someone from the police who would formally accuse her of the crime she'd committed. Any abnormal noise caused her to tense. No one came.

The swaying of the train sent her lurching to the lavatory where the contents of her stomach gushed from her mouth. This was followed by several minutes of dry heaving that left her weakened and damply feverish. By the time she arrived back at the house on Kenilworth Road she was quivering uncontrollably and went directly to the bathroom to immerse herself in a tubful of hot water.

To her mother's anxious enquiry through the door, Frances wearily replied, "I think it's a touch of 'flu. I'll be fine. Just leave me be, please."

Deirdre went off, apparently satisfied with this explanation, and Frances sank down into the water, the mental re-enactment of all that had taken place the previous night reviving the tremors throughout her body. It was, she reasoned, merely a matter of a short time before someone from the police or

Scotland Yard presented himself at the front door to confront her with the details and evidence of her violence. On the one hand she was terror-stricken; on the other, she suspected she'd be relieved not to have to continue living in her present state of anxiety.

No one came.

Arthur's infrequent telephone calls were without nuance. He asked after her and Deirdre, spoke briefly with the children, and ended each time with his promise to be in touch again at the first possible opportunity.

Daily she bought the London papers, fully expecting to see banner headlines. Some three days after her return, several of the papers carried obituary notices that said simply that Edwin had met his untimely death as a result of an air-raid attack, then went on to note his academic and business achievements. Elsa was mentioned, as were his next of kin, who consisted of a number of aunts, uncles, and cousins. That was all. There was no hint from any source that his death had been anything but an accident; Edwin appeared to have become another casualty of the war. She was dumfounded. Surely this was nothing more than a clever police ploy meant to endow her with a sense of false security. After all, she'd left behind evidence. Hadn't she?

She scoured her brain, trying to go back over every last detail, slowly arriving at the conclusion that there was something she was missing, some, perhaps subconscious, item lodged like a sliver in a lost corner of her memory. Again and again, she reviewed what had happened, each word they'd spoken, every action. There was something, she was certain, but she just could not get to it.

As days, and then weeks, passed, she began to tell herself she had to have imagined all of it. She stopped leaping to attention each time the doorbell or the telephone sounded; she no longer went out to purchase all the daily newspapers. But her ongoing sleeplessness was wearing her down, and when she did manage to doze for a few hours, she was back in the flat off Kensington Church Street, bringing the poker down over and over on Edwin's skull. She killed him nightly; he died ceaselessly.

While at the greengrocer's, or the chemist's, or in the kitchen, she'd find herself viewing the commission of her crime, and had to force herself to attend to whatever it was she was supposed to be doing. The only help available reposed in the drinks cabinet, and regularly she handed a discreetly folded pound note in under-the-counter transaction with the proprietor of the local off-license in order to replenish the supply of scotch. In similar fashion, she obtained cigarettes.

In the course of each day she'd have several swallows of scotch directly from the bottle, followed by two or three legitimate drinks of an evening while she sat with her mother in the lounge, daring Deirdre even so much as to comment on her new habits. She smoked openly, and Deirdre came along after, without comment cleaning the ashtrays that appeared everywhere in the house. Having sensed her daughter's defiance, Deirdre kept silent. Frances was daily becoming less recognizable, and Deirdre couldn't think of any casual way in which to find out just what was responsible.

Frances was, in fact, so unlike herself that Deirdre covertly studied her with fascination. It was almost as if an actress had taken over the role of Frances and was doing so inept a job of portrayal that, surely, it would be no more than a short time before the actress departed in disgrace and the real Frances resumed the role.

Yet, by spring nothing like that had occurred, and their dealings were growing increasingly uncivil. Frances was openly hostile to everyone, but particularly to Hadleigh. Deirdre was reluctant to intercede on the children's behalf for fear of exacerbating the situation. Frances was growing as volatile as an incendiary device, one of those dreadful German buzz-bombs that made such a fearful racket, then were silent for a moment or two before exploding.

What most worried Deirdre was that Hadleigh seemed to trigger something ugly in Frances. For the slightest of misdemeanors, Frances would shout at the girl and order her up to her room. Several times it was only Deirdre's presence that prevented Frances from actually beating the girl, although Frances certainly showed no compunction about administering slaps and pushes and screams of invective at the unwitting child.

While previously Hadleigh had seemed fairly able to handle her ongoing rejection by her mother, she now was dwindling visibly beneath her mother's constant attacks. She ate less and less, and jumped every time Frances entered the room. She couldn't concentrate on her studies, and Deirdre took to helping her with her work of an evening. She tried to be extra kind to the child, at bedtime reassuring her, "It's a difficult time, dear, for all of us. Mummy's under a good deal of pressure. Certainly you can understand that, what with being unable to live in her own home, and being away from all her friends."

"She hates me, Nana," Hadleigh confided in a whisper. "Honestly, she does."

"Of course, she doesn't!" Deirdre smiled to mask her dismay. "It's simply a time when we must pull together, and make do without a lot of the things we're accustomed to."

Hadleigh clung to her grandmother's hand. "Nana, I've been a good girl, haven't I? I know I've done nothing naughty, except for eating those French chestnuts. I thought no one wanted them. They'd been there for ever such a long time."

"You've been a *very* good girl," Deirdre declared, "the best possible girl. And no one minded about the *marrons glacé*."

"Then why is she always so cross with me?"

"Everyone's feeling the strain, Haddy. I'm sure that's all it is. Now give Nana a kiss and let me tuck you up."

Deirdre most definitely felt the strain, not from the wartime privations so much as from the full-time responsibility of two children at an age when she'd thought she'd do nothing more strenuous than tending the garden in good weather, and going off on outings with her friends. But someone had to see to Ben and Haddy. Patently, Frances had lost interest in the girl, and retained only a rapidly diminishing fondness for Ben. The only times Frances at all resembled herself were on the odd weekends when Arthur managed to get home for a night or two.

Arthur's presence in the house had an extraordinary effect on Frances. Whereas always in the past she'd appeared to take her husband completely for granted, Frances now doted on him almost slavishly. She was, during his brief stays, so preoccupied with Arthur that she forgot to be angry with the children. Everyone relaxed and breathed more deeply when Arthur was home.

The moment he left, though, Frances's rage seemed to renew itself. Deirdre began to catch whiffs of alcohol on her daughter's breath early in the day; it alarmed her, but she said nothing, although she longed for an opportunity to talk privately with Arthur.

There was simply no opportunity either during his visits or in the course of telephone conversations to interject any comment on Frances's deterioration. As if suspicious of this very thing happening, Frances took to hovering close by, apparently ready at any moment to snatch away the handset. This new habit of monitoring what was said to Arthur unnerved Deirdre and the children further. Frances herself replaced the receiver at the end of each call wearing an expression of extreme satisfaction. It was the one area of their existence she scrutinized with near fanaticism. Meals, overseeing the children, queuing for rations at the shops, and cleaning the house all gradually fell to Deirdre who, from sheer weariness, enlisted the children's help. Duties were assigned. Ben's job was to collect the bread daily from the bakery. Hadleigh made up both her own and Ben's beds, and washed the tea dishes. With the advent of warmer weather, both children were put to work clearing the garden. The three of them labored while Frances seemed to drift, distracted and scented too often with scotch whiskey. Nightly, Deirdre fell into bed exhausted, and wondered when, if ever, things would improve.

In her weakening condition, the daily unfolding events of the war took on utterly personal meaning for Deirdre. She wept at Chamberlain's resignation, and was jubilant at Churchill's installation. She fretted over the increased rationing and what the food shortages might signify to those less fortunate. She wept again in April when the Germans took Denmark and Norway, and listened fearfully to the nightly reports of the *Blitzkreig* in Holland. With pride, she heard Churchill's broadcasts on the wireless, and read in the newspaper, awed, his statement in the House of Commons: "Victory: victory at all costs, victory in spite of all terror, victory however long and hard the road may be, for without victory there is no survival." It *was* personal. The menace of the German forces swept ever closer, seemingly, to Deirdre's mind, in direct proportion both to Frances's abdication of her role as mother, and to Deirdre's flagging energy from picking up what her daughter left undone.

Hadleigh's birthday was in mid-June, and Deirdre thought she should have a small party.

"It's a frivolity!" Frances stated, waving her arm in a gesture meant to be dismissing but which appeared merely drunken and uncontrolled.

"I feel it's a necessity," Deirdre held fast. "I'll be more than happy to see to the details. Just a few children for tea, with a cake. I'm quite sure I can assemble the makings for a small cake."

Hadleigh listened from the top of the stairs, fingers crossed, praying her mother wouldn't refuse.

"What did she say?" Ben asked in a whisper, creeping up beside her on the landing.

"Hush! She hasn't said yet."

"By the time we return to London," Frances said, "they both will have become absolutely impossible, thanks to your overindulgence."

"Frances, it's her *birthday*. I should think you'd want to make a bit of a fuss."

"Oh, do as you like." Frances walked somewhat unsteadily from the room.

"I will, then!" Deirdre vowed, suppressing any hint of triumph in her voice. "You'll be there, of course?"

Frances stopped in the doorway, her mouth drawing downwards, her eyebrows arched. "Naturally," she spat. "Where else would I be?"

"Oh, good!" Ben said happily. "You're to have a party. Smashing!"

"Be quick! She's coming!" Hadleigh jumped up and ran along the hall to her room, dragging Ben with her. Safely behind her closed door, the two of them danced ecstatically for a moment, then fell silent at the sound of their mother's footsteps ascending the stairs. Once they heard the master bedroom door close, Ben relaxed and went to sit in Haddy's rocker, asking, "How many, d'you suppose?"

"Not many. Perhaps four or five. But still," Hadleigh smiled, "I'm to have a party. I can't wait to tell Daddy. Perhaps he'll be able to be here for it."

"I expect he'll be able, if he explains to everyone it's your birthday."

"I do hope so," she said fervently, thoughts of her father causing her eyes to fill. She yearned to see him. It had been ages since he'd last been able to come. "I'll wear the frock Nana gave me at Christmas, the pink one. And maybe," she continued, working herself back into a festive spirit, "maybe she'll put up my hair."

"It looked jolly nice last time she did it for you," Ben said supportively, leaning forward on the edge of the rocker with his small hands placed flat on his bare knees. "I expect it will be a super party."

"Oh, I do hope so," she said again.

Deirdre and the children sat together in the kitchen to plan the guest list and the menu. There was to be fizzy squash; cress, jam, and cucumber sandwiches; blancmanges and jellies; and a proper cake with icing. Hadleigh's three best friends were to come, along with Ben's best friend, Magnus. Nana planned to set the table with the good linen cloth, the Spode service, and the silver. Using the silver meant a polishing session, in which the children eagerly assisted.

Frances eavesdropped on the trio, annoyed and guilt-ridden. Had it been Ben's party, she might have found the motivation to contribute. Since all this, however, was in aid of celebrating Hadleigh's tenth birthday, the most Frances could feel was some small astonishment at having managed to tolerate the girl for so many years. She'd have preferred to have nothing to do with the occasion, but her conscience wouldn't allow that. She helped Deirdre launder the table linens, and diligently lined up for rations of margarine and sugar, hoarding these staples over a period of weeks in order that they'd have enough to bake the cake.

The excitement of the others was contagious and she found herself feeling less fraught, more alive than she had in months as she ironed the serviettes and Hadleigh's pink organza party dress. In the days just prior to the party she stayed away as best she could from the drinks cabinet, and her store of energy seemed to become replenished. She was quite looking forward to the day of the party, and to the arrival of the invited children. Arthur had said he'd try to get the time away. She hoped he'd be unable. Her new dependence upon him made her hate herself. He seemed now to take great pleasure in controlling her sexually and beamed with unfeigned delight upon the successful conclusion of yet another encounter. Since the night of Edwin's death, Arthur's attitude toward her—at least sexually—had altered radically. Whether it was because of his knowledge of what she'd done, or due to her abandoned behavior during the air-raid, he'd embarked upon totally new directions, displaying imagination and mastery that caused her both to crave and despise those moments when he coerced her into seismic convulsions.

The morning of the day of the party, Frances was unaccountably nervous. She'd scarcely slept, and had had to resort to several drinks in order to attain the few hours of rest she'd, finally, managed to get. She dressed and applied her makeup, then had to go downstairs to the drinks cabinet. Returning, a steadying drink near to hand, she sat for more than an hour contemplating the despicable reflection in the oval glass. Her features, as they were so often nowadays, were puffy—from alcohol, from lack of sleep, from tension and fear and barely suppressed anxiety that was never far from the raw wound of her guilt. She didn't look like a murderess; neither did she look recognizably herself. The double rings of the telephone below caught her attention. She waited, listening, then Deirdre called.

"For you, Frances."

"I'm coming," Frances answered, and took her time going down the stairs.

"Are you well, Frances?" Mandy's voice asked. "You've been out of touch a terribly long time."

"I'm not, ah, all that well, actually."

"That *is* too bad." Amanda didn't sound in the least sympathetic. "I thought you'd be in touch with me before now, Frances. I was almost certain you would be."

"I've been very busy. Look, could I get back to you? Today's Hadleigh's birthday and we're in the midst of preparations."

"Call me, Frances. There are things we *must* talk about."

Frances put down the receiver, snatching back her hand as if the instrument had gone suddenly hot.

"How is Amanda?" Deirdre asked. "It's ages since we've seen her. I've always been fond of her."

"Do shut up, Mother." Frances glared at her, then ran back upstairs to the bedroom to her seat at the dressing table, and to her scotch.

The glass drained, she turned once more to her reflected image. Why had Mandy really called? Did she know or suspect something? Frances pressed her fists to her temples, worried. Was it conceivable Mandy knew anything? No. How could she? But in all likelihood she'd seek to place blame for

Frances's having been a source of irritation during Edwin's last weeks alive. That would be just like her, she thought, her eyes narrowing. *We're close friends. We see each other, socially, regularly. We talk.* Had she gone away from their disastrous luncheon encounter to tell tales about her to Edwin? Had she poisoned Edwin's mind against her? Could that be why he'd rebuffed her so unfeelingly? It was possible, very possible. Mandy was dangerous, to be avoided in future at all costs.

She could hear the children romping in the garden below, giddy and shrill with excitement. Hadleigh's sharp-edged laughter was lacerating to Frances's ears. She got up and went to the window, seeing, with a sudden ignition of fury, that Hadleigh was darting about on the grass in her party frock. Throwing open the window, Frances bellowed, "Come in at once, the two of you!" then slammed shut the window and stormed down the stairs and through to the kitchen door where she stood, arms held tightly to her sides, foot tapping furiously, as the children, exchanging bewildered glances, came running across the grass toward her.

"Go to your room!" she told Ben. "And stay there until I say you may come down." She gave him a not-so-gentle push and he hurried off, looking back over his shoulder.

"I do not recall giving permission for you to put on that dress!" she coldly addressed Hadleigh.

"But Mummy . . ."

"You've *soiled* it!" Frances hissed as she grabbed hold of Hadleigh's upper arm and yanked her inside. "You will *not* listen, will you? You simply do not comprehend what's told to you, do you?"

"But Mummy, it's only water. And Nana said . . ."

"I have no wish to hear what Nana said." Frances marched the girl through the kitchen to the front entry where, opening the cloakroom door, she gave in to her fury. "You will stay in here until *I* say it's time for you to come out, until *I* give permission, until *I* can stomach the sight of your characterless little face." With that, she thrust the girl inside, slammed shut the door in Hadleigh's dumb-struck face, and turned the key in the lock.

"But Mummy," Hadleigh cried, "I haven't *done* anything! I've been ever so good. Please don't make me stay in here!"

"If I hear one more word from you," Frances threatened,

"you may find yourself spending the better part of every day for the rest of your life in there!"

She stormed into the lounge, grabbed the bottle of scotch and carried it with her upstairs, settling once more at the dressing table, her chest heaving with irate indignation. So angry was she that it was a good five minutes before she was sufficiently in control to pour herself a fresh drink.

Upon returning from the greengrocer's with the cucumber and the cress for the children's sandwiches, Deirdre went, as was her habit, directly to the cloakroom to hang away her cardigan, and halted in surprise at finding the door locked.

Slowly tuning in to Hadleigh's sobs and Deirdre's soothing murmurs, Frances leaped up and raced to the top of the stairs. "*She's to remain in there!*" she shouted, causing the two below to jump apart in surprise. "She's been disobedient and I haven't yet decided on her punishment."

"What on earth has she done?" Deirdre wanted to know, touching her hand to Hadleigh's hot, wet cheek.

"She was not to wear that frock until tea-time!" Frances thundered, descending the stairs—like a storm-trooper, Deirdre thought.

"But I told her . . ."

"I am sick to *death* of your countermanding my authority with my children!" Taking hold of Hadleigh's arm, she wrenched the girl off balance and shoved her back into the cloakroom, again locking the door. Hadleigh began to scream, begging to be let out, and Deirdre moved to do just that.

"*Don't you dare!*" Frances warned, positioning herself between her mother and the door. "It's not your place to interfere. I *will not* have it!"

"You're mad!" Deirdre whispered disbelievingly, still holding the bag with the cucumber and the cress. "It's her birthday, for God's sake, Frances. And whatever she's done, it couldn't possibly have been so wicked that it warrants this sort of treatment. What's the harm in her wearing the dress? Another few months and she'll have outgrown it in any case. Don't you think you're being rather irrational?"

"Mummy, please!" Hadleigh wept, pounding her fists against the door, further upset by hearing her mother speaking to Nana in that horrid way. "Please!" she begged, unable to breathe properly in the dark, confined space. "*Please!* I'll be very good, very careful. Truly I will! Truly!"

"Let her out at once, Frances!" Deirdre ordered evenly, taking a step forward.

"You will *not* interfere!" Frances insisted menacingly. "She is *my* child, not yours."

"*You* are *my* child, I'm sickened to say. And *you've* completely lost your reason. You're not a well woman, Frances. Something's terribly the matter with you."

"*Give me that!*" Frances snatched the bag from her mother's hand. "I've a good mind to ring round and tell everyone not to come."

"Please don't do that, Frances. You'll break her heart. And Ben's. Why are you doing this?" she asked, wrenched by Hadleigh's cries. "*Why?*"

Holding the bag to her breast, Frances ordered, "Go to your room, Mother! I'll let you know when to come down."

The madness Deirdre saw in her daughter's eyes made the breath catch in her throat. At that moment she fully believed that if she went to her granddaughter's aid, her own daughter was capable of killing her. Under the frenzied heat of those eyes, Deirdre's resolve was destroyed. She looked at the locked door, then again at Frances, then slowly exhaled and started toward the stairs. "There will come a day," she said quietly, pausing at the foot of the stairway, "when you will remember this and be as appalled as I am right now. I can only hope that day comes very soon, Frances. I no longer know you. The things you do and say are utterly without logic or reason. I fear for you." Deirdre waited, hoping for some response. She got none. Grieved, she climbed the stairs.

Feeling huge with accomplishment, Frances took the bag to the kitchen and set it down on the counter. It was high time she'd regained control of the situation, and she'd done it. She spent the next few hours patrolling the upper landing, making sure neither her mother nor Ben left their rooms while, below, Hadleigh's cries diminished to a steady whimpering, and then to silence.

At two-thirty, the doorbell rang signifying the arrival of the first of the children. She announced through the door to Ben, "You may come down now and entertain your guests."

"But, Mummy . . ." he began.

"Come along," she dictated, and he obeyed.

Magnus was first to arrive, looking most unlike his usually

mussed self, in a blue velvet suit with short pants and a cream-colored satin shirt complete with carefully looped bow. He stood in the doorway holding his gift of hand-embroidered handkerchiefs made by his mother for Hadleigh, breaking into a gappy smile at the sight of Ben.

"Go into the lounge," Frances said, and Ben led his friend away.

"I say," Magnus whispered once inside the lounge, "this is odd."

Unable to think of what else to do, Ben got the cards and sat down with Magnus for a game of Snap.

By three-fifteen, all the children were sitting together on the sofa, fidgeting and exchanging puzzled looks. Frances, in the armchair, drank scotch and studied their faces. By far the best-looking of the lot was Hadleigh's best friend Millicent. She really was gorgeous, Frances thought, noting the girl's jet black hair, milky skin, and luminous deep green eyes. Amused by the children's solemnity, Frances suggested, "Play some games, why don't you?"

The others looked to Ben who said, "I'll get Hadleigh, shall I, Mummy?"

"I think not," she answered imperiously. "Carry on without her."

Infected by Frances's mood, the children continued to sit together in a row on the sofa. She was greatly amused by their inability to sit still. They shifted, squirmed, knitted their fingers together, stretched, and generally behaved as if ants were crawling over their bodies. It was all Frances could do not to laugh aloud.

"We could play in the garden," Ben offered quietly. "Perhaps French cricket."

Frances was already shaking her head. "It wouldn't do to send everyone home with soiled clothes, would it, Ben?"

"No, Mummy," he said softly, increasingly afraid, and wondering why Nana didn't come down.

They listened to the clock ticking on the mantel as they alternately watched Ben and Ben's mummy who kept on drinking brown stuff from her glass. Their hands were sweaty, and someone's tummy made a gurgling noise which caused Lillian, Hadleigh's second-best friend, to giggle. No one else laughed and, after a moment, Lillian grew still.

After an hour, Frances lifted herself from the armchair. "I

expect it's time for tea," she said, and went off to the kitchen.

The instant she was gone, Magnus whispered, "I say! This is most peculiar, Ben. Where's Haddy? And your Nana?"

Ben, in an agony now of confusion and fear, felt on the verge of being sick. He opened his mouth to reply when, all at once, Hadleigh started screaming and pounding at the cloakroom door. The children stared in horror, seeking an explanation, and Ben tried frantically to think of something to say. Magnus, who'd just turned seven, but who wept easily, grew pale and his chin trembled as he asked in a whisper, "Whatever's wrong with your sister, Ben?"

Lillian boldly rose and took several steps toward the entryway thinking to investigate, when the front door opened and Arthur came smiling in. He stopped, cocked his head to one side, and said, "It's Lillian, isn't it?"

"Yes, Mr. Holden."

Hearing her father's voice, Hadleigh began to scream with renewed energy, beating her bruised fists against the cloakroom door. Arthur's smile vanished. In three steps he was at the door, had it unlocked, and was lifting Hadleigh into his arms.

"Is this a part of some game you've been playing?" he asked the children who were now clustered around him, gazing up in bewilderment at the deeply flushed, utterly undone Hadleigh who'd wound her arms around her father's neck and sobbed against his shoulder in hiccoughing gusts.

"Mummy put her in there ever such a long time ago," Ben confided, placing his hand a little fearfully on his father's arm, as if concerned that Arthur, too, might have suffered alarming changes in personality.

"Where is Mummy, Ben?" Arthur asked, briefly hugging the boy to his side before freeing his hand to support his daughter's weight.

"In the kitchen, fixing the tea."

"And Nana?"

"Shall I fetch her?" Ben asked eagerly.

"By all means."

Ben scooted off up the stairs and Arthur looked down at the quartet of small faces, summoning up an encouraging smile while trying to imagine what might have gone on here today. Hadleigh's sobs were broken by her efforts, in gulps, to tell him what had happened. Her words were unintelligible.

"There, there," he soothed her. "We'll set it all straight. Why don't you," he addressed the four young guests, "go into the lounge for a few minutes while we clarify the situation. Then we'll see to tea. All right?"

"I don't like it here," Millicent announced to the others. "This is a horrid party. I want to go home!"

"But we're going to have tea now," Lillian told her.

"I should *hate* being shut away in the cloakroom," Magnus admitted.

"Oh, so should I!" Hadleigh's third-best friend, Margaret, concurred. "I think Haddy was ever so brave."

"I want to go home!" Millicent repeated.

In the kitchen, with Hadleigh literally cringing from the sight of her mother and pressing herself even tighter against her father, Arthur quietly demanded to know just what had transpired. Frances, unfazed, replied, "She was disobedient. It was imperative to punish her."

"I see. Well," he said on a breathless intake of air, "we'll discuss this later. Right now, I've got to organize an outing." He turned and carried Hadleigh to the lounge. "I won't be a moment," he promised, breaking her tenacious hold and giving her his handkerchief.

He made a quick telephone call, then returned to announce to the children and a grim-faced Deirdre, "We're having tea at the Pump Room."

The children burst into excited cries and ran for the door.

"Ben," Arthur said softly. "Be a good lad and help your sister and me carry the gifts."

"Is Mummy coming too?" Ben asked, looking doubtfully toward the kitchen.

"Not this time," Arthur told him. "Nana will help you freshen up at the Pump Room," he told Hadleigh. "Won't you, Nana?"

"Of course," Deirdre said, rising to the moment. She reached for her bag, took Hadleigh's hand firmly in her own, and they were off.

The tea was a resounding success. Jan Barenska and his string trio played "Happy Birthday"; there were crustless sandwiches, and jellies, and even a small cake with a candle for Hadleigh to wish upon. She exclaimed happily over the crayons, the soap, the sweets, the embroidered handkerchiefs, the Milky Ways from Millicent, the bath cubes from Nana, and the lovely new book to read, *What Katy Did*, from her father.

No one mentioned Frances or the dreadful hours that had preceded his return home. The waitresses made a fuss, and joined with the children in singing another chorus of "Happy Birthday" before they left to climb back into the Rover to deliver home each of the guests who claimed, after all, to have had a lovely time.

Eight

Arthur controlled his temper. It was difficult. His immediate instinct was to take hold of Frances and inflict upon her some small measure of the pain she'd caused Hadleigh. A stronger influence, though, was his inbred belief that no responsible adult male ever laid hand on a woman. It was loutish behavior to strike a woman, something done by those who'd never learned to reason their way through matters.

"*Why* did you *do* it?" he demanded of her, his temples throbbing with the effort he was making to keep a grip on his anger.

Under the impression that he was at last about to deal with the events of that night months earlier, Frances declared, "It was an accident!" She held herself very erect, tautly prepared for the onslaught of accusations and recriminations that was bound to come.

"How in the name of everything sacred could it possibly have been an accident?" he wanted to know.

"It *was*! It was never my intention to have anything like that happen." She was trembling and wild-eyed, and longed to dash downstairs for a tumbler full of liquid fortification. If he pushed her with any significant degree of forcefulness, it seemed to her eminently possible she'd disintegrate.

Slowly, he said, "Perhaps, Frances, you could explain to me how locking a ten-year-old child in a cloakroom—on her birthday, no less—could, to anyone's mind, be construed as an *accident*. Perhaps you'd be good enough to elucidate." As he spoke, he watched her eyes alter.

"Oh, for heaven's sake!" Her mind skipped about, trying to reassemble whatever rationale she'd had earlier in the day for punishing Hadleigh. "She was disobedient. Mother spoils her terribly, allows her to do whatever takes her fancy. I felt the time had come to put a stop to it before the girl turns completely intractable."

"From what I'm given to understand, Hadleigh's innocent of any wrongdoing. Certainly, whatever minor transgression she committed against you didn't warrant her being locked up for the better part of an entire day."

"Hardly an entire day."

"Five hours," he amended.

"Very well, five hours."

"That seems reasonable to you, does it?"

"Yes, it does."

"And how would it be, Frances, if I were to lock *you* up for an equal amount of time? Would you consider that fair punishment for your recent behavior?"

"It would depend," she said with bravado, "on the offense you believed I'd committed."

"You truly are not rational!" He was stunned by how true this seemed to be. "You've been behaving irrationally since well before last Christmas."

"What nonsense! I've been nothing of the sort." She held her hands clasped in front of her in the hopes of steadying them. Tremors surged through her and she looked longingly at the bed, wishing she could climb beneath the bedclothes, shut her eyes and sleep her life away. If she could just sleep through one night, she was positive she'd awaken come morning once more familiar to herself, and at peace. It she could just sleep.

He watched her closely, searching for some chink through which he might penetrate her staunch self-defense in order to get her to view her actions with some sort of viable perspective. "Frances," he said tiredly, "I want you to try to think about what you did today, to see if you're able, even to the slightest degree, to view what you did from Hadleigh's viewpoint, or your mother's, or Ben's, or mine. If you could manage that, you might just realize that you behaved monstrously to everyone involved, including those four, poor, beleaguered children who've undoubtedly gone home to tell their parents about the horror show they attended here today."

"And what do you mean by that?" Her alarm was renewing itself.

"I can almost promise you that at this very moment there are four sets of parents sitting, trying to make sense of what their children told them the instant they came through their front doors. This isn't London. News travels quickly in areas like this. I can only hope that those children will, in future, be allowed to play with Haddy and Ben."

"Whyever wouldn't they?"

"*Think* about it!" He was growing more and more frustrated. "Why *would* they? They had the sterling opportunity to spend several hours watching you drink, while their friend screamed and begged to be freed from a locked cloakroom. If you don't think that's worthy of mention, then you're even more seriously deluded than I'd suspected."

"I'm going to get ready for bed." She was determined not to hear any more of this. "I was acting fully within my rights as a mother. You're never here to do your share, yet when you do manage to appear for a few hours, the first thing you do is begin attacking me, making accusations, and declaring me not in my right mind. I believe I've heard quite enough, thank you." She went to the wardrobe for her nightdress and robe and draped them over her arm before opening the bedroom door and going along to the bathroom.

He remained unmoving, sifting through his feelings. On Hadleigh's behalf, he was still very angry. He was also disturbed that his wife's behavior had spilled beyond the arena of these immediate walls and into other lives. He feared that Frances was sliding beyond anyone's control, and that he'd be obliged to seek outside help in dealing with her. In no way did he want to have to do that, and hoped with all his heart that she'd consider what she'd done and, upon review, choose to take herself in hand. He did love her, but at this moment it very much felt as if he loved his children more. He was absolutely not prepared to sacrifice them on the altar of his wife's aberrant behavior. Had there been more time, and had there not been a war going on, he was certain he'd have been better able to cope. But there was a stringent premium on his time, and he could do no more than hope Frances would see reason and pull herself together. With a sigh, he began his preparations for bed.

By the time she returned from the bathroom, Arthur was asleep. Relieved, she swung about at once and went directly downstairs to fetch the scotch. She was about to pour her drink when she heard Hadleigh cry out.

"Damn!" She set down the glass and bottle, and raced up the stairs to her daughter's room.

At the sight of her mother, Hadleigh commenced screaming and huddled in an hysterical knot against the headboard of her bed, refusing to allow Frances to come anywhere near her.

For a second or two, her thoughts chillingly clear, Frances realized the extent of the damage she'd done, and continued to do, to her child, and felt physically ill with shame and remorse. But it was only a moment, then her vision seemed to shift and she saw Hadleigh as a scene-making, petulant, horribly spoiled little monster.

"Stop that at once!" she said from the foot of the bed. "You'll wake everyone, you foolish girl!"

Hadleigh couldn't stop. She'd emerged from a nightmare of being locked away only to find the source of her anguish looming in the doorway. She fully believed her mother was determined to drag her from her bed and lock her up again.

"Come away, Frances." Arthur directed Frances toward the door as Deirdre rushed in to begin comforting the child.

"*You see!*" She pointed an accusing finger at her mother. "She's doing it again: trying to take my place."

"You're frightening her, Frances," Deirdre said calmly, holding Hadleigh to her breast. "Please, Arthur. Haven't we had enough for one day?"

He nodded, easing Frances back to their bedroom.

The moment the door was closed, Frances began again stating her case. "You saw for yourself! You can't say you didn't see! She's made my own child fearful of me."

"You've done that all by yourself," he said sadly. "I wish I knew what was to be done."

"I should think that would be obvious," she said hotly. "We simply cannot stay on here."

"No," he said, thinking it through. "Other arrangements will have to be made. Why did you go into her room?"

"Why? Because she cried out; she'd had a bad dream. Why else?"

"I see. It's time for bed now, Frances." He turned off the light. "We'll talk further in the morning."

"I hope you *do* see. You will insist on blaming me when it's *she* who's responsible."

"Lie down now. We'll talk in the morning."

She feigned sleep for hours until, certain Arthur was deeply asleep, she crept from the room and downstairs to where she'd left the scotch and her glass. Settled in the dark on the floor with her back against the sofa, she poured a badly-needed drink. After the first good swallow, she let out her pent-up breath as some of the stiffness seeped from her limbs. "Bloody hell!" she whispered inaudibly to the unlit room, trying to force the shadows to assume familiar shapes. She didn't mind the dark, but she did prefer to be able to identify the masses around her. She drank again, reviewing the scene with Arthur.

Obviously, he and her mother were conspiring against her. And that loathsome lump of a child, carrying on in that ridiculous fashion! If anyone's reason were in doubt, the prime candidate was Hadleigh. First, she was flagrantly disobedient, then she made a ludicrous fuss over perfectly reasonable punishment and, finally, she made an hysterical display for purposes of revenge. It was all Deirdre's fault, and her own for allowing her mother too free a hand. The net result was this: all of them gathering against her. Aside from Ben, she could well do without any of them. Perhaps she'd suggest to Arthur that Hadleigh stay on here with Deirdre, while she and Ben returned to London. That would leave Deirdre free to cultivate her already disproportionate nurturing instincts with Hadleigh, and give Frances an opportunity to undo whatever damage had been done to Ben. It was a most sensible solution. Arthur was bound to see that.

Using the tip of her finger as a gauge, she added more scotch to the glass. God, but she hated the night! Wide awake while everyone else slept, she had nothing to do, no one to be with. She'd tried reading, but her attention wandered. There was nothing on the wireless, of course, and nowhere to go. She could do no more than drink and wait out each night as it came.

The days weren't very much better, but, somehow, with light, she had more of a purpose. There were meals to prepare, laundry, endless odd jobs to be seen to. Time got used up one way or another while she thought yearningly of the night to come, and the possibility of a sleep that was always denied her.

Having had enough to drink, she fumbled her way past the furniture to return the depleted bottle to its place in the cabinet. On her way to the kitchen with the glass, she tripped and fell, the glass smashing in her hand. The pain across her palm was immediate and sobering. On her knees, she felt about for the pull on the table lamp, got the light on, and stared at the mess of glass and blood.

Hoping no one had heard her fall, she quickly collected up the fragments and in the kitchen wrapped them in newspaper. The bulky package set to one side, she held her gouged hand under the cold water, wincing as the flow whitened and separated the lips of the wound. "It's deep," she said aloud, without thinking, awed by the blood that continued to gush from either side of the cut that nearly bisected her palm. Captivated by the graphics of her injury, she watched until her flesh was almost blue and the blood stopped flowing. Anaesthetized by the cold, there was no sensation in her hand. Dizzily, she held onto the sink with her free hand, trying to overcome an immense impulse her body seemed to have to slide sideways into a heap on the floor. "Musn't allow that," she cautioned.

She lost track of time, but after what seemed hours, she had sufficient momentum to wind a tea towel around her hand, get the kitchen door open and push the newspaper package into the bin. Returning indoors, she congratulated herself on remembering to lock up. Lights out, she worked her way through the house, up the stairs, and back into bed. She'd managed everything very cleverly, she thought.

Arthur emerged from the bedroom the next morning to find Hadleigh sitting at the top of the stairs, waiting for him. He smiled at her. She stood, and they went down to the kitchen hand in hand.

"I'll put on the kettle," she offered. "I know how to do it. Nana's shown me how to light the stove."

"Clever girl. You make the tea and I'll see to some toast."

They worked together in harmonious silence, then carried the food out to the garden, where they sat on the brick rim of the small ornamental pond Deirdre had built years before. The fish that had once inhabited the pool had long-since died, their population replaced by frogs. Deirdre promised each summer to have the pool thoroughly cleaned and the fish replaced, but she never did.

Arthur watched Hadleigh eat two rounds of toast between gulps of the hot tea. He chuckled and reached out to lay his hand on her glossy blonde hair. "Are you still hungry? There's another round left, if you'd care to have it."

"Oh, no," she said solemnly, her eyes on the plate poised on his knee. "That's yours."

"Have it, if you like."

She shook her head and looked away down the garden. "When are you going back?" she asked, dreading his departure.

"Midday."

"I don't suppose you'd take me with you?" She turned to look up at him.

"I've been giving that some thought," he replied, and at once saw hope illuminate her eyes. "It's most awkward, Hadleigh. At the moment, the offices are chaotic. Beside each of the secretary's desks is a mattress. Few of us have had any time outside the ministry to speak of. It simply wouldn't be possible to take you there."

"Oh!" Crestfallen, she shifted her eyes.

"I've been trying to think of alternatives and I do have an idea. Only an idea, mind."

"What?"

"I'd prefer not to tell you until it's been settled. Less disappointing that way, don't you think? I know you'd like some time apart from your mother."

"She hates me, Daddy," she whispered, looking at the house. "Honestly, she does." She paused, taking several deep breaths to prevent tears. "Please don't make me stay with her. Please!"

Putting aside his cup and plate, he took hold of his daughter's hand, forever astonished that he was responsible for this little girl's existence. "Have there been other incidents?" he asked. "If there have, I'd like you to tell me about them."

"I try ever so hard to be good, not to do anything to make her cross . . ." She shrugged, unable to explain. "A fortnight ago, I stopped on the way home from school at Millicent's house. It was only fifteen minutes, honestly. Ben got back before I did because I'd stopped with Millicent, you see. Only fifteen minutes, but when I got home, Mummy'd locked the door and wouldn't let me in. I rang, and knocked, but no one came. I looked through the letter slot and Mummy was standing in the entryway, just standing there. I asked her, please, to let me in, and she went away. She wouldn't allow him to open the door either. I know, because I saw him come downstairs and I called to him to unlock the door, and he was going to, but she came and took him into the kitchen for his tea."

"Where was your grandmother?" Arthur asked.

"It was Nana's afternoon for tea with her bridge friends. She used to go every Thursday, but she doesn't now. She says it's because she's lost interest, but I think it's because she's afraid Mummy will do something to upset me. When Mummy did finally open the door, she said I was to go to bed straight-away, without my tea. It wasn't fair, Daddy. Ben stops with Magnus all the time, and she's never ever locked him out. I think she only let me in because she knew there'd be a row if Nana came home and found me sitting out there."

"Your mother seems to be going through rather a rough patch just now," he said, giving her hand a squeeze.

"Nana says that too, and that we must make allowances. But, Daddy, I don't understand. She was horrid to Nana before you came; she said frightful things to her." Her voice had grown heavy with hurt and indignation; her eyes brimmed.

"I'll see what can be done. I may not be able to arrange anything on such short notice, however. It may take a bit of time."

"I see." She nodded. "I didn't mean to make a scene last night. It's just that I was frightened. I don't want to get Mummy into trouble. I was just so frightened she was going to lock me up again."

"I'll do my best," he promised.

"Arthur Holden here. I do hope I'm not catching you at a bad time."

"Arthur! Hello. Not at all. How are you? And Frances?"

"Look, there's a bit of a problem and I'm rather pressed for time. I did ring the office but they said you've given up your position, which is why I'm taking the liberty of ringing you at home."

"It's quite all right. What seems to be the problem? And how might I help?"

"I think Hadleigh and her mother need to be apart just now, for a number of reasons I can't go into on the telephone. My first thought was to take Haddy back with me, but it's quite impossible under the circumstances. You came to mind, and I was wondering . . ."

"I'd be delighted to have Hadleigh," Mandy said with enthusiasm. "When would you like to bring her?"

"You would?" He'd anticipated reluctance and was thrown by the immediacy of her interest. "You mean you truthfully wouldn't mind? I don't know how long it might be . . ."

"However long you like," she told him. "Food's not yet impossible to obtain, and I'm sure we'll manage beautifully. Oh, but what about school?"

"I hadn't thought that far. I wanted to see first . . ."

"If I'd be willing. I'm perfectly willing. Are you with her now? You could bring her at once. Do you have the address?"

"I do, unless you've moved recently." He laughed with relief.

"I haven't moved an inch. When should I expect the two of you?"

"This afternoon?"

"Splendid!"

"This is terribly good of you, Amanda."

"I'm delighted you'd think of me. Frances has no objections?"

"Oh, I think not. Well, I'm most grateful. We'll talk about the financial arrangements this afternoon."

"That won't be necessary. You needn't even consider it. It will be my pleasure to have Hadleigh here. And you have my word, I'll take the greatest care in the world of her."

"Bless you," he said, and rang off.

Hadleigh was overjoyed, but had the wits to contain her excitement in front of her mother. She ran off to pack a bag, leaving Arthur to present Frances with the news.

"It's madness!" Frances raged.

"Oh, I disagree. It's all too obvious the two of you need to be apart temporarily."

"Amanda Adams, of all people? Have you lost your judgment entirely? The woman knows nothing about children, nothing at all.''

"The woman *wants* Hadleigh. That's ample qualification as far as I'm concerned.''

"She wants a good deal more than Hadleigh," Frances thought aloud. "Am I to take it, then, that if *I* were to want something, that would, to your mind, be sufficient reason for me to have it?''

"We're not discussing you, Frances. We're talking about Hadleigh, and the fact that Amanda's been good enough to say she'd have her. There's to be no debate on this. Hadleigh's returning to London with me, and that's the end of it." He looked hard at her. "I should think you'd be thrilled, Frances. You're getting what you wanted. Perhaps you'd like me to make arrangements for Ben, too.''

"I would not!" Something was pushing at the corner of her brain, trying for her attention. Something to do with Mandy. She couldn't quite take hold of it. "You won't rob me of both my children!''

"No one's robbing you, Frances. When you're past finding Hadleigh such a thorn in your side, she'll come home.''

Frances smiled suddenly, alarmingly. "I quite like the irony, actually, now that I think about it. We'll let Mandy see what it's like, being a mother. Perhaps you're cleverer than I gave you credit for being. How ever did you think of it?" Without awaiting an answer, she sailed off to the bathroom to start the tub filling.

After a moment, defeated in his attempt to follow his wife's circuitous thinking, he gave up and went to supervise Hadleigh's packing.

Nine

Hadleigh's absence bothered Frances almost more than her presence had. Having lost the major outlet for her anger, and in a permanent-feeling, seething state, Frances continued for weeks to anticipate the girl's arrival home from school, her greedy attendance at meals, her endless quest for approbation. She'd remember that Mandy now had the task of overseeing Hadleigh, and her anger broadened. How dare Arthur decide unilaterally to elect Mandy as Hadleigh's guardian! The woman was a tart, with no discernible moral stature. She was also wildly jealous of Frances's relationship with Edwin. Arthur had played right into her hands, and given Mandy a substantial weapon. What Deirdre had started, Mandy would see to completion: Hadleigh would evolve into a monster. Mandy would do everything in her power to turn Hadleigh against Frances. She was even capable of going after Arthur, intent on stripping Frances bare. Why was she the only one who could see the dangers inherent in the situation?

"It's best for both of you," Deirdre said, refusing to allow herself to be drawn into a dissection of Amanda's character.

Thwarted, Frances withdrew into sullen silence, to review the terms of her discontent. Her fear of discovery had appended itself to, and gradually overtaken, her anger with Arthur. What he'd done in placing Hadleigh with that woman was to effect a one-step-removed domestic set-up that was even more bothersome than actually having Hadleigh underfoot. Now there were regular telephone calls from the girl, and pathetic little pencilled notes—primarily to Deirdre who made a point of reading them aloud at tea-time—accompanied by surprisingly talented sketches; there were requests to pack yet another bag of clothing and toys to be seen onto the London train. For all the trouble she was, Hadleigh might just as well have stayed in Leamington.

Frances had gone beyond exhaustion into a state where she now no longer seemed to require more than three or four hours' sleep each night. She spent the dark hours slowly sipping scotch and smoking cigarettes while she made entries in the journal she'd started to keep. Occasionally, in the midst of penning random thoughts, she'd be overcome by longing for her old self. It was as if the woman she'd been only months before had been a well-loved friend who'd suffered an unfortunate death. She'd search backwards, examining the remembered aspects of this other Frances. For fifteen minutes or half an hour, she'd grieve for the loss of someone she thought she'd known well and understood perfectly. At these times, she was able to see that the person who'd replaced her was only the poorest facsimile—a secret drinker in a state of perpetual fear and rage, this woman lived on the edge of her nerves, and was capable of saying and doing things that the other Frances would have deplored. She knew this, could see it. Why then was she unable to call back her former self? It should have been possible. It should have required nothing more than disposing of the cigarettes and the alcohol, the fear, the guilt, the confusion. Simple. Yet she'd end up in bitter laughter, acknowledging the permanent loss of good old Frances.

She'd take herself to bed, stretch out to sleep and, three hours later, awaken to look toward the window where, with the pallid glow of morning, nothing awaited her but more of the same. She was imprisoned, caged by her own acts. There was nothing to be done; nowhere to go, nothing to do.

Aunt Mandy was so unlike her mother that for the first two weeks Hadleigh couldn't stop comparing the two, finding one area of difference after another. Aunt Mandy urged Hadleigh to eat. Seated at the table, smiling, she said, "It's lovely to have someone to cook for again. Cooking for oneself is such a bore."

"I don't know how to cook," Hadleigh said. "Nana promised to teach me."

"I have a number of cookery books somewhere." Mandy craned around to look at the room. "We'll find them, shall we? I think we could start with a few simple things—Welsh rarebit, soups. They're fun, and not terribly difficult."

"You'll teach me?"

"I might learn a few new things myself." She leaned on her hand, watching the girl eat. "How pretty you are!"

Hadleigh shook her head, setting down her knife and fork.

"But of course you are!" Mandy said. "Why do you shake your head?"

"I'm not," Hadleigh disagreed. "You're only being kind." Aunt Mandy was a very kind person. It showed in all sorts of ways. "It's very good of you to have me to stay with you."

"It's very good of *you* to stay with *me*. I was becoming very old-maidish, fussing with my plants and forever polishing the furniture."

"Is it possible to be an old maid if you've been married?"

"A figure of speech. Certain habits tend to be considered those of women who've lived too long alone."

"Did you want to leave your job?"

"I thought I'd like more time to myself. I even thought I might go to the seaside, but all I've done is walk every day to the shops, and read a great deal, see a few friends now and then. It's been a lonely time."

"You were lonely?" This seemed to Hadleigh an exceptional thing for a grown-up to admit to.

"Everyone has lonely periods. It's not necessarily a bad thing. It was just . . . quiet. I had a very close friend who died. It left me feeling rather down, and so I preferred to be on my own. Aren't you lonely sometimes?"

"Ever such a lot," Hadleigh admitted. "But not now. I do like it here, with you."

"And I you. We could be very naughty," Mandy grinned, "and try for a film this evening. What would you think?"

"Would they allow me in?"

"I expect so. We'll find something suitable, and keep our fingers crossed the sirens don't go off halfway through."

"I love films!" Hadleigh said eagerly. "Mummy and Daddy used to take us. We saw *Snow White and the Seven*

Dwarfs, and *Goodbye, Mr. Chips*, and *Wuthering Heights*."

"You haven't seen *The Wizard of Oz*?"

"Oh, I'd *adore* to see it! Do you think we could?"

"We'll try, shall we?"

"Yes, please."

Mandy wondered what it was about the girl that had so upset Frances. Arthur had hedged, offering only the skimpiest of explanations, along with profuse declarations of gratitude. "Do you miss your family?" she asked.

"I miss my Nana, and Ben, and my Daddy." Hadleigh stopped a moment, then out of loyalty, added, "My Mummy, too, of course."

"Of course. You must feel free to ring them whenever you like."

"Thank you." Hadleigh neatly folded her serviette and returned it to the silver ring Mandy had said was to be hers. "That was very nice. I could do the washing up."

"Could you?"

"I could. Would you like me to?"

"It's not necessary."

"But I'd like to." Hadleigh looked doubtful. "Nana sometimes let me."

"Why don't we both do it?" Mandy compromised. "Then we'll see if we're in time for the film."

Arthur couldn't quite decipher Amanda's enthusiasm, couldn't decide if it was genuine or merely drummed up to suit the situation. She continued to maintain it even after Frances began making harassing telephone calls, in the course of which she accused Amanda of everything from attempting to subvert her role as wife and mother, to seeking some bizarre form of retribution. Since she made similar calls to him, he had no difficulty in imagining the text of her declarations against Amanda. Amanda bore it all with grace, however, waving away Frances's periodic tirades with a tolerant hand.

"She's overwrought," Amanda stated. "The alcohol doesn't help, I'm sure. Perhaps professional help is called for. On the other hand, it may just pass. Some women tend to fall to pieces when they turn forty."

Arthur wasn't sure it would pass, nor was he convinced that his wife's age was relevant to what was happening. Yet the recognition was unavoidable that Frances's behavior had grown worse since Hadleigh's relocation. He didn't give voice to his misgivings, though, both from loyalty and his desire to enjoy his daughter's company in relaxed, pleasant surroundings. Hadleigh seemed to shine under Mandy's care. They'd decided there was no point to enrolling her in a new school for the month or so that was left of the school year, so she and Amanda were on an extended holiday, seeing films, having picnics in the park, making do in the underground for a night when a raid occurred.

What struck Arthur most strongly was the general assumption, when the three of them were out together in public, that they were a family and Mandy was Hadleigh's mother. Their coloring was very similar—both blonde-haired and blue-eyed—and their ease together was remarkable. Seeing how well they got on only highlighted the radical differences between his wife and this woman. Amanda seemed so incredibly serene. Conversation flowed effortlessly; silences were free of tension. The more difficult dealing with Frances became, the more good-humored and affable were his encounters with Mandy. Invariably, the time went too quickly and he had to tear himself away to return to the ministry.

He did manage the odd trip to Leamington, but the atmosphere in the house there was so weighted with negative emotions that he'd have preferred not to go. Deirdre seemed to age months in only weeks. Ben was totally confused and asked repeatedly when he, too, could come to London. And Frances was like something feral, barely containing the volume of rage that gave her, despite her thinness, a look of immensity. He had to take special care with what he said to her, and the era of near-demented lovemaking had ended. He still wanted her, but couldn't get past his own wariness and her ready temper. He did suspect she'd been having an affair in London, back when she'd been making weekly trips in to the flat. He supposed the affair had ended, and its end was responsible for her present mood. He had no wish to know of her possible affair; he simply wished he understood.

She looked progressively worse each time he visited. She'd grown gaunt, yet her torso was bloated, so that her clothes didn't hang properly. She looked unkempt, her hair lankly hanging, her eyes glittering from deeply shadowed sockets.

When he asked after her health, she insisted, "I am perfectly well. Why do you go on and on about it?"

"I'm concerned for your well-being."

"Well don't be. I hang," she pronounced dramatically, "in animated suspension. It's possible that the full blast of unfettered emotions might just be the breeding ground for contempt. Have you ever thought of that? I confess to wondering why it falls to women to be the housekeepers of men's untidy minds. Have you ever thought of *that*? It may be the concept of the ultimate state of sharing that perpetuates all private dreaming. Have you *ever* considered *that*?"

"I'm afraid you've lost me."

"How odd! It's perfectly clear to me." She sighed heavily, then said, "It's been a long, hateful day, Arthur. Another in a series of long, hateful days. I'm coming to think of myself as a freckle on the ass of a baboon. But who's to notice? Almost everything important remains forever undiscovered, lost beneath clever quips and the need for routine conversation. This will pass eventually, and then I'll be able to live my real life again. Do you remember me? I do, sometimes, very clearly. Other times I think she's lost forever. I may no longer have a real life. I may be nothing more than an underfleshed puppet dangling from invisible strings."

Alarmed by the disjointed nature of her words, he said, "I do wish you'd pop over the road and have another visit with Dr. Connors. He might be able to prescribe something . . ."

"Have you ever considered how fascinating, how compelling, pure intelligence and humor can be? In the end, though, it's the search for the corresponding thought that promotes all human endeavor. I do believe it's the search itself, rather than the actuality of attainment, that moves everything forward."

He didn't dare admit to being unable to make sense of her words, so he merely listened as she strung more and more of them, like beads on a long chain, growing afraid of her as well as for her. Between her invective-ridden telephone calls and these baroque monologues that had evolved into a regular feature of his visits, it was becoming plain that her grasp of everyday matters was all but nonexistent. It was her drinking, he thought, but there was something more as well.

After leaving Frances, he managed a late visit to Amanda. And while Hadleigh lay asleep beyond the closed bedroom door, he confided his fears by way of revealing some of what had been going on. "I'm at my wits' end," he confessed. "I simply don't know what to do."

Amanda thought carefully before attempting a reply. "There was a party New Year's Eve. Frances attended."

"I believe she mentioned something about it. But what . . . ?"

"I thought she was acting rather out of character then, but I wasn't sure of it until some weeks later when we met for luncheon at the Cumberland. She was most definitely off the mark that day, hearing only what she chose, and nothing more."

"That's it exactly! She spoke today as if she were lecturing on some rare philosophical tangent: all sorts of odd remarks about the search for the corresponding thought promoting human endeavor." He shook his head. "I haven't the foggiest what she was on about." Even as he spoke, he was feeling immensely disloyal to Frances. Yet Amanda did seem concerned with helping him solve the riddle Frances had become. "I suspect she was having an affair," he said hesitantly, the walls of propriety thoroughly breached.

Mandy studied him, trying to decide how best to answer. "It didn't happen, Arthur. She had hoped it would, but it never came off."

"Oh!" He sat back. "I see."

"I don't know that *I* do," she told him.

With traces of anger, he explained. "In a way, I'm absolved, don't you see? I mean to say, I had no idea, really, that she considered our marriage at an end."

"Oh, I don't know that she thought that."

"It's my personal interpretation of what an affair represents."

"But, Arthur, it didn't happen."

"That's beside the point. She was willing."

"I suppose so."

"Therefore, I am now at liberty to make certain decisions."

"What do you mean?" she asked, somewhat apprehensive.

"Something must be done," he said decisively, getting to his feet. "I find myself once again indebted to you. I'm most grateful for this conversation."

"What will you do, Arthur?"

"I'm far too angry to think logically right now. But something must be done about Frances."

"It's your decision, of course. But please, go slowly. I don't honestly think she's aware . . ."

"As I see it, that's the problem entirely: her complete lack of awareness. We have two children, Amanda. Already the family's been separated. Either it must be separated altogether, or I must take steps to make it all of a piece again."

"Frances didn't actually *do* anything."

He made a face. "Perhaps it's somewhat Catholic of me, but as far as I'm concerned, the thought's as good as the deed." His words came out with more strength than he'd intended. Nothing with Frances had ever been decidedly black or white; nor were his feelings for her. "I wish I were able to make the fine distinctions people make in situations like this, but I can't. I feel *betrayed*. It's not very pleasant. I apologize for coming by so late at night, but I did want to talk."

Her hand on his arm, she asked, "Will you be able to get back all right?"

"I'll manage." He looked down at her hand, then at her indecipherable expression. "I'd like to throttle her," he said, anger showing in the whiteness around his mouth, "but she's too far gone for it. I couldn't, in any case. Thank you again." He slipped from beneath her hand, and left.

Mandy closed and locked the door, reviewing what had been said, deciding she was satisfied. She went to look in on Hadleigh, admiring the child's rounded limbs in motionless sleep. She, too, could have throttled Frances, for a dozen different reasons. But Hadleigh was here, and the weeks they'd so far spent together had been most fulfilling. Eventually, though, Hadleigh would be returned to her mother. Frances really didn't deserve the child. Some elements of life were simply galling in their unfairness.

As she creamed off her makeup in the bathroom, she concluded two things: First, she was glad that she hadn't told Arthur more than she had about Frances and Edwin; and, second, that she was willing to offer him any degree of comfort within her means.

It was such a pretty place, with armchairs and a sofa covered in flowered chintz. On a round mahogany table beside the sofa was a collection of antique paperweights. Hadleigh examined each of the smooth, heavy weights repeatedly, turning them this way and that, entranced by the swirls of color, the tiny formations and air bubbles held permanently within the solid translucence.

In the mornings after breakfast, while Aunt Mandy bathed and made up in the bathroom, Haddy sat in the center of the sofa and looked around, silently listing her favorite features of the flat. There were the paperweights, of course, but there were also many other things to admire: an etched crystal lamp with an ivory silk shade; the unfurled paper fan concealing the grate of the fireplace; the ornately framed miniatures clustered above a bow-legged table just inside the entryway; in a small, glass-fronted cabinet mounted on the wall were a number of snuff boxes in gold and silver and painted porcelain; magazines and newspapers were stacked symmetrically on a table in back of the sofa. Every week Aunt Mandy discarded some and added a number more so that the stacks always remained the same height.

Mandy's bedroom was simply wonderful, like something in a fairy tale, with a canopy bed and filmy white curtains on the windows and a full-skirted white coverlet on the bed. Even at night, with the blackout curtains drawn, the room seemed to be lit from within, as if each object contained its own power source. All the rooms were fragrant with Aunt Mandy's scent. The clothes in the wardrobe smelled of it, too.

Sometimes, while Mandy was bathing, Hadleigh went to stand by the open wardrobe in the big bedroom to breathe deeply, tempted to throw out her arms and gather together everything she could hold—the silks, and fine wools, and starched cottons—and bury her face in the scented textures. She didn't dare touch anything that didn't belong to her, but she thought of what a fine feeling it would be to fill her arms with those pieces of Aunt Mandy, and breathe her in.

Her own room was blue and white, cool and crisp, with white walls and a blue comforter, a pair of white lamps and a white-painted chest of drawers with blue porcelain knobs, a deep blue carpet that always felt warm under her feet. At moments, Haddy wanted to beg to be allowed to stay here, in the blue and white room, for the rest of her life. Just the thought of being allowed to stay made her want to cry. She'd begin taking in air in huge gulps, and all the reservoirs within her would fill in anticipation of tears. She did so love it here with Aunt Mandy, whose face never shrank in anger, whose mouth never flattened to spit out enflamed accusations.

Whenever she thought of her mother she grew afraid, and guilty. She knew she wasn't supposed to feel the way she did, the way she had for as long as she could remember. But she couldn't help believing that she'd failed in some dreadful way that had never been explained to her. For hours on end, she'd scour her memory, trying to recall what it was she must have done to make Mummy hate her so. She could think of nothing specific, and so she reasoned it must be her entire self that was wrong. Mummy preferred Ben, and she wasn't one bit like him, although she did love Ben terribly, and missed him. Ben was a boy, though, and perhaps it was that. She had tried once, for an entire week, to be like Ben in every way possible. But that had only resulted in Mummy's taking hold of her and shaking her until Haddy had thought she might fall apart. She'd pictured her head shaking free and rolling off into the corner, and her arms simply coming away in Mummy's hands, her legs toppling over to lie abandoned on the floor. She'd been able to see it very distinctly; she still could. Sometimes, when she thought of herself, she saw the scattered Haddy pieces strewn about on the floor and felt a rushing despair because she had no idea how she might reassemble herself. This image, and the repeated nightmare of being locked again in the cloakroom, were the two worst things she could think of.

And yet she did love her mother. She loved her for reasons she knew other people would think were ridiculous: the way Mummy looked when they used to go out together, when she wasn't cross and smiled a lot, and the terribly funny things she'd say, especially about strangers they'd see on the street; the patient way she'd potty-trained Ben, getting him to laugh by singing him silly songs; Mummy's wonderful cleverness when she read stories aloud and did all the different voices. Mummy wasn't that way anymore, but perhaps she would be again, and then she'd no longer be so frightened of her. Her best dream was of being reunited, of having Mummy catch her up, laughing, in her arms, the two of them running off hand in hand. She had to be sensible, though. That might never happen. And Mummy had been ever so mean to Nana, even to Ben. Why? Always before, when she'd said quite frightful things to Haddy about her appetite, and her table manners, Haddy hadn't truly been bothered because she'd known it was just Mummy's way to be sarcastic. Way before the war, when people used to come for dinner, everyone had laughed and said things like, "How dreadful of you, Fan!" but they'd said it admiringly, because Mummy had been so terribly clever, and Haddy had been very proud of her.

Mandy wasn't at all like that, and, in a way, it was ever so much easier. Whatever Haddy did seemed to be all right. Mandy didn't find fault, nor did she make sharp, clever remarks about people. It was very confusing. There were moments when, seated side by side at the cinema—they went as often as possible—Haddy would think of her mother and grow giddy with guilt at being away from her and having such a pleasant time with someone else. She'd wonder then if Mummy could possibly know that she sometimes thought she'd rather have Aunt Mandy for a mother, instead of her.

Mandy got awfully close at times to sensing Haddy's thoughts, and Haddy had to be very careful not to reveal herself because she didn't want anything bad to happen to Mummy or to Aunt Mandy. And if Mummy were to find out how happy she sometimes was here, she might harm one, or both, of them. Then, Aunt Mandy might convince Daddy to do something awful, like get rid of Mummy, divorce her.

It really was horribly confusing.

Sitting together on the sofa, they'd listen to the war news on the wireless, or to "The Children's Hour with Uncle Don," and Mandy's perfume would swell her nostrils, expanding her chest. Then, she'd wish she were invisible so that no one could find her, and that way she'd be able to remain here for the rest of her life, snug behind the blackout curtains, close enough to absorb every particle of texture and color that was Amanda.

There was her hair, thick and smoothly rolled, or free-hanging in a fall over her shoulders; there was the straight line and narrow tilt of her nose, and the curve of her chin into her jaw; her eyes were blue and perfectly round, the lashes almost white at the very tips; the line of her throat was a long arc, dissolving into shoulders, and arms, and tiny wrists, and delicate hands with fingernails lacquered pure red with never a chip. Unlike Mummy, Amanda was composed of softnesses and plummeting lines of invitation. Unlike Mummy, Amanda had no reluctance about showing herself, and sat for ages in the tub, dreamy, with damp tendrils of hair clinging to the column of her neck as she laughed softly and smiled, recalling this or that to share with Haddy, who sat on a white enamel stool, leaning with her arm on the rim of the tub, keeping Amanda company while she bathed lazily, soap froth slithering over her shoulders and sloping breasts. Haddy, dazed by this intimacy, wished she could make drawings of the many Amandas who kept revealing themselves to her: Amanda with the cookery book in the kitchen, reading directions as Haddy followed; Amanda in the bedroom, turning before the long mirror to straighten her stocking seams; Amanda sitting, elbows on her knees, listening as Mr. Churchill spoke again on the wireless; Amanda sliding with a sigh into the thick-steaming water.

Late that summer, leaning against the rim of the tub while Amanda bathed, Haddy said, "I wish I knew how to draw properly."

"Do you?" Mandy squeezed the water from a large sponge. "Why?"

Haddy was a little bothered by the question. She sensed her mother wouldn't have asked it, although she couldn't have guaranteed that. It was merely a sense she had that Mummy would somehow have known why. There were times when her mother knew things no one else seemed to understand. She regretted saying anything, but it was too late to retract.

"You'll think I'm ever so silly," she said.

"Do tell me why," Amanda urged.

Hadleigh shifted, resting her chin on her folded hands. "I'll have to go back, I expect," she said, her heartbeat accelerating. "Go home, I mean. I'm sure I will, and then I don't know when I'll be able to visit again. If I could draw properly, I'd have pictures, and then it would be almost as if I were still here."

Mandy let the sponge drift away. "Perhaps," she said, "you'll be able to stay for a time."

"I would like to. But if I could draw, I'd always be here, in a way."

"One doesn't lose people in the same way one misplaces one's gloves," Mandy smiled. Hadleigh seemed not to notice.

"I lost Mummy," she said. "No matter how hard I try, I can't think how it happened."

"That's not quite the way things are," Mandy disagreed. "If anything, I think the reverse might be true."

"How?"

"I think your mother's been unhappy for a very long time. And being unhappy, there were things she forgot. Important things."

"Do you think so?" Hadleigh asked, intrigued.

Taken off guard by the girl's grasp of what Mandy considered a fairly elusive insight, she said, "These things do happen, you know. I will say I don't think any of this has to do with you directly, but rather with the circumstances."

"What circumstances?"

It was Mandy's turn to wish she'd said nothing. "Oh, the war, for one." Her mind raced, searching for answers.

"And what else?"

"Your father's work, for another." She smiled again all at once, saying, "I hope we'll be together for a good, long time. I believe your father thinks so too."

"You do? Why?"

Christ! Mandy thought, feeling inundated by the girl's doggedness. "Perhaps we'll see if we can't find someone to give you drawing lessons."

"I'd like that very much. I'm sure Daddy would pay for them."

"That's not important."

"Oh, it is!" Haddy argued. "We always decide together on special things."

"Well, I'm sure there'll be no problem."

Hadleigh looked down at Mandy's shiny knees that rose above the water like two little mountains, her brows drawing together as she tried to pinpoint what it was about all of this—her being here and away from her mother, her mother's frightful anger, and her father's occasional late-night whispered conversations with Mandy when they both thought her asleep—that felt just the tiniest bit peculiar. She couldn't make it come clear.

Raising her head, she said, "You're ever so pretty, Aunt Mandy."

Retrieving the sponge, Mandy said, "You're prettier."

Hadleigh laughed. "Oh, never! Mummy's always said Ben would make a much prettier girl than me."

"Your mother," Mandy said rashly, "isn't always the kindest or most tactful woman alive."

"Sometimes, she is," Hadleigh defended her. "She doesn't

mean to be unkind." Why had she repeated that comment about Ben? Why? At the time, they'd all laughed and laughed, because they'd rigged Ben out in an old frock Haddy had outgrown, and he'd been very pretty, far prettier than his sister. She couldn't possibly explain that now to Mandy. She didn't think Mandy cared very much for Mummy anymore.

Ten

In order not to remind Hadleigh in any way of her mother, Mandy cut back sharply on her drinking. It wouldn't do to have Hadleigh see her sitting about with a full glass in her hand, so she limited herself to sherry before dinner and one drink in the evening. It was a part of the evolving routine of her life with the child.

Since the air-raids were sporadic and light during July and August, they took to remaining in the flat when the intermittent siren blasts signalled the start of a raid. Their experiences in the underground had been unpleasant, what with the massive overcrowding and terrible airlessness; with the stench of overflowing lavatories, and the suitcase boundaries erected between row upon row of people. There were infants that cried for hours, and angry, impatient people spreading improbable tales of the destruction going on above; there was constant coughing, murmurs from all sides and, somewhere, the sound of water dripping. With the steady scream that indicated the all-clear, she and Hadleigh had emerged more upset and exhausted than they'd have been had they remained in the flat. So they agreed, at least for the time being, to take their chances above ground.

Being a surrogate mother proved a more trying task than she'd thought it might be. It was important to gain Hadleigh's trust, but they were travelling together over unfamiliar terrain, and regularly came up against obstacles created by their different ways of doing things. Hadleigh tried not to point out that her mother, or her Nana, did things in such and such a fashion, but sometimes it just couldn't be avoided. There was, for example, the way in which her hair had always been washed. Mandy wanted her to sit with her back to the basin and tip back her head. It was horribly uncomfortable, and Haddy had to say, "My mother always does it frontways." There was the matter of her bedtime: She'd always been allowed to stay up until ten; Mandy insisted on her retiring at nine-thirty. All kinds of ordinary everyday things that had been done one way all her life were now not so ordinary or everyday because Aunt Mandy had never done any of them.

Mandy had never listened to "The Children's Hour," and so knew nothing about Toy Town or Larry the Lamb, and the Mayor, and Dennis the Dachshund. She didn't know how to play Strip Jack Naked, or even Snap. She strongly objected to Haddy going downstairs to skip rope on the pavement, and while she did make an effort to seem interested, she really had no desire to play with Haddy's dolls.

Haddy badly missed Millicent and Lillian, and even Magnus, and couldn't help recalling how her mother used to get down on the lounge floor and play Old Maid, or Chinese checkers with them. It really was very nice to be with Aunt Mandy. Haddy just wished she could see her old friends, or find some new ones. But the vast majority of children had been evacuated from the city.

All in all, though, they did get on well together.

"I do hope you're not too terribly bored," Mandy said often, to which Hadleigh replied each time, "Oh, no. I'm very happy, really."

Mandy couldn't begin to fathom why Frances found Hadleigh such a difficult child, and ventured to express this thought to Arthur on one of his infrequent visits in early September.

"You must understand," he told her, "that children behave differently with adults who aren't their parents. Children have a license of sorts to express themselves to their mothers and fathers in ways they never would to other adults. I concede that where Frances is concerned, there's always been something not quite right. Almost from the day Haddy was born, Frances seemed to view her as something of an opponent. I thought she'd get past it in time, but in retrospect, matters were growing worse for years. Then I thought this recent separation would help, but it doesn't seem to have."

"You don't like talking about her with me, do you?" Mandy asked. "It makes you feel disloyal, doesn't it? We all seem to be suffering from it. Certainly Haddy is. She's desperate not to say anything that might reflect badly on Frances. And I think you feel fairly much as she does: that it's unthinkably improper to discuss someone who can't be here to defend herself. You're married, yet here you are talking about your wife with another woman. It must feel dreadful."

"It's beyond describing," he admitted. "But it's been such a help to be able to talk matters over with you. Right now, Deirdre's rebelling, and I can't say I blame her. She's worn out from the responsibility, first of two children, now of Ben. And poor Ben's caught in the line of fire. He's afraid to have his friends in, and if he stops, even for five minutes, to visit with one of his schoolmates on the way home from school, Frances holds a full-scale inquisition of the poor lad, railing away at him with her drunken logic. I wish I knew if it were just the drink; or if . . ."

"Or if it's Frances herself," she completed his thought. "I'll tell you this much: The last time I saw her, she was cold sober, only had one drink. I found her terribly . . . absent. I scarcely knew her. This *is* hateful, isn't it?"

"I can't think why you'd want to become embroiled in this mess," he said truthfully.

"I don't see why I shouldn't. Before Hadleigh came, I was simply using up time, socializing a fair amount when Edwin was . . . Everything's changed with the war. So many of the men I knew have gone into one service or another. It hardly seems right to dine out every night simply because one can afford it, when others barely have enough rations. I was feeling . . . fraudulent. I'm not even able to knit, or else I'd have been here of an evening, doing something that might be construed as remotely useful. Now, I'm serving a useful purpose. Hadleigh will be starting school soon, and I do think she's beginning to thaw. She's still fearful, but I'm most optimistic, really. We've found someone who'll give her drawing lessons twice a week, and she'll be starting with that in another fortnight. She's becoming quite a good cook, and constantly offers to help. She's a *wonderful* child, Arthur. I'll hate it when she has to go back to the Midlands."

Arthur had to wonder why, when contrasted to Amanda,

Frances seemed so brittle and self-involved. "Why has it all turned so ugly?" he mused aloud.

"Oh hell, Arthur! You married the wrong woman. I'm sorry, but there it is."

He felt imprisoned. For the first time in his adult life, he looked ahead at the vague outlines of his future and felt only despair. The Intelligence information was all menacing; his wife had become an alcoholic and seemed on the verge of mental collapse; his mother-in-law was an elderly woman growing daily more fatigued from contending with her problem daughter and a six-year-old boy. He himself rarely now got to see the light of day, and there was no end in sight to the war. If anything, the war seemed to be everyone's future. Perhaps there was no point in caring anymore. They might all soon be dead.

There were times, like now, when he loathed his privileged position. There was a titanic unreality to watching pins get moved on enormous wall charts, to seeing WAAF personnel shifting ships or planes on vast table-sized maps of the British Isles; it hardly seemed possible that he was privy to knowledge not only of military movements on both sides, but to telegraphed messages of formidable import. At moments it was like some lunatic game being played by grown men. Yet it was hardly a game, and vast numbers of people were dying; countries were overrun, entire populations displaced. He spent eighteen and twenty hours a day with personnel who hadn't been above ground in weeks. His own random hours of leave he took in order to preserve his sanity, and to confirm the relative well-being of his family. The thought of his placid pre-war existence almost made him laugh in view of the diametrical swing to his life now.

And here was this woman, his wife's friend Amanda, whom he'd known socially for years, but with whom he'd never had more than a passing acquaintanceship. In just a few months she'd assumed a key role in his life.

"You've gone very quiet," Mandy interrupted his thinking.

"Sorry."

"You're exhausted. I've never seen you so worn out."

"It's a permanent condition," he said impatiently. "What odd times these are! Here am I, saying and doing things I'd never say or do in ordinary circumstances."

"We all are."

"No. I'm sitting here asking myself if I feel about you the way I do simply because I need to feel this way, or if it's because I've never really had an opportunity to know you."

"This is risky," she said, her eyes on Haddy's door. "What . . . Are you suggesting something, Arthur?"

"I have no idea. I find myself thinking of the two of you, you and Haddy, and I begin looking forward to coming here. It's such an oasis. When I'm met with the necessity of going up to Leamington, it's all I can do to fulfill my obligations. I don't want to go; I don't want to have to try to deal with Frances as she is now. I'm repelled by her evolution into a self-righteous sot. It's so intolerant of me that I'm repelled by my own repulsion." He ran his hands through his hair, distraught.

"It's only human," she contradicted. "No more than that."

"She's my *wife*, Amanda."

"On paper, perhaps. I could make love to you," she said carefully. "I'm not sure it wouldn't just complicate matters more."

"Sorry?" He was so tired his attention kept fading in and out.

"Frances already believes we're having an affair," she said matter-of-factly. "The prospect of turning her fantasies into reality doesn't concern me. I've always found it a source of comfort and, heaven only knows, both of us could use a little of that just now. But I do have doubts about being able to deal with her accusations if the situation undergoes a change. And then there's the matter of an intuition I have that you'll keep Frances as your wife, regardless of what happens." She paused, then asked, "I'm right about that, aren't I?"

"I should go," he said. "We're ranging too far afield here. If I may, I'll look in on Haddy before I go."

"Of course."

He got up and went to open the guest-room door. Mandy rose and took several steps, stopping halfway between Haddy's room and the entry, to wait.

"She's sleeping beautifully," he said quietly, returning.

She crossed her arms over her breasts and smiled at him.

"If I were at least in some branch of the military, I could come with tins of coffee, or silk stockings."

"I have a decent stock of both." She put a hand on his

shoulder. "I expect you're in need of fresh clothes. If you like, bring your laundry and I'll see to having it done for you."

"I haven't been to the flat in ages," he said, looking more discomfited by her talk of laundry than by their earlier discussion of lovemaking. "I must make a point of fetching a few things, collecting the post . . ." He trailed off, and they stood looking at each other. "You've been a brick," he began, but stopped when she laughed. For a second or two, he felt like a fool, but heard himself, saw her delight in the cliché, and laughed with her. "It's all so damned ridiculous," he said apologetically. "I'll ring, if I'm able, and I'll stop by again, when and if."

"Lovely." She walked with him to the door, where they stood, each casting about for appropriate parting words. "Take care," she urged him. "We'll be here."

He opened the door, gave a little wave from the top of the stairs, and went on his way.

She went to make a cup of tea. While the kettle was coming to a boil, she leaned in the doorway, gazing in at the lounge, telling herself that Frances would, in all likelihood, be more than happy to be the one to break up the marriage. But were Arthur to ask for a divorce, Frances would go to her grave refusing, especially if she discovered that he'd formed an alliance with Mandy. Frances's perversity was easy to see; she'd displayed it in the course of every harassing telephone conversation; she'd aired it in her dealings with poor, darling Edwin. Arthur was right to wonder, because it wasn't the drink that was to blame, it was Frances. Something in her yearned for ascendance, and if it proved unobtainable, she'd play hell with every life that touched hers. Hadn't she already done precisely that?

Not bothering to warm the pot, she spooned in several measures of tea, then poured on the water. She wished, as she so often did, that she could ring up Edwin. She missed their long chats, and the impromptu invitations, and that marvellously silly flat where they'd sat for hours before the fire, bringing each other up to date over a bottle of wine. Thinking of him, she felt angry, but tamped it down. Anger would serve no useful purpose.

Haddy could draw. Mandy was most impressed by the first sketches she brought home from her class.

"These are very good!" she complimented the child. "You're quite the artist."

"Miss Braden said I'm too tentative."

"Be that as it may, I think these are splendid. Do you think you'll be a painter when you grow up?"

"I think I'd like to be an architect."

"An architect. That's an impressive ambition. You'll have to do very well in school in order to go to university to study. What sort of buildings do you think you'd like to do?"

Haddy didn't think Mandy was taking her seriously. She was asking the kinds of questions, making the kinds of remarks, grown-ups made to children when they were not really interested but wanted to be polite. "I don't know," she answered, trying to imagine how her mother might have responded. Mummy would certainly have said something funny. Haddy could almost hear her, and laughed suddenly. "Perhaps I'll do dollhouses," she declared. "Tiny little houses, with each room properly done up, tiny little stairways, and tiny little loos."

Mandy laughed. "Tiny little loos, indeed. Are you ravenously hungry?"

"Yes, I am."

"You're in luck. I've been craving custard tarts all afternoon. Shall we walk down to Lyon's? Does that appeal?"

"I'll just have a quick wash."

"We could do fish and chips, if you'd prefer."

"Lyon's," Hadleigh called back.

Mandy looked at the several sketches spread across the dining table. They were boring, but good: a very lifelike bowl of fruit, a wine bottle positioned before a potted plant, several renderings of Haddy's left hand, another view of the fruit.

As they walked through Portman Square on their way to Marble Arch, Haddy said, "I think I'll send some of my drawings home for Ben and Nana and Mummy."

"I'm sure they'd like that."

"Miss Braden said there'll be several other people attending the next class, and perhaps she'd try to get a life model. I'm not very good at doing people, but she said it's important to try."

"She's quite right. You'll have to have tiny people in those tiny little houses, won't you?"

Hadleigh laughed and swung on Mandy's hand.

"Do be careful!" Mandy warned, concerned that the girl might collide with someone in the darkness.

Chastened, Hadleigh went very quiet and walked along in silence until they arrived in Oxford Street. "You don't really believe I could be an architect, do you?" she asked.

"Of course, I do. Why shouldn't you, if it's what you say you'd like to do?"

"I don't know. Sometimes grown-ups say things to children they don't really mean."

"Has that been your experience?" Mandy wanted to know.

Hadleigh considered. "Not in my family," she answered at length.

"You're a very lucky girl," Mandy commented, suppressing the small stab of irritation she felt each time Hadleigh dredged up her family as a reference.

In the five months since Arthur had taken Hadleigh off to London to live with That Woman—Frances refused to name Amanda—her outrage had snaked its tendrils through every part of her consciousness. Ben and Deirdre didn't dare refer to Amanda, or Hadleigh, or even Arthur, for fear of setting Frances off on another tirade. She'd drop her voice to a disgusted level, declaring, "I do not wish to hear about That Woman, or that Hateful Child. I hope with all my heart the lot of them get blown sky high."

It was all Deirdre could do not to strike her. She restrained herself, saying, "Hadleigh is a perfectly fine child. You go too far, Frances."

At the merest hint of an incipient confrontation, Ben's face took on an agonized, pleading expression. Often, he'd tug at Deirdre's hand or cardigan, silently reminding her of his presence and entreating her visually to ignore his mother's words.

Seeing this, Frances would snatch the boy to herself and hold him captive against her jutting hip while she verbally excoriated her mother. "It wasn't enough you had to turn That Child into a piggish little sluggard. Now you're trying to turn Ben against me as well. I swear you've gone senile!"

"You're drunk," Deirdre said flatly. "Why don't you go up to your bedroom and lie down?"

"I am *not* drunk!" Frances flared with exaggerated dignity.

"How dare you say such a thing to me in front of a small child?"

Ben squirmed miserably, wishing he could go live with Magnus, or in London with That Woman and Haddy. That Woman was sure to be a lot nicer than Mummy was. Even Nana expressed a similar view when, tucking him up for the night, she confided, "I'll have a word with your father. This can't go on."

"Is Mummy crazy?" he asked in a hushed voice.

"I don't know anymore," Deirdre sighed. "Perhaps she is. I do know that if this goes on very much longer, *I* shall go mad."

She shouldn't have said it. Ben was immediately frightened; he grew pale and began to cry. "I want my Daddy," he sobbed, clutching at his grandmother's sleeve. "I want to go to London with my Daddy."

"We'll see what's to be done. In the meantime, how would you like to go to Coventry for an afternoon? We could have a lovely luncheon out."

He sniffed, recovering himself. "I'd like that, Nana."

"There's a good boy. You close your eyes now and don't worry your dear self. Nana's not going to go mad. You have my word."

Deirdre wanted to take Ben on the bus. Frances wouldn't hear of it.

"I'll drive you in the Rover."

"Oh, I don't think Arthur . . ."

"To hell with Arthur! I'll take you in the Rover."

"But I promised Ben an outing . . ."

"And you'll have it. Have your outing, the two of you, and I'll look in Coventry's tatty shops. We'll meet late afternoon and come home together."

"All right," Deirdre relented.

The short drive to Coventry was uneventful. Frances appeared to be entirely sober, and looked more like herself than she had in almost a year. She'd washed her hair, dressed with some care, and applied makeup. She actually hummed to herself as she took the large car over the narrow roads.

"I've promised Ben luncheon at The Geisha Cafe in Hertford Street. If you wouldn't mind setting us down there."

"Not at all," Frances said pleasantly. "I'll collect the two of you from in front of the restaurant at four-thirty, and we'll be home, with luck, before dark."

After dropping them off, she lost her momentum and couldn't think what next to do. If she kept driving, she'd use up all the petrol. Spotting a pub, she decided to have a drink and plan out the afternoon. She had to go to Hammon's to get new undergarments for Ben, and, at some point, she'd get something to eat. One thing at a time. First, she'd park the car, then she'd go into that charming-looking little pub and have a drink. She might even have her lunch in the pub, thereby killing two birds with one stone.

Eleven

"She's bound to be along any moment," Deirdre told her grandson every few minutes as they stood outside the restaurant scanning the road. They'd been waiting more than an hour, and it was already dark. She was trying to conceal her anxiety, but Ben, too, was worried.

"Perhaps she's forgotten," he said, trying to distinguish one vehicle from another. "She forgets ever such a lot of things. She forgot last Thursday was early closing and sent me to the bakery, and I had to walk all the way there and then all the way back again because I'd forgotten, too. But I'm only little," he protested. "I'm not supposed to remember everything."

"Of course you're not," Deirdre concurred, trying to think what to do. They couldn't very well stand here indefinitely. "I'll try to ring her. It's possible she could've gone home. Do you recall seeing a call box?"

"I saw one! It's back there"—he pointed—"near the corner."

"I'm sure I have pennies." She led Ben back along the street toward the call box. "It's a lovely, clear evening, isn't it?" she noted, encouraging him to look up at the moonlit sky.

The ringing went on and on while Deirdre waited, pennies at the ready. "No reply," she said at last. "We'll just go back and wait a bit longer. She may be having trouble finding her way."

"I *do* hope she hasn't forgotten us," Ben said, skipping

along at his grandmother's side, his light movements an extreme contrast to his concerned tone.

"If it comes to it," she thought aloud, "we have several alternatives. We could make our way to the station and get a train back. Or we could try for the number five-seventeen bus. Or we could book into a hotel and go home in the morning. You're not to worry." She looked around, determined to climb aboard one of the familiar Midland Red buses, should she see one.

Back in the doorway of The Geisha Cafe, Deirdre feared now that Frances might have come and gone in the brief interval while they were ringing home. Frances wouldn't do that, Deirdre told herself. She'd stop and wait for them. "Where *could* she be?" she wondered aloud, feeling a nip in the air. This really was too much! she thought. She'd give Frances a strong talking-to once they got home.

"I don't know," Ben answered, his small voice lonely sounding. "I wish I did know. It's my tea-time, Nana. And yours," he added stalwartly, holding fast to her hand.

"We'll give her another half hour, and then we'll book into a hotel for the night and be done with it."

"I've never stopped in a hotel."

"We'll go to the King's Head." It was the first and only name that came to her mind. "We'll book a room, have a wash, then go straight to the dining room for our tea."

"Good!" He gave another little skip. "It's getting ever so cold, Nana."

"It is, isn't it? We should've brought your scarf. Never mind." She chafed his hand, in the process warming her own. Her back was starting to ache and her feet hurt. She was becoming very angry with Frances.

Throughout the afternoon Arthur rang the Leamington house every half hour. The unanswered telephone was distressing, and he wondered where they all could be. He prayed they hadn't gone to Birmingham for the day, or to Coventry. He was fearfully obsessed by the notion that they had, and so kept excusing himself to go back to the telephone. By seven he was forced to abandon his attempts to make contact. It was too late.

*   *   *

Just when Deirdre decided they'd make their way to the King's Head, the siren sounded. Her instant fear transmitted itself through her suddenly damp hand to Ben, who let out a cry and threw himself against her.

"Not to worry, dear heart. We'll find a shelter." They hurried from the doorway into the street, joining the others rushing along, apparently with a definite destination in mind.

"Wait, Nana!" Ben said urgently, dragging against her hand. "I've lost my shoe."

She stopped as Ben hopped back to retrieve his shoe, and dared to glance up at the sky. She could actually see bombs falling through the air. Her heart lurched. She could see the bursting flames, hear the aftermath explosions, and it felt as if they were going off in her chest and in her ears, eyes, and mouth. Terrified, she lifted Ben into her arms and ran lumberingly after the people who'd now all disappeared off the street. Where had they gone? She hadn't thought a small boy could be so heavy. Her lungs ached from the effort of breathing and she ducked instinctively, almost falling with Ben, as a bomb hit less than fifty yards away and showers of glass descended on the pavement, following by the thudding impact of bricks striking the ground. Dear God! she thought, her eyes darting here and there, seeking some safe place. The noise was dreadful, the reverberations painful. Ben was screaming and she cupped the back of his head protectively with her hand, holding him secure against her shoulder as she struggled along the road.

The ceaseless noise awakened her. She opened her eyes and tried to generate some moisture in her parched mouth. She had no idea where she was, nor who the man determinedly bellowing at her might be.

"Do shut up!" she told him.

"There's a bloody raid going on! I'm getting the hell out of here!"

"Do, by all means," she said, sitting up and discovering to her thorough disgust that her belly and thighs were covered with dozens of foreign hairs, pasted to her flesh with seminal fluid.

"By the way," her companion said at the door. "My name's not Edwin, and it's not Arthur. It's Charles."

"How lovely for you!" she said disdainfully.

"No need to be unpleasant," he said, the door open. "I paid for all your bloody drinks."

"How kind!" She looked about for her clothes.

"It wasn't worth it!" he said angrily, ready to leave.

"Oh, I say!" she summoned him back, smiling sweetly.

"Yes?"

"Just thought I'd mention: I've got syphilis. Thank you for the drinks."

With a look of horror, he slammed shut the door and took off at a run.

"Cretin!" she mumbled, making her way to the sink in the corner of the room. Although there were two faucets, only the cold water one worked. Shaking from the combination of cold air and cold water, she washed quickly, dried herself on a worn-thin towel, then began to assemble her clothes. Suddenly remembering, she looked at her wristwatch. Six-forty. "Oh, my God!" she exclaimed, and frantically dragged on her clothes.

She had no idea where she was, and it was no use looking for landmarks to give her some clue. Everything seemed to be ablaze, or in the process of crumbling. Smoke rose thickly into the air, obscuring her vision. Where was the Rover? Eyes tearing, she ran to the corner and spotted the car. The keys, thank heaven, were in her bag. There was a call box between her and the car, and she halted, deliberating. Perhaps they'd given up and gone home. Her mother was a sensible woman. She wouldn't have waited in the street for more than two hours. Groping in her bag for pennies, she closed herself into the box. There was no reply.

Ignoring the shouts of firemen and air-raid wardens, she drove up one road and down another and, finally, had to stop at the end of the road. She leaped from the car, determined to get to the restaurant but she could see it was impossible. The entire street was in flames, the roadway blocked with rubble.

She returned to the car and tried to think what to do. The raid was still going on. Explosions seemed to occur every few seconds. She had to look for them. For a second time, she left the car, dashed past the firemen and ran, tripping, down the street, calling, "Mother! Ben! Mother? Ben?"

She was forcibly removed from the area by two burly, soot-covered firemen. "Get out of the area at once!" they told her, escorting her to the car. "Are you mad?"

She had no choice but to reverse and drive away.

So many of the streets were impassable she had to resort to laneways and alleys, working her way out of the city. The only other vehicles she saw were fire engines as, at last, she gained the outskirts and spotted a road marker. She'd gone miles out of her way, and there was very little petrol left. All she could do was continue toward Leamington until the car stopped. When and if it did, she'd have to walk the rest of the way.

The house was empty. Her head throbbing, she went directly to the telephone for the directory. With the book open across her lap, she began ringing each of the hotels in Coventry. At those establishments where the telephone was answered, she was advised there was no Mrs. Chapman registered. Next, she rang the local constabulary who suggested she ring their associates in Coventry. She couldn't get through, despite repeated efforts. Closing the directory, she began to weep in fear and exhaustion. She hadn't run out of petrol but it had still taken her the better part of two hours to get home.

She wanted to ring Arthur, but dreaded what he might say. There was no question in her mind that if anything had happened to her mother and Ben it was entirely her fault. The implications of her failure to be at the restaurant at the appointed time were limitless. She dared not consider them. She couldn't think what she could do next, but sit and wait and hope they'd turn up. The only way she could deaden herself to further speculations reposed in the drinks cabinet.

Remaining close by the telephone, she proceeded to drink steadily well into the night, coming to with a start every time she heard a motor passing in the road. She awakened at six the following morning to find herself on the floor in the entryway, the carpet sodden and reeking of scotch. She was attempting to blot up some of the spilled liquor when the telephone went. It took her a full minute to collect herself sufficiently to be able to approach it.

"*Where have you been*?" Arthur bellowed. "I've been worried sick. I spent hours trying to reach you all yesterday afternoon and evening."

Her control gone, she wept into the mouthpiece. "Oh, Arthur! I don't know where they are. I've been on to everyone, the hotels, the police, everywhere I could think of.

Arthur, I'm so terribly afraid something's happened to
them."

"I'll arrange transportation and be there as quickly as possible." He rang off without another word.

She was filthy, covered in oily black soot from head to toe.
Examining her trembling hands, she told herself she must
bathe. Arthur was coming.

It was one of the very few times in his life when he pulled all
the stoppers and let his emotions dance about visibly on the
surface of his words and in his actions. The result was a
ministry vehicle and a driver. They set off at once.

Throughout the trip, Arthur worked to convince himself
that by the time he arrived at the house, Ben and Deirdre
would be safely home. He couldn't bring it off. A quiet inner
voice warned him of further disasters, all personal. He was
never again going to see Deirdre, or his son, and, worse, he
believed they were casualties not of the war but of his wife's ir-
responsibility. Nothing had ever been more painful or of
longer duration than this drive toward what he knew in his
bones would be the worst possible news.

The bodies were discovered beneath the rubble late that same
morning.

Frances, sober, was ashen with grief.

"You'd best tell me what happened," Arthur said, unable
to comfort her until he could be satisfied of her innocence.

"Oh, please, Arthur," she wept, her thin arms wrapped
around herself. "Must we go into that now?"

"Why were they there? The raid didn't start until after six-
thirty. Deirdre was a practical woman. Unless plans had been
made, she'd have brought Ben home well before tea-time.
What was the plan, Frances?" he asked, loathing the yellow-
ish tinge to her skin and the whites of her eyes; loathing the
self-pity and the reek of whiskey oozing from her pores. He
wouldn't have believed himself capable of the hatred he felt at
that moment. His entire being screamed in favor of striking
her, of beating her senseless with his fists.

"I won't lie to you. I was to collect them. I was late. By the
time I got there, the raid was in full swing and most of the
streets were barricaded."

"What did you do, Frances? Did you get drunk somewhere

and forget about them? That's it, isn't it? Isn't that what you did?"

He expected her to lie, and was taken aback when she answered, "Yes. That is what I did."

"How *could* you?" he railed at her. "How could you place your own mother and child in such danger? I don't understand."

"Don't you think I'm suffering? Can't you see that I am?" Swaying slightly, she swore, "I won't drink again, ever."

The scene impressed him as being so farcical he simply couldn't deal with it.

"Where are you going?" she cried, chasing after him to the door.

Enunciating slowly, he said, "I am going to have a word with my driver. Arrangements must be made. I think it would be best if you stay away from me just now. You're in jeopardy here, Frances. I suggest you go upstairs and remain there. After I've spoken with the driver, there are several telephone calls to be made. I don't want to have to see you. Just keep out of my sight. I'll advise you on the details." He swung open the door, then turned back. "I will give you this final opportunity to pull yourself together. If you fail, I shall have you committed."

"*Committed?*" She backed away. "I'm not mad."

"Only by your own definition. By anyone else's you are completely, hopelessly mad. You're dangerous, Frances. You're a truly dangerous woman."

He closed the door between them. Unable to catch her breath, she turned and raced clumsily up the stairs. She couldn't believe he'd spoken to her as he had, threatening her with commitment, calling her dangerous. If anyone were in peril here, it was she. He'd become unhinged by the deaths, and was trying to heap the blame upon her. She locked the door behind her and sat on the edge of the bed, alternating between spasms of sorrow and fear of her husband. Her only clear thought was that Mandy, in some way, was responsible for placing poisoned ideas in Arthur's mind.

Hadleigh watched Aunt Mandy as she talked on the telephone, and knew from the way Aunt Mandy listened, her features tight, that something very bad had happened. All Hadleigh could think of was that Mummy was going to force her to come back to live with them. She didn't want to go. She wasn't ready yet. Her mouth was dry and her throat hurt.

At last, the call ended and Mandy said, "Come sit with me."

"Am I going to have to go back?" Haddy asked tremulously.

Mandy shook her head. "It's most distressing news, I'm afraid. That was your father on the telephone."

"Is he all right? Has something happened to my Daddy?"

"He's all right," Mandy said, taking hold of her. "There's been an accident, Haddy."

"An accident? With the motor?"

"There was a very severe air raid on Coventry two nights ago. Your grandmother and Ben . . ."

"But we live *eight miles* from Coventry."

"They were there, Haddy."

"What's happened to them? Are they in hospital?"

"They were killed," Mandy said very quietly.

"Killed," Hadleigh repeated. "My Nana and Ben?"

"I'm afraid so."

"And Mummy? Is my Mummy all right? Was she killed as well?"

"Your mother's at the house in Leamington, with your father. She wasn't injured."

"My Nana? And Ben? *How* were they killed?"

"They were . . . A great number of bombs were dropped. There was terrible damage. Much of Coventry's been destroyed."

Haddy was shaking her head back and forth, the action sending tears from her eyes. "He's only little," she wept. "And my Nana. I want my Nana. I want my little brother. I'm never going to see them again?" She looked beseechingly at Amanda.

"I am terribly sorry." Amanda put her arms around the girl. "We'll go up on the train tomorrow morning, for the funeral."

"You're going with me?"

"Of course I will."

"But, I'll be coming back here with you?"

"If you wish to."

Haddy chewed on her lower lip, her eyes and nose streaming. "I want my Nana," she gasped. "I want my Nana."

"I'm so sorry," Mandy repeated, stroking Hadleigh's hair.

"Six isn't old enough to die!" Hadleigh cried, anguished. "It's not fair."

"No, it isn't," Mandy agreed.

"I'm so glad," Hadleigh said fervently, "that Mummy didn't die, too."

Twelve

It was torture. Her body was being deprived of something Frances had to have merely to function. She could think of nothing but her need for a drink, just one to quiet the noise below the surface of her skin, the blood that sizzled through her system. Nothing diverted her from the need. She tried to relax in a tub of near-scalding water and watched, mesmerized, the tremors that jolted her limbs and rattled her hands. Being sober preoccupied her more than the fact of the deaths; no activity slaked the thirst rooted in her very cells.

When she was able to sleep, she dreamed of liquids, and bottles, and bedewed glasses; of her desiccated mouth welcoming the medicinal flow that would put an end to the ceaseless twitching. She came up from sleep as if emerging from perilously deep water, having been seconds away from death. Awake, she examined with repugnance a body with arms and legs like those of a victim of starvation. Her belly was an inflated sac, hung impossibly between scrawny, wasted hips. Her breasts were shrivelled, fallen pouches that lay against the prominent bones of her chest like disused balloons. An old woman's wasted cadaver had replaced her formerly lithe figure. She'd been left behind as caretaker of this ruin, which she doubted it was possible to return to its proper condition.

Darling Ben was gone, as was her mother, and Arthur despised her. Edwin, too, was gone, and Amanda was seeking vengeance. She sat naked on the side of the bed, her bony hands gripping her gaunt thighs, listening. Silence. Arthur had left the house. Hope shot through her. She could run downstairs, quickly fortify herself. A drink would allow her to attend the funeral services with some semblance of calm; it would loosen the knot of her stomach so she could eat something. She couldn't remember when last she'd had a meal.

She crept stealthily to the door and stepped out onto the landing, head to one side, listening. The silence held. He'd gone out. Good. She ran down the stairs and through to the lounge, her eyes on the polished cabinet at the far side of the room. Salvation sat in bottles just twenty feet away. Mouth open in anticipation, she lurched across the room.

He saw her appear in the doorway and was too shocked to do anything for a moment. He had to remind himself that this mobile skeleton was Frances, a woman he'd once loved beyond all others. He couldn't believe this was the same woman or that, thinking the house unoccupied, she was rushing towards the drinks cabinet.

"What are you doing, Frances?" he asked quietly, causing her literally to jump with fright, and turn crazed eyes upon him.

He'd been there all along, perhaps hoping to trap her. She had to make a rapid mental shift, wetting her lips before changing directions. With only the slightest hesitation, she swung around and came straight to the armchair where he was seated. Falling to her knees, she laid her head in his lap, sliding her arms along his outer thighs.

Looking at the prominent knobs of her naked spine and the thin skin barely concealing the bones of her shoulders, he felt a terrible pity for her. His hand covered the too-vulnerable nape of her neck, and he said, "You have to have it, don't you?"

"Oh, I don't!" she lied, lifting her head.

"You do," he said sorrowfully, understanding suddenly that it wouldn't be possible for her to stop cold. She'd have to be weaned from her bottles, like an overgrown infant. Her eyes had lost the depth of their hue; they appeared pale and watery, red-rimmed, the pupils dilated. "You must eat," he told her, slipping into the role of attendant. "If you have one small drink, will you be able to eat something?"

His kindness was worse by far than any of his threats, and left her feeling enfeebled and totally dependent. "I could try," she agreed, moistening her lips again. Was this a ruse of some kind? she wondered, scouring his eyes for some clue. He looked only fatigued, and dreadfully sad. She couldn't bear his eyes and buried her face once more in his lap.

"I know you hate me, Arthur," she said miserably, "and I don't blame you for it. Everything that's happened has been my fault, everything. I never dreamed any of it would end up this way. It's impossible for you to believe a word I say now, and you're more than justified in doubting me. But I did search for them. They made me leave, the wardens and the firemen. I'd have stayed." She looked up at him. "I'd have done everything, anything, to find them." As if it were too much of an effort to keep her head raised, she lowered it once more. "My head's very clear right at this moment, and you must believe me when I tell you that I loved my mother and my son. I know it hasn't seemed as if I've cared for any of you in a very long time, but it's been as if something came to stand between my feelings and the people most important to me. Please *hear* what I'm saying, because it is the truth." Again she lifted her head to gaze at him. "I don't deserve your kindness, but I am so terribly grateful."

"I'll give you one drink," he said, easing her aside. "And you'll have it where I can watch you. Put on some clothes, then come down to the kitchen."

"Oh, Arthur!" she cried. "That isn't what I was talking about."

"Frances," he said evenly, "I cannot hold a conversation with you just now. Please dress and come to the kitchen."

She rose and went to do his bidding. He watched her withered flanks as she walked away, defeat rising like bile into his throat. It was impossible for him to remain here and play watchdog over her drinking. He was glad now he'd thought to go to the surgery to have a word with Dr. Connors.

Having had no alcohol for some sixteen hours, the small measure Arthur allowed her had amazingly revitalizing effects. She shuddered once, violently, then waited, feeling the elixir spread miraculously through her, undoing the multitude of small knots and pulses in her system. She was able to eat the Bovril-spread toast and boiled egg Arthur set before her, although well before she'd finished her stomach constricted hotly while her bowels were flushed with cold fire. She thanked him with pathetic formality, then excused herself and went upstairs to the lavatory where she remained for so long that Arthur finally came to stand outside the door, asking, "Are you all right, Frances?"

"I will be," she answered and, forced to be content with that, he went to dress.

When an hour later she came down, she looked reasonably like herself. In a black suit, with a bit of makeup and rouge to relieve her pallor, she seemed like the old Frances. A whisper of optimism touched at him, and he hoped she'd been shocked back, once and for all, into reality. She'd even applied a dab of scent and, mindlessly, he breathed in the fragrance of roses appreciatively as they sat together in the back of the ministry automobile, en route to the church.

Her first sight in months of her daughter came as a surprise. In spite of the pinched, grieving expression she wore, Hadleigh really was a lovely-looking girl. It was almost as if she'd never seen her before, and Frances had to admire her charming profile and thick waving hair. She was inexplicably moved, and bent to embrace Hadleigh, mindful of the fact that this child was all she had left. For a moment, Hadleigh remained stiff within the embrace. Frances willed her to soften, to respond, and all at once Hadleigh's resistance left her and her arms closed gratifyingly around her mother's shoulders.

Haddy had been very fearful of this reunion, had even dreaded it. But Mummy seemed so pleased to see her, and even dropped to her knees to hug her—something Haddy couldn't remember her doing in ages. For the duration of the embrace, Haddy thought things might come right now. She'd be able to come back, now that Mummy loved her again. They'd be together, and have more of these lovely hugs. But suddenly, everything went horribly wrong.

Amanda, having watched from a few feet away, said, "Hello, Frances," and saw her greeting take its effect.

Frances shot upright and glared at Mandy, whispering fiercely to Arthur, "How dare you bring That Woman here at a time like this! How *could* you?"

"Be reasonable," he pleaded in an undertone. "She was good enough to bring Hadleigh. How else did you think she'd get here?"

"You don't understand!" she tried to explain. "She's engineered every bit of this! You're playing straight into her hands."

"Oh, Lord, Frances!" Mandy entreated. "Don't make a scene!"

"You conniving, venomous bitch!" Frances hissed and darted forward, as if to strike out.

Arthur stepped between the two women, his face setting into hard lines. "Get a grip on yourself!" he warned. His hand fastened around her upper arm—simply a long bone beneath the fabric of the suit—to subdue her, but it was too late. Frances was drowning in rage, and words spewed volcanically from her mouth as the assembled mourners stood by in horrified, riveted silence.

"I won't *have* it! It's bad enough she's got her claws firmly embedded in my daughter's flesh, but to bring her here, at a time like this. Haven't you any decency?" she shouted at Amanda.

Hadleigh stood midway between Amanda and her father and mother; the minimal trust established moments before was torn away by Frances's hysteria. There was a choice to be made. She could go to her mother, and seek to comfort her, explain that Aunt Mandy wasn't trying to do anything bad. Or, she could go to Aunt Mandy who, she knew, would offer comfort. A split second, and she flung herself against Amanda, sobbing dryly with fear and in humiliation of what her mother was doing in front of all these people when, inside the church, Nana and Ben lay in their coffins. She huddled beneath Amanda's encircling arm, fearfully watching as her father tried to calm her mother. Her father made a gesture to someone in the crowd. Someone else managed to get the mourners moving into the church, and Hadleigh separated herself from Amanda in order to see what was happening. She could hear her mother struggling, crying out, and Hadleigh pushed past people, suddenly finding herself in a clear space.

Two men in suits and a woman were there, the men holding her mother's arms. Frances's skirt was lifted briefly, a needle was plunged into her thigh; then the woman, with the help of one of the men, wrapped her in a garment that prevented any but leg movements. A few seconds more and she was incapable of any movement at all.

Hadleigh screamed and ran forward, pounding her fists against the thighs of one of the men. "Leave her alone!" she screamed. "Leave Mummy alone!"

Arthur grabbed Hadleigh and held her tightly, her head

pressed firmly against his chest.

Frances wanted to say something; her brain continued to send urgent messages to her body, to her tongue, but the signals were intercepted and she simply sagged into the three sets of expectant arms.

"Come along," Dr. Connors said, propelling Arthur and Hadleigh along the walk.

Arthur let himself be moved forward, but couldn't help looking back to see Frances being parcelled into the rear of a black sedan. Another moment and the car was speeding off.

"It's for the best," Dr. Connors was saying. "She'll be well looked after."

His arms still securely around his sobbing daughter, Arthur whispered, "Oh, Christ!" He needed time to absorb this. His wife had just been carted off to Hatton, for which he'd given signed permission in advance, on the offchance that something might go wrong. And everything had gone wrong. If not for his intercession, Frances would have set upon Amanda with her fists. She'd have inflicted injuries on the woman. He had no doubt of that. But knowledge of the truth in no way ameliorated the horror he felt. He doubted he'd ever be able to forget the terror and humiliation that had overtaken Frances when her skirt had been raised and the needle was pushed deep into her thigh. He'd *never* forget it. Whatever she'd done, she paid for it a thousandfold in that moment. He could only hope she might forget it because he knew that for the rest of his life, every time he looked at her, he'd remember.

"Where have they taken Mummy?" Hadleigh demanded. "Why did you let them do that to her?"

He squatted before his daughter and, at eye-level, explained, "You could see for yourself how unwell your mother is, Haddy. I had no choice. I had to arrange for her to be taken to a place where she'll get help."

"It didn't *look* as if they were helping her," Hadleigh argued, her fists on his shoulders.

"I promise you she'll be in good hands."

"I think . . ." She couldn't go on.

"What?" he urged. "Tell me what you think."

She wanted to tell him about the feeling she'd had, just for the briefest moment, that her mother had been telling the truth, that there was something about Aunt Mandy, something about her eyes and the way she'd made Mummy look at her that had caused Mummy to get so angry. But she didn't know how to explain it, and it was only a feeling, just a kind of niggling tickle in her brain, and not anything concrete she could find words for.

"They'll look after her?" she asked, looking at the roadway as if the black sedan might still be there.

"They will."

Holding her hand, Arthur walked leadenly down the center aisle of the church. They sat and, like someone drugged, Hadleigh sagged against him. His arm curved around her shoulders as the service began.

Hadleigh sobbed throughout the first half of the drive back to London. Then, abruptly, she fell asleep. Arthur held her on his lap and gazed steadily out the window, thinking that the fast-falling rain would be turning the graves to mud. His son and mother-in-law lay beneath the mud, shielded by their coffins. His chest felt overfull with unshed tears. He was startled by Mandy's hand on his and turned to look at her. He couldn't speak and looked away again.

Following Mandy's orders, Arthur set his daughter down upon her bed, then went from the room. In the lounge, he automatically drew the blackout curtains against the encroaching night then, addled by thoughts of Frances, he helped himself to a measure of Mandy's gin. He stood looking down at the square outside through a slit in the curtains, sipping the gin, aware of Amanda quietly closing the guest-room door, and then of her receding footsteps. There was a far-off rushing of water, and then she was directly behind him saying, "I'm drawing you a bath, Arthur."

He didn't question it, but gulped down the gin and went with her to the bathroom.

"Give me your clothes," she told him, "and I'll see what I can do to freshen them."

Moments later, he leaned around the door to say, "You needn't bother."

"I'll see to this"—she accepted his clothing—"while you bathe."

He fell asleep in the tub. She had to wake him. "There's a warm towel on the rack."

He nodded, and she went out.

Coming from the bathroom, the towel wound around his

waist, he said, "I'll be on my way, let you get some sleep."

"It's you who needs the sleep. Come along with me now."

The sheets were cool, the room fragrant. He allowed his head to sink into the welcoming pillows, and came awake some minutes later at a slight sound to the realization that he was in her flat, in her bed, and she was removing her dressing gown. He saw her breasts sway forward, and a flash of thigh as she leaned to switch off the lamp. There was the slithering fall of the discarded gown, the bed tilted slightly, and then shock as her body came up against his.

He simply hadn't considered the possibility of something like this happening. It was, in fact, so far beyond the realm of his immediate thinking he didn't know how to react. She put her mouth to his, but he was unable to respond.

"I'm not prepared . . ." he began.

Misunderstanding, she said, "It's entirely safe. I'm sterile."

"Oh, Christ, Amanda!" he exclaimed softly. "I'm terribly sorry."

He was rejecting her. She would not reveal her hurt, her terrible embarrassment. "I quite understand," she strove for a lightness of voice.

"I wonder if I do," he said, "if anyone does. Poor Frances. That was nightmarish." He was seeing again the way they'd raised her skirt before stabbing the needle into her thigh. It made him feel ill.

"It was," Mandy concurred. "I don't think I'd be able to live, knowing I was responsible for the deaths of others."

At her side, Arthur sat up and turned on the bedside light. "It's a *shared* responsibility," he said emphatically. "I could have prevented it happening, but I didn't."

"What do you mean?"

"I'm not at liberty to elaborate, I'm afraid. You'll just have to accept that it's the truth." He found the towel on the floor beside the bed and wrapped it around his waist. "If I may, I'll sleep on your sofa."

"Of course," she said quickly. Retrieving her dressing gown, she found blankets and a pillow and carried them to the lounge.

"I apologize—for everything," he told her.

"No need." She touched her mouth to his, then returned to her bedroom.

He sat on the sofa in the dark, his head in his hands, regretting his failure to absolve Frances to some appreciable degree from the burden of responsibility. The ministry had known the raid was to take place, but the decision had been made to allow it to go ahead, because any extraordinary precautions they might have taken would have tipped the Germans to the fact that their code had been broken. He could have warned them, told them to stay well away from Coventry, but he hadn't dared violate the secrecy. The result was the deaths of his sweet-natured little boy and his ever-forgiving mother-in-law, for which Frances carried the full burden of guilt.

It wasn't that he hadn't been tempted to lose himself in Amanda's embrace, because he'd been mightily drawn to her. It was, rather, that he couldn't stop imagining the sort of things that might be happening to Frances at Hatton; couldn't stop wishing Hadleigh hadn't had to be there to witness her mother's forcible removal.

He stretched out on the too-short sofa, trying to shut down his brain, to resist the impulse to go back to the bedroom and lose himself in Amanda's body. But it couldn't go anywhere; congress with her could lead only to further pain. Yet this might be all there'd ever be. A day or two more and they could all be dead, blue beneath the rubble.

At daybreak, having slept as if bludgeoned, he tiptoed into the bathroom. Amanda had left shaving gear on the basin. Automatically, he began to scrape clean his face, when grief engulfed him and he had to set down the razor as he folded over, weeping. He saw again the bodies as they'd been when he'd made the identification: gray with plaster dust, brown-black trails of dried blood on the exposed areas of skin. His son, so small, and gone for all time, with staring eyes and dirt-clogged mouth; Deirdre, her skull split like a melon, her features surprisingly serene. He saw Frances being strapped into a straitjacket as the needle was plunged into her flesh.

"Is there anything at all I can do for you?" Mandy asked from the doorway.

His head shook from side to side. He wanted to reassure her that he'd have himself in hand in just a moment or two, but was unable. She picked up a face flannel and wiped clean his face, then put her arms around him. His resistance was gone, finally.

In the bedroom they collided urgently and locked together,

writhing in common desire to blot out everything but their mutual destination. Like Roman candles, sparks of awareness illuminated his brain as, from moment to moment, he catalogued the unsettling differences between this woman and the wife to whom he was accustomed. At the end, he had a sudden, deathly intimation of the extent of his disloyalty to Frances, and was compelled to acknowledge it.

"I had no idea they'd treat her in that dreadful fashion. I thought they'd take her quietly. She'd go off with them, and that would be the end of it. I'm terribly afraid for her, but I truly had no choice. Alone, I'm powerless to help her."

"You did the only thing you could. There's no cause for you to feel guilty."

"But I do, and I always shall. Look, Amanda," he began, but she stopped him.

"Don't say it. All you feel toward me is gratitude, and I know it."

"I . . ."

"It's no good, Arthur. I saw your face when they took her. She may be any number of things, but you love your wife."

Desolate, he gazed into space without replying.

As she was seeing him off at the front door an hour later, she was on the verge of telling him about Edwin, but she couldn't. The timing was wrong. It was wiser to maintain her silence. Eventually, when everything had settled, she'd reveal what she knew.

Thirteen

When freed from the restraints, Frances at once created a commotion. Her shouted demands for her right to freedom upset the others. So she was medicated again, returned to the restraining garment, and placed in a room alone. She came round from the medication some hours later focusing on the screened light in the ceiling. The walls of her enclosure, she saw, had been covered with quilted material. She laughed in bitter disbelief and said aloud, "My God! They've actually put me in a padded cell." Her amusement was short-lived. The women who, during the first few days, brought her food, who took her to the lavatory and oversaw her activities there, who stripped her and then installed her in a vast canvas-covered tub of bone-numbingly cold water, who dressed her hours later after hauling her from the tub, all advised her to stop fighting, to quit making demands. "The sooner you're able to demonstrate control of yourself, the sooner you'll be allowed in the ward."

"The *ward*? The WARD? I'd rather stay where I am."

The food was inedible, grayish muck.

"If you don't eat voluntarily, we'll have to force-feed you."

She wouldn't eat. They held her down, fed a thick tube down her throat, and poured liquid nourishment into the funnel-like opening at the top of the tube. The feeding equipment was withdrawn, but she remained strapped in place on the table for three more hours, to ensure that she didn't immediately force herself to vomit.

She begged for a cigarette. One of the attendants propped her against the corridor wall and held a cigarette to Frances's mouth, tipping the live ashes into the cupped palm of her hand until Frances had finished. She threw the cigarette end into the uneaten muck on the food tray, pushed Frances back down onto her mattress and went away.

They came for her one afternoon and led her along corridors to a small room filled with odd-looking equipment. Her jacket was removed and she was positioned on a table, her body fastened neatly into leather straps. One attendant applied jelly to Frances's temples with a thick spatula, another pushed a large, padded stick into her mouth, electrodes were put into place over the jelly and then the man in charge threw a switch.

Her first session of electroconvulsive therapy left her disoriented, shocked into temporary silence; the muscles throughout her body ached, and she lay unmoving, back again in the jacket, on her mattress. In a state of utter disbelief at what was being done to her, she began to protest even more strenuously. The next day she was again led back along the corridors to the small room, but this time she fought with everything in her against being placed on the table. She lost the fight, and came to consciousness some time later once more in her cell.

In time, she begged to be removed from the restraining jacket, convinced that her willingness to cooperate would prevent further trips to the small room. She promised not to raise her voice; she promised to eat the unidentifiable food. They went away with the jacket, leaving Frances seated on the floor with her useless arms dangling at her sides. Renewed circulation brought pain. Curling into herself on the mattress, she cried, and prayed for Arthur to come take her out of this place.

The next afternoon, they came again to take her for her shock therapy.

"But I've stopped arguing. I've eaten the food."

"Come along!" they ordered, their rough hands fastening around her arms.

Days became nights, became days, on and on, but Arthur didn't come. They were killing her with the interminable hours in the gelid tubs, and the monstrous jolts of electricity, and their inhuman surveillance of her every bodily function. If she had to die, it would not be at the hands of these people, in this place.

She ate the food and begged again, this time to be allowed to keep the blunted tin spoon, her only utensil. Failing to see what harm she could possibly come to with a spoon, she was permitted possession.

She obeyed all orders and rules. She disrobed of her own volition before climbing into the icy water. She was rewarded by being allowed to go to the lavatory unattended, although one of the women waited directly outside the door. She closed her eyes in silent prayer as she lay upon the table in the therapy room. She followed every instruction scrupulously. And during every unsupervised moment in her room, the spoon was in her mouth as she chewed on the rim, hourly, daily thinning it with her teeth, until, at last, the bowl had a sharp, jagged edge that drew blood when she tested it against the underside of her thumb.

When next night came, and the overhead lights had been shut off, she traced with her fingers the vein in her left arm. It was prominent; she could feel the blood shunting along beneath the fingertips. Her lower lip caught hard between her teeth, she embedded the spoon in the vein halfway between her elbow and her wrist, and slowly dragged it down through the protecting flesh. Blood spilled from her upheld arm. She dropped the spoon and lay back on the mattress to wait, her ravaged arm resting on the floor.

When she regained consciousness, Arthur was there.

She wept, and turned her face away.

He sat at her bedside in the infirmary looking at the heavily bandaged arm that was strapped in place, out of harm's way. There were more straps, across her midsection, her thighs, and feet. For some reason, her right hand had been left free. He hated seeing her this way, and reached for her hand, shocked by its coldness, and by the racking continuation of her sobs.

Given hope by his gesture, she gripped his hand. "Please, Arthur," she pleaded, "don't leave me here. Whatever I've done, I don't deserve this. If I have to remain here, I'd prefer to die."

"I don't know what to do," he said honestly.

"I'm not threatening you," she said weakly. "But I'm

being destroyed here. Are you *aware* of their methods of treatment? Are you aware I'm left for hours on end in tubs of freezing water? Did you know that they're running electricity through my brain? *Arthur*! They're *killing* me!''

She did look endangered. He wouldn't have believed it possible for her to look worse than she had before she'd been brought here, but she did.

"How long have I been here?" she asked.

"Almost four weeks."

"Four weeks?" She'd survived here for four entire weeks, yet it felt as if she'd been here for years. "If you *want* me dead, go away now and leave me here. You have my word I'll be dead in very short order. I *cannot* bear this!"

He believed her. He didn't want her dead, but he couldn't believe she was ready yet to return home. "Perhaps, if I could find some other place?"

"*Anything*!" She jumped at once on this suggestion. "Please! I know you don't trust me. I know it. I understand it. Just don't leave me here. If you still care anything at all about me, you'll take me out of this place."

She was asking him, he realized, to get her out of there at once, then and there. Along with this realization came the conviction that if he didn't obtain her release the next time he saw her she would be dead. "I'll take care of it," he said and let go of her hand.

"You're not *going*?" she gasped, attempting to rise against the straps.

"I won't leave here without you. Rest now. I'll be back shortly."

The administrator argued against letting her go.

"I realize," Arthur told him with tired patience, "that she's nowhere near healthy. I also believe it's dangerous for her to remain here. I plan to take her with me."

"She'll be back," the man smiled with knowing smugness.

"She will *never* be back!" Arthur closed the discussion.

He drove her back to Leamington in the Swallow. For much of the drive she slept, her body crumpled against the passenger door. Upon arrival, he carried her upstairs—she was all but weightless, no heavier than Hadleigh—and into bed, then went to ring Dr. Connors to explain what had transpired.

Connors sounded as shocked as Arthur felt. "I had no

idea," he exclaimed. "I'll make inquiries at once. How dreadful! How simply dreadful!"

Frances was only able to drink a small amount of the warm milk Arthur brought her, but was most appreciative, thanking him repeatedly for every slight attention he paid her. It was depressing, and he wondered if he sounded this way to Amanda when he repeatedly declared his gratitude to her. He hoped to God not. He despaired of anyone viewing him in the same light he viewed Frances just then.

He set about changing the dressing on her arm, and drew in a sickened breath at the sight of the wound. "My God, Frances! This is becoming septic." Red threads of infection snaked outward from the distended lips of the ragged tear. Her entire arm was swollen and the torn flesh was enflamed, straining against the crude black threads holding together the two sides of the long laceration.

He went directly to the telephone to ring Connors again. "I'll come immediately," Connors promised.

"I think it's best he see you," Arthur told her. "I don't like the look of this at all."

"You don't?" She gazed almost fondly at her arm. "I thought I did rather a splendid job. It's a great pity I failed."

"You failed," he shouted angrily, "because you did such a 'splendid' job. The blood ran beneath the door and one of the nursing sisters saw it." Why was he behaving this way? he asked himself. She wasn't really responsible. "I'm sorry. I have no right to be angry with you."

"Oh, but you do," she disagreed. "You have every right."

He sat down on the side of the bed, wondering aloud, "How has all this come about?"

"I've been mad," she said unemotionally. "I do believe I've been to another place. This all looks and feels familiar"—she gazed around the room—"but *I* don't. I went *somewhere*, Arthur." She groped for his hand. "Ages ago, I went. Part of me watched, not understanding, but the other part of me was so keen to go. I would be forever grateful for a cigarette."

"Of course," he said, and lit one for her.

She inhaled deeply, letting her head fall back. "If it's what you want, I'll give you a divorce. I won't cause a scandal. I'll do nothing to hold you back." Her voice dropped and she looked deeply into his eyes. "I believe I'll spend the remainder of my life split between the part of me that wants to go and the part that was never truly either happy or unhappy. I've been here, watching most of it, from the distance, as it were. You've been most generous. Really most generous. This is making me ill.'' She gave him the cigarette and he put it out in the ashtray on the bedside table. When he straightened, she was Frances as he'd always known her. She smiled at him with infinite sadness and recognition. Then her eyes rolled back into her skull, and she fell heavily across his lap.

For one heart-stopping moment, he thought she might be dead, and he badly wanted her to be alive. He felt beneath her breast, reassured by the steady beating of her heart.

"I thought she'd died," he told Connors when he arrived, "and all I could think was how would I tell Haddy?"

"We'd best take her over to the Warneford," Connors decided, concluding his examination of her arm. "This is a bloody mess, and she's in even worse condition that I'd imagined. Come on. We'll take her in my car.''

While he paced the corridors, Frances received a transfusion, and the wound in her arm was opened, cleaned, drained, and stitched up again. She was unconscious for six hours, during which time Arthur either sat or paced the floor by her bed, pausing every so often to study the glucose dripping steadily into a vein in her right hand, and the tranquility of her unconscious features.

He reviewed his entire life with Francis, from the first day he'd met her until now, all the while examining her features from different angles, retrospectively relishing her acerbic wit and her moments of unparalleled insight. Interspersed throughout these recollections came snippets of dialogue with Amanda, hearing himself say, "This is very unfair to you," before leaving her bed.

"The serenade of the married man," she'd said, with a smile. "I've had affairs before with married men."

Then, later, she'd said, "I was glad to have Haddy. I'd have agreed to take in anyone, even Frances, had you asked me to."

"Why?" he'd asked her, at sea.

"Because when Frances conversationally disclaimed you, I decided I'd be more than happy to have you. I never thought it would come to anything, but I thought I'd be glad of you. I'll go on wanting you as long as you want me."

He'd been flattered but primarily made uncomfortable by Amanda's words. He wanted to come to her home, but not as someone illicitly visiting his mistress. He wanted to be able to visit with his daughter, and Amanda seemed to have forgotten altogether about Hadleigh. Or perhaps he was overly sensitive.

On his last visit, just a week earlier, Amanda had made it clear he was welcome to stop the night in her bed. He'd refused as gently as possible. She'd taken his refusal lightly, with a shrug, but he'd sensed a very real anger beneath her lightness.

Very late that same night, while sleeping on the mattress in his office, he dreamed of Frances. They were outside the church, and the two men were holding her as the woman lifted Frances's skirt to reveal her naked thighs. The woman stabbed a spoon into Frances's thigh, and she screamed. There was then a brief silence, during which his wife's eyes fastened to his, and he could read her thoughts. Why are you allowing them to do this to me?

His sadness was immeasurable; he mourned his failure to console her appropriately, and his failure to take action upon his impulse to embrace her and tell her how wretched her desire for death made him. In his dream, he'd spoken to her at length of his feelings for her, and of his hope that they might, some day soon, be able to continue on together.

Into the center of his dream had come Amanda, her naked body as white as marble, and as smooth. His lust for her was immediate. He yearned to delve to the very core of her being so that he might fully comprehend the meaning of her kindness. With Frances standing by, tap-tapping her foot impatiently, he fell upon Amanda and moved frantically within her, every few moments turning to confirm that Frances was taking no interest whatsoever in any of this. She kept looking at her wristwatch, waiting for it to be ended. Everything was terribly wrong. Amanda's molten interior caress and Frances's *ennui*-filled tolerance were in reverse order. He wanted it to be Frances within whose body he found solace and courage, but he couldn't free himself from the steely hold of Amanda's thighs.

Why should he love her? he wondered now. And why did he

fly to her when summoned, like a puppy? Why was he always turned toward Frances, as if she were the sun and he were doomed without her radiance?

Back and forth and back again, he paced out the hours while Frances slept unheeding. He thought of her offer to divorce him, and felt again the fear her words had provoked. What he wanted now, and had wanted all along, was to have everything the way it had always been. They'd both dishonored their marriage vows, and each other. He'd made love to another woman. It had been a purely mechanical exercise, heartless and impersonal; he'd felt only drained and guilty at having succumbed to his temporary weakness. It wasn't what he'd wanted; all he'd thought of since was that he'd committed adultery while his ten-year-old daughter slept in an adjoining room. Everything in their lives had gone so terribly wrong. His wife had opened her vein, bent on escape. They'd done unspeakable things to her, but she'd fought back. In attempting to take her own life, she'd been trying to preserve what remained of her identity. He could see that, and it made sense to him.

He went nearer the bed to look closer at Frances's waxen features, trying to absorb the significance her life had to his. She opened her eyes, closed them, then opened them again.

"You'll be here at least a fortnight," he informed her quietly.

"Here, where?"

"Warneford Hospital, here in Leamington."

"Oh!"

"Have they a mental wing?"

"I really don't know."

"I'm very thirsty," she whispered.

He held her head while she sipped some water, finding all that was going on almost dreamlike in its quality of inevitability.

"I want to believe in you, Frances," he said, holding her hand. "There's a voice in my head that says I'm the damnedest fool that ever lived, that you've done everything possible to destroy whatever we had together. But I still want to believe in you. We're two people who never speak of love, except at times of emergency or disaster. Have you any feelings for me?" he asked.

"I do," she answered. "Of course, I do."

"I no longer know what to do—about any of it. I've always thought of myself as a clear-thinking, decisive sort of man. But that's no longer true." He pulled over a chair and sat down, framing his next words with care. "I'm as much to blame for what happened as you are, Frances. I could've prevented it happening but I chose to go on playing by the rules when, this one time, I should've listened to my conscience. We knew the raid was to take place. I could have warned you, but for all sorts of reasons, I didn't." He drew a deep breath, and said, "Perhaps I should've confided in you a long time ago, and none of this would've happened. I'll tell you now that once it's over, I'll ask for a transfer and the three of us will leave here, perhaps go abroad. I'm not cut out for the work. I haven't the heart for it. Whatever happens, I'll leave Intelligence."

"Intelligence?" She stared at him, absorbing this information. "I should have guessed," she said at last. She gave him a small smile. "It must have given you heart-failure every time I made some caustic remark about the ministry."

"It did a bit," he allowed, returning her smile.

"What's to happen after my fortnight here?"

"I don't know. We'll be into the new year then. Perhaps we could wait to decide."

"I'll abide by whatever decision you make."

"Let's leave it until the new year," he said, "and go from there."

"Arthur?"

"Yes?"

"I'm never going to be the sweet, domestic type. You do know that?"

"I know it."

"We'll undoubtedly do battle right to the bloody end."

"I know that, too."

"I very much want my daughter back."

"We'll see, Frances. We'll see."

Fourteen

The Germans had cut back on their bombing raids. Instead of sounding nightly, the sirens went off only a few times a week. There was no raid Christmas Eve. Christmas day fell on a Wednesday, and Arthur was able to steal an hour to visit at the flat in Portman Square. He had very little time in which to present his daughter with the chocolates he'd managed to buy under-the-counter the previous week, and the small gold brooch he'd purchased more than a month earlier in an antiques shop on Bond Street.

"I wish I could stay, Haddy, but it's simply impossible. It was all I could do to get away at all."

"I understand," Hadleigh lied, having prayed nightly for weeks that he'd be able to spend the entire day with her. She and Aunt Mandy had prepared a meal, on the offchance that he'd get to share it with them. "Thank you ever so much for my lovely presents."

"I know you hoped for more of a celebration," he said, sitting with her on his knee. "I'd hoped for it myself. One day, I'll make it up to you."

She sat with her arm around his neck, her head on his shoulder, thinking that if she remained very very still, he might forget to go.

"I'm going to put your lovely drawing up in my office, and every time I see it, I'll think of you. You really must keep on with your lessons. You're very gifted."

He didn't forget. He eased her off his knee saying, "I want

157

a quick word with Amanda and then I must get back."

She sat on the edge of the sofa, watching the way Aunt Mandy listened and nodded, wondering if they were discussing her.

Arthur pressed a small package into Amanda's hands, saying, "I want you to take Hadleigh to a shelter for the next week, until after the new year. Will you do that?"

"If you wish, but . . ."

"Please do it," he insisted. "You must trust me on this."

"If you insist, of course we will."

"I know Haddy's disappointed, and I wish I could stay, but there you are. You won't forget now, about the shelter, will you?"

"I won't."

"Good." He turned to beckon, smiling, to Hadleigh. "Come give me a hug before I go."

Mandy discreetly moved away to give them some privacy.

"How's Mummy?" Hadleigh asked in a hushed voice.

"She's much better, very much better."

"Good. She was ever so funny on the telephone when I rang her to say happy Christmas."

"Funny peculiar, or funny nice?"

"Funny nice. She said I'd forced her to walk miles to get to the telephone, and she made panting noises to show how exhausted she was. She said she missed me, Daddy, and she said she hoped I was happy. We talked for ever such a long time. Will I see her soon?"

"Would you like to, Had?"

"I think I would," she replied with seriousness. "When she was funny, it made me feel peculiar right here." She held her hand flat over her chest.

"I know how that is," he said, kissing the tip of her nose. "I must go."

She hugged him hard, reluctant to have him leave. After each of his visits, she was very afraid she'd never see him again. And it wasn't until he'd gone that she remembered the many things she'd wanted to tell him: about how she'd made that sketch for him ages ago but, lately, hadn't been able to draw at all; about the dreams she had of Nana and Ben and sometimes Mummy; about how she frequently woke up in the middle of the night when there was a raid, and she went to peek through the curtains to watch the spotlights raking the sky, pinpointing airplanes not far away at all; about how she could see fires nearby, and almost feel the heat from them; about how several times she'd fallen asleep right at the window and had had to rush back to bed and pretend to be waking up when Aunt Mandy came in with her morning cup of tea. Now he was going again, and she was afraid it would always be this way.

"The two of you enjoy your Christmas," he said, setting her down. And then the door closed and he was gone.

Haddy burst into tears.

"Try to cheer up," Mandy said, patting the top of her head. "I've got a surprise for you. We've got tickets for Monday afternoon to see *Where the Rainbow Ends* at the New Theatre. It's a super new comedy-panto."

"I feel afraid," Hadleigh admitted.

"Come sit with me and tell me what of," Mandy invited.

"I'm not sure," the girl said. "I don't want to go to the drawing classes anymore."

"You don't have to if you'd prefer not to."

"Are you angry?"

"Not in the least. Perhaps you'll go again in the spring."

"Perhaps," Hadleigh allowed, thinking she'd never go back. She no longer had any interest in drawing. "What did Daddy give you?"

"I don't know. Shall we open it and see?" Amanda reached into her pocket for the small package. "What do you suppose it is?"

"Jewelry, I expect. He always gives Mummy small boxes with jewelry."

"Do you mind that he's given me a gift?"

"Why would I mind?" Hadleigh looked addled by the question.

"Because I'm not your mother, but he's given me a gift."

"Oh, but he gave her a lovely necklace. She told me so this morning."

Mandy didn't say anything.

"Aren't you going to open it?" Hadleigh asked.

The box contained a gold ring with a small, black pearl. Amanda sat staring at it while Hadleigh leaned to look, exclaiming, "It's very pretty, isn't it? Daddy always finds such unusual things. Are you going to wear it?"

Amanda took a cigarette from the crystal bowl on the table.

"I expect so," she said, lighting the cigarette.

"You don't often wear rings, do you?"

"I never seem to remember to put them on."

"But you have a wedding band and one with a big diamond. Are they from when you were married?"

"They are."

"Is it because they make you think of an unhappy time?"

"No. I rarely wear them because it feels a little dishonest when I do."

"I see. You wouldn't want people to think you were still married when you're not anymore."

"Something like that."

"I do think you should wear this one," Haddy said decisively.

"Oh, I will."

"What were you talking about with Daddy?"

"Your father would like us to spend the next few nights in a shelter. I thought perhaps we'd go the Marble Arch station."

"Do we have to? It's so awful."

"We have to."

"For how long?"

"Just until after the new year."

Haddy sagged. "Now I'm afraid again. And you're cross."

"No." Amanda puffed once more on the cigarette then put it out. "It's a dreadful way to live, but we haven't any alternative. I've given your father my word I'd take you to the shelter, and I will."

"Perhaps it'll be this way forever," the girl ventured. "Bombs and fires until there's nothing left."

"It will end eventually."

"No one can be sure of that."

"Let's not be morbid!" Mandy's voice rose. Then, as if hearing herself, she gave Hadleigh a smile, saying, "It's Christmas. What would you like to do?"

"I am a little hungry."

"Then we'll eat. And after, we could go take a walk."

"I wish we didn't have to go to the shelter."

"So do I. But your father did ask."

When they got to the tube station at four-thirty that afternoon, it was already packed with people. Dismayed, Mandy stood looking around when a young man approached her.

"I'm supposed to be holding that spot for a friend." He pointed out a bundle of rags over the way. "He hasn't come. I'll let you have it for half a crown."

"I could book a hotel room for that," Mandy said indignantly.

He shrugged and moved off, saying, "Up to you, dear."

"Cheeky bastard!" she murmured, offended. "There must be some free space here somewhere."

There wasn't. In the end, her temper frayed, she paid the young man two shillings for the privilege of using the space. Whistling, he collected the bundle of rags and hurried to give his sales pitch to an elderly couple just entering. As Amanda got Haddy settled, she watched him sell the pair another space a bit further along the platform. In the course of the next two hours, he did it half a dozen more times. Then, carrying his bundles, he worked his way to the extreme end of the platform where his personal spot had been reserved by yet another bundle of rags. "He ought to be arrested," Mandy said hotly, arranging the bedding they'd brought while Hadleigh looked at the people crowded the length of the platform. Each family or group had a small space and, within its confines, carried on as if no one else could see or hear them. Immediately to her left, two women were drinking tea from a flask and playing cards. Beyond them, a mother had tucked up her two small children, and was reading to them from a storybook. To her right, a couple sat with their backs to the curving wall, their extended legs crossed in front of them. The man was reading a newspaper while the woman opened packets of sandwiches she'd prepared at home.

It was terribly noisy, what with all the people and the trains pulling in to let off even more people. Those arriving on the trains could barely move because of the crowds, and several heated arguments sprang up between those camped on the cement platform and those departing the trains.

The good thing about the trains was that they brought air with them, which eased the heat and smell of so many tightly-packed bodies. The tunnel reeked of urine, beneath which were the various odors of sweating feet, and foodstuffs, of perfume and hair lotion, even of camphor. Hadleigh wrinkled her nose, and prayed she wouldn't have to go to the W.C. here.

The place was too terrible, not to mention inadequate for the number of people. There were always great long queues of women and children waiting.

She and Amanda had worn loose, comfortable clothes for their sojourn below ground, and they'd brought pillows and comforters as well as a wicker hamper with leftovers from their Christmas dinner. There was a flask with soup, and a bag with some of Haddy's chocolates. Mandy had also thought to bring the checkers board, and books for each of them. "We'll make the best of it," she'd said as they'd decided on what and how much they could carry.

Now, looking around, Haddy thought there was no possible way to make the best of a situation as unpleasant as this. There was ever such a lot of coughing and sniffling, so much noise. She couldn't imagine how those two small children were able to sleep as they did. She doubted she'd be able to shut her eyes at all. Time dragged, and she refused the invitation of a girl her own age who suddenly materialized to ask if Haddy would like to play naughts and crosses or, possibly, a game of checkers.

"No, thank you very much," Haddy told the girl, reasoning that if she settled in and began to play, it would mean something. She wasn't sure what, but it had to do with accepting the necessity of their being in this place. "Perhaps later," she told the girl.

"Right-o," the girl said cheerily, and made her way back along the platform.

"It would have helped to pass the time," Amanda said. "Why did you refuse?"

"I didn't mean to be rude," Hadleigh explained. "It's just that I'd rather watch."

"What's there to see?" Mandy asked.

"All sorts of things. I like to watch people."

"What an odd little girl you are!"

"I am?"

"Well, perhaps not odd. But I'd've thought you'd jump at the opportunity to spend time with someone your own age."

"I would, really, but it feels odd to play in here. I could go find her," she said with sudden enthusiasm, "and ask her to come round to the flat to play."

"Oh, I wouldn't do that," Mandy dissuaded her.

"But why?" Hadleigh asked, already halfway to her feet.

"She seemed very nice. Perhaps she lives nearby."

"Sit down, Hadleigh!" Amanda said sharply. "I'd prefer you not to invite her round."

"Oh!" Fuddled, Hadleigh sat down.

"I've brought your pencils and sketchbook. Perhaps you'd like to draw."

"Yes, all right."

"They're just there, in the bag."

Hadleigh crawled over and sat on her knees to open the bag. She really had no desire to draw, but she sensed it would be unwise of her not to take her sketching block and pencils and, at least, make a pretense of it. She resumed her seat and leaned back against the wall, turning her head from time to time.

Satisfied Hadleigh was finally settled, Amanda opened *The Grapes of Wrath*, found her marker and began to read.

Amanda dozed off. Hadleigh continued to sit, watching the people on all sides arranging themselves for sleep. The time dragged terribly, and she felt she might have to go to the loo, but looked at the line of women waiting and told herself she could wait.

The girl came back some time later and, with a smile, said, "Shall I keep you company?"

"All right," Haddy whispered.

"My name's Claire. What's yours?"

"Haddy."

"I know a funny story," Claire said. "Would you like to hear it? My brother told it to us when he was home on leave."

"All right."

"It's ever so funny," Claire chuckled with amusement. "He did it with a very silly accent. I don't think I can tell it quite so well, but it's still very funny." She shook back her hair, squared her shoulders, and began. "There was this chap named Findish," she said, "who lived somewhere abroad—Poland or Russia, it doesn't matter. He decided he wanted to come to live in England, but before he left his mother said, 'Be sure you call me now, Findish,' and he promised he would. But he was gone for ages and he never once called. So, after a few years, another young chap from the same village was going to come to London and this lady heard about it. She went to see him, and she said, 'My son vent off to England and never vonce did he call me. Ven you get to England, I vant you should find my son and get him to call me.' The young man said he'd do it, but he had to know his name and where he lived. 'His name is Findish, and he lives in London W.C.' So the young man arrived in London and the first thing he saw in Piccadilly was a big sign that said W.C. and he thought, 'Aha!' He went inside and walked along until he came to one of the loos that was engaged. He knocked at the door, shouting, 'Are you Findish?' and the man inside shouted back, 'Yes.' So the young man shouted, 'Well, if you're Findish, vy don't you call your mother?' '' Claire fell about laughing, and Hadleigh wet herself.

The noise woke Mandy as well as the two children sleeping next to them. Mandy was livid.

"Do go back to wherever it was you were!" she told Claire. "And you," she rounded on Hadleigh, "ought to be ashamed of yourself."

"But it was a very funny story," Hadleigh tried to explain.

"It's the *middle* of the *night* and people are *trying* to *sleep*."

"I'm sorry, Aunt Mandy."

"Luckily, I brought a spare change of clothing for you. I don't know what we'll do about the comforter. I expect it's ruined."

"I'm very sorry," Hadleigh said again. "I'm sure my daddy will buy you a new one. Please don't be cross with me."

Mandy tamped down her anger and put her arm around the girl's shoulders. "I'm sorry. Tempers are rather short. Please forget it."

They both remained awake after that. At daybreak, they gathered their belongings and moved, with dozens of others, toward the surface. There'd been no raid during the night.

When it came time the next afternoon to return to the shelter, Hadleigh pleaded not to go.

"Please, couldn't we stay here? I hate it in the underground. It smells horrible, and it's so stuffy."

"I gave your father my word we'd stay in the shelters until the new year. I'm responsible for your well-being, Hadleigh. And aside from that, if I gave *you* my promise that I'd do something, then changed my mind and didn't do it after all, you'd never trust me again, would you?"

"But this isn't the same."

"It's exactly the same, and we're going to the shelter. I know it's unpleasant, and I don't care for it any more than you do. As you witnessed last night, it tends to bring out the worst in me. I don't think there's a soul down there who cares for it, but we really must go."

Grudgingly, Hadleigh began collecting things from her room, then went three times to the loo.

The raid that night proved Mandy's point. Haddy sat, as the night before, with her knees drawn forward, her back against the wall, her eyes periodically on the ceiling as faint reverberations seemed to shiver through the concrete.

For the next two nights, Haddy collected her bedding without having to be told. Lack of sleep was having its effects on both of them. Haddy looked pale, her movements were lethargic, and Mandy feared she might be coming down with the influenza that was going around. Periodically, she fell into spasms of what Mandy had learned was called "shelter cough."

By Sunday morning of the twenty-ninth, as they trudged home with their bundles, Mandy was relenting. If they kept on this way, they'd both become ill.

"We'll stay in the flat tonight," she announced. "Four nights in that hell-hole is quite enough."

"Oh, thank you!" Hadleigh crowed, winding her arms around Amanda's waist.

"We mustn't tell your father," she warned. "I did promise we'd go tonight as well."

"It'll be our secret," Haddy swore, then ran off to fling herself happily on her bed, holding the pillows in a contented embrace.

"A bath's in order," Mandy called. "We both reek."

The last of the verbena foam went into the tub, and they shared it. Hadleigh sculpted the froth into odd formations, even creating a diadem for her hair. As she played, she said, "Ben and I used to bathe together, when I was little. He was ever such a funny little boy. He liked to pretend his legs were scissors and he was going to cut off my feet with them. We'd make a frightful mess in the bathroom and Mummy would pretend to be cross with us, but I knew she wasn't, not really.

"One time I asked her if she liked Ben better than me because he was a boy and she said I must learn to be more tolerant because even though I was a girl, I was cleverer than most boys, and it wouldn't do me the least bit of good, because out in the real world being clever was a social disadvantage for girls. Is that true, do you suppose?"

"Well, usually it's the boys who go to university and are expected to make careers. So, from that point of view, being clever doesn't necessarily do a girl all that much good. I'm just paraphrasing what your mother said," she qualified.

"Does that mean you don't believe it?" Hadleigh asked.

"I don't see why girls can't do any number of things. It's a matter of tradition, really. The most important goal for a girl is, of course, to make a good match, marry, and have children. Just now, everything's turned wrong-side-up with this war. A great number of women are doing men's jobs and doing them very well. Once the war's over, those women will go back to being wives and mothers."

"But you had a job. Didn't you like it?"

"I liked it very much."

"Then why did you give it up?"

"I told you: a dear friend died, and I was very sad. I didn't feel up to going to my job."

"But will you once the war's over?"

"Possibly. I have no idea. We'll have to wash your hair. It's sticky with soap."

Hadleigh slid beneath the surface of the water, then popped upright, declaring, "It's not sticky anymore. Now we won't have to wash it!"

Shortly after six, as they were dawdling over a late tea, the sirens went off and, almost simultaneously, the first of the bombs began to fall. Intuition told Amanda they'd made a serious mistake in not going to the shelter, and it was far too late to go now, not to mention too dangerous even to consider going down into the street.

"Damn!" she cursed, rising to clear the table. "I think we're in for a very bad night."

"I'm sure we'll be all right," Hadleigh said placidly. "I'm certain of it."

"I wish I had your certainty," Amanda said.

"I know we will," Hadleigh insisted, then went to look out through a crack in the curtains at the fire bombs falling in the distance that created rather beautiful bursts of light in the blacked-out streets.

"Come away, Haddy!" Amanda drew the girl back from the window.

"They're ever so pretty." Hadleigh was flushed with excitement, and thrilled at not being trapped in the tube station with all those people and the sickening smell.

"They're doing damage," Amanda corrected her. "They're destroying historic buildings and churches, places we'll never see again. It *isn't* pretty."

The bombing continued hour after hour.

"You may think it foolish," Amanda said, "but you're going to sleep beneath the dining table. It's far safer than either of the bedrooms."

Hadleigh actually thought it was fun, and helped Aunt Mandy drag the cushions from the sofa to lean them against the legs of the table. The result was a cavelike effect Hadleigh liked very much.

"Try to sleep," Amanda said, kissing the girl's forehead, then standing back as Hadleigh ducked under the table and out of sight.

"It's lovely and cozy in here." Hadleigh's smiling face came back into view. "There's loads of room, if you'd like to come in, too."

"I'll stay out here, thank you. If you need anything, call me."

Secure in her pillowed nest beneath the massive mahogany table, Hadleigh fell almost immediately into a deep, sound sleep. Bending to check on her, Amanda was amazed. She wouldn't have thought it possible that anyone could sleep with the noise of the bombs.

As more time passed and there was no hint that the raid was anywhere near an end, Amanda became progressively more frantic. Risking a look through the lounge window, she was astonished to see the sky bright with the glow of fire in the City. It appeared that the German barrage was being concentrated on the east end and, judging from the brilliance of the sky in that area, they were succeeding. She thought sadly of Edwin, and of the offices in Lombard Street. She fully believed that when this night was over, all of it would be gone.

She'd disregarded Arthur's wishes and had kept Hadleigh in the flat during the worst and most prolonged raid to date. She wasn't afraid for herself, but quaked at the idea of any harm coming to Hadleigh. *Why* hadn't she kept her word?

Pulling back from the window with a start as a cluster of bombs detonated not far away, she swore aloud, thinking what a fool she'd been to take such a risk. She gazed at the heavily covered window, listening to the bombs falling outside, and understood finally the dimensions of the responsibility she'd undertaken in so blithely accepting guardianship of this child. Her thoughts at the outset had been of herself, and not of what might actually be involved in looking after a child twenty-four hours a day, week after week, for months on end.

Tomorrow, if the theatre was still standing, and the two of them were still alive, she'd take Hadleigh to see *Where the Rainbow Ends*, and Haddy would, undoubtedly, look upon this outing as some sort of reward. When you came right down to it, everything with children was either punishment or reward, and she had no aptitude for doling out either. She no longer wanted to be responsible for Hadleigh, who was a moody, gifted child with some small talent for manipulation. After all, hadn't it been Haddy to whom she'd listened, instead of heeding her promise to Arthur?

Don't blame her! she told herself. It wasn't reasonable to blame a ten-year-old for one's own failures, especially when one's promise had been given in good faith. A sudden spasm of comprehension shook her. *Arthur had known this raid was coming*! That's why he'd been so determined they spend their nights in the shelter.

"My God!" she said, turning to look at the enclosure she'd created of the sofa pillows. Arthur was far more than merely another member of some ministry or other. He had to be with the Ministry of Defense, or even Intelligence. "God!" she whispered. Who *were* these people: Arthur Holden with his privileged knowledge, his ceaselessly inquisitive daughter, and his deranged wife? It seemed as if the floor beneath her feet actually tilted, so rattled was she.

As the bombs went on falling, she moved restlessly through the flat cringing with each explosion, periodically pulling aside one of the cushions to confirm that Hadleigh was still asleep.

If they survived this night, she wanted Hadleigh to be returned to Frances. The two of them deserved each other. "I can't be responsible," she said, hugging herself fearfully. "It's too much, too much."

Throughout the night she paced the flat, reviewing the past year, deciding nothing had come about as she'd hoped. Nothing. None of it. She could keep on, wear down Arthur's resistance with her continued displays of kindness and understanding. She could, but what would she gain?

By daybreak, the raid at last ended. The all-clear sounded, and she went to draw the curtains. Her joints ached, her eyes felt gritty with sleeplessness, but they'd survived. She leaned on the sill, breathless at the sight of the fires raging in the distance. Such an immensity of damage was almost inconceivable. Yet the proof was in the air itself which lay against the window wreathed with smoke and ash particles. Her arms trembled and she pushed herself upright. She pictured people in the City beginning to clear the debris. Trains would soon pull into Waterloo and Victoria, loaded with people who'd make their way to the City only to find that the place where they'd worked no longer existed. The travelling canteens would come to begin dispensing tea, and befuddled workers would stand about with cups of tea, trying to decide what to do next.

With a quick motion, she drew closed the curtains, sending the room back into darkness. It was over, she thought, and headed for her bed. When Arthur next made contact with her, she'd explain that new arrangements would have to be made. She could not, after all, be responsible.

She stretched out on her bed, still suffering from the twitching that had assailed her throughout the bombing. She lay with her arms at her sides, staring at the wall. Exactly one year ago, Edwin had given his party. An entire year had passed since that night when they'd all had such fun.

In the distance sirens on ambulances and fire engines sent their shrill cries into the early morning air. And beneath the dining table, Hadleigh slept on.

PART TWO

New York 1948–1960

Fifteen

"How could you be such a fool?" Frances sputtered. "I simply cannot credit it."

"Perhaps if you'd ever told me the things I needed to know . . . It was only once." Shame pushed color into Hadleigh's face.

"Quite obviously once was enough. Do I even know this young man?"

"Of course you do. Please don't pretend now that you don't know who he is. He came to the house quite a number of times during the summer."

"The one with the teeth? Is that who we're discussing?"

Hadleigh groaned. "Yes. The one with the teeth."

"Good Lord, Hadleigh! You could do far better than that for yourself."

"It's rather academic now, wouldn't you say?"

"Have you told him about this?"

"Not yet. I've only just . . . found out about it myself."

Frances shook her head. "Have you told your father?" she asked.

"No! And *please* don't tell him! He needn't know. I'm certain Chris will do whatever's right."

"What do you suppose the right thing is in this situation?"

"I planned to ring him this evening, when he's back from classes."

"You do realize," Frances said with disgust, "that this will

173

put paid to your plans to study architecture?"

"I realize that," Hadleigh acknowledged unhappily.

They were headed toward a full-scale battle, and Hadleigh was in no mood for it. Right now, she had to solve the problem of her pregnancy, a fact that set her mind reeling every time she thought of it. She hadn't even any idea of why she'd given in to Chris. The experience had been unpleasant and painful, and she'd never dreamed she'd find herself pregnant three months later. She almost wished she'd kept it a secret, but Frances would have guessed somehow. She had an uncanny knack for uncovering all Hadleigh's secrets. At times, it seemed as if she could see right into Hadleigh's skull; she browsed there, as if in a lending library.

"What will you do," Frances was asking, "if this toothy young man doesn't wish to marry you?"

"I'm sure he'll want to do the proper thing."

"Where *do* you manage to find such archaic expressions? The proper thing," Frances repeated. "Marriage to this Chris may, in no way, be what's 'proper' for you. We could," she suggested, "have you declared mentally incapacitated and arrange an abortion on those grounds."

"*Mother!*" Hadleigh was deeply shocked. "How could you even *think* something like that?"

"It's one clear solution," Frances said judiciously. "It's not as if you'd actually have to be committed."

God! Hadleigh hoped Frances wasn't going to go off on a tangent and begin elaborating on the details of her confinements—to the place in Ottawa, and the one in Connecticut, the two in England. "Please, let's not go into that," she said. "I know you're well acquainted with that sort of establishment, but I have no intention of starting a family tradition, thank you. And anyway, I quite like the idea of having a child."

"You 'quite like' the idea? You haven't the remotest notion what's involved in giving birth, let alone tending an infant."

"Only because no one's ever bothered to enlighten me."

"Hadleigh," Frances said calmly, "is it your intention to spend the rest of your life blaming my supposed sins of omission for all your acts of commission?"

"No one's blaming you for anything."

Frances gave a soft laugh.

"I'll learn!" Hadleigh argued. "It can't be that difficult. Women do it every day."

"If there's the least bit of resistance from this boy, I'll have your father get on to his parents. This will not be allowed simply to drift."

"What are you talking about, drift? What does that mean?"

"According to the law, you're underage. I believe that what has occurred does, in certain parts of this outsized colonial plantation, constitute statutory rape. I've read of several fascinating cases in the newspapers."

"I was *not* raped!"

"Nevertheless, you are a minor. One doesn't engage in sexual congress with eighteen-year-old girls. There are penalties for that sort of thing."

"Yes, and *I'm* the one who's going to pay them. I don't want you to do *anything*. I'll talk to Chris. I know he'll make it good."

"He'll have to," Frances said. "Or he'll have me to reckon with."

Hadleigh couldn't help it, she laughed. It was just so ludicrous that her mother should think of herself as someone to be reckoned with when, too often, what she was was a source of profound embarrassment. She'd been arrested for public drunkenness in Ottawa and it was only because of Arthur's position as vice consul at the British embassy that the charges had been dropped. She'd been found, roaring drunk on Fifth Avenue, and carted off to Bellevue. Again, because of her father's position in the New York embassy, Frances had been released. After her release, she'd embarked upon a series of shopping sprees, spending thousands of dollars in the course of three weeks. It had fallen to Hadleigh to go round to the stores returning the purchases her mother had made.

They'd had to leave Ottawa, her father requesting a transfer, in order not to compromise his position entirely. Ottawa was an insular, completely political city, where everyone knew everyone else, and gossip was the order of the day. Word got out very quickly about the vice consul's wife. At least New York was a big place, where it was easier to conceal some of Frances's more inventive escapades. But not all, because on those occasions when Hadleigh met up with her father at the consulate for lunch, the staff smiled with knowing eyes, and she'd felt the humiliation all the way into her bones. She didn't know how her father withstood it; she'd never really understood the dynamics of their marriage. But he handled everything routinely, as a matter of course. The only saving aspect was that her mother's forays into alcoholic madness were becoming less frequent, and, usually, it was something Frances viewed as too traumatic to deal with that set her off.

"What is so amusing?" Frances asked with regard to Hadleigh's peals of laughter.

"Oh, you are," Hadleigh answered. "You see yourself as some sort of avenging angel."

"Hardly!"

"Look. I'll take care of it. If there's a problem, I'll let you know. But I'm sure there'll be no problem."

"I wish I shared your confidence in the morals of someone I doubt I'd allow to park my automobile."

"I'm up to my ears in exams, Had," Christopher told her.

"I really must see you. There's a problem."

"A problem?" There was silence on the line and then he said, "Oh, shit! *Tell* me it's not *that kind* of problem!"

"I'm afraid it is."

"Jesus H. Christ!"

"We really must talk about it."

"We *are* talking about it. What the hell are we going to do?"

"I thought I'd take the train up. I can be there by seven-thirty."

"I guess you'd better." He sounded resigned, even angry. "I'll meet you at the station."

She put down the receiver filled with hatred of him, and of herself. She scarcely knew him, wasn't even sure if she liked him, but if he failed to agree to marry her, her mother would come up with even more outrageous solutions, and probably tell her father. *Why* had she allowed it to happen? She'd liked him reasonably well the summer before, and he'd paid her a lot of attention while they'd been staying at the seaside in Old Saybrook.

Her father had rented the house for two months thinking the sea air and walks along the pebbly beach would be therapeutic for all of them. Frances had come down the walk from the house exactly once. She'd looked out at the waters of Long Island Sound, then down at the bleached stones on the beach, turned around and went back indoors where she'd remained the entire two months, reading anything she could lay her hands on and playing symphonies on the record-player. For an hour or more a day, she'd attempted to resurrect her sight-reading skills at the piano, repeating certain phrases over and over until Hadleigh was convinced the neighbors would drag her mother from the house and break her fingers with a hammer if she didn't desist.

Hadleigh had been left to amuse herself and, after their then-housekeeper had quit, had watchdogged her mother and made sure that the delivery boy from the market in town didn't smuggle in bottles of scotch. It was a wasted effort since, for her always arbitrary reasons, Frances was having a prolonged dry spell.

Her first sight of the rickety, yet imposing, beach houses had thoroughly charmed Hadleigh. While all constructed during the early twenties and differing in detail, the dwellings had shared a common builder and therefore had interesting similarities. Each had wide porches on the waterfront sides, and shutter-framed windows overlooking the beach; each had several chimneys that serviced the fireplaces in the dining, living, and master bedrooms; each had dormers on the top stories, and round, latticed windows at either end of the attics. All the houses were painted white, the shutters varying in color from black to dark green. Two of the places had stained-glass panels inset above the living room windows and front doors; three of them had boathouses and jetties leading down to the water. They were quirky, whimsical houses, with scalloped shingles and fanciful weather-vanes.

Haddy began to sketch each of the houses, painstakingly crosshatching the details with pen and India ink. She'd been at work on the third of them when Christopher MacDonald had come to stand looking over her shoulder.

"Say, you're pretty good," he'd said. "Are you a professional?"

"A professional what?" she'd answered, not bothering to turn.

"You know! Painter."

"I am not."

"Oh! You're in the Ormand house, aren't you?"

"That's right."

"I'm Chris MacDonald. That's our house you're working on."

At that, she'd shifted to have a look at the young man who belonged both to the voice and to the house. He had sandy hair, the front of which seemed to fall continually into his brown eyes. His features were small and well-placed, unspecial. His teeth, though, were exceptional: perfectly even and very white. She decided at once that his smile was the most attractive thing about him, although his easy manner was refreshing. She hadn't yet managed to accustom herself to the casual friendliness of Americans, especially after their eighteen months in Ottawa with the dour Canadians who'd been incredibly British in their attitudes and behavior. She was still overcoming her wariness of Americans. Their very ease and openness was suspect. It was almost too easy to fall under the charm of their friendly enthusiasm. She'd had a better understanding of the Canadians, and of the necessity of overcoming *their* suspicions before entering into the slow process of friendship. Americans seemed to offer instant friendship, and anything so hasty had to be of doubtful quality. Still, she told herself she hadn't the right, as a guest, to criticize.

"I'm Hadleigh," she introduced herself, then prepared to go on with her work.

"I've seen you down here," he said, his hands jammed into the rear pockets of his baggy trousers. "You're here with your mom, right? And your dad's some kind of ambassador, or something, and he comes up on the weekends, right?"

Politely, she corrected him. "My father is the vice consul at the British embassy. And he does try to come at the weekends, although he's not always able. And, yes, I am here with my mother. Are you always so curious?"

"Oh, sure." He grinned, showing again those remarkable teeth. "So what d'you do?" he wanted to know. "Are you in school in New York?"

"I'll be going to Columbia University in the autumn."

"Majoring in?"

"Sorry?"

'What're you studying?"

"Oh! Architecture."

"Wrong school." He squatted on the sand, crossing his arms over his knees. "Yale's way better."

"Is it? You attend Yale, do you?"

"Yup. Going into my junior year."

"And what is *your* 'major'?"

"B and E."

"Breaking and entering?" she asked, with a smile.

He laughed, dropping his head on his crossed arms. "That's a good one!" he complimented her. "Business and economics."

"Ah! I see."

"Gee," he laughed. "I just love that Limey accent of yours."

"English."

"English," he stood corrected. "It's just great. Where're you from over there?"

"London."

"London," he said appreciatively, then shook his head. "Boy, they bombed the hell out of you guys, didn't they?"

"That's right. They did."

"Must've been something." Again he shook his head.

"It was certainly something." She was beginning to wish he'd go away. He was tiresomely repetitive.

"I was dying to go fight the Nazis," he said, "but I was too young. My brother went." He looked off along the beach. "He never came back. My folks still get all choked up whenever his name is mentioned."

"And do you?" she asked.

"Me?" His eyes returned to her. "Sure I do. Ben was a good guy."

"Ben?" At once, she softened toward him. "Your brother's name was Ben?"

"Yup."

"I had a brother also named Ben. He died in the raid on Coventry."

"Gee, that's tough," he sympathized. "Was he stationed there?"

"He was six years old."

"Six years old. That's really tough. My brother got it at Dunkirk."

"But the Americans weren't in the war then."

"He took off, joined the Canadian army. Anyway, listen. I'm here to find out if you want to come up to the house for lunch. My mom sent me, but," he added hastily, "I was gonna come on my own anyway. What d'you think?"

"I'll have to discuss it with my mother." The one wonderful thing about having Frances as her mother was the limitless range of excuses and alibis that could be offered with regard to her.

"Oh, she's welcome to come, too."

"My mother almost never socializes," she said. "I'll fix her meal, then come at . . . What time?"

"Whenever you like. Say one?"

"All right. I'll come at one."

"Great!" He stood up. "I'll go tell Mom you'll be coming." He walked off along the beach whistling, his hands once more in his pockets.

Frances had broken off her sight-reading practise to say, "You're not seriously going to sit down to a meal with that frightful woman."

"How do you know she's frightful?" Hadleigh had challenged.

"My darling, one has but to look, and one *sees*. She has teeth like Eleanor Roosevelt."

Hadleigh laughed, then asked, "What's so terrible about that?"

"Well, better you than I. *I* certainly couldn't swallow one mouthful had I to sit watching those tractor-like mandibles hacking their way through the roughage."

"You're awful!" Hadleigh had laughed. "Do you want me to fix you something to eat before I go?"

"You know, Hadleigh"—Frances swivelled around on the piano bench—"you're beginning to believe your own propaganda concerning me. I'm more than capable of putting something between two pieces of bread, or of opening a tin. I don't mind you placing me in an advanced state of senility as your rationale for refusing invitations. I merely wish you'd remember that, in reality, I'm still flourishing in my prime."

"I'll try to remember," Hadleigh had promised.

She hadn't liked Mrs. MacDonald, and could never afterwards be certain she hadn't been influenced by her mother's remarks. Several times throughout the meal she looked up to see food being pushed past those forwardly prominent teeth and nearly choked trying not to laugh.

Mrs. MacDonald was a woman who smiled coldly and often, and spoke with that odd accent Hadleigh had heard a number of times before, the words delivered as if from between paralyzed jaws. Mrs. MacDonald had been superficially forthcoming, but she'd managed to make everything, from her *Mayflower* lineage to her husband's affluence, very clear without ever stating facts. She was a woman born to innuendo and seemed to have no need for expressive, specific language. Square-shouldered, darkly tanned, hair carefully crimped into Marcel waves, she gave the impression of being a well-placed member of a closed society to which even a vice consul's daughter would have extreme difficulty gaining access.

Throughout the lunch, of salad and slices of blood-rare roast beef—Hadleigh ate only the salad—Mrs. MacDonald made references to people with some of the most improbable names Hadleigh had ever heard. There were Kippy and Muffy, Itsy and Macky, Cappy, Pansy, Sandy and Bobo; there were also Sonny, Buddy, Martha (a notable exception) and, incredibly, Fudge. Haddy simply had no idea who any of these people might be, nor did Mrs. MacDonald choose to inform her. The woman simply sprinkled these names over the conversation like croutons.

Afterwards, Chris explained. "Kippy and Muffy live over there." He pointed to the adjacent house. "And they have two kids, Itsy and Macky. The next house over, you've got Cappy and Pansy and their kids, Sandy and Bobo. Sonny and Buddy live in the last house, and Martha and Fudge own your place. They couldn't make it this year. Buddy's been hitting the sauce pretty hard, so he's down at a place in Baltimore, getting dried out."

"Dried out?"

"You know, getting off the booze."

"Oh!" She thought of her mother rolled between thick layers of absorbent towelling, being "dried out." It was an hilarious image. She told herself she must remember to repeat this expression to her mother. Frances would love it.

"I don't think your mother cared very much for me," she told Chris as they walked along the beach.

"Oh, don't worry about her," he said. "That's just the way she is."

"Sorry? How is she?"

"She liked you just fine," he said, either oblivious to or unconcerned with his mother's coldness to Hadleigh over lunch. "So, listen," he sailed blithely onward. "We're going to have a get-together tonight on the beach. Some of the gang're coming. You want to come?"

"I'm not sure."

"Oh, come on!" he cajoled. "You must be bored out of your skull just sitting around all day drawing houses. D'you ever do anything at night?"

In the end, he persuaded her to attend, and her acceptance of this invitation had led to more offers until she'd found herself spending the better part of each day with Chris and his friends.

Frances said, "This is a golden opportunity for you to examine first-hand a proliferating subspecies of males. The breed is typified by their exquisitely advanced dental work, clammy palms, and brains the consistency of library paste. Study them closely," she told Hadleigh. "They're utterly fascinating."

"How would you know about their clammy hands?" Hadleigh asked.

"You'll simply have to trust me," Frances had replied airily.

Hadleigh had liked only two of Chris's friends. One was a rather retiring young man they all called Sheffie, but whose full name was Elmo Sheffield. He was Chris's roommate, and was studying history. It was his habit to position himself on the periphery of the group, where he sat fussing ritualistically with his pipe while watching and listening to the others with an amused expression. He seemed to be the unofficial voice of reason in the crowd and regularly capped an evening's activities by making comments like, "I think the festivities are about at a close, ladies and gentlemen." The others appeared to rely on him to make these declarations and abided by his referee-like calls.

The other was a girl from Hartford, a student about to enter her last year at Miss Porter's School and who seemed unpretentious and genuinely friendly. Augusta had none of the garish effusiveness of the three or four other girls who regularly joined the group. When Augusta laughed, it was with true amusement. The first time Hadleigh heard her laugh, she remembered Claire, the little girl she'd met in the underground shelter, who'd told her that ridiculous joke about Findish. She'd warmed at once to Augusta because of her contagious laugh, and her apparent ability to decide what, of all that was said, was actually funny. Hadleigh thought Augusta found more humor in the group's quest for sophistication than in anything they actually said or did.

Although Chris ushered Hadleigh directly into the middle of the group, and kept her with him there throughout her stay at the seaside, she would have felt more at ease on the sidelines with Sheffie. Augusta made an ongoing effort to include her, for which Hadleigh was overtly grateful.

"Don't let them bamboozle you," Augusta told her. "There's not one mental giant here, with the possible exception of old Elmo who'd like everyone to believe he's just a year or two younger than God and just the least little bit less wise. He's okay, though. Boy!" Augusta rolled her eyes. "The rest of them give me the pips."

The group liked to drink. With bottles of hard liquor or beer they'd purloined from their parents' bars, the parties on the beach usually culminated with someone's staggering off to the bushes to be violently ill. Hadleigh watched these goings-on with distaste, but near the end of her stay allowed herself to be persuaded to have a go.

"It won't kill you," Chris said, holding out a bottle of gin.

"Yeah!" agreed one of the girls. "Come on, Holden! Loosen up a little!"

"Take it," Chris urged, pushing the bottle at her. "It'll relax you, let you have a little more fun."

Everyone was watching and telling her to do it. The heat of their eyes, more substantial than the fire where potatoes roasted and hot dogs skewered on green twigs were propped over the flames, moved her to accept the bottle. She took a mouthful and swallowed. Her eyes watered, her throat felt stripped raw. The taste was foul, and she wondered if it hadn't been another of their foolish practical jokes, with one of them switching some sort of medicine with the gin.

"Great, huh?" Chris said approvingly, throwing his arm

around her shoulder and crushing her against his side.

She said nothing, and didn't think she could have spoken in any case. She was tracking the gin's passage to her stomach where it sat radiating heat as if she'd ingested live coals. The taste clung to the interior of her mouth and the lining of her nose. How, she wondered, could her mother drink foul stuff like this? It was disgusting, medicinal-tasting poison. She fully expected to be the one to rush for the bushes to be sick.

It didn't happen. She did begin to feel somewhat more relaxed, and gagged down another mouthful when the bottle came her way a second time. Later on, having taken her turn again at the bottle and passed it along with a laugh, she'd happened to look over and see Sheffie's eyes on her. He looked sober, and disappointed. In her. Or so it seemed. She couldn't quite decipher his expression, and thought of going over to ask why he was staring at her that way, but she felt too comfortable to move. She did, however, pass on the next half-dozen rounds without bothering to drink anymore.

Very late that same night, after all the others had gone, she finally gave in. Chris had been nagging and pleading with her for weeks, and she'd steadfastly refused in spite of her enormous curiosity. Then, suddenly she wondered why she'd resisted, and relented. It had been over very quickly and she'd sworn to herself she'd never do it again. She'd hated being squashed beneath his thrusting weight, and couldn't imagine why people made such a fuss about lovemaking, if this was all it amounted to.

Now, she was on her way to New Haven to find out if Chris was someone honorable who'd assume his share of the liability for those few minutes on the beach. The whole affair struck her as being so tawdry she had to wonder why her mother had been as restrained as she had upon being told. She'd left the apartment with misgivings, after having warned their new housekeeper that her mother might very well be in a mood to go off on a spree.

"Please try to keep an eye on her, would you, Mrs. Walsh? My father should be home by seven. And I'll be back by midnight at the latest."

"I don't know that I 'ired on to be a bodyguard," the Cockney Mrs. Walsh had complained good-naturedly. "Don't know's I like 'aving to watch over 'er ladyship." She'd begun referring to Frances this way on her first day of employment a week earlier. She even did it in front of Frances who found it wildly amusing.

The train snaked along through the tunnels, out from Grand Central, and Haddy halfway hoped Chris would prove himself an absolute bastard by refusing to marry her. She didn't mind the idea of a baby, but the thought of marriage, and to someone she barely liked, was most depressing. She was only eighteen, after all. It was rather young for marriage.

She sighed and looked out the window as the train came above ground.

Sixteen

Having heard from Sheffie of the impending marriage, Augusta called up to ask if Hadleigh needed any help.

Touched by the offer, Hadleigh said, "I do, actually. My mother's not well just now and I haven't the faintest notion where to begin."

Frances, in total opposition to this marriage, had opted, in view of her failure to change Hadleigh's decision to go through with it, to retaliate by entering one of her drinking phases. She was, at the time of Augusta's call, in her third week of what threatened to be a monumental binge. The only positive thing to be said for her drinking was that since she was a chronic insomniac she spent the night hours, when everyone else slept, listening to her symphonic recordings while working her way through a bottle of scotch. By mid-morning, she was in bed, soundly asleep, and usually didn't rise until three or four in the afternoon.

"I'd love to shop with you," Augusta said. "Why don't I come down from school on Friday and we can spend Saturday doing the stores?"

"That would be perfect."

Haddy met her at the station and brought her back to the Central Park West apartment, apologizing for the necessity of their having to share Hadleigh's room. "The housekeeper's occupying the guest-room because Mother decided to redecorate Mrs. Walsh's bedroom, then stopped halfway through. I do hope you don't mind.''

"It's more fun, sharing.''

Augusta's relaxed acceptance of things was impressive, Hadleigh thought. Over dinner, she charmed Arthur with tales of Miss Porter's School, and even got Frances laughing with a story about how, as a small girl, she'd been the principal accessory in her housekeeper's affair with the local grocery store manager. Mrs. Walsh took an immediate liking to her and insisted on offering her third and fourth helpings of everything, from the braised chicken with celery, to the lemon sillabub, for which Augusta developed an instant passion.

"This is scrumptious! What is it? How do you make it?'' she asked Mrs. Walsh who, beaming, explained, "It's just cream, dear, mixed with wine and sweetened; a bit of lemon juice and rind added. It's traditional, you know. 'Undreds of years old, is sillabub.''

"I just love it!'' Augusta insisted.

"Glad you like it, dear.'' Mrs. Walsh returned to the kitchen, glowing with satisfaction.

It was impossible not to like Augusta. For a girl of seventeen, she had remarkable grace and composure. Nothing seemed to surprise her, yet many things were sources of a delight she shared with disarming generosity. It was she who introduced Hadleigh to "going-away" outfits, and bridal garters, and negligees, and everything else that went along with getting married.

Over lunch at 21, where Augusta was greeted as if she'd been known there all her life, Hadleigh had to ask, "How do you know all these things?''

"Well, in the first place,'' Augusta explained, "they *have* known me all my life here. And in the second place, I have two older sisters who are both married, *and* my mother's been married three times with the whole works, including white satin dress with French lace and seed pearls. She's sentimental about the dress. She's worn it every time, but all the other stuff had to be new. Both my sisters used her peignoirs and stuff. Marriage is very big in my family.'' She laughed, then became serious. "Are you sure you know what you're doing?'' she asked. "I mean, I could be wrong, but you and Chris hardly even know each other. And you didn't seem to like him all that much last summer. Are you pregnant?'' she guessed. ''Is that why this is happening?''

Mortified, Hadleigh confided, ''We only did it once.''

''Boy oh boy!'' Augusta whistled softly between her teeth. ''That's really lousy. What luck! Well, I sure hope it works out. I mean, Chris isn't a bad guy or anything, but, no offense, he's not exactly a heavyweight. Boy, I just hate it the way the girl's the one who always winds up paying. I hope this turns out all right for you.''

''I'm sure it will,'' Hadleigh said with unfelt confidence.

''Well, just remember. If there's ever anything I can do, you let me know. I hope you're not mad at me for saying what I did.''

''Not at all.''

''You're sure?'' Augusta asked.

''You're the only one—aside from my mother, who lives in another dimension altogether—who's been truthful with me. The other girls have all rung up cooing their congratulations and giggling. I very much appreciate your being honest.''

''That's a relief.'' Augusta smiled. ''Most of the time, being truthful only winds up getting me in trouble. I'm not supposed to have any sense. I'm just supposed to be pretty, so I can nail myself a husband. I watch the girls who do that and it looks like too much work, all that simpering and playing patty-cake. I can't name one boy who's worth the trouble, except maybe Elmo. And he's in another dimension, too. Sometimes I think he may just be the smartest one of us. Other times I think the whole thing's a big act, and maybe he should be going into the theatre instead of history.''

''I quite like him,'' Hadleigh admitted. ''He always seems so . . . calm, I suppose.''

''Sure. And underneath that calm surface, who knows what evil lurks?'' Augusta laughed, slapping the flat of her hand on the table. ''D'you want steak? Or would you like to try something outrageous?''

On the morning of her wedding day, Arthur invited her to have a cup of tea with him in the breakfast nook. Reaching across the table to take hold of her hand, he said, ''I can't help but feel this marriage may not be the wisest course of action for you, Hadleigh. I don't want you to think your mother's influenced me in this. As you well know, I make my own decisions. But this is one of those times when I'm somewhat inclined to take her view. There's still time to call it off, if you'd like to. I realize there'd be some loss of face, but that might be preferable to entering into something as hastily arranged as this."

"I haven't changed my mind, Daddy." Her pregnancy, so far as she knew, was still a secret, although her weight gain was becoming visible, and she'd had to purchase a sturdy girdle to wear under her wedding dress.

"Well," he said doubtfully, "if you're certain."

"Honestly, I am."

"I've given your young man the official parental gift, but there's something I want you to have, solely for yourself." He freed his hand to delve into his inner jacket pocket. Producing an envelope he placed it in her hand. "This is for you, Haddy. In case the men in your life let you down."

"Oh, Daddy." Close to tears, she took hold again of his hand and squeezed it. "Thank you. I will miss you so."

"We'll expect to see you often. New Haven's not that far away."

"No, it isn't." She sniffed back the tears. There wasn't anyone who thought this marriage was a good idea.

"I hope you find happiness," he said, then pushed away from the table. "I must go check on your mother, see what sort of day she's likely to have."

"How can you *bear* it," she asked rashly, "year after year?"

He smiled rather mysteriously. "Never," he said, "make the mistake of judging solely on appearances. There's far more to a marriage than what shows on the surface."

"I'm sorry."

"No need," he said gallantly. "In time, any number of things will make sense to you."

In her bedroom, she stood staring at the bridal gown laid across her bed. It was a pretty dress, of white peau de soie, with a rounded neckline and full, pleated sleeves. Chris had said, "I guess we'd better get married," and she'd wanted to strike him for his pitiful display of chivalry. What was she *doing*, marrying him? She'd have to sleep in the same bed with him for the rest of her life, and suffer the intrusion of his naked body in hers. It seemed an enormous price to pay simply because she'd been curious, and anxious to please, and so had allowed herself to be persuaded.

She turned to look at her image in the mirror. In profile, there was a definite swelling at her middle. And she was fatter than she'd ever been. She either ate constantly or went days on end scarcely eating at all. It drove her mother and Mrs. Walsh crazy, but, luckily, they'd written it off as premarital jitters. She had something a lot worse than jitters, she reflected, thinking she looked like a pig. She had a case of dread that, from one moment to the next, had her wishing she'd never been born.

The envelope contained the deed to a three-acre parcel of land in Connecticut, and a note that read, "Here is the land upon which you may one day realize some personal piece of architecture. With all my love, Father."

In case the men in your life let you down.

Insurance.

If only she'd never set eyes on Christopher MacDonald.

If only someone had told her in graphic terms of the connection between her monthly periods and the act she'd allowed Chris to perform.

If only she'd had the courage to ask.

Sighing, she began her preparations for the day.

Frances got drunk at the reception, tripped, and fell face first through a glass-topped coffee table. Hadleigh cried out and ran pushing through the guests, very afraid this time Frances had really injured herself. Her father and Mr. MacDonald were already there, lifting Frances from the wreckage. She looked around, apparently unaware of the blood seeping from a number of cuts into her gray silk dress, until her eyes found Hadleigh.

Hadleigh stood a foot away watching her mother's eyes until they located her. Frances gave her a sadly apologetic smile, and Hadleigh rushed to embrace her, wondering as she did why she cared as much as she did whether or not her mother hurt herself, and whether or not Frances approved or disapproved of her actions.

"I'm sorry," Frances murmured in Hadleigh's ear.

"It doesn't matter," Hadleigh said, mildly dazed by the reek of alcohol.

"God, I hope you have something left at the end of this," Frances said feelingly. "I truly hope you do."

"Go along back to your guests now," her father advised Hadleigh in an undertone. "I'll see to your mother."

"No harm done," Mr. MacDonald, a jovial, kind-hearted man told her. "We'll get your mother squared away in no time flat."

"Who," Frances asked Mr. MacDonald, "appointed you to be in charge of my squaring?"

"Oh, you're such a kidder!" Mr. MacDonald laughed. "She's some kidder, your wife, Art."

"Call him Arthur," Frances told him in a stage whisper. "He *loathes* diminutives."

"Diminu-whats?"

"Nicknames, Mr. MacDonald," Frances instructed, as the two men helped her away from the party. Patting the man on the stomach, she observed, "What a portly little fellow you are, Mac!" which set MacDonald off in peals of laughter.

"She okay?" Chris asked Hadleigh upon her return to his side.

"She'll be fine," she said thickly, dredging up a smile for the inescapable photographer whose prints would be documentation of these proceedings.

"You look kind of seedy," Chris told her. "Why don't you go get changed and we'll make our getaway. The party's kind of fizzling out now, anyway."

"I do hope," Hadleigh turned on him, "that's not meant to be some sort of dig at my mother."

"Hey! I didn't mean anything. I just thought maybe you'd had enough of all this."

She gathered up the skirts of her gown and went to change into her "going-away" outfit, selected by Augusta. Augusta, at that moment noting Haddy's course, broke off her conversation with Sheffie and arrived in Hadleigh's room in time to help her out of her dress.

"How are you?" she asked, watching Hadleigh tug at the girdle. "Too tight?"

"I've never worn anything more uncomfortable. Otherwise, I'm as well as can be expected. Did you see what happened?"

"Your mother, you mean? I guess everybody did. I wouldn't worry about it, though. People always get bombed at weddings."

"Is that what everyone will think?"

"Oh, sure." Augusta was reassuringly offhand. "You'd better get a move on." She lifted the hanger with the navy suit from the back of the closet door. "You worry way too much about your mother. Half the time, I think she's just putting on a show for the crowd. Boy, she sure is funny. Did you hear what she said to Chris's dad?"

"About his being portly?"

Augusta laughed. "I didn't hear *that* one. Boy! She's a scream. No, it was during the ceremony. Everybody was sitting there watching, and your mother leaned over to Mr. MacDonald and said, 'Does your son have a birth defect?' Well he shot around and stared at her like she'd just landed from the moon, saying, 'What d'you mean by that, Mrs. Holden?' Up till then he'd been calling her Fran and Frannie, and maybe that's what made her do it because you could tell it was driving her nuts his calling her Frannie. So she said, 'The teeth, Mr. MacDonald.' And his face got all wrinkled, and his voice got a little loud and he said, 'What *about* his teeth?' and she said, 'I just wondered if all the members of your family were given full sets of dentures at birth.' Then she turned away and left him scratching his head. I thought I was going to wet my pants. I missed half the damn ceremony listening to the two of them."

Before leaving the bedroom, Hadleigh had to give her friend a hug. "You've been wonderful, about everything. We'll keep in touch, won't we?"

"We sure will. I'm getting a car for graduation, so I'll be able to drive from wherever I decide to go to school to see you on weekends and stuff."

"I expect I'll need you again, to help me get rigged out for the baby. Do your sisters have children?"

"Naturally. And I'm even better with layettes than I am with weddings. You'd better get going. And don't forget to throw the bouquet in the opposite direction to me. Wait a minute! Make sure you look to see where I am and throw it to me after all. I don't *ever* want to get married, but I definitely want those flowers!"

Because it was the middle of the semester, they were to spend their three-day honeymoon at his family's summer house in

Old Saybrook. Mr. MacDonald had given Chris the choice of down-payment money for a house, or a new car, and Chris had opted for the car.

"We can get a house later," he'd reasoned, "but the car will make life a whole lot easier. I've found us an apartment not too far off campus. Fixing it up'll give you something to do while I'm away all day."

This seemed to make as much sense as anything else, so she voiced no argument. They drove towards Old Saybrook for the most part in silence, each considering the future.

"And anyway," Chris said some time later, as if continuing an ongoing conversation, "after graduation next June, who knows where we'll be. We might wind up in the city, if I decide to go in with Dad. Or maybe we'll just relocate downstate, in Greenwich, or Darien. A lot of my classmates are from Greenwich. And it'll probably be a whole lot more practical, as far as money goes, to stay in Connecticut. Manhattan can be expensive as hell."

"We'll have to wait and see," she said to prove she was listening. She'd formed no fixed ideas on how she wanted things to be. Her sole focus was the coming night.

"Boy!" he said some time later. "That was really something, the way your mother went through that coffee table. She really throws down the sauce, doesn't she?"

"My mother's an alcoholic," she replied. "She can't help herself."

"I know that. But it sure was something. I thought half the guests were going to shit themselves when she came up all covered in blood."

"She might have been badly hurt, Chris. It's jolly good luck that she wasn't."

He glanced over at her, stung. "I wasn't taking potshots," he said. "I was thinking out loud, that's all. I mean, you've got to admit it was pretty astounding, the way she went flat out, right through the goddamned coffee table."

"Please could we drop it? She *is* my mother, and I dislike talking about her this way."

"Don't be so touchy! I mean, Christ! She's *my* new mother-in-law. I'd drop dead if she ever did anything like that in front of . . ." He wound down, realizing she'd already suffered quite a mishap with all his friends and family as witnesses.

"I'm sorry. I guess I shouldn't shoot my mouth off that way. I just can't get over it, that's all."

Neither could Hadleigh. She kept recalling the intensity of their embrace, and her mother's words. Since she and Frances almost never came close physically to one another, it had been an exceptional moment. She could still feel her mother's substance in her arms, could still smell, beneath the alcohol, the scent of roses that had always been Frances's. It had been a moment when she'd loved her mother fiercely, utterly, and had been shaken by the depth of her feelings.

When they arrived at the house, it was dark.

Chris said, "You go on in, get the lights on and I'll see about some firewood. It gets cold as hell here at night."

He left her to carry in her bag and the oversized hamper packed by the caterers. Leaving her bag just inside the front door, she lugged the hamper to the kitchen. Chris's friends had been here. There was an empty ice bucket on the table, beside a vase of red roses. A note, signed by Sheffie, said ice had been delivered and put in the icebox, and champagne was cooling. Under a wrapping of protective gauze was a roasted chicken, with white ribbon looped in an elaborate bow around the drumsticks.

"Wiseguys!" Chris laughed, entering. "This is swell, huh!" He chipped ice into the bucket before pushing the champagne bottle deep into it. Exuberant, he put his hands on her waist, grinning. "Well, we finally made it. Married, by God! It wasn't too bad, was it?"

"Not too bad." She felt awkward, with no idea, what, if any, protocol existed for this situation.

"I guess you'll want to get out of those clothes and into something more comfortable," Chris said, making her laugh. "What's so funny?"

"You've heard that in films," she accused. "People don't actually say things like that. Do they?"

"Well, I just did. C'mon." He took her hand. "I'll bring up the bags, see if they've left any other surprises. I wouldn't put it past those guys to French the bed."

He was being very sweet, she thought, feeling less tense. She could have done far worse, she reasoned. Chris was obviously prepared to make his best effort, and the least she could do was try equally hard.

*   *   *

They ate the chicken and drank the champagne in front of the fire in the master bedroom.

"No sense moving too far from where we're going to end up," Chris laughed, then added, "What a day! You must be whacked."

"I am rather tired."

"And how's my kid?" he asked, throwing himself across her lap to press his ear to her belly. "Must be sleeping." He propped himself on his elbows, looking up at her critically. "I'll say one thing for you, Had. You're sure one of the prettiest girls I've ever seen."

"Thank you." She was uncomfortable with compliments, always wondering if there were ulterior motives beneath them. "I know I'm not, really. But you have a lovely smile."

He flashed one for her, saying, "You think so?"

"Yes, I do."

"You're so cute!" he chortled. "So proper. I'm crazy about that accent of yours. Maybe you could teach my kid to talk that way, too."

"You give the impression you think it's going to be a boy."

"Do I? Well, yeah, maybe I do kind of think it will be. But a girl'd be okay, too. I like kids."

"That's a good thing, I'd say, since we'll be having one in a little less than five months."

He yawned and sat up, grinding his fists into his eyes. "I'm ready to hit the sack. What about you?"

"I'll clear away the food."

"Leave it. We'll do it in the morning."

"All right." Apprehensive again, she collected her overnight bag and closed herself into the bathroom.

"Don't take forever!" he called, going off to use one of the hall bathrooms.

She knew she was taking far too long but after putting on the filmy blue nightgown and matching peignoir she felt too ridiculous to allow herself to be seen, so she removed them and pulled on her favorite long, flannel nightdress that was worn soft with use.

When she finally came out, he'd turned off the overhead lights and there was only a small puddle of light cast by the lamp beside the bed. He was waiting, the blankets folded neatly across his chest.

It wasn't as unpleasant as it had been the first time, perhaps because his new status as husband freed him to experiment in rather a wistful fashion. Passively, she accepted his exploration of her breasts, and could only wonder at the urgency that suddenly overtook him and had him burrowing between her thighs. He seemed almost unaware of her as he struggled to achieve his goal, looking, to boot, as if he were strangling in the process. Then, it was over. He'd withdrawn, and turned away to commence the deep breathing that signalled sleep.

She could bear it, she told herself. She'd learn to accept his attentions. He was an awfully good sport, really, the way he'd fallen in with the plans once they'd agreed they'd have to marry. And he did have a splendid smile.

During the first months of their marriage, she was kept busy sorting the gifts and writing thank-you notes. She returned two of the three toasters, four carving sets, six trays, two silver tea services, one set of steak knives, five waffle irons, and two of the seven crystal water jugs. The nearly seven hundred dollars went into a savings account she opened in her own name, without bothering to tell Chris. She rearranged the furniture that came with the rented apartment, but gave up trying when Chris pointed out that by June they'd be out of there and could start buying things of their own.

"It *is* pretty crummy stuff," he allowed, "but it'll do for now."

For want of anything else to do, she turned her attention next to cooking, and prepared lavish meals until Chris came out of the bathroom naked one night to show her his growing paunch.

"You're going to wreck me, kid," he complained. "Half the time I'm so logy from your big breakfasts I can hardly keep my eyes open during the lectures, and I've got term papers coming up."

"I thought you should start the day with a good meal, but if you'd prefer, I won't bother."

"Listen," he said, pulling on his pajama bottoms. "Don't stop cooking altogether. Just try not to make so much. You've got to remember that cooking in my mother's house consists of picking up the telephone and phoning in the order." He came over to her side of the bed where she was propped against the pillows, reading. "What's the kid up to?" he asked, putting his ear to her belly.

"Nothing at the moment. She moved a short time ago. It was as if she was shifting in her sleep."

"Hey! Maybe if I hang around, I can wake her up, get her to talk or something."

Haddy laughed and pushed at his shoulder. He caught hold of her hand and sat smiling at her. "You hardly ever laugh," he said. "And that's a real shame, cause you look so nice when you do."

He wondered about her sometimes, wondered what she thought about. He seemed to be the one who did all the talking, while she came up with answers and comments. He figured since they were stuck together they might as well make the best of it, but she didn't seem to know how to try. Altogether, the Holdens were a pretty peculiar family. But maybe it was only because they were English. He couldn't figure them out. The feeling he had was that instead of living in the dorm with Sheffie, he'd switched over to another kind of a dorm now, with a girl. It wasn't all that different. They took turns sharing the bathroom; he studied at the kitchen table while she sat in the living room listening to the radio and knitting baby stuff. All right, he wasn't crazy in love with her, but he liked her, and she was definitely better-looking than most of the girls his friends dated. The funny thing about that was that she didn't act good-looking. She didn't do any of that hair-tossing stuff, or messing with makeup the other girls did. Now that he thought about it, she acted the way the plain Janes did. He just couldn't figure it. But at least he wasn't ashamed to be seen with her. In fact, he really liked taking her out and watching her get double-takes. He only wished she'd loosen up a little, relax and let herself have some fun.

The one thing she was definitely crazy for was the movies. So they went once a week, and every so often he'd turn to look at her and think she looked just like a little kid, with her hand poised over the popcorn box, her eyes fixed on the screen, and this heated look of absorption as, her lips slightly parted, she watched the action.

Sometimes, looking at her in the movies, he'd feel a kind of lurching in his chest, and he'd want to figure out some way to get inside that part of her. A couple of times he put his arm around her shoulders and leaned over to kiss her cheek or forehead. He was surprised every time by how warm she was, as if her concentration actually generated heat. She didn't even seem to notice him; her eyes didn't so much as flicker. She kept right on watching the screen, and when the movie was over he'd have to wait for her to snap out of it, like someone coming out of a trance.

One night, on their way out of the theatre, he told her to wait, he'd go get the car. But when he got back she was nowhere in sight. He couldn't see her anywhere, and started driving up and down the streets, getting scared. It must have been fifteen minutes before he spotted her walking in the wrong direction. When he got her into the car, he asked, "Where were you going, Had?" and she looked at him blankly, as if she didn't recognize him.

"Sorry?"

"I told you to wait, I'd get the car."

"Oh! I'm afraid I must not have heard."

"Scared the hell out of me," he admitted.

"Did it?" Again she looked at him. "Why, Christopher?"

"Why? Because I expected you to be there, and you weren't. Anything could've happened. There are all kinds of crazy people in the world, you know, guys who go around raping and murdering women."

"But nothing happened."

"No, but it could have. Boy! Trying to talk to you at the movies is a complete waste of time. You don't hear a thing."

"I love films," she said ardently.

"I can tell." He laughed and patted her on the head. "Boy! A guy's really got to keep an eye on you. You're a real fruitcake."

"It's just that I get very involved with the story."

"That's the understatement of the century. If I could concentrate on my term papers the way you concentrate on movies, I'd have a Ph.D. in about two weeks flat. Not that I intend to spend one extra minute here. I want to get out and start making money."

"Do you? Yes, I suppose you would be eager for that." They were living on allowances given by both families. It was only natural he'd be anxious to start providing for her and the baby.

"Sure I would. You bet."

She'd never have believed she could become accustomed to lying naked nightly with a man, but she did. By the end of their second month of marriage, she didn't mind it at all. Chris was familiar; she'd learned to recognize his signals; and he didn't immediately turn away once it was done, but curled against her and talked quietly about his plans until his voice dwindled off and he was asleep.

Seventeen

Frances had long since become acclimated to her nightmares, although, too often, they tended to become confused with reality. There were events she was certain had actually taken place, yet she could never gather together enough facts for verification. The majority of these shadowy occurrences had to do with Edwin's death and its immediate aftermath. Even eight years after the fact something still nagged at her from time to time, insisting upon being remembered. Yet, try as she would, she couldn't bring the complete picture into focus.

There were also memories she insisted belonged to the realm of her troubled sleep that seemed perversely rooted in reality. Days, even perhaps weeks, of her life had been lost in an attempt to unravel the snarled strings that led from the past, or her dreams, into the present.

Since her course of electroconvulsive therapy she sometimes had presentiments, even a foreknowledge, of events. She also saw and heard things, now and then, that vanished, or went silent, in the briefest spaces of time. When this happened, she was mystified, frightened, and captivated, but never for a moment doubted that what she'd seen and heard had been real— if not to anyone else—at least to her.

Hadleigh, and her feelings about her, constituted an area of Frances's life that had two clearly defined halves. On the one side, her daughter was as tiresomely curious and unfathomable as she'd ever been. But on the other, there were periods when Frances suffered beneath a threatening weight of affection for the girl. The love she felt was almost as unpleasant as the disagreeable reactions Hadleigh fostered. And what bothered her most was her inability to remember, prior to her last epic binge, whether or not she'd actually expressed to her daughter her escalating concern for her well-being.

When they visited, Frances would look at Hadleigh, taking note of the weight she was accumulating—almost as one watched—and had to restrain herself from commenting. It was as if Hadleigh equated food with security, and if she managed to consume enough of it, she'd be insulated forever purely by her poundage. Yet there was something so forlorn about her that it came as a shock every time to find Hadleigh had the ability to take a stand and maintain it with stolid obstinacy. She kept on expecting her daughter to be as malleable as she looked, but there were areas where Hadleigh was immovable as a mountain. One of these areas was her absolute devotion to her father. She refused to see or hear of any failing he might have. To her, he was incapable of errors of judgment. She would leave the room if Frances expressed, even in jest, the slightest criticism of Arthur.

It was a pity, Frances thought, because she'd waited years for the time when Hadleigh would be old enough and sufficiently mature to talk about all that had happened in 1940. It was ground she and Arthur had covered to both their satisfaction, but there were details and thoughts she'd have liked to share. Hadleigh failed to become a candidate for her confidences. So that left the psychiatrists, and the majority of them—once she got past her fear of their power to keep her confined for limitless periods—were easily duped. She amused herself by sending them on wild-goose chases while never revealing the horde of feelings she kept, like a secret fund, beneath the floorboards of the modified behavior she'd had to adopt in order to regain the freedom she seemed to misplace with dismal regularity.

She knew Hadleigh would have been greatly surprised to learn of the amount of space she took up in her mother's thoughts. Yet Hadleigh was tied in pivotal fashion to Frances's ongoing anger with Amanda. Hadleigh had been used as a pawn in a dangerous game Mandy had attempted to play with Frances's life; she'd been an unwitting victim, and the unfortunate witness to the manipulation of her father. She could never forgive Amanda or forget the extent to which the woman had gone to accomplish her goals. She was determined that one day, somehow, Amanda would be penalized for her subtle acts of sabotage.

Of the disastrous tenth birthday party, she had no recollection. In her memory, Arthur had one day announced his intention to separate mother and daughter and had, stupidly, foolishly, selected Amanda as her replacement. She did remember subjecting Hadleigh to some fairly terrible abuses, and had made a concerted effort since regaining parental control of her daughter early in 1941 to repair some of the damage done. She hadn't done so bad a job of it, she thought, and her guilt was considerably reduced with respect to her acceptability. At least the girl had a decent sense of humor, for which Frances took full credit.

Now she was preoccupied with the forthcoming birth of Hadleigh's child, and by a morbid premonition that the delivery would imperil Hadleigh's life. And so she began telephoning daily to check up on her—a move, she acknowledged, that displayed an unprecedented amount of interest on her part.

"I'm perfectly fine, Mother," was Hadleigh's daily response. "Don't you think Chris would let you know if something happened?"

Since Frances didn't think for a moment she'd be the first person that young man would call should some emergency arise, she had to say, "Given that your husband considers me about on a par with certain rather unpleasant social diseases, I must answer no."

"None of that's true," Hadleigh argued, bewildered by this new tack her mother had taken. She was touched and impressed, but she also mistrusted Frances from long habit. She didn't dare allow herself to capitulate to the sentiments aroused by the regular calls. "I do appreciate your staying in close touch. Truly, I do. And so does Chris," she added, although this was flatly untrue. Chris was afraid of her mother, afraid of her talent for outrageous remarks and public displays of an alarming nature. "If anything happens, we'll let you know straightaway."

"I would like to be with you," Frances said hesitantly. "And you'll need help with the baby during the first weeks."

"We've arranged to have someone in."

"Paid staff never take the same sort of interest as a member of the family."

"She's a very nice woman, Mother. Chris and I both interviewed her, and she'll do beautifully, we're sure."

Rebuffed, Frances cut short the call to stride back and forth across the living room, more certain than ever that disaster lay just ahead.

"You really mustn't keep on with this," Arthur told her at dinner that evening. "They've just moved house and Haddy has quite enough on her plate without your ringing daily to voice your fears. It's most unthinking of you, Frances."

"It's nothing of the sort. It's precisely because she has so much on her plate that I am worried. She doesn't even have a char to help with the cleaning. I would like to *help*. I don't know why everyone insists on viewing my offer to help as if it were a reconstruction of the last days of Pompeii."

"You know *precisely* why," he disagreed with a smile. "Why, Frances, have you chosen to involve yourself with Hadleigh at this very late date?"

"My daughter's about to have a baby," she said reasonably. "Since I've been through the process a time or two myself I know what's expected. She doesn't. I simply wish to be there on the offchance I'm needed."

"They've arranged for live-in help. The hospital's a very good one, and Hadleigh's in perfect health. Chris is less than an hour away by car during the day, and at home with her every evening. Aside from that, Augusta is staying weekends to lend a hand setting the house to rights. I'd say she's well covered on all sides."

"I don't expect you to understand," Frances forged on. "I'm not sure I do myself. I just know I must be with her."

Impressed, finally, by her sincerity, he agreed to talk with Hadleigh.

"I do think she means well," Hadleigh said, "but it's so awkward. I honestly don't know *what* to do."

"Let me suggest a compromise. Could we not agree she'd come to stay with you, say, a week prior to the time the baby's expected? It's been almost five months now since her last episode."

"I'll have to discuss it with Chris."

"Of course. But please take into account that people have been known to change."

"Are you trying to say that Mother's changed?"

"I'm saying it's possible."

"I've spent my whole life wanting to believe she could."

"Perhaps it's beginning."

"I'll see what Chris says."

Having eavesdropped blatantly, when the call was completed, Frances wound her arm through Arthur's, saying, "She'll listen to you. I'm most grateful." Her smile was one whose meaning only Arthur would have recognized. It was a signal that galvanized him every time, without fail; one she gave him with gratifying regularity. He looked at her mouth, then slowly returned her smile.

Chris hated the idea. "She'll drive you crazy! Not to mention the fact that I'll have to hide all the booze, and watch every stinking word I say."

"She very much wants to be with me."

"Jesus Murphy, Hadleigh!" He stared hard at her, wishing, not for the first time, that he'd never laid a hand on her. Oh, her father was all right. But Frances! "I don't want her here. It's bad enough we're up to our asses in boxes, and the baby's room isn't even organized yet. I spend all day at school, then drive back here and try to get my studying done, as well as helping unpack this stuff. Where the hell did it all come from, anyway? And, on top of that, I'm up at five-thirty so I can get to New Haven in time for my first lectures. Since we moved in here three weeks ago, I've had to spend every weekend trying not to fall over you and Gus. I've got final papers to do, and at the rate things are going, I'll be lucky if I don't blow the whole thing. And now, *now* your mother wants to come. I say no! It's too goddamned much!"

"It's very important to her, Chris. And what harm could her being here do?" She was becoming very angry, and in her anger decided Frances could come at once, and never mind waiting.

"Plenty! Christ! I'm still not over what she did at the wedding."

"I want her to come. She's the only mother I'm ever going to have, and her coming to stay for a month means a lot to both of us. And I could use the help."

"You've got Gus, for Pete's sake."

"Only on weekends. I don't know what's in half these

boxes, and it's very hard trying to sort through it all on my own. Daddy says she hasn't had a drink in months, and she's promised to be on her best behavior. Please, Chris. If it was *your* mother, there'd be no argument at all. She'd simply come, regardless of how *I* felt about it."

"I'll tell you what," he said hotly. "She comes to stay for a month, I'll spend the month bunking in with Sheffie. The two of you and Gus can have the whole place to yourselves. You're the one who wanted to move now, instead of after the baby was born. You picked the place. Go ahead and have your mother, and maybe I'll be able to get my stinking paper done."

"You agreed to the move, and to this house," she retorted, wounded by his attempting to make it sound as if she'd engineered matters. "You said you couldn't spare the time to look, so I was the one who went round with the real estate agent. You said I should find something I thought we'd both like, and so I did. You said you'd get your father to give us the down-payment money, but he wouldn't, because you accepted his offer of the car. So it was *my* father who gave us the money. I didn't do any of this without your consent, and I won't have you accusing me this way!"

"Okay, okay," he backed down somewhat.

"*And*," she raced on, "it's the money from Nana's trust that's paid for the appliances, and the carpet, and the furniture, and the mortgage payments, and will keep on paying them until you start your job with your father's company. I've done my fair share, and I haven't made a fuss because we're married, after all, and everything's as much my fault as it is yours. I've asked nothing of you, but I *want* my mother to come. If you choose to stay that month with Elmo, fine. That's your decision, and I wouldn't dream of interfering. I quite understand how you feel about my mother. I do. She's a difficult woman and I won't deny it. But she *is* my mother. And while we're about it, Augusta's been wonderful with all the help she's given us. It's dreadful of you to speak as if she'd forced herself on us uninvited. And, furthermore, she hates being called Gus, yet you will insist on calling her that, even though she's asked you a dozen times please not to do it."

"It's just a goddamned nickname," he defended himself, aggrieved. "And I've got a right to my opinion."

"Of course you do," she agreed, seeing the pouty little boy

in him, disliking it. "So do I. This has been difficult for us both. I know you don't love me, and that none of this is quite what you had in mind. It's not what I had in mind, either. Could we *please* make the best of a bad lot and try to work together?"

"I'm trying to. But when your mother comes into it, boy, that's asking too much. The woman's a goddamned lush who falls through glass coffee tables. I can't believe you're not worried about having her around your baby."

"We've got Mrs. Santelli coming. She'll be the one looking after the baby, not Mother."

"You don't love me, either," he said quietly. "And what makes you so sure I don't love you?"

"You've never said that you do."

"Neither have you."

"Because you haven't."

"Well, maybe I haven't because you haven't."

"This is silly. It's the sort of circular conversation small children have. It doesn't matter how you feel about me, Chris. But, this once, I'm going to have it my way. My mother's coming to stay."

"Have her. If it's all the same to you, I'll spend the time in New Haven. It's really got nothing to do with you and me, Had. I just get nervous as hell with her around. If you think you can handle her, fine. It'll probably do us both good to be apart for a little while. I can get my work done, and you can get the house organized. And then, on the weekends, we'll be able to relax." He shoved his hands into his back pockets and gave her a smile. "You know, this is the longest conversation we've ever had."

"I suppose it is." As always, she found herself responding to his smile. "It wasn't my intention to say hurtful things, and I apologize."

"Oh, that's okay," he said expansively. "Arguments are bound to happen, I guess. You should hear my folks. This was nothing, compared to them."

"Really? They argue?"

"Not too often, and my mom always wins. She's one tough cookie."

"I would imagine she is."

"You don't like her, do you?"

"I don't think she cares very much for me."

"I'll let you in on a little secret." He looked for a moment at the scuffed toes of his saddle shoes before returning his eyes to her. "I don't think she cares much for anybody. She's all set, you know. Everything's just the way she likes it. She's got the club, and her cronies to play golf and bridge with. And they all sit around talking about the people they don't think measure up. She's a full-time critic. It's like, if she doesn't let everybody know about all the people and things she doesn't like, then it's not official." He laughed and gave her a shy hug. "It really would be a break if I could spend a month just studying. So, maybe it'll work out for everybody. You can have Frances to stay, and I'll bunk in with Sheffie. Okay?"

"Yes, okay. Thank you."

"And about all that other stuff? We'll just forget about it. Okay?"

"Yes, okay."

Frances arrived in a long, black limousine with enough luggage for a family of five making a permanent move. The chauffeur carried the bags inside and up to the guest room, accepted the five dollar tip Frances gave him, touched two fingers to the brim of his cap, and departed.

"It's not all clothes," Frances hastened to explain. "Two of the bags have gifts for the baby. You look rather tired." She frowned slightly.

"I'm fine. *You* look marvellous!" Hadleigh complimented her. When Frances wasn't drinking, she took great pains with her hair and makeup and clothes. Today she was wearing a smartly tailored, nip-waisted black broadcloth suit; a wide-brimmed, flat-topped black hat; wrist-length black gloves above which on her left wrist rode the heavy-link gold bracelet she always wore; and very high-heeled black leather pumps. Sober, she looked to be at most in her early forties. When she was drinking, she had the appearance of someone in her sixties. Right then, she looked young and very energetic. She unpinned the hat, removed her gloves, and looped her arm through Hadleigh's saying, "I'd adore a cup of tea. I'll put on the kettle, shall I, and then perhaps you'll give me a tour of the house. It's lovely and large, isn't it? And so sunny." On the threshold of the kitchen, she stopped to say, "A month is more than I'd dared hope for. However did you persuade him to allow it?"

"Oh, it wasn't difficult," Hadleigh answered. "I simply threatened to disable him permanently."

Frances laughed and clapped her on the shoulder. "Well done! Ah, yes, tea!"

Frances was so helpful, so noncritical, so relaxed, that Hadleigh found herself wondering if the time hadn't at last come when Frances would stay sober and continue her evolution into a parent. Certainly her deferential treatment of Hadleigh was a most optimistic sign.

Frances appeared with a tray of tea things in the nursery where Hadleigh was arranging the baby furniture; she was awake and dressed, preparing breakfast every morning when Hadleigh came down to the kitchen; her hair protected by a scarf, and wearing some of Arthur's old clothes, she insisted on unpacking the remaining boxes.

"Just keep me company," she instructed, "and tell me where it's all to go."

Most evenings she made the dinner and, generally, coddled her bemused daughter. It continued this way right through the first week of her stay.

Chris telephoned every evening to report on his day and to ask, guardedly, about hers. And Hadleigh had to admit, "She's been simply wonderful, won't let me do a thing. It's quite incredible."

At the weekend, with both Augusta and Chris in residence, Frances maintained her distance, entering into the conversation only when asked direct questions, and retiring early to bed in order that her presence would in no way be deemed an intrusion.

The first four days of the second week were pleasantly uneventful. With Augusta gone back to school and Chris up in New Haven, Frances and Hadleigh spent the evenings in the underfurnished living room. Hadleigh knitted while her mother studied fashion magazines. The radio pushed symphonic music lightly into the air. Every so often, Hadleigh would look over at the lean, elegant woman curled into one of the armchairs, marvelling at her mother's new-found capacity for stillness. With ingrained skepticism, Hadleigh found it hard to believe her present behavior could be maintained.

Her confusion intact and her curiosity aroused, on the

morning of the fifth day, she just had to ask, "Has something happened?"

Frances looked up from the *Times*. "Sorry?"

"You don't seem like yourself," Hadleigh said, wondering if she was running the risk of triggering some sort of explosion in her mother. "I mean, you've been most helpful and kind, and I appreciate it more than I can say. But I can't help wondering . . . I mean, what was it made you decide you wanted to be here with me?"

"I shouldn't have thought that would require explaining. You are my daughter, after all. And your first child's due in a matter of weeks. It's only natural I'd want to be with you."

"I really don't understand," Hadleigh persisted. "I've *been* your daughter for almost nineteen years and . . . well . . . You know what I'm trying to say. One could hardly call any aspect of our relationship natural. Now, suddenly, you are the way you are, and I want very much to believe we'll continue on this way, but I can't quite manage it."

"They say, you know, that I'm manic-depressive," Frances said, unruffled. "The symptoms are illustrated by extreme swings of mood. It's quite fascinating, all the textbook terminology. Although I do object to being so readily definable, much of their description does seem to apply. In all likelihood, I'll swing back the other way soon enough. But right now I'm trying to do what I feel must be done. Now that I think of it, it really isn't that surprising you'd be confused." Carefully refolding the newspaper, she said, "Did you know they gave me twenty-seven sessions of shock therapy at Hatton? It's unimagineable. They dab some frightfully cold jelly on one's temples, and apply the electrodes there. A piece of thickly padded wood is inserted between one's teeth. One's arms and legs are, of course, strapped down. And then they switch on the current, shooting electricity through one's brain. The object of this arcane exercise is, I'm told, to short-circuit that segment of the brain responsible for one's depression. Clearly," she smiled, "it's effectiveness is debatable. What it does do is create blind spots in one's memory. I try to perform some perfectly ordinary bit of business and find I cannot, for the life of me, remember how it's done. I'll see someone I'm certain I know, but just cannot recall his or her name. There are any number of things I simply don't remember." She gave a slow shake of her head, then reached for her cigarettes.

"I've never been an especially 'nice' person," she said, holding the unlit cigarette between her long fingers. "I've never aspired to niceness. I've always believed being nice was the domain of women content merely to be wives and mothers, those frightfully boring women you see poking the produce in markets and who, without the slightest hesitation, will whip out twenty or thirty of the latest snaps of their babies to show you. They're the tedious little drones who refer, with fabricated *ennui*, to the tiresome habits of their midget-minded husbands. I do hope you'll never volunteer to join their ranks, Hadleigh. Whatever you do, don't ever compel innocent bystanders to look at snaps of your baby."

"I wouldn't, in any case," Hadleigh told her.

"Good!" Frances said a little absently, then finally lit her cigarette. "Have you ever wondered what those places are like? They range from the utterly primitive—Hatton, for example—to the grand deluxe sort of nut-farm the Americans have created for the mentally bankrupt but financially sound members of the community. The odd thing is that one actually becomes fairly philosophical in the end. A large part of me," she confided, leaning across the table, "prefers madness. Ah! You're shocked!"

"Well, of course, I am!" Hadleigh answered. "You've just finished describing the most dreadful things, and in the next breath you say you prefer it. I find that very shocking."

Frances turned slowly and gazed out the window at the grounds. "If one is mad, one is not responsible," she said softly. "It's often the safest path. So much of what happens can be safely attributed to the madness, thereby absolving one of direct responsibility." She was silent a moment, then turned back. "You are quite right not to trust me. I'm completely unreliable. But I will *be* reliable until your child is born. You have my word on that."

"But why?"

"I have no idea. I simply had, and have, an overpowering intuition that I must be here. It's most gracious of you to humor me."

Again, Hadleigh had to wonder why she kept on seeking this strange woman's approval, forever hoping she'd alter to fit more closely her personal vision of what a proper mother should be. "You'll always be welcome in my home," she said at last.

Frances smiled. "They may succeed in someday scorching what's left of my brain to the point where it's like an over-cooked Sunday roast. Expect nothing of me, Hadleigh. This is purely temporary."

"I don't know why you talk about yourself the way you do. It's as if you want to be shocking. I really don't understand you."

"Oh, but you do," Frances disagreed. "Even at my worst, you've understood in some buried part of you. And, in any event, what does it matter?"

"It does matter. It's supposed to matter."

"Is there a document somewhere that you signed with your blood swearing undying love and allegiance to me? Naturally not. You're in no way obligated to me. Only your father is, and I to him, for reasons I couldn't possibly enumerate."

"If you're unreliable, as you say, and all the rest of it, then how do you know you're not mistaken about your having to be here?"

"I'm not entirely mad." Frances laughed, as if at a private joke. "Someday, you'll discover I didn't fabricate nearly so much as you thought."

"I'm totally confused," Hadleigh complained. "Could we please stop?"

"Certainly. Let me get you a fresh cup of tea. That one's gone cold." She got up to tip the contents of the cup into the sink, and Hadleigh watched, her head reeling with the contradictions and inconsistencies of her mother. She felt a little queasy, as if the conversation had tainted the air in the kitchen, and her breathing in of that air was making her ill.

As Frances made another pot of tea, Hadleigh continued to follow her movements, trying to work her way through all that had been said. Did recognition of one's madness render one safe from the judgments of others? she wondered. Or had her mother made use of the ultimate weapon in her arsenal: self-admitted failure. If one acknowledged in advance one's predilection for failure, no one could condemn the end results.

She was getting a headache, and, on top of that, she suddenly realized Frances hadn't actually answered the question. She still had no idea why her mother was there.

*   *   *

Frances sat that night on her bed in the dark, still fully dressed, watching the moonlight play tricks with the contents of the room. A slight breeze toyed with the branches of the trees outside, and the light that travelled through them and entered shaped itself and shifted like something alive. She watched, very awake, alert to the sounds of the house and those outside. She chain-smoked, lighting fresh cigarettes from those just finished. The room smelled, she thought, like an old man's breath, but she didn't move to open the window and allow fresh air to enter. It was important she remain alert, and so all that moved was her hand with the cigarette.

At two o'clock that morning, Hadleigh slowly came awake. Not only was she in pain, but the bedclothes were sticky wet. Reaching to turn on the light, she struggled upright and pushed back the blankets. With a cry, she saw that the sheet was drenched in blood.

Frances appeared in the doorway, as if she'd been awaiting this moment, took several steps closer, saw the blood, then whirled and ran off, saying, "Don't move! I'll ring for an ambulance."

The call made, she returned and, without a word, stripped off Hadleigh's nightgown, bathed her as best she was able, gently placed a folded towel between Hadleigh's thighs, got her into a fresh nightgown, then softly said, "Lie down absolutely flat," as she helped Hadleigh from the bed onto the floor.

Until the ambulance came, Frances knelt on the floor, holding Hadleigh's hand and stroking her hot forehead with cool fingers, saying over and over, "Be very still. Everything will be all right."

She continued this litany throughout the ride to the hospital, so that Hadleigh was all but hypnotized by the whispered repetition.

There was a brief skirmish when two nurses began pushing Hadleigh's stretcher off along the corridor in the maternity wing. A third nurse tried to hold Frances back, saying, "You're not allowed in there."

Frances placed her hands on the smaller, younger woman's arms and literally lifted her aside. "I am allowed wherever I damned well choose! Don't even *think* of attempting to stop me!'' With that, she tore off after the departing stretcher, arriving just as the two nurses were rather impatiently attempting to undress a weakly protesting Hadleigh.

"I'll do that!'' Frances announced. "Go along and ring her doctor, and do whatever else needs doing!''

"She has to be prepped,'' the more senior of the nurses argued.

"Squander one more minute and my daughter will bleed to death, you imbecilic, insensitive cretin! Get someone in here who knows what he's doing! *I* will see to this.''

Cowed by her fierce authority, the two nurses exchanged a glance, then hurried off, muttering threats. Hadleigh watched the whole thing with bursting pride, then, suffering, moaned, "This is all wrong! It hurts terribly. I'm frightened.''

"There's no need to be,'' Frances told her. "Your doctor will be here any moment to sort out the situation. Prep indeed! They're all enema mad, nurses! As if the solution to all the world's problems reposes in one's bowels!''

Hadleigh laughed, then her eyes went wide. "It feels as if the baby's coming. What should I do?''

"Hold on!'' Frances slammed the heel of her hand against the call button and kept it there. "Just hold on, Hadleigh! Try to calm down. It won't help matters if you become hysterical. Clearly, the placenta's coming before the baby.''

"How do you *know* that?''

"Call it an educated guess! We'll just get you up here on the bed so you can stretch out flat, and then we'll take one step at a time.''

The doctor came flying in, hastily examined Hadleigh, confirmed Frances's diagnosis, and went dashing out again. Within minutes, Hadleigh had been taken off to the delivery room, and Frances was left to study the blood spatters on the floor, infuriated at having been refused entry into the delivery room. She tried to look in through the window in the door, but a nursing supervisor came along and ordered her away.

"There's a waiting room down the corridor. Stay there! We'll let you know your daughter's progress.''

Frances went to the telephone and put in a call to Chris. Some young man answered after the ringing had gone on for several minutes.

"Put Christopher MacDonald on the line at once!'' she commanded.

"Who?" the sleep-dazed voice wanted to know.

"Christopher MacDonald. *Get him!*"

Finally, Chris got to the telephone.

"I suggest you come straightaway. They've taken Hadleigh into the delivery room. She's had a hemorrhage. I shall stay here until I know she's well out of any danger and then, I expect, I shall go somewhere and have a drink."

"Oh, Jesus Christ! I'll be there as fast as I can. She's okay?"

"So far as I know!"

"Okay! I'm on my way. And thanks for letting me know."

Frances positioned herself by the window in the waiting room where she resumed her chain-smoking. She felt thoroughly vindicated by circumstances. When, some forty minutes later, the doctor came, he congratulated her on her fast actions before informing her that Hadleigh had had twins by caesarian section. Frances thanked him, nodded to herself in satisfaction, then went to ring for a taxi.

She was gone for nine days. Then a telephone call from the night manager of the Ritz in Boston summoned Arthur to collect her.

"Has there been any problem?" Arthur asked.

"No, sir. None at all. She asked me to call, said to tell you it was time to come get her."

"Is she sober?"

"She is now, sir. Hasn't had a thing from room service since yesterday."

"Thank you. I'll make arrangements. Good of you to call."

Eighteen

Frances was right. There was a part of Hadleigh that understood perfectly why her mother did the things she did. But understanding didn't prevent her from being bitterly disappointed by the discovery that her mother had gone off again. She'd been hoping that Frances's recent display of interest would continue. She told herself her hope was merely a reckless indulgence, and chided herself for her ill-founded optimism. Yet Frances had been so nearly accessible that it scarcely seemed possible she'd removed herself with so little compunction.

Chris, of course, could see only the positive side. "Boy! It's just amazing," he commented several times. "As if she knew something like this was going to happen. It's a damned good thing she was here."

"She didn't even wait to see the babies." Hadleigh heard the incipient whine in her voice, and hated herself for her dependence upon someone as flatly undependable as her mother. Still, she'd almost attained a genuine sense of the woman; she'd come closer than ever before to being able to identify the specific traits and qualities of someone who, at best, had been only intermittently familiar. Nevertheless she was hurt by Frances's ability to be present and caring at one moment, and gone bag and baggage the next.

Her father, when he came, looked fatigued, as if under a great strain.

"It's best not to expect anything of your mother," he told

her—as indeed, Frances herself had told her. "She stayed as long as she felt there was some need."

They were walking together along the corridor to the nursery to see Bonita and Benjamin. They moved slowly, and Hadleigh wasn't sure which of them had set the pace, she, because of her sutures, or her father because of his near-palpable weariness. At the viewing window, she eagerly pointed out the twins, and her father stood with one hand flat against the glass, looking in at the tiny enflamed faces and waving fists of his grandchildren.

"You've got two, fine, lusty babies there, Hadleigh." He draped his arm around her shoulders. "Well done!"

She laughed softly, awed at having produced not one but two infants. "An entire family all in one go," she said, not yet able to connect the babies to herself. "I can't quite believe it. How are you?" She looked up at him with concern.

"A bit on the tired side, but fine," he answered.

The nurse lifted Bonita from her crib and brought her over to the window. At once, Hadleigh pressed close to the glass, gazing at her child. "I feel so odd," she admitted, her eyes on the baby, "as if I'm here under false pretenses, visiting someone else's newborn. The only times I feel as if they're truly mine are when they're brought to me for feeding. And then I don't seem able to do it properly. I'm so astonished by their tiny fingers, their ears, the absurd *smallness* of them, that I forget to feed them." The nurse returned Bonita to her crib and fetched Ben. "They're not identical," Hadleigh continued. "I thought at first they were, but I'm able to see differences in them now. It's all so very strange. I'll be in my room and suddenly I'll wonder what it is I'm doing here. I'm frightened about taking them home."

"But you've got live-in help, and Augusta at the weekends."

"It isn't that." She turned from the window and they started walking back along the corridor. "I suppose the truth is: I thought she'd want to stay. I so hoped she would." Again she looked up at him. "How is she?"

"Come, let's sit down a moment." He directed her into a small waiting area near the elevator where they sat together on a leatherette sofa. "Haddy," he began, "I'd hate to think you're angry in any way with your mother for some area in which you think she's failed you. We've both of us told you, and often, that if you expect nothing, you can't ever be disappointed. I realize that may seem a very hard line to take, but it's the best possible course. You have a family of your own now, and driving yourself half-mad attempting to analyze your mother's behavior will only complicate your life unnecessarily. There are certain things, certain people, one must simply accept on faith. Your mother is one of those people. She does what she wants to do, and undoubtedly always will. Her reasons don't always coincide with our preferences, but that doesn't render them any less valid."

"Why didn't you divorce her and marry Amanda?"

"Oh, dear." He laughed. "Would you have preferred that?"

"No," she said slowly. "But why didn't you?"

"It was never an issue, Hadleigh. I love your mother. I always have."

"She doesn't love you," she blurted out, then regretted it instantly.

He measured his words carefully. "What your mother and I share goes beyond ready definition. You're not nearly old enough, nor have you lived sufficiently, to be able to make assessments of something that doesn't fall within the realm of your experience."

"But Amanda was in love with you," she argued.

"That may well be true, but whatever state she was in, she put herself there, not I. I wanted your mother. I still do."

"I don't understand any of it."

"Stop trying," he advised quietly, then was caught up for a moment in contemplation of the very tangible ways in which Frances displayed her caring. Without reservation, he succumbed always to the indecipherable mystery of her appeal for him. "One must," he said at length, "simply accept her."

"I can't just 'accept' her, and I don't see how you can." Even as she spoke, images of her mother drifted across her vision, compellingly inscrutable.

"I think we've exhausted the topic," he said, pushing back his cuff to check the time.

"Must you leave so soon?" she asked.

"I'm afraid I have to."

"Will she be coming to see me?" she asked, looking very young.

"I'm certain she'll be in touch with you." He kissed her

forehead and got to his feet. "We'll talk at the weekend," he said, then proceeded on his way.

There were certain of her dreams Frances could never outrun. Sooner or later they caught her up, and then her nights turned too bright, too busy with scenes that played themselves until even the smallest detail was highlighted. Sequentially, she met and spoke with Edwin. They kissed, and anticipation filled her like helium so that, weightlessly, she rose, a living bubble. They talked and planned; they met again. This second meeting was fraught with misunderstandings, loud with the rage of rejection. She silenced him, and blood seeped from the unseen wounds in his skull. Magnified a thousand times, each drop lived independently, falling forever. She fled into the heart of an air-raid. Bombs whistled to detonation on all sides; bits of debris hurtled through the smoky air. Then, shedding her clothes, she made love in the sheltered courtyard of an abandoned church, the damp mossy bricks grinding their impressions into her flesh. It was Edwin she made love to, but not Edwin she craved. Shredding his features until his image was nothing more than drifting tatters lifted by unseen winds, she impaled herself upon her chosen Arthur, cloaked herself in his love. Edwin was, for all time, dead.

She no longer believed anyone would come for her; too much time had passed. Yet upon waking, she turned each time to study the long figure at her side, held in willing bondage to the only person alive who, she thought, knew of what she'd done. Straight from her dreams, she often awakened Arthur with caresses, eager in doomed fashion to have him reaffirm her value to him. There were times when she prayed she would one night die in her sleep. In the event of her death, he might have some more reasonable sort of life. As long as she continued to live, she had to endure the recriminations, her own and those he'd never voiced.

Sometimes, making love with her husband, she felt as if she were holding death in her arms, guiding it deep into her body where she held it locked to her striving interior with elation and despair. "We're animals," she told him occasionally, "bloody animals."

Once past his initial shock at this comment, he was able to respond, "It's how you prefer it, Frances. It's you who's set the tone, and the pace, for all our dealings."

She couldn't believe that he didn't somewhere, secretly, hate her for her crimes, and she sought to goad him into displaying this hatred. She failed consistently.

"What are you trying to get to?" he'd asked her frequently over the years. "What is it you think you'd like to hear me say?"

When she was unable to frame any suitable answer, he said, "It will always be you who pushes against the fairly elastic boundaries we've set up together, not I."

This depressed her because she felt she'd corrupted him. "Have I," she asked, some weeks after her return from Boston, "made you into someone you despise, Arthur?"

"Of course not," he answered, poised above her. "Why would you think a thing like that?"

"I can't help thinking that my death would solve any number of people's problems."

"And what if *I* were to die, Frances?" he countered. "What would you do, sleep with my corpse?"

"Isn't that what *you've* been doing all these years? We both know I died years ago. We simply seem to have a problem with a body that won't lie down."

He laughed, grazing the back of his hand on her breast. "You love melodrama!" he accused.

"I despise it! You know full well it's never been my favorite art form."

"Why do you do it?" he asked. "Why do you toy with people's lives?"

"I wasn't toying with her," she said, affronted. "I knew I'd be needed. I went, and I was indeed needed. When that need no longer existed, I left."

"One cannot come and go in people's lives with such blatant disregard for their feelings."

"Oh, please! Hadleigh's as self-contained as an air-raid shelter at the bottom of one's garden; everything one might need for survival's stored neatly on shelves."

"What a simply awful thing to say! And how untrue!"

"You see!" she said, as if having proved her point. "Were I to die, I'd no longer be a contemptible source of embarrassment. Unfortunately, I'm in excellent health."

"Hardly unfortunate."

"Whatever. One day, you know, I might evolve into a purely social drinker, or even a non-drinker, and then the consulate staff will have to find itself another topic of conversation. How boring it would all be!"

"Doesn't that cast a lovely light on me!" he chided her. "You give me no credit for my debonair charm."

She laughed and pinched him. "You're quite wrong. I give you full marks. Now, why don't you do something wonderfully charming for me?"

Hadleigh vowed she'd pay the sort of attention to her children she herself had never received. It was far more difficult than she'd imagined. Not only were there two babies squalling for attention, draining her with their incessant requirements, there was also Chris, who seemed to take no more than a passing interest in his children.

After his graduation, they spent a month with his parents in the Old Saybrook house, with Mrs. MacDonald furrowing her brow disapprovingly each time one of the babies began to cry. Mrs. Santelli simply couldn't cope alone. One baby's crying usually set off the other, and it took two people to get the infants fed, or bathed, or into clean diapers. It might have been a most agreeable occupation, had it not been for Mrs. MacDonald's long-suffering expressions. Her attitude made Hadleigh feel inept, and by the month's end, she was glad to begin loading the car to return to Greenwich.

"I'm beginning to think there's something about me mothers don't like," she told Chris the night of their return home.

"I told you my mother hates everybody," he said, tying his pajama bottoms. "It's got nothing to do with you personally."

"I'm serious, Chris. I haven't heard a word from *my* mother since the birth of the twins, and *your* mother insists we come visit for a month, then spends the whole time we're there looking at me as if I were a nasty stain on her carpet."

"She looks at Augusta and Sheffie that way, too, not to mention just about every living soul on earth. Boy, I'm going to be glad to start work. I'm really putting it on." He patted his stomach. "I can't stand sitting around all day doing nothing."

She looked over at him and, all at once, she could *feel* Frances inside her brain. Clever, hurtful words crowded into her mouth and she had to work hard to keep them from escaping. It was an exceptional, bewildering moment and she wished she could prolong it, but Chris pushed back the bed-clothes and bounced in beside her.

"What is Elmo going to be doing now?" she asked.

"Didn't he tell you? I thought he did. He's going on for his master's. Then he'll try for a doctorate."

"In what?"

"Hadleigh, have you got amnesia or something? *History*. He'd like to wind up one day teaching at Yale. I think he sees himself with a pipe and an old tweed jacket with leather patches on the elbows, conferring his great knowledge on the lowly freshmen."

"It's easy to picture him that way."

"There's no money in it, that's for sure."

"Not everyone does things for money."

"Well, you're looking at one guy who does. No more living off loans from the parents. From now on, we pay our own way." He folded his arms behind his head, smiling. "We'll have a nice cabin cruiser, a new car every year. Be nice to me, toots, and I'll buy you mink."

She smiled back at him. "I have no interest in mink."

"Oh, you will have. Women always do."

"What I'd really like someday would be a shop of my own."

"A shop? Selling what?"

"I'm not sure," she hedged.

"You've got two kids and this house to keep you busy."

"I won't always, and then I'd like to have a dollhouse . . ."

He cut short the conversation by reaching across her to turn off the light. "It's been almost two months," he said by way of preamble. "If we don't start doing it again, I might forget how."

She turned to look at him, waiting for him to laugh, but he wasn't joking.

"Still kind of mushy," he said, pressing his hand into her belly. "You need to start getting some exercise, lose some of this weight."

"It takes time to lose it," she justified herself, humiliated by the way he was pushing her flesh around, as if it were a blancmange on a plate.

"Hell! I don't care."

She might have been anyone, she thought, bracing herself to

bear his weight. As long as she was female and he could attach himself to her, her particulars were of no significance. She felt anonymous. It made her cry.

"Hey! Is something wrong?" He paused.

"No, nothing's wrong," she answered, and he went back to his labor.

Along the corridor, one of the babies awakened and gave a high-pitched cry. She listened, hearing Mrs. Santelli's footsteps. She was paying such close attention to the removed sounds she lost her awareness of Chris. He finished quickly, hiked up his pajama bottoms, gave her a pat on the behind, then rolled onto his side away from her, and slept. In tears again, she heard Mrs. Santelli going back to her bedroom, then silence. She longed to go look at the babies, but she didn't move. After a time, she blotted her eyes on the pillow case, then lay staring at the night, waiting for sleep to claim her.

She found herself caught in something black and glue-like from which no amount of sunlight or laughter could release her. She watched Mrs. Santelli play with the babies on the lawn, and tried to make herself feel some connection to them. She couldn't. She was filled with apprehension of the day when Mrs. Santelli would leave to tend some other woman's newborn, leaving Hadleigh to cope alone with the babies and this house. The only activity that managed to hold her interest, that eased the blackness she felt to a shade of gray, was gardening.

While Bonita and Ben lay napping on a blanket in the shade of the copper beech tree, with Mrs. Santelli keeping watch over them, Hadleigh turned the earth and marked out the perimeters of the flower beds. She placed seeds at meticulous intervals along precisely marked trenches, then scooped earth over the seeds; patiently, she knotted pachysandra roots before implanting them at strategically designated areas where they'd spread to provide ground cover. The flower beds grew broader and more elaborate almost in direct proportion to the growth of her children.

Chris's homecoming each evening from the city marked the end of yet another day she'd somehow managed to get through. They sat together in the dining room to eat the meal she'd cooked while, above, Mrs. Santelli bathed and readied the babies for bed. Dutifully, Hadleigh asked about Chris's day, then forgot to listen as he narrated his growing acumen with stocks and bond offerings. He didn't seem aware of her inattentiveness. He ate whatever she gave him and only commented if she happened to serve something he didn't like.

After dinner they climbed the stairs to the nursery where they stood looking at their sleeping children. Then, an appropriate amount of time having passed and the ritual completed, they descended the stairs to the living room where he read profit and loss statements, and prospectuses, while the radio provided a low drone of background noise. She sat and watched him turn pages, periodically aware of bursts of laughter from some comedy show on the radio, trying to make sense of her position here.

At ten o'clock, he replaced the paperwork in his briefcase and switched off the lamp beside his chair. She followed suit, turning off the radio and whatever other lights were on. While he went about checking that the downstairs doors and windows were secured, she went up to prepare for bed. Most nights he climbed aboard her body as if she were an express train with only one stop and, within minutes, he reached his destination and departed. His capacity for sleep and the ease with which he claimed it seemed to her remarkable. She envied his ability to shut his eyes and leave the world, while she lay feeling trampled and lacking an identity, wide awake.

She began getting up at two or three in the morning to creep down the hall to the nursery where, with the aid of the night-light, she studied the faces of her babies, deeply moved by their seemingly genetic talent for sleep. Like their father, they plunged effortlessly into it. They napped at specific times during the day, and awakened eager for the world. She wondered, examining the completeness of the sleeping household, why she felt there should be more to life than eating and sleeping.

Her days and nights were directed toward facilitating the passage of those around her from one state into the other, yet she couldn't find any pleasure or satisfaction in her own acts. She was able to handle the babies with offhanded skill, finding within herself an affinity for those small, scented bodies that fit so readily against her hip or shoulder. She adored their faces and their toothless grins of recognition. She loved their tiny pummeling fists and pudgy thighs, their wispy blond hair and ever-curious eyes. She couldn't, though, connect them to the back-bending weight she'd carried for almost eight months; as the beings responsible for the strange inner pokes and prods she'd become accustomed to and now missed, as if one of her limbs had been amputated.

"You've got post-partum depression," Augusta declared.

Hadleigh looked at her auburn-haired, brown-eyed friend, thinking she'd never actually *looked* before at Augusta. She really was a lovely looking girl, with her fair freckled skin and long eyelashes.

"It takes a few months," Augusta went on, "but you'll get over it. My older sister moped around the house for ages after her second baby was born."

"Is that what it is?" Hadleigh asked.

"I'll bet it is. You wait. Another few weeks and every-thing'll look a whole lot better."

"I hope so," Hadleigh said. "There's nothing wrong, really, and yet I've felt so terribly detached. I'm dreading Mrs. Santelli's leaving."

"You'll be fine. Line up a couple of babysitters and make sure you get out regularly. Check with the high school. They've always got a list of kids who want to sit."

"I'll do that. Thank you. Isn't it extraordinary?" she said. "One wouldn't think that merely putting a name to something could make such a difference. I feel quite a bit better already."

It didn't last. After Mrs. Santelli's fairly emotional depar-ture, Hadleigh found herself still floundering beneath waves of darkness that threatened to cut off permanently the little light illuminating her life. Periodically, she'd come to to find one of the babies being held too tightly against her breast, emitting squeals of protest she then had to soothe to silence. Diligently, she placed a blanket on the lawn and allowed the twins to twist and squirm in the sunlight as they tested their strengthening muscles. She watched them, seeing only their outlines, as if they were sketches brought magically to life, moving about and gurgling contentedly. She talked to them as she spoonfed applesauce or puréed vegetables into their little liquid mouths, then wiped clean their faces. She bathed them in the double sink in the kitchen where they splashed and cooed and offered their ecstatic faces for her approval. And very gradually they became recognizable to her; she learned their preferences, their quirks.

Ben could always, instantly, be placated with a bath. Bonita found contentment in anything chewable, from arrowroot biscuits to small rubber rings. Hadleigh learned that they were distinctly separate people with differing interests and dissimilar natures. They did everything with gusto, from eating whatever food they were given, to bellowing when in discomfort. Bonita, however, was easier, more readily appeased, while Ben seemed to savor his misery, reluctant to surrender it.

They were, after all, people, and Hadleigh fell victim to her fascination with them. Her depression lifted slightly, and she worked at preventing its return by involving herself more and more with her children. She knitted and sewed for them; she played with and kept them amused during their every waking hour.

"I told you you'd get over it," Augusta said some months later. "I knew you would."

"You were right," Hadleigh agreed. "I'm enjoying being a wife and mother."

Augusta accepted this, but with reservations. It seemed as if Hadleigh had gone overboard and, if anything, was growing too involved with her family. She didn't dare comment on this to Hadleigh, though, for fear of returning her friend to her depression.

"Sometimes," she confided to Sheffie at a dance she attended at Yale as his date, "I really worry about her."

"Why?" he asked, with an intensity of interest that never failed to surprise her. Any mention of Hadleigh invariably got his immediate attention.

"I'm not sure. She just has such scary highs and lows."

"Which is she now?" he wanted to know, as if he were a doctor hearing a patient's symptoms.

"Up, at the moment."

"Maybe she'll just stay up. Maybe it's exactly what you said it was."

"I hope so. But sometimes I get the feeling she's trying to be just like her mother."

Nineteen

Frances was deep in a medicated sleep, so Mrs. Walsh took the call from the consulate, then tried to push her information past the black borders beyond which Frances reposed.

"You've got to get up!" Mrs. Walsh insisted repeatedly, pushing and pulling until she succeeded in getting Frances to open her eyes.

"What *are* you doing?" Frances demanded hoarsely, eyelids prepared to lower.

"Mr. 'Olden's been taken to 'ospital! You've *got* to *get up!*"

"Mister Holden," Frances argued, "is behind his highly polished desk at the consulate, refusing passage home to disenchanted wretches lacking the price of the fare. He is wielding the Parker pen of authority with all due dignity, and will arrive home promptly at six-fifteen anticipating steak and kidney pie." She tried to turn over, but Mrs. Walsh wasn't having any of it.

"A right bloody nutter, you are!" cried the exasperated woman. "The man's been taken to 'ospital, and you're to go there! Open them eyes! Don't you go back to sleep!" She dragged Frances from the bed and into the bathroom where, despite Frances's struggles, she managed to get her positioned beneath an ice-cold shower that shocked her into wakefulness. "You stay there, you stupid git!" Mrs. Walsh ordered. "You move, and I'll 'ave a real go at you!"

It took her another half hour and two cups of coffee to bring Frances to the point where she was sufficiently coherent to understand that Arthur had been taken ill at the office and was presently in critical condition at Mt. Sinai Hospital.

"Course that was an 'our ago," Mrs. Walsh stormed, dragging a sweater over Frances's head. "Don't know why I bother with you. Demented you are, what with the drink and them little pills you're so fond of. The doorman's 'olding a taxi downstairs. Go get yourself in it and see to your 'usband." Her body still under the influence of the Seconal and Miltowns she'd taken to help her sleep, Frances felt as if she were trudging through oceans of mucilage as she accepted her handbag from Mrs. Walsh, and then aimed her feet at her shoes. Mrs. Walsh propelled her out of the apartment, down the corridor and into the elevator, then ran back to warn the doorman Mrs. Holden was on her way down.

The hospital was certainly real enough, and travelling along its disinfectant-scented hallways helped wake her up. But Arthur's body seemed some bizarre effigy concocted by others to trouble her. The color was all wrong, for one thing; his flesh had a distinctly blue tinge to it. For another thing, he'd stopped breathing and no one had bothered to enlighten her. She'd come prepared to taunt him, smart words having to do with his malingering at the ready. The words melted like ice on her tongue as she stared, thinking he didn't look remotely like himself.

Someone from the embassy approached to offer consolation, but she dismissed him, puzzling over the possible reasons why this demented ruse was being played out. Throwing aside the sheet some fool had draped over him, she examined the body at very close range, searching for the seams, or the valve by which they'd inflated this life-size doll. It was his wedding ring, finally, that pulled her directly into a state of gelid wakefulness and brought home the truth of his death.

"It was very sudden," the consulate official ventured. "He simply slumped over at his desk."

"This is monstrously unfair!" she said, turning the wedding band round and round on Arthur's finger.

"Indeed, it is," the official agreed.

The voice, like an echo, was an intrusion. Turning she addressed the man. "I'd be most grateful if you'd leave."

"Of course." He gave one of those tedious little demi-bows the consular staff were so fond of, and backed out of the room.

She sat down and held Arthur's cold heavy hand, waiting for him to open his eyes. She'd never known such frustration. It simply wasn't supposed to be this way. When she'd spoken of death, when they'd talked banteringly of it, she'd been embracing emotional and philosophical concepts, not anything literal. There was supposed to be an opportunity for final words, for a summation of their years together. There were so many things still left to be said, and only she was left to say them. He wasn't meant to keel over dead of a heart attack at fifty-five, leaving her with absolutely nothing resolved.

There were voices in the corridor and they interfered with her attempts to marshal her sentiments. Letting go of his hand, she went to close the door. Then, drawing the chair closer, she sat again, retrieved Arthur's hand and tried to get on with the sorting process.

She was appalled to discover that she hadn't the least notion of even the next step to be taken. This was all so poorly planned. Death wasn't supposed to trip you up like a step you hadn't noticed was there. It was something to be eased into, with due warning and appropriate farewells. Arthur had quit living, disuniting himself from her.

He'd never done anything she'd expected, not from the first. Each time she decided he was predictable and as easily read as the *News of The World*, he'd taken a half-turn to the left to reveal a new facet of himself. He'd never allowed anyone undue influence on his decisions, refusing always to follow the urgings of any voice but that of his own conscience. He'd more than compensated for her early dissatisfaction by his willingness in the last thirteen years to seek new routes to understanding and pleasure. He'd partnered her with a vengeance without ever losing his unique identity in the process. He'd remained Arthur even *in extremis*. Nothing either of them had ever done had been potent enough to defuse his identity. He'd died with it intact. He'd taken with him all the charm, and generosity, all the kindness and tolerance she'd depended on.

She looked around the room, slowly considering how, for so many of the early years, she'd thought him her adversary.

They'd been posted at opposite ends of a playing field and she'd assumed the positions signified their roles as opponents. Yet he'd been her one true friend. She'd rewarded him with irregular doses of public shame, and frequent displays of private nakedness. She couldn't imagine what she'd do next.

"This is unlike you, Arthur," she whispered, again twisting the gold band on his finger. "Of all the punishments you might've devised, this is the cruellest. What *am* I supposed to *do*?"

As she turned the ring round and round on his finger, something began to build low in her body, rising along with the words tumbling from her lips. "Who'll be there when I ring up, wanting to come home? And where do you expect my bloody home to *be*? I rely on you. How . . . ?" The flow of recriminations was halted by her sudden, unbidden, animal-like bark of grief. So many years of guilt and fear, of anxiety; all the venom she'd spewed at him, that he'd simply waved aside; the ritualistic savagery with which they'd mated, had all stemmed from her sometime desperation and his unqualified refusal to stop loving her. Her thoughts had a sudden linear rationality that terrified her more than any institution in which she'd ever been confined, and it was hateful to be clear-minded, to have to admit so very late in the day that the one person she'd always loved to the fullest extent of her capacities was now gone.

Sorrow overwhelmed her and for several nightmarishly uncontrolled minutes, she was gripped by pain as those barking cries tore out of her. Her bones, even her teeth, ached as she clung to Arthur's hand, attempting to imagine how she could possibly continue on into the future alone. She was rescued by Hadleigh's arrival.

The door flew open, and Frances turned to see her daughter hang, for a moment, in the doorway before she cried out and hurled herself across the room, flinging herself upon her father's body. Frances watched, impressed by Hadleigh's ability to display her emotions. Her daughter's tears were a veritable flood. The entire bed shook with the force of her grief. She went on and on with her awe-inspiring show while Frances lit a cigarette, a spectator at this pyrotechnical display.

At last, after ten minutes or so, Hadleigh pushed herself upright and looked over at her mother.

"Why are you just *sitting there*?" she shrilled.

After the briefest pause to consider what sort of response she'd give, Frances said, "I'm afraid I haven't your gift for performing an entire Greek chorus single-handedly. What I am doing is watching you. I had no idea you were so emotional."

"My father's dead! I'm sorry I can't suppress my *unseemly* sorrow and sit smoking a cigarette as if I were at an embassy cocktail party for some visiting dignitary."

"That's not quite how I feel," Frances said, rather liking Hadleigh's retort. Hadleigh might, one day, develop into someone with true wit.

"You don't *feel* anything about anyone except yourself. You never have. You didn't care about him!"

Frances turned away, paying close attention to putting out her cigarette. "You're quite wrong, but it's of no consequence." She stood up, debating whether or not to attempt explaining herself. The prospect was too exhausting. "I'll leave you to perform privately," she said, heading toward the door.

"*You're a heartless bitch!*" Hadleigh flung the words like daggers.

Frances turned back, shaking her head. "No," she corrected calmly. "I'm not some simpleminded warm-blooded feline whose emotions are centered squarely in her groin. You can't sum me up that easily, although I'll wager you'll spend your life trying. I lived with that man"—she pointed at the housing that had contained Arthur—"for twenty-four years. There are some experiences that surpass one's abilities either to describe or to fully comprehend. Don't think for a moment that you know anything, Hadleigh, because what you think you know will turn itself about and show you only your own confusion. I'll ring Mrs. Walsh to prepare your room. You'll want to stay, of course, to be sure I don't make a complete shambles of the funeral." She got the door open and left Hadleigh gaping after her.

In the women's rest room just down the corridor, Frances closed herself into one of the stalls. She put the lid down on the toilet, then seated herself, her stomach quaking and her knees rubbery. It was too late to change the habits and behavior of a lifetime, too late to begin offering explanations for the things she said and did. Arthur had known and understood, and that alone was important.

Hadleigh thought she'd seen something in her mother's eyes. But what? A challenge? Fear? Grief? She couldn't interpret the message, although she tried after Frances was gone from the room, leaving behind her a silence that seemed underscored by a thousand whispers. The harsh words weren't the key to Frances, and Hadleigh bemoaned her lack of deciphering skill. Why couldn't either one of them get past their self-erected protecting barricades to share this loss?

She looked again at her father with the sense that the world was disintegrating. He'd always been there, had always offered solutions to her problems. Who'd perform that service now? Certainly Chris lacked the initiative to take decisive action, even when he could see it was badly needed. He was a man so hotly in pursuit of success and money that he was impervious to everything else.

The twins bounced off him like small rubber toys he seldom had the inclination to play with. They appeared to accept that he would only occasionally turn his attention to them, and when he did, inevitably, some mishap occurred. His roughhousing was too gregariously incautious. He defied his children to pit their four-year-old strength against his. And when they showed themselves willing, he outran, outplayed, outmaneuvered them at every turn, and then expected them to applaud his superior abilities. When their shoulders curved inward with defeat and bewilderment, he was annoyed by their failure to respond as he'd wished. When he did choose to play with them, the games he elected to play were beyond their abilities in every way, yet he neglected to commend them on the valiance of their efforts. The result was that Ben, defeated in advance, kept offering to meet his father's challenges, but was rendered increasingly miserable by his failures. And Bonita, with wisdom remarkable in so young a child, simply thanked her father politely but turned down his invitations.

Arthur had had such kindness, such endless patience with the twins. He'd read Kipling to them for hours in his low, lyrical voice; he'd taken them on long walks—a distinguished, smartly suited man with a child tethered to each hand—pointing out wildflowers and small animals in summer, Canadian geese arrowing south in the late autumn, snowdrift sculptures in winter. He'd accepted with enthusiasm their splattery watercolors and random crayon portraits; he'd lavished thoughtful gifts upon them, and had loved them with quietly smiling tolerance, more than once tending to their skinned knees, bad dreams, and runny colds.

Even Frances showed more interest in the children than Chris did. She seemed particularly fond of Bonita and never passed up an opportunity to spend time with the little girl. Hadleigh had, any number of times, come across her mother and her daughter playing with paper dolls, or sitting on the nursery floor with coloring books and crayons while Frances transported Bonita with stories made up on the spot solely for the little girl's pleasure.

Her parents' presence in her house had made it home. Now her father was dead, and she felt homeless. All she had left was a mother who defied anyone's understanding, and a husband who, in the past few months, had taken to spending occasional nights in the city, with excuses she accepted but didn't for a moment believe as truth. The scent of his cast-off clothes had undergone a minimal but nevertheless discernible alteration. Traces of his passage through another woman's life showed in small ways, but she saw them all: the faintest smudge of lipstick on the edge of a handkerchief; a single strand of dark, almost black hair clinging magnetically to his shorts; a pair of theatre ticket stubs forgotten in his trousers pocket. She'd been willing to ignore the signs because the burden of his attention had shifted elsewhere, thereby relieving her of its full weight. Let some other woman lie breathless beneath his annually increasing girth. It meant less time Hadleigh had to spend being the repository for his urges. She certainly didn't mind foregoing the need to sleep on cold, slimy sheets, her thighs welded closed with the evidence of his ejaculations. She'd been willing to tolerate all sorts of things, until now. Her father's lifeless body rendered her entire existence meaningless.

She wished there were someone to grieve with her, someone who'd verify the greatness of this loss. She thought of Augusta, and knew she'd call her as soon as she got back to her mother's apartment. Augusta would understand; she was someone with a capacity for loving. She herself constantly told the twins how much she loved them, yet felt a pang when they failed to parrot her sentiments. It was ridiculous to expect children to reciprocate an emotion they accepted as their due, but of which they had no larger concept. They didn't know what love was, they merely required its constancy. They thrived on it, gobbling it up like sugar. It was a form of food to them, and they ate and ate from a never-empty bowl. She'd kept her own supply replenished from the well of her father's limitless goodness. Now the well was dry, and all at once she could feel aridity soldering her joints.

An orderly came to remove her father to the pathology laboratory. An autopsy was to be performed; a formality. As if she were invisible, the man moved around her. The concealing sheet was drawn up, then the bed was pulled out from the wall, turned and aimed at the yawning doorway. The muscles bunching in his arms and shoulders, the orderly directed the bed out through the door and away down the corridor toward the bank of elevators. Hadleigh was left alone. She went out of the room and was taken aback by the sight of her mother in conversation with one of the aides she recognized from the embassy.

Even without makeup, with her hair pinned into an untidy knot, and wearing a gray flannel skirt and a plain black cashmere pullover, Frances commanded attention. Fifty-two-years old, yet there wasn't a thing about her that indicated her history of drunken madness. She was smoking one of her brown Nat Sherman cigarettes and turning every so often to tip the ashes into a wall-mounted receptacle. She didn't look her age; she looked soberly concerned, but not grief-stricken. Yet that indefinable something still adhered to her. Perhaps it was a softening of her usually abrupt gestures.

Hadleigh looked at her mother's slim hips and shapely legs, and wanted to scream with the feeling of grossness she had at being at least twenty pounds overweight and tastelessly dressed. She hated the roll of fat around her midriff, the chunky heft of her thighs.

The aide was saying something. Frances listened. Then she spoke. It all seemed so goddamned casual that Hadleigh felt more than ever like screaming, so that she might crash through the damnable poise her mother had even when blind drunk. Hadleigh leaned against the wall, watching them, trying to understand yet again why she admired and loved this woman. Frances had never done anything to earn anyone's love. Yet Arthur had loved her, and Hadleigh did too.

The conversation ended, the official departed, and Frances

extinguished her cigarette. She turned, saw Hadleigh, and they studied each other from twenty feet apart. Hadleigh disintegrated. Her mouth fell open and tears spilled down her cheeks. Like an inquisitive bird, Frances's head dropped slightly to one side. She stood that way for several seconds, then closed the distance between them and, slipping her arm through Hadleigh's, said, "We might as well go back to the apartment. There's nothing more to be done here."

They walked together and Hadleigh was aware of their similar height, of her mother's much smaller bone structure, of the fragrance of roses; she noted her mother's aggressive strides forward and the susurrating slide of her nylon-covered thighs, the strong but not unpleasant aroma of tobacco; she was aware of her own blotchy, dishevelled state and her pathetic need to cling to an arm that didn't seem substantial enough to support her gargantuan weight.

As they waited for a taxi, Hadleigh mopped at her face with a sodden tissue. "Why do you hate me so?" she asked forlornly.

Frances's features lifted with surprise. "I don't hate you, Hadleigh. I've hated only one person in my life, and he's dead."

"I knew it!" Hadleigh wrenched herself away. "He didn't deserve to be hated."

"I am not," Frances said patiently, "referring to your father. I cared very much for Arthur."

"You did?" Hadleigh's grief cleared temporarily, as if a cloud had travelled past the sun.

"Well, of course, I did. I may be a great many things, but I'm certainly not masochistic enough to spend nearly a quarter century with someone I disliked."

The cab driver actually got out to open the passenger door. It was something that happened all the time for Frances, regardless of her condition. It had never happened for Hadleigh even once. What the hell did people *see* in this woman that even New York cab drivers, some of the rudest men alive, danced attendance on her?

Once in the back of the cab, Hadleigh had to ask, "Then why aren't you . . . Why don't you . . . ?"

"Why do you insist on believing people have reasons for everything they do? Not all of us do, Hadleigh. And your determination that we all explain ourselves endlessly is positively maddening. Since you were first able to speak in full sentences you've been demanding explanations. I am the last person on earth qualified to supply them. I do not hate you, and I did not hate your father. There were, I will admit, times when neither of our actions indicated fondness, but that happens in all marriages. No one cares for anyone *all* the time. It's not possible. It's simply not human. I have not in the past, and will never in the future, be someone to tie lavish bows on information before I pass it along. I do wish you could accept that. Matters between us would be considerably easier.''

"I'm to go along with the things you do and never question any of it. Is that it?''

Frances sighed and looked out the window. "If you will insist on coming to mad people searching for truth, it's to be expected that the answers you receive will make little, if any, sense to you. We have our own convoluted logic.''

Slowly, Hadleigh said, "I've believed for years and years now that you're not in the least little bit mad, that it's something you perform at.''

Frances swivelled around to confront her. "How frightfully clever of you!'' she exclaimed, looking pleased. "You may very well have hit upon a significant truth.''

This declaration muddied Hadleigh's thoughts. It was her turn to look away, thinking as she did that it was impossible. She and this woman could never be close. What lay between them was a wasteland of unendurable dimensions. It was startling, then, when Frances's hand fell lightly on her wrist, and she said, "It may not be worth the effort, Haddy. Why not give it up as a bad lot and get on with your life? I'm no one's idea of a mother, least of all my own. It is possible that one day we'll meet on a more equal footing, without the weight of ancient history bearing down on us.''

"I don't see why it can't be now,'' Hadleigh pleaded, longing to be able to tell about the shambles her life had become.

Frances withdrew her hand. "This is the last answer I'm going to give today,'' she said. "It is because I'm having a crucial debate just now about whether or not to drink myself into permanent oblivion. The difficulty, you see, is that I alone would have to take full charge of the situation, and I don't care for that thought at all. I'm going to have to plan very carefully for what comes next.''

Hadleigh simply had to see how her mother looked saying this, and shifted to find Frances staring straight ahead. She did indeed seem deeply involved in her admittedly convoluted thought processes. I could never count on you, Hadleigh thought, stricken anew. Not ever, not for anything.

"Oh, God!" she said, and took hold of her mother's hand.

Twenty

Throughout the service, and the interment after, when people came forward to express their condolences, Hadleigh could respond only with movements of her head. Speech was impossible. Her throat and facial muscles were at work stoppering her tears.

Chris was impatient, embarrassed by his wife's grief and, for once, preferred the company of his mother-in-law who was handling the proceedings with laudable self-control. Augusta had volunteered to stay with the twins once it had been decided they would not attend. Hadleigh had wanted them to come, believing it was their right to say goodbye, in whatever fashion, to their grandfather, but Chris had been adamant. "It's goddamned morbid of you to want them there! They're too young to know what it's all about. It'd probably just scare the hell out of them, especially with you carrying on the way you are."

She'd wanted to lash out, to beat him with her fists for his lack of sensitivity, but she'd been immobilized by her grief. She was also dismayed by this further evidence of his absence of feelings for her. They remained strangers, as unfamiliar to one another as they'd been on the day they'd married.

It was Elmo who seemed best to understand her pain. He materialized at her side as people began leaving the cemetery and took hold of her hand, saying, "I'm really sorry, Haddy. I know how close you were to your dad. When my mother died

237

a couple of years ago it was about the worst I've ever felt. I still can't believe she's gone.''

She wanted to thank him but couldn't form the words. Instead, she hooked her arm around his neck and embraced him. His body felt alien, a complete contrast to that of her husband's. Elmo was taller and thinner. She was oddly comforted by the smell of pipe tobacco that lay deep within the fibers of his clothing, and the summery scent to his hair that reminded her of her son. The embrace lasted longer than she'd expected, but his sympathy was so welcome she was reluctant to be separated from him.

"It takes a long time to get used to the fact that they're not around anymore." He had hold again of her hand and was looking directly into her overflowing eyes. "If there's anything I can do, let me know." He almost started to tell her that he'd always thought she'd made the worst possible mistake in marrying Chris, but managed to stop himself from uttering something so inappropriate to the occasion.

"Are you coming back to the apartment?" she asked. "Or do you have to get back to New Haven?" She knew he was halfway to his doctorate and teaching part-time to subsidize his degree.

"I don't have to get back right away."

"Then come with us," she asked. "I know Chris would like it."

"I'll do it for you," he said. "I don't think Chris gives a damn one way or another."

"Is it that obvious?" she asked fearfully, shamed to think that all the people here could see so clearly that she was married to someone so unfeeling.

"Only if you happen to know him," he told her, as they started across the grass toward the row of waiting limousines.

She looked ahead to where Chris was holding open the door as her mother climbed into the rear of the lead limo. "Will you ride with me, Elmo?"

"If you like. I kind of tagged along out here with some people I don't know. I came down on the train this morning."

Sheffie broke the silence on the ride into the city to ask, "D'you mind if I light up?"

"Not at all. I've always enjoyed the aroma of your tobacco."

He proceeded to push the bowl of his pipe full of tobacco, then got it lit with a wooden kitchen match. She breathed in the sweet density of the smoke appreciatively, asking, "Why did you come today?"

"Out of respect," he answered. "When I read the obituary in the *Times* I knew I had to come. I liked your dad, the few times I met him. He never seemed to me to be out to prove anything, and he never patronized me. We talked a couple of times about the war, and Churchill, about the work he'd done. He was very well informed, and kind of reminded me of my grandfather, who was English, too. He had the same sort of bearing, the same kinds of attitudes. I've always been an admitted Anglophile. As a matter of fact, I'm hoping to take three months in England when it comes time to research my dissertation."

"I really thought you came because of Chris."

"No. It was because of you."

"It's very good of you."

"It's pretty selfish of me, actually. It was a chance to see you, even if the circumstances weren't what either of us would have preferred. Where are the twins?"

"At home. Chris thought it best if they didn't come."

"Oh!" His expression didn't alter, but her impression of his dislike of Chris was growing.

"Have you and Chris had a falling out?" she asked.

"No. Why do you ask?"

"I think perhaps I've assumed you were better friends than you are."

He smiled around the pipe stem, the fingers of his left hand propping up the bowl. "Assumptions can be dangerous," he said. "We've been acquaintances a very long time, but according to my definition of it, I don't think we've ever been friends. Augusta and I are friends. You and I have more of a friendship than anything I've ever had with Chris. I'm not even sure he actually *has* friends. Does he?"

"Oh, I'm sure he must. But how can you consider the two of us friends when we don't see each other more than three or four times a year?"

"Time's not the quotient. It's content. Chris is okay, as far as he goes. I personally happen to prefer people who go just a little further than that. As a topic of conversation, money has its limitations. I tend to get a little bored watching someone get ecstatic over some company that's about to go public. I'm sorry. I shouldn't be saying any of this to you now. It's hardly the right time."

"It might be the only right time," she disagreed. "In another ten minutes we'll be at my mother's apartment with masses of people on all sides wanting to tell me how sorry they are, when they have no idea how it feels to know I'll never see my father again. I *want* to have this conversation. It seems as if it's been years since anyone actually spoke to me. Please tell me why you think what you do."

"Oh, a lot of reasons. Some of it has to do with the nature of acquisition and the majority's hunger for it, and Chris's position smack in the middle of the majority. And some of it has to do with the fact that I've always wondered why you married him."

"But I was . . ."

"I know that," he interrupted. "But you went ahead with it. You didn't have to. Your dad and I talked at the wedding. He'd have stood by you, if he'd known. He didn't know, did he?"

"No."

"I didn't think so. *We* all knew. That crowd," he went off tangentially, "they were such cookie-cutter kids. Augusta was, is, different. And so were you. The rest of them were jokers, following their fathers from Choate or St. Paul's into Yale—or their mothers from Miss Porter's to Vassar—to get their pieces of paper so they could keep on following down to Wall Street or to the family insurance brokerage in Hartford. I used to sit and listen to them with my eyes closed and I couldn't distinguish their voices, one from the other. They all sounded the same, had the same silly interests, the same rabid passion for money." He paused to take a breath, then recovered his original track. "One thing I'll say for Chris, at least he did the right thing."

"You think so?"

"I would've been willing to bet anything that he'd find some way out. I'm sorry, Haddy. I'm way out of line."

"It's all right. I'm simply not clear on *why* you're saying all this now."

"Maybe I'm only defending my own position," he thought

aloud, "protecting my right to live differently, be different. Sometimes it comes to that. Going after an academic life tends to cast a lot of doubt on you. After all, you're passing up opportunities you ought to be grabbing with both hands, and there's something mighty peculiar about that, about you, for letting less-than-tangible values take precedence in your life."

"I wanted to be an architect. Did you know that? I did. Now I spend my time thinking about dollhouses. I've even started constructing one. I expect it's the closest I'll ever come to creating a real house. I used to draw rather well as a child."

"D'you still do it?"

"Not for years. Once or twice, I've tried. It's completely gone."

"You might get it back."

"No," she said. "I don't think so."

They were in the city now. A few more minutes and they'd be on Central Park West.

"Will you come to visit again soon?" she asked.

"We'll stay in touch, I promise."

"Thank you for talking with me, Elmo."

"I'll be around, and you've got my number."

"Yes, I do."

"I meant what I said. If I can help, in any way, just let me know."

The car had pulled up in front of the apartment building and Hadleigh had become visibly distracted. She was ready to leave the car even before the driver had come round to open her door. Elmo was tempted to tell her how well she looked, how the black garments highlighted her fair hair and lovely complexion. He said nothing, just walked along at her side into the building.

Once upstairs, enisled in the inflowing tide of mourners, Hadleigh struck him as both sad and desirable. He wished it were possible to take her somewhere and make love to her. He didn't believe anyone had ever delved beneath her surface, and he'd have liked to try. But more would be required than a few hours of naked investigation, and the most he could offer her was temporary consolation that would, without question, further complicate her life. He watched her listen to the people who ebbed and flowed around her, touched by how young she seemed. Chris was intentionally keeping well away from her, as if her ability to grieve was a form of cancer he might contract.

"Why is it," a voice close by suddenly asked him, "you are forever on the outside, watching all of us?"

"I'm at my best on the outside," he answered readily.

"And why is that?"

"Because I'm free to observe without involvement. I don't have to participate if I don't choose to, but I like to see what's going on."

"Fascinating. A question?"

"Sure."

"Do you find me attractive?"

"Oh, very," he said without hesitation.

"Really? That *is* gratifying. You don't consider my somewhat advanced age repelling?"

"Not if you don't find my relative youth repelling."

"You're very fond of my daughter, aren't you?"

"Yes, I am."

"She's married to a dolt. But then you know that, don't you?"

"Yes, I do."

"Quite an exceptional number of people here, wouldn't you say?"

"It's quite a crowd," he agreed.

"It's not likely anyone would notice a brief absence."

"Not very."

"Would you, in that case, be interested in a few minutes' private conversation?"

"It's not conversation you're suggesting, is it, Mrs. Holden?"

"I do admire your directness. It wasn't precisely what I had in mind, no."

"D'you think this is the right time for what you have in mind?"

"Most definitely. I'd consider it an enormous favor, actually."

"Favor's kind of demeaning. To you, I mean. You know, don't you, that I'm more than fond of Hadleigh?"

"This hasn't anything to do with her. Or with you, for that matter. It's not as if I'm proposing taking from her something she already has."

"That's true," he allowed.

"There is rather a large dressing room off the master bedroom, with a door that locks. It's not difficult to find."

A slight backwash of air indicated she'd moved away. He remained where he was, deliberating. He hadn't lied about finding her attractive. There was about her an aura of aloofness combined with sexuality that defied her years and his ability to ignore it.

He simply backed through the archway where he'd been standing and ducked down the corridor to the bedroom. The dressing room was to the left and he went across the thick carpet, cracked open the door, then slipped inside.

Her body had a certain softness that belied her age but she was astonishingly limber. When it was ended and they were collecting their clothes in the dark, she said, "I'd like you to understand that this was something of a farewell for me. In my own fashion, I was honoring what is gone for all time and can never again be duplicated. We each have ways of burying our dead. I'd appreciate it if you'd try not to judge any of this."

"Maybe, when I'm in town . . ."

Her hand touched against his mouth. "If you are in town, and you still find me attractive, Mr. Sheffield, I very much doubt I'll be unavailable." Her mouth replaced her hand just for a moment, and then she was gone. The door quickly opened and closed, and he was left with the impression of her lips moving against his.

"I really can't stay," Hadleigh said. "I want to go home, see the twins. Mrs. Walsh is here. Will you be all right?"

"Go home," Frances told her. "I'll be perfectly all right. I have no intention of drinking other people's leavings. There are things I must think about. Ring me, if you like."

Chris was waiting near the door, looking pointedly at his watch. Hadleigh glanced over at him, then turned back to her mother. "If you'd prefer me to stay . . ."

"Hadleigh, go home! Your husband's about as subtle as a ticking bomb, and the caterers are anxious to clear up. I intend to go directly to bed. There's no need for you to stay."

"Hadleigh!" Chris had the door open.

She lingered, hoping her mother would say something of

significance, something that would memorialize this day. A strand of her hair had come free, and Hadleigh wanted to fix it. But even as she thought of it, her mother's hand rose, she pulled a pin from the back of her head, swept back the escaped bit and pinned it into place. There really wasn't anything Hadleigh could do.

"*You can talk to your mother on the phone!*" Chris bellowed. "Can we *please* get going?"

Frances was about to intercede on her daughter's behalf when Hadleigh whirled around, and shouted, "*Get the bloody car!* I'll be along in a moment."

He flung open the door and stalked off.

"He has no feeling for occasion, does he?" Frances observed. "Extraordinary, isn't it, how unaffected by others some people are? I can't think why, or how, you live with him."

"He's my husband," Hadleigh said defeatedly.

"That doesn't preclude one's having other options. Do go along! He's really very cross, and you've an hour's drive ahead of you."

Hadleigh no longer wanted to go. If her mother said anything at all of importance, she thought she might just sit down and never leave. She tried to think of some statement that would inspire Frances to commit herself, but all she could think to say was, "I can't believe Daddy's gone, that I'll never see him again."

To her horror, Frances became livid. "Why is it," she demanded, "all your sentiments are couched in terms of your own precious store of emotions? My husband dropped dead a few days ago. I'm sorry you've lost your father, Hadleigh, but I'm infinitely more concerned just now with my own losses. Go home! I'm not up to this. I'm truly not. You have that boorish, incipient tycoon and two children to console you. I have the option of inebriation, should I care to avail myself of it. I don't wish to do that. For the first time in years, I would prefer to go to bed sober and spend my energy trying to decide what I'm going to do with the rest of my life. You keep changing your mind, deciding first you must go, then looking to me to make the decision that you should stop here. I know you want me to say I'd like you to remain here, but I simply cannot do it. *I'm not responsible*," she said hoarsely. "You *must* decide for *yourself!*'' As if hearing how close she sounded to hysteria, she brought her voice down. ''Please go along now. Life goes on, unless we actively seek to end it, and, inevitably, we get through the nights and find some way or other to muddle through the days. *Every one of us is alone.*''

Hadleigh gulped down a mouthful of air and ran off, leaving the door open. Allowing her spine to relax, Frances walked across the foyer to close it. ''Bloody hell!'' she murmured, leaning for a moment against the door.

Mrs. Walsh was working with the catering team, muttering under her breath as she collected glasses.

''Will you be staying on?'' Frances asked her, adding several glasses to the tray.

''Not if you're gonna get pissed every night, I'm not.''

''And if I'm sober?''

''I fancy I'll continue. I'm just warning you, though. I've 'ad it with all the nonsense. You want a 'ousekeeper, that's lovely. I don't mind at all, but I'm too old to be babysittin' a middle-aged widow. I'm one of those my bloody self!''

Frances laughed. ''I do enjoy you, Emma. I'd like it if you'd stay.''

''Right you are, then. Leave this lot. I'll see to the clearing up.''

''Thank you.'' Frances placed the last of the glasses on the tray, then went to the bedroom.

On the dressing room floor, she found Elmo's pipe and stood holding it for some time before placing it in the drawer of her bedside table. He'd come back for it.

Hadleigh felt doubly betrayed—by her father's too sudden death, and by her mother's refusal to capitulate and come close. Much of what Frances had said made her feel limited and stupid, as if she were suffering from some form of retardation so rarefied that it was detectable only by someone with privileged information. And that someone was Frances. She couldn't argue the truth or falsity of her mother's declarations because she was unable to make the distinction. She felt reduced by each failed attempt to infiltrate her mother's clever armor, and had no idea why she kept on trying, when every successive foray left her battle-fatigued and scarred.

She and Chris drove home to Greenwich without exchanging a single word. He was furious. She had no idea why, and lacked the desire to find out. She hated him for neglecting to show her the sympathy she needed, as well as for the flagrantly mounting evidence of his extramarital activities. The only person who'd been kind was Elmo, and he'd left without saying goodbye. Or perhaps he had, and she'd failed to notice. She'd accepted several glasses of white wine from the trays being offered around by one of the catering staff, and the wine had blunted the edges of her grief. It was the first time in her adult life she was able to see clearly the purpose alcohol might have. It was effective in creating a barrier between one's self and the world, behind which one could hide in plain view. The wine had made everything look less crisp, less angular. With muted vision, the occasion had, temporarily, been almost pleasant. Chris and her mother had brought her brutally to earth, and resentment buzzed in her ears and clutched at the vertebrae in her neck, causing her head to ache.

They arrived home to find Augusta waiting, her bag packed.

"I'm glad you decided to come back after all," she told them frantically. "My mother's just given the heave to number three and wants me home to console her." She smiled sheepishly. "I'm sorry to run off on you, but she really sounds miserable."

Hadleigh walked out with her to her car and stood with her hand on the front fender as Augusta tossed her bag into the back seat. "Thank you for staying. Did the twins behave?"

"They were fine. We had a picnic in the living room, so don't have a fit if you're up to your knees in crumbs. How did it go?"

"It went. Elmo was there. Will you be able to come at the weekend?"

"I'll have to let you know. Number three's lasted longer than the other two, and she's really mad because she was the one who dumped numbers one and two, but this time she got dumped. He's moved in with his twenty-two-year-old secretary. I mean, for God's sake! The man's almost sixty. It's just puke-provoking! I'll call you as soon as I can, but I can't promise when that'll be. I'm months behind on my final paper and if I don't get it done, they'll never let me leave Sarah goddamned Lawrence."

They hugged, then Augusta asked, "Are you okay? You look kind of . . . I don't know."

"I'm fine. Drive carefully."

"This is such a pain in the ass. I swear to God I'll *never* get married. It just doesn't work. Ask my mother if it works!"

Her tires spitting gravel, she reversed, then drove off. Hadleigh turned to look at the house, overwhelmed by apprehension. The two-story white clapboard house with the mint-green shutters and black front door seemed menacing; the coach lamps flanking the front door looked like gaping eyes. Feeling a thousand years old, she made her way to the door. She was twenty-three. Inside, waiting for her, was her twenty-six-year-old husband who, in all likelihood, was sleeping with *his* twenty-two-year-old secretary.

Chris was in the kitchen making himself a sandwich. She put on the kettle for tea, then watched him consume the sandwich while he stood with one hand braced against the refrigerator door.

Mouth full, he complained, "The longest goddamn day of my entire life! There must've been two hundred people there."

"My father had many, many friends."

"Jesus! You're not going to start up again!"

"No." She cleared her throat and directed her eyes to the countertop which was a collage of globules of jelly, smears of peanut butter, and scatterings of bread crumbs. The sink was crowded with dirty dishes and the linoleum floor had a visible path from the back door to the interior door. Changing her mind about the tea, she turned off the burner beneath the kettle and started the water going as she shifted dishes to clear one of the sinks.

"Why don't you leave all that for the cleaning lady?" he asked, drinking milk directly from the bottle, a habit of his that sickened her.

"She's not due for another two days. It'll only take a few minutes."

"I'm going to bed. I've got to work tomorrow."

He returned the bottle to the refrigerator, slammed shut the door, and left, saying, "Don't forget to lock up!"

She opened the refrigerator, got the bottle and poured its contents down the sink. She hated him. She couldn't believe he didn't feel it. The vapors of her hatred floated on the air, and sent invisible needles through his temples, poured scalding oil into his ears. Why, when they'd agreed to marry, hadn't it occurred to her that it was to be a life sentence? She'd thought only of the immediate problem and its need for a solution. She'd never seriously considered what it would be like to live day after day, for years, with someone who had come to represent everything she disliked. He was callous, self-centered, superficial, greedy, and a disinterested father. And the natty-dressing, duplicitous son of a bitch was going to want to push himself inside her as soon as she got to bed, to prove, once again, that it was he who held the reins and she who'd agreed publicly to obey.

Before going upstairs, she invaded his liquor supply, gulping down two burning mouthfuls of neat gin. Fortified, she headed toward the stairs.

Twenty-one

Hadleigh turned to the creation of dollhouses. The first one—completed some months after her father's death—was carted off at once to the attic by the twins who spent the entire summer furnishing the many small rooms with pieces made from old gift boxes, matchboxes, parts of broken toys, and small celluloid dolls Hadleigh found in a five and dime store. To her mind, the house was too crude; it lacked precision and, more importantly, charm. And so, before starting another, she made a cardboard model to scale, using those evenings when Chris stayed in the city to cut each piece with the aid of a mat knife and set square. Sitting in the kitchen surrounded by pots of glue, large pieces of cardboard, pencils, scissors, and a cutting board, she painstakingly assembled the model. Then, having studied it from all angles, she made certain modifications in the doors and windows, in the placement of the interior stairways and retaining walls, in the pitch of the roof. Finally, satisfied, she took it all apart and, using the parts of the model as patterns, she began cutting plywood to size.

With the radio for company, the children in bed for the night, she worked until her eyes itched and her back ached. Then she stored her supplies in the pantry, poured herself a drink from the bottle she'd bought in the liquor store next door to the supermarket, and wandered through the house, listening to the variations in tone of her footfalls as she moved from linoleum, to hardwood, to carpet. Stopping here and there, she admired the gracious dimensions of the house, the quality of the workmanship and materials, the soundness of its structure. She thought often how wonderful it would be if Chris one day decided never again to return home. She'd be more than content to stay in this house with the children, working on her models, and simply existing. In the warmer weather, she spent her days in the garden, refining the beds, dragging rocks from one place to another to situate them with more precise appeal. She shopped for food, delivered the children to the houses of their friends, had an occasional cup of coffee with another mother, and tried not to think at all. Augusta's visits gradually grew less frequent, probably, Hadleigh reasoned, because she'd all but given up telephoning anyone and Augusta likely felt she'd done her fair share of keeping in touch; if Hadleigh wanted to see her, all she had to do was call her. Elmo telephoned from time to time, to talk for five or ten minutes, but he, too, rarely visited. As for Frances, Hadleigh spoke with her weekly, reporting on the children and their activities or accomplishments. Of herself, Hadleigh volunteered nothing. Frances seemed disinclined to press. The calls were a formality, Hadleigh believed, something Frances did to ease her conscience. If Frances hadn't called, Hadleigh doubted they'd ever have spoken to each other. It seemed, at last, they'd nothing left to say to one another.

The children turned five almost a year to the day of Arthur's death, and went off the following September to attend kindergarten half-days. Hadleigh felt some sort of linchpin had been pulled from the wheel of her personal machinery. From eight-thirty in the morning when they climbed onto the yellow school bus until one in the afternoon when another bus deposited them at the foot of the driveway, she hurried through the bedmaking, the laundry, and the preparation of meals only to find herself unable to fill out the hours. Chris had given in to her request for a deep-freeze, and in a matter of weeks she'd crammed it full with pies, and casseroles, and cuts of meat she'd bought on special.

When Augusta or Elmo would take the impetus and come crashing through the silence to announce their intended arrival for a weekend, she'd prepare lavish meals; she'd put fresh-cut flowers in their rooms and crisp, carefully ironed linens on the beds. She left an ashtray for Elmo, a carafe of water and a box of biscuits for Augusta who liked a snack before bed. When one or both of them came, she felt heady with her capacity for nurturing, eager to have them bask in the luxurious perfection of her caretaking.

After three months of interviews, the best job Augusta was able to land was as a script reader for the Manhattan offices of a Los Angeles-based film production company.

"The worst garbage you've ever seen," she moaned, slogging her way through a minimum of a half dozen scripts each visit. "*I* could write something more intelligent than this crap, *if* I were interested, which I definitely am not. I'm supposed to be prime editorial candidate number one, not the eyes and judgment of a bunch of thugs who wouldn't know correct English on their best day." Her plan was to put in sufficient time to garner a reference, then go after an editing job with a good publishing house.

Elmo had completed his doctorate without taking the trip to England. He still mentioned the possibility of going one day, but the plan had been temporarily shelved. He was angling for a full-time teaching position at Yale but in the meantime continued to lecture part-time and supplemented his income waiting tables at Mory's.

"The cookie-cutter kids just keep on rolling in," he said privately to Hadleigh. "It's as if they're specially bred in hatcheries, à la Huxley, for the sole purpose of stumbling through prep school, and then Yale, so they'll be able to point out their initials carved here, there, and everywhere, and their chunky-faced portraits in full hockey gear on the walls at Mory's. I think I'm going to switch over to a pizza parlor. I can't take many more little lost lambs bleating over their beers."

On weekends when Elmo was the only guest, she toured the house imagining she might encounter him in one of the rooms, and how they would embrace with guilty haste. It never happened, but knowing he slept nearby made her feel less of a phantom. He was good with the children, too, joining them in lengthy games of Monopoly or Snakes and Ladders, or improvising plays in which everyone was given an identity appropriate to some historical occasion. They acted out the signing of the Magna Carta, and the formation of the Round Table; they played General Custer and the conquering Indians; the twins performed their favorite Kipling stories, with Elmo prompting from the sidelines.

From moment to moment during these performances, Hadleigh would feel herself swell with heady pleasure as she transposed Chris and Elmo. Elmo was so engagingly inventive with the twins, so interested in the interpretations they offered for his stories. Even Augusta fell in wholeheartedly, emoting her assigned roles with much tossing of her long auburn hair and waving of her arms. Hadleigh thought it might be possible to sustain the life she and Chris led here if only Sheffie and Augusta could always be counted on to be present. But they'd leave on Sunday, and she'd forget to get in touch with them, and it would be weeks before one or the other of them got around to calling.

During his nights in the house, Elmo listened to Hadleigh's steps as she roved about, and fought his recurring impulse to creep down the stairs and surprise her. As long as he continued his involvement with Frances, Hadleigh remained off-limits. He'd long-since discounted Chris and would have had no compunction whatever about sleeping with his wife. What held him back, aside from his affair with Frances, was his certain knowledge that Haddy would expect him to assume Chris's role as head of the family. And, as much as he liked the children and desired their mother, he had no interest in taking over as a replacement for Chris. He could see the deterioration of the marriage. It was hard to overlook. Chris and Haddy seldom spoke directly to one another. When they did, their conversations had to do with the children, or the house, or one of the cars. They were perfectly polite, superb hosts, and worked together by rote. It was dreadful, and with each visit, Elmo could see the chasm widening between the two of them. The children were beginning to see it as well, and offered casual explanations for the wedges of silence that inserted themselves into the dinner table conversation.

At work on one of the skits, Ben was overheard by Elmo to say, "They had another fight. They're not talking." Or Bonita, clambering into Elmo's lap with a storybook, would whisper, "Mummy's in her bathroom, crying. Daddy was mean." He tried to jolly them away from their somber journalism with distracting anecdotes, but he couldn't always avert the spillover of their parents' anger from falling directly onto the heads of the twins. Having been rebuked by Chris, Hadleigh would snap at the children for some imagined misdeed. The children would argue the unfairness of it and then Chris, his temper frayed, would dictate the terms of unwarranted punishment for their having dared to protest.

Worst of all were those Friday evenings when Elmo arrived to find Haddy flushed with the good humor generated by a solid day's slow drinking. Initially, it happened once in a rare while, but in less than a year, she was greeting him almost every time with effusive alcohol-inspired warmth.

"She's developing a real problem," Augusta said worriedly one evening that winter. "With the kids in school all day now she says she doesn't have enough to do. I know she starts drinking by ten in the morning. When I tried to say something, she had her excuses all ready. Remember the way her mother used to be? The way she was at Haddy's wedding?"

"I remember."

"I'd hate to see Haddy go that same route, spending half her time sucking a bottle and the other half in some fancy drunk farm getting dried out. Maybe you could talk to her."

"What would you suggest I say?" he asked, the words sounding colder than he'd intended. He felt she was pushing him into a potentially dangerous situation, involved as he was with both mother and daughter.

"Oh, that's very nice," she said sourly. "You're supposed to be a friend. Can't you think of something?"

"The only thing I can think of to do for Hadleigh would just create more problems."

"And what would that be?"

"I could take her to bed."

"Jesus! That's crude. Why is it men always think that's the only thing that'll set a woman straight, that it's the only thing any woman really needs?"

"I don't happen to subscribe to the idea as a general rule. I just think it in this case."

"Why? Are you in love with her?"

"I don't know how to answer that. I care a lot about her. I always have. I do know I don't want to take everyone on. If it was Hadleigh on her own, I'd be glad to jump right in with both feet. But I'm in no position to do battle with Chris, or to slide into the role of father to two six-year-olds. Don't look at me that way! You asked me a question and I'm trying to answer it."

"You stink, Sheffield!"

"You know I don't. I don't know why the truth always makes people so angry."

"Maybe because your truth happens to have such a personal

bias to it. Nobody's suggesting you have to move in and start running things. I just asked you to try to talk to her."

"I'll try. All right? But don't hold it against me if I don't get anywhere. People who drink tend to have hearing problems."

"Well, well, well! When did you get so smug and self-righteous? When did you decide your shit don't smell, bud?"

"And who appointed you Haddy's official guardian? And what makes you think *anybody's* words will work miracles? Chris has a girlfriend in the city, and it's not his first. And Hadleigh may not say anything, but she damned well knows about it. The kids don't know what the hell's going on, and their mother's started drinking in a big way. I haven't told you one damned thing you don't already know, so, please, don't try to pile a load of guilt on my shoulders just because I show up regularly and happen to consider the woman a friend."

"You know something?" Augusta narrowed her eyes. "People who claim to be friends do more than just 'show up regularly,' Sheffield. They get involved and they don't always take the easy way out. I used to think you were kind of a swell guy, quiet but nice; somebody who actually had a functioning brain. Now, all of a sudden, I don't think you're all that nice. In fact, I think you're nothing more than a goddamned freeloader. You come here for free weekend vacations with the best to eat and drink. And all you have to do in return is play with the kids for a couple of hours, say 'thank you' politely, then take yourself back to New Haven. Do me a favor and let me know next time you're planning to be here. I'll make it a point to stay away that weekend." She raced off up the stairs to her room.

"Augusta and I had kind of an argument," he told Hadleigh on his next visit, a month later. "That's why she didn't come this weekend. I thought it only fair to tell you she's staying away because of me."

"But why?"

"Because she wanted me to talk to you about your drinking and I said I didn't think it'd do much good."

"My drinking? What about it?"

"Has it ever occurred to you," he asked her, "that you started drinking right about the time your mother quit? Have you ever thought of that?"

She laughed, as if listening to a foolish child. "I can take it or leave it. There are days on end when I don't drink at all. Are you trying to imply I'm like my mother?"

"I might as well leap in with both feet," he said, squaring his shoulders. "I'll tell you how it looks to me. Okay? You people have a chain-of-command shouting order around here. Chris fights with you, then you fight with the kids. The kids don't like it and say so, then Chris jumps in and orders them up to their rooms for talking back. Why don't the two of you get a divorce and stop all this? The kids are getting hurt, and so are you."

"Chris would never divorce me."

"Don't kid yourself! As soon as he thinks the time is right, he'll be out of here like a shot. Come on, Haddy! Pull the rug out from under him and get yourself a divorce!"

She was shaking her head. "It was so good to have something to look forward to, with you and Augusta coming for weekends. All those super games, and the plays you staged, and the lovely talks we'd have. We'll never be able to have that again. Why did you have to spoil everything?"

"I'm not trying to spoil anything," he said, wishing he'd taken his own advice and stayed out of this. "I want to help. I guess I thought maybe I could shock you into taking some kind of action before it's too late. I love coming to visit, being with you and the kids. I love *you*, for chrissake!"

"Do you?" she asked, softening.

"Of course I do. As a friend. And as a friend, I want to see you happy." It was all going wrong, he thought wretchedly, and going more wrong with every additional word he spoke.

Her eyes slid away from him. "You think I'm a drunk," she said, "but I can do without it. I don't have to have it."

"Start some kind of business," he suggested. "Get into something you enjoy. You can't sit here all day long doing nothing, then spend every night wandering around the house, drinking."

From her neck to her hairline her features took on a deep-rose hue. "How do you know that?" she asked in a whisper.

"I've heard you," he admitted. "I like to read before I go to sleep. I've heard you walking from room to room."

"Why didn't you come down?" she asked soulfully.

"I couldn't."

"Why?"

"Because I can't give you what you need."

"How do you know that?"

"I know it. My making love to you wouldn't solve any problems. It would just create more. I couldn't, Haddy. The timing's all wrong."

"When will it be right?" she wanted to know.

"Maybe never. Look at this place! Think about the kind of money it takes to keep a house like this running. And the kids. I can't do it. I don't want to be anyone's husband or father, and you could never cope with something on the side."

"I've coped for *years* with 'something on the side'!"

"It's not the same thing. You're not the one setting up the times and places, the one who's always checking to make sure there's no one who knows you in the restaurant or hotel. It takes a strong stomach and a stronger ego to carry it off, and you're not equipped for that kind of thing. You need the traditional trappings, the security, the family dinners, and everything else that goes along with having had money all your life."

"You see," she said almost inaudibly. "I'm not at all like my mother."

He was suddenly afraid he'd gone too far, tipped his hand. "Meaning?" he asked fearfully.

"For years we'd get telephone calls from strange people saying my mother had asked them to ring up and let us know where she was, and would we please come collect her."

"Oh!" Relief pounded through his system. "She didn't know what she was doing."

"She knew *exactly* what she was doing. And that, you see, Elmo, is the difference between us. I've *never* known what I was doing. I keep expecting I'll wake up one morning and suddenly everything will make perfect sense. It may never happen. I think perhaps it might be best if you didn't stay the night after all. I've got a headache."

"Don't cut me out, Hadleigh. I'm only trying to help."

"Shall I tell you something funny, Elmo?" She gave him a strange, distorted smile. "It really is terribly funny. I'm sure you'll see the humor in it. For all this talk of making love, the truth is I don't care for sex at all. I never have. I was willing, though, to try it with you. I find that very funny. Don't you?" The smile held a moment longer, then she got up and left him sitting alone.

After her talk with Elmo, her single purpose became remaining sober until the children were put to bed at night. The unfinished dollhouse sat in pieces in the pantry where she came to stare at it from time to time as if it were a portion of an archeological dig. Her life was a barren place to which she added a looping voice-track of remembered dialogues. She couldn't think of anything positive in her life, and wondered if the kindest service she could perform would be to end it. Chris would be glad, and the children would recover rapidly, once past their initial shock. She couldn't decide on the best method, though, and gave up her late-night travels to sit in the kitchen considering all the alternatives, rejecting those too painful or too messy. Ideally, she'd have preferred simple disappearance, but she knew leaving the scene of her present unhappiness wouldn't put a stop to it.

She lacked the drive to do anything more than maintain the house and keep Chris and the twins in clean clothes, with clean sheets on their beds, and their breakfast and dinner on the table. Food no longer had any appeal and she served herself ever-smaller portions, watching with interest as her family consumed what she'd provided. Their eating habits were most intriguing, especially Chris's. He ate like a robot, delivering food to his mouth, chewing until it was gone, then taking in more. True to her perception of him, he took in everything but gave nothing out, except ever-larger measures of anger.

He arrived home from the city one evening, dropped his coat and briefcase in the front hall, stalked through to the kitchen where she was at the stove and, without any warning, hit her quickly and furiously half a dozen times before dropping his arms.

Momentarily oblivious to the pain, utterly bewildered and instantly guilty, she asked, "What have I done?"

"*I'm sick of you!*" he shouted. "You'd better start shaping up or you'll be damned sorry."

"I don't know what you mean," she said, daring to touch her fingertips to her battered face. "What's wrong, Chris? What's happened?"

"*You're* what's wrong! And I'm warning you, I'm not going to put up with much more of this!" He stomped out, cursing under his breath.

Not knowing what else to do, she turned back to the stove, automatically stirring one of the pots. It was several minutes before what he'd done impacted on her and she began to tremble, tears splattering from her eyes. She'd purposely stayed away from the gin all day. The laundry was done, and she'd even prepared one of his favorite meals. Why was he so outraged?

At dinner, in front of the children, they both pretended that nothing had happened. In bed he heaved himself over on top of her in his usual fashion. The only difference was that he kept his head averted, as if pretending she was someone else. After he'd finished, she put her hand on his shoulder, asking, "Will you talk to me, tell me what the matter is?"

He shrugged her off. "Go see someone!" he told her. "See your doctor or somebody and get yourself pulled together. You're turning into your goddamned mother and I have no intention of going through the kind of crap your father had to."

She went to see their family doctor in Old Greenwich who, upon hearing how frequently agitated she felt, prescribed Equanil.

"What will that do?" she asked, watching him write out the prescription.

"Calm you down," he answered. "If this doesn't help, come see me again, and we'll try something else."

The pills made it hard for her to function. Even the slightest physical effort seemed too strenuous. After the children left for school in the morning, she'd sit in the kitchen drinking coffee, trying to rouse herself. She'd sit there and somehow it would get to be noon. By two in the afternoon she was rushing, with wildly pounding heart, to set the house to rights and see about dinner, in a fever of anxiety, and in defiance of her body's preferences. She made another appointment with the doctor who, upon hearing of the effects of the medication, decided to try for something that wouldn't make her quite so lethargic, something that would help maintain her energy level.

The new prescription energized her so thoroughly that she couldn't sleep at night without the help of several drinks. After a few weeks of this, she decided to try alternating her medications, using one prescription to combat the effects of the other. She felt physically as if she were inhabited by two vastly different populations, one that was sluggish and dozy; the other was constantly on the rampage, seeking to oust the laggards.

On the second occasion when Chris arrived home and went directly to the kitchen and began hitting her, he failed to notice the twins in the corner at the table. Bonnie leaped up screaming and tried to insinuate herself between her parents. Ben watched open-mouthed, reaching out automatically to lift the receiver when the telephone rang.

"What *is* all that racket?" Frances asked him.

"Daddy's hitting Mommy," he told her, "and Bonnie can't make him stop."

Frances threw down the telephone, then snatched it up again to call the limousine service. Just over an hour later she marched through the front door without ringing the bell, went straight to the dining room where four faces turned in unison toward her, and came to a halt in front of her son-in-law.

"I understand you've taken to using your fists on my daughter." She glanced over at Hadleigh's bruised and swollen face for confirmation. Hadleigh lowered her eyes and covered her face with both hands. "I'm here to tell you that if I learn you've raised your hand to her ever again you will regret it for the rest of your life. Do you understand?"

"Now wait just a minute . . ." He half-rose out of his chair.

With the strength of one hand, Frances shoved him back down.

"Don't say a word!" she cautioned. "I'm taking the children back with me to the city for the next few days. Go collect what you need!" she told the twins who at once ran off to their rooms. "You," she pointed one long finger at Chris, "are a walking, talking obscenity. There are parking lot attendants and cinema ushers with more to recommend them. Elevator operators, construction workers. All sorts of people with far more decency than you'll ever possess. But it happens my daughter elected to marry you, you dreary little overpaid clerk! *No one strikes my child!* Be very careful, young man, or I will do everything in my power to destroy you. And that is not an idle threat. For all your Brooks Brothers suits and smartly polished shoes you're nothing more than a prematurely pompous, basically illiterate eight-year-old. Hadleigh, do you wish to come with the children?"

"I'll stay," she whispered, agonized.

"Very well. I suggest you try to use the time, both of you, to come to terms."

The twins came clattering down the stairs with overnight bags, and stuffed toys under their arms, and stood waiting in the hall.

"You're quite sure, Hadleigh?" Frances asked again.

"Quite sure."

"Fine!" She turned on her heel and, shepherding the children ahead of her, departed. The door slammed resoundingly.

There was a terrible quiet that lasted for some time until Chris said, "What did you tell her?"

"I've told her nothing."

"Then how did she know?"

"I have no idea."

"You're lying!"

"Oh, God!" she exploded. "If you want to kill me, now's your perfect opportunity. There's nothing left. You've humiliated me utterly. I just don't care anymore. Pick up the bread knife and cut my throat, why don't you?"

"You're disgusting!" He got up and leaned on the table beside her. "I've had all I'm going to take. I was going to wait, but now I'm not. I don't want anything more to do with you." He made to leave the room.

"What are you doing?" she asked tiredly.

"You'll be hearing from my lawyer. And one other thing. I'll fight you for the kids. You're not fit to look after them."

It sounded like a film she'd seen dozens of times. The dialogue was so familiar it couldn't possibly be real. She remained at the table staring at the half-eaten meal, and continued to sit there long after Chris had left the house with two bulging bags and his briefcase. Motionless, she paid close attention to the beating of her heart and the throbbing in her bruised cheek, the stinging of her split lip. She was aware of every pulsing point of her body, and of her aloneness in the house. What distressed her most was that it had been her mother who'd brought everything to a head, her mother who'd come to her defense.

At nine-thirty, she went upstairs to the bathroom where, seated on the rim of the tub, she swallowed every pill in every prescription bottle in the house.

Twenty-two

Elmo marvelled constantly at Frances. There were other, much younger, women he socialized with, but none were as infinitely appealing as she. He stayed away for weeks at a time, not even bothering to telephone, yet his behavior had no apparent effect on her. She received his calls, his visits, even his lovemaking, with baffling placidity. She never questioned him, nor made demands of any sort. When he announced his wish to visit, she responded each time, "Come ahead," and greeted him at the door as if it had been merely hours since he'd last been there.

They ate together very formally, usually meals Mrs. Walsh had prepared before going off for the night to see friends. Frances offered him his choice of alcoholic beverages but drank only mineral water herself, chain-smoking cigarettes with the casual explanation, "I have an addictive nature," when he commented that she smelled, not unpleasantly, of tobacco.

Their conversations were minimal, limited by her disinterest.

"You're not here to talk," she said bluntly, "and I've no interest whatever in the sophomoric activities taking place at your hallowed institute of higher learning."

What they did do was make love in the most abandoned, utterly satisfying fashion. And no matter what they might be engaged in at any given moment when he chose to study her, she was never lacking in grace. Her capacities seemed entirely elastic. She was able to go on as long as he, and never revealed fatigue. Because he couldn't fathom either her motives or her appetites, he was driven to investigate the limits of her endurance, and failed every time to measure them with any degree of accuracy.

Only when positively glutted, when they lay sprawled together upon her bed, did they ever talk with any real significance. He had asked her, soon after they'd become lovers, if she had behaved this way with her husband, and had been startled by her amused response of, "Naturally. Did you think I only began at his funeral?"

"You must miss him like hell," he said, mentally revising his memory of Arthur.

"Of course I do. There was an adversarial aspect to our marriage that triggered some of our most successful campaigns upon one another's bodies and minds."

"Why did you stop drinking?" he wondered aloud.

"Does that have something, in your mind, to do with what we've been discussing?" she asked.

"I'm not sure. Maybe."

"I stopped because there was no longer any reason to continue. I am bored by this conversation, Mr. Sheffield."

"Then we'll stop," he said readily.

"Good!"

He liked and disliked her. If he chanced to raise the subject of Hadleigh, she became vague and uncommunicative. It irked him because he missed Hadleigh and his visits to the house in Greenwich. Since their parting of ways he thought of her often, and he had hoped Frances might keep him informed. She refused.

"If you're curious about my daughter, find out for yourself," she told him flatly. "I'm not some form of Indian drum you beat to get the most recent news from the next valley. I don't care for the notion that you'd use me to stay close to my daughter."

He liked her for her loyalty, but was irritated by her suspicions, especially since they came, every time, to within inches of the truth. He didn't like being so easily read, yet Frances had the ability to swing him about endlessly, and it was why he kept returning. It was also why the other women he sometimes slept with seemed so relentlessly dull by comparison. He dared to refer only once to his, in his view, inordinate sexual capacities.

With a positively merry laugh, Frances declared, "You're no more over-sexed than any other typical thirty-year-old self-satisfied American male. How simply ludicrous! What an extraordinary hypothesis!" she went on. "Were I to concur with your thinking, that would have to qualify me for special mention in Ripley's 'Believe It or Not.' You really must learn never to reveal thoughts of such a self-indulgent nature, Mr. Sheffield. You might be surprised to discover that there are literally legions of women who've been hearing that same remark, in all its infinite varieties, since men first discovered they had what amounted to little divining rods between their legs. Really!" she laughed.

When apart, considering the twenty-five-year difference in their ages, he felt mildly disgusted. Yet there always came a moment when he visualized himself making a connection with her, and he knew he couldn't stay away. No matter how he tried, he couldn't wear her down to a point where she became familiar. Had that been possible, he'd have been able to break away from her.

He'd be in his office grading papers and would suddenly become aroused at imagining her rising from the dinner table to begin disrobing. It was something she did often, and without warning. Expressionlessly, she'd remove her clothes and present herself. He'd take the time to study the way the flesh adhered to her bones, and the lift of her small breasts, while his own flesh was vulcanized by the sight of her slightly parted legs, and long, blue-veined arms. But it was the prominent ridge of scar tissue that ran half the length of her inner arm he found most erotic. He was fascinated by the scar and, finally, asked its cause.

"Ah!" she said, looking down at her arm. "You wish to know the origins of my wound, do you?"

"I've been wondering what happened," he admitted.

"This, Mr. Sheffield," she told him, "is where my third hand was, before they removed it."

"What?"

"You ask far too many questions!" she admonished, refusing to give him a direct answer.

Within the confines of her home she was shameless, making love with him on the sofa, or the floor, or bent forward over the arm of a chair; standing against the hallway wall, or sitting on the edge of her bed while he knelt between her outflung thighs.

He brought her flowers, or books he thought she might like; he arrived with tiny measures of her perfume, or bars of imported chocolate. Bringing her gifts satisfied his need to feel equal on some level other than the sexual one—and even there, he felt constantly challenged. She accepted his offerings with polite gravity, causing him to feel very like his neutered tabby with its gifts of dead mice and mangled sparrows. Yet he continued presenting her with tokens he hoped might please her. He thought that were he able in some way to ingratiate himself so that she became dependent upon him, he'd be able to go away and never return. He simply couldn't understand their relationship, and so he kept going back to her in the hope of finding some satisfactory definition.

It was only because of her extreme anger with Chris that he learned of Hadleigh's suicide attempt when he telephoned Frances a week after it happened.

"I cannot possibly see you," she said with unusual ferocity. "The children are here, and Hadleigh's in hospital. That importunate bastard had been beating her, but she insisted on remaining in the house. He announced he was going to seek a divorce, and she took quite a number of pills. It was simply sheer good luck he decided to go back to the house for something he'd forgotten, and discovered her unconscious on the bathroom floor."

"Jesus Christ!" Elmo exclaimed.

"Now, he's acting out the role of concerned husband, dashing to her bedside directly the train arrives in the station each evening. It's perfectly clear he's setting up a public impression. He's not in the least interested in her well-being."

"I think I'd better drive down there right away," he said.

"Why?"

"Because I want to. What d'you mean why?"

"For what reason? What do you imagine you'll accomplish?"

"I don't want to accomplish anything. I care about Haddy. She's got to be feeling rotten."

"And you hope to improve upon that, do you?"

"This is one of those times when I don't like you," he said, very annoyed. "How the hell can you be so cold about this?"

"Like most people, you dislike what you fail to understand, because it's threatening in some nonspecific fashion."

"What bullshit! I don't feel threatened, but I'll admit I sure don't understand most of the things you say and do.''

"I doubt you ever will. However, I will ask you not to muddy the waters. Hadleigh has too much on her plate as it is.''

"Is that motherly concern I detect?'' he asked sarcastically. "Or are you just protecting your own interests?''

It bounced right off her. "Keep away from my daughter just now, Mr. Sheffield. Whatever happens, only Hadleigh herself can set this right. No one else can do that for her. And you admit freely you're a temporary man at best.''

"I want to see her,'' he said less forcefully.

"You will *not* see her. If necessary, I'll instruct the hospital to refuse you admittance.''

"*Why?*''

"Because it is your undying conviction that the best medicine you could possibly offer any woman reposes between your thighs. Hadleigh is in no condition to recognize what motivates you. But I do, and while it's acceptable to me, it is utterly unacceptable for her. Good day, Mr. Sheffield.'' She put down the receiver.

Finding herself still alive was the single most depressing moment of Hadleigh's life. To be told she'd been as close to death as she had, only to have been rescued—by bloody Chris, of all people—struck her as the ultimate ineptitude in a lifetime crammed full of examples. On top of that, to be presented nightly with his flagrantly dishonest show of caring simply added to her hatred of them both. She had no idea what he was trying to prove, and watching him work to impress the nurses and her attending physician disgusted her. They seemed unable to recognize his lack of real acting talent. She thought anyone should have been able to see he was performing something he'd seen or read about somewhere, and doing a very bad job of it, to boot. His visits were an agony she endured only by clenching her teeth and refusing to speak to him. When he left, the nurses clucked and tut-tutted, addressing her as if she were a naughty, willful child who didn't deserve such a devoted, loving husband.

Mercifully, she slept for hours at a stretch and was thereby able to avoid both her own thoughts and the opinions of the hospital staff. It was Augusta's arrival, the night before she was to be discharged, that enabled her to break out of her silence. At first sight of her coming through the door, Hadleigh burst into tears and automatically held out her arms. She clutched Augusta fiercely, grateful for this one true friend.

"God, you're so thin!" Augusta said, feeling the bones of Hadleigh's rib cage beneath her hands, before pulling away to sit in the chair beside the bed. "I have to look at you," she said, holding both Hadleigh's hands as she examined her face. "I can't get over how thin you are!"

"Suicide as a diet," Hadleigh said with grim humor. "How did you know I was here?"

"I kept phoning the house and when nobody answered I got worried, so I called your mother. I was afraid something like this would happen."

"You did try to warn me, didn't you? It had nothing to do with drinking," she said in a rush. "I was completely sober."

"Haddy, you don't want to kill yourself," Augusta rebuked gently. "You're too young to think it's the only way out of this mess with Chris. Look at my family, for God's sake! We've got divorces from here to there, and nobody's killed herself over it yet. It's so dumb. He's not worth it."

"I don't want to live anymore. Truly I don't. I'm so tired." She pulled free her hands and folded them in her lap. "Chris comes every evening and sits where you are, just staring at me with eyes filled with hate. The moment anyone comes near, he begins talking very quickly, a lot of nonsense about how much he wants me to get well and come home; the children need me and so does he. He intends to get a divorce, and to take the children away from me."

"Fight him!" Augusta told her. "Judges usually give custody of children to their mothers. Fight the bastard!"

"He came last night with all sorts of legal papers. I pretended to be asleep so I wouldn't have to listen to him." She wet her lips and looked toward the window. "I'd so love a drink. Or a cigarette. You don't have a cigarette, do you?"

"I can go get you some."

"Would you? I'd be so grateful."

"Sure. I'll be right back."

In a few minutes, Augusta returned with a pack of Luckies and some matches. Hadleigh tore off the cellophane and got a cigarette lit, at once becoming nauseated. Dropping the cigarette into the ashtray, she stumbled from the bed to the bathroom. Augusta's view was of her naked backside as the hospital gown flared open. She looked away, trying not to hear Hadleigh's retching, but it went on and on. Finally, she went out to pace the length of the corridor until she thought sufficient time had passed.

"I thought you'd gone," Hadleigh said from the side of the bed where she sat leaning on her hands, her newly thin legs dangling.

"I just wanted you to have some privacy." She stood in front of Hadleigh trying to think how she could fire her into defending herself. "What can I do for you, Had?" she asked, placing her hands on Hadleigh's shoulders.

"Nothing," she answered, not meeting Augusta's eyes. "There's nothing to be done."

"There's *a lot* to be done," Augusta argued. "Why are you just giving in this way? Why won't you fight back?"

"How? With what?"

"First thing, get yourself a lawyer. He'll tell you what to do."

"All right," she said listlessly. "I'll do it on Monday. Did my mother tell you when she's bringing the twins home?"

"She said she's waiting for word from you. We're *all* waiting for word from you. Don't just let things happen, Haddy! He'll steamroller you, if you do."

"It's hard to think," she said, her speech growing slow. "I'm sorry. I keep falling asleep."

Augusta helped her get back under the bedclothes, then watched her eyelids fluttering with her effort to remain awake. "If you need me for anything, let me know. I want to help, but you've got to help yourself."

"I've always liked you, Augusta."

"I've always liked you, too. I just wish you'd protect yourself, fight for your rights. There are people who'll help. I will. Your mother will . . ." She stopped, realizing Hadleigh was asleep.

Two days and a night after her release from the hospital, Hadleigh was starting to feel more awake. And as the drugs' hold on her system diminished, her fury grew. Augusta was right. She couldn't allow Chris to do whatever he liked without contesting it. She would fight him.

When he telephoned on the Sunday evening saying he wanted to come over to talk, she was geared up for it.

He arrived with his briefcase, and went directly to the living room where he began to spread papers on the coffee table.

"What is all this?" she asked, holding a mug of hot tea with both hands. "I thought we were going to talk."

"We are," he answered curtly. "We're going to talk about all this." He indicated the papers.

"What is it?"

"This represents the groundwork," he explained, as if addressing a small child. "Just so you know exactly where we stand. My lawyer has collected affidavits from the nursing staff, from your doctor at the hospital, and the one in Old Greenwich. There are also a couple from two of the liquor stores in town, and one from the guy who delivers the groceries."

"What are you talking about?"

"*Proof*!" He waved at the papers. "These prove you're not competent to look after the twins."

"*How* do they prove that? What *are* you talking about?"

He began grabbing up documents, shaking them in her face. "This one says you were drunk out of your goddamned mind at least half a dozen times when groceries were delivered. This one says you buy your booze in his store, and so does this one. These"—he snatched up another sheaf of pages—"all document your erratic behavior. Buying useless crap in five and dime stores, sitting around most nights making cardboard cutouts. You want more? I've got *dozens* of them."

She threw the tea at him, mug and all. He let go the papers and went at her with his fists. Abandoning her passivity, brimming with hatred, she grabbed handfuls of his hair and pulled with all her might while kicking at his shins. He threw up his arms, chopping outward to break her hold on his hair, then fastened his hands around her throat and began to squeeze. Certain he intended to kill her, she jerked her knee upward into his groin, and he screamed, releasing her. Seizing the advantage, she grabbed the nearest thing to hand, and hit him squarely across the head with his briefcase. He reeled, his hands cupping his bruised testicles, and she hit him again.

In the grip of fury, she threw herself upon his back, dragging her fingernails across his face, digging them into his neck before sinking her teeth into the point where his neck joined his shoulder. She believed she could kill him, and wanted to. Pushing herself away, she ran through the room picking up objects and hurling them at him.

"YOU'LL NEVER HAVE MY CHILDREN!" she screamed. "I'LL SEE YOU DEAD FIRST! I HATE YOU! I'VE ALWAYS HATED YOU. I know all about you, all about your bloody women! I'll get my own documents and we'll see who has the right to the children. You've never paid a moment's attention to them, and when you did, it was to compete with them. You're not a father! My mother was absolutely right: You're an eight-year-old!" She began gathering his papers, crumpling and tearing them, throwing the pieces at him. At last, she picked up his briefcase and ran with it to the front door where she heaved it out onto the lawn. "GET OUT OF HERE!" she bellowed. "GET OUT AND DON'T EVER COME BACK!" She stood panting, both hands holding the door open.

Dripping blood and tea, one fist raised, he staggered to the door. "You'll regret this!" he choked. "I was going to make sure you were provided for. Now I'll see you *naked* in the fucking *street*."

She began pushing the door shut while he was going through it. From the living room window, she watched him hobbling around on the lawn, collecting the spilled contents of his briefcase. She laughed briefly, then went to report to Augusta.

"Good for you!" Augusta cheered. "Finally! Listen, I've got a lawyer for you. His name's Carter Leggett, and he's an old friend of the family. Call him, Haddy. According to my mother, who's an expert, he's one of the best. He'll make sure you come out all right."

"I will. Thank you."

"You sure do sound a whole lot better," Augusta said. "Keep it up!"

"I will."

"And call Leggett!"

"I will, I promise. Thank you for everything."

"You'll keep me posted?"

"Positively."

"Go get him!" Augusta urged.

It was too quiet. Weeks passed and Hadleigh kept waiting for something to happen. Leggett assured her everything was under control, and she had no option but to believe him. She stayed sober, looked after the children and the house, and waited. In the evenings she worked once more on the doll-house, periodically climbing the stairs to check on the children. Since her appetite hadn't returned, she spent a good part of each day taking in the seams of her clothing. Every time the telephone rang, she expected it to be Chris, with a list of demands. He didn't call. She spoke with Augusta several times a week, and cherished her company on those weekends when she was able to visit. She spoke with her mother, maintaining the distance between them, striving to be pleasant as she reported the lack of progress. She changed supermarkets in order not to run the risk of encountering either of the liquor store owners who'd been willing to sign papers against her. She cooked, and cleaned, and played with the children; she waited.

It was the first time Elmo and Frances had seen each other in more than three months. She'd been receptive as always on the telephone, saying, "Come ahead. I'll have Mrs. Walsh fix a meal, then send her off to her friends for the night." He was surprised and pleased by her obvious refusal to hold grudges, or to remain for long in an angry state.

The longer-than-normal gap between visits had heightened his interest. As she was returning from the dining room with his drink, he ventured to say, "I don't think I want to wait."

She smiled, handing him the bourbon. "The one lovely aspect of your youth, Mr. Sheffield, is the exquisite frequency of your erections."

"I'll drink to that." He tasted the drink, then set down the glass to take hold of her, his hands skimming appreciatively the length of her silk-covered spine. She drifted forward, pressing into him with a delicate twist of her hips. "Someday," he said, his cheek against hers, "I'm going to find out what makes you tick."

"And then what will you do?"

"Don't know." He unzipped her dress to the waist, then took a step back to undo the belt. "Probably sneak into some geriatric home to get you as you climb out of your wheelchair."

She laughed and kissed him, then said, "Let's adjourn to the bedroom, shall we? I don't fancy the floor this evening." Pausing to step out of her dress, she then led the way down the hall.

"Why don't you *seem* as old as you are?" he asked wonderingly, pressing his face into the yielding warmth of her belly.

"Don't be absurd!" she said lightly. "I seem precisely as

old as I am. You are a man of somewhat degenerate interests."

"Maybe I am," he agreed.

They'd stopped to rest. He'd gone to the living room to retrieve his now-watery drink, and they were sitting against the pillows, drowsily chatting, when the telephone rang.

"I'll ignore it," she said, stroking his belly.

"It's your telephone, your right to ignore it." He ran his tongue across the top of her breast while caressing the slight swell of her inner thigh.

"You're insatiable," she observed. "I'm not sure whether to be flattered or alarmed."

"Take your pick."

"The bloody thing's going to go on forever," she said after the tenth ring. "I'm afraid I'll have to answer. I've never been good at ignoring ringing telephones." She took her time, hoping whoever it was would give up by the time her hand connected with the receiver. She said hello, heard Hadleigh's voice, and knew at once there was a crisis.

"What's happened?" she asked.

Hadleigh was completely hysterical. "He's taken the children! He came, there was someone from the sheriff's office, and they had papers to take them. Leggett warned me but we didn't know anything about all the other things . . . *There's nothing left*! He's taken the money from my trust funds, all of it, signed documents in my name, stripped every account. He's got the children! I don't know what to do."

She was talking so loudly Elmo had no difficulty hearing her. He put his hand on Frances's arm and whispered, "Help her! She needs you." Frances shook him off, trying to listen to what Hadleigh was saying.

"My lawyer's going to prove fraud or something, but I haven't anything left. I'm to pack up the children's things and have them ready. He's *taken* them! Oh, God! I don't know what to *do*! How could he just take them away when everyone promised I'd have custody? He doesn't care about them; he doesn't. Even they know it."

"Try to calm down," Frances interjected. "I'm having difficulty following."

"*Help her!*" Elmo whispered fiercely, his hand tightening around her arm. "I swear, if you don't, you'll never see me again."

She pushed him away and swung her legs over the side of the bed. "What is it you'd like me to do?" she asked Hadleigh.

"I tried to reach Augusta but she wasn't . . . Everything's happening all at once. I knew . . . I was waiting. I thought we were making progress but I can't . . . He's taken my *children*! He had papers, and people who've sworn I'm not competent. I can't bear it . . ."

"Is it money you need right now, Hadleigh?"

"Money. But the children. What should I do?"

"What has your lawyer said?"

"He talks about procedures, filing this and that, court dates. None of it makes sense. How can he have the right to take them? He forged my name. He's a thief. He should be in jail, not with the children. He'll turn them against me. He's already started. I can tell by the way they look at me when they've been to visit with him. And he brought *pills*! My God! When the man, the sheriff, I don't know what he was, he wasn't looking and Chris left bottles everywhere, trying to make it look as if they're mine, but he's the one. I haven't any . . ." She went suddenly quiet. Her voice, when she spoke again, was deadened. "I don't know why, but I thought perhaps you'd help. I can't think why I thought that." There was a metallic click and the line went dead.

Elmo was frantically pulling on his clothes.

"You're leaving?" she asked, putting down the telephone.

"What *are* you?" he demanded. "What the holy hell are you?" He jammed his feet into his shoes, then whipped up his jacket from the floor.

After hearing the front door slam, she sighed and picked up the telephone.

Twenty-three

The drive to Greenwich lasted forever. Elmo had visions of ar-riving at the house to find Hadleigh dead. He saw her crum-pled body cast adrift on a sea of blood, imagined her hanging from the rafters in the garage, or with her upper body resting on the open oven door. He jumped lanes, keeping a fearful eye on the rearview mirror as he raced up the highway. He passed slow-moving vehicles either on the left or right, depending on the available gaps in the traffic. He flashed his bright lights to signal his intent to pass, and shot by dozens of cars as his sweat-slicked hands threw the steering wheel from one side to the other. In the event that he might be pulled over either by the New York or Connecticut state police, he had his state-ment all prepared. He would tell the truth: He was on his way to avert a death. If they tried to detain him, he'd just drive off and let them catch up with him later.

By the time he was halfway there, the traffic had thinned a little and, between grotesque scenarios wherein he discovered Hadleigh's remains, he reviewed his parting exchange with Frances, deploring her detached attitude. Could it be that what had seemed the elusive key to her character had, in fact, been her lack of feeling? Christ! It incensed him to think he'd endowed her with all kinds of qualities she didn't have, that she was nothing more than a highly sexed, pathologically in-ventive, middle-aged woman with a craving for younger men. And if she was all that, what was he? He'd made love dozens of times with the mother of the woman he'd always wanted,

thinking the act might in some way bring him closer to the
daughter. They'd done it on the day of her husband's funeral,
and he'd seen nothing particularly wrong with that at the time.
It had been, in truth, one of the more titillating experiences of
his life, one about which every detail remained with embossed
clarity in his mind. He could remember the small shock he'd
felt fumbling about in the dark dressing-room only to collide
with her naked body and entwining arms. He'd found her ravenous mouth and slippery groin utterly irresistible—the first
woman of his adult life who'd not only been willing but who
hadn't required hours of foreplay before reluctantly accepting
him into her body. Frances had needed only his complicity.
They'd gone to the floor before he'd even managed to remove
his trousers, her hands guiding him with a sureness he'd never
thought to question. Preferring to concentrate on the more
dramatic, less grubby aspects of what had been taking place,
he'd gladly thrust into her, their hipbones grinding together
until, biting down on his hand to keep from making any sound
that might have been overheard, she'd lifted right off the floor
and held there for one breathtaking moment before, as if elec-
trocuted, dancing uncontrollably beneath him. He'd been impressed as hell by the whole show, and by the fact of how well
she'd known her own body. He had yet to encounter any
woman who knew herself to the degree Frances did. For more
than three years he'd been driving down from New Haven, at
least once, and usually three or four times, a month to spend a
night performing with this woman every sexual act he'd ever
heard of, read about, or imagined. Now, in the immediate
aftermath, he felt scummy. He'd wanted Hadleigh all along,
and the very fact of his long-term affair with Frances would
inhibit any feelings he might show toward Hadleigh. He
pounded the steering wheel with his fist, then wrenched the car
over into the right-hand lane; the Greenwich exit was coming
up.

 As he raced along Round Hill Road, he suddenly wondered
what he was doing, and why. He'd jumped out of bed and
gone charging into the night because Frances had refused to
listen to him. He had no idea what he might find when he arrived, or even what he'd say to Hadleigh. Maybe this was a
mistake, he thought, nevertheless keeping his foot down on
the accelerator. Was he crazy? he wondered. He was about to
throw himself into the middle of a very messy divorce, simply

because a woman twenty-five years his senior had refused to do what he'd wanted. He was probably making the biggest mistake of his life. He'd just check to make sure Haddy was all right, then get the hell back to New Haven and stay there.

The house was dark. He picked his way across the lawn hoping not to fall over one of the kids' bicycles or some abandoned toy. As he got to the steps he could see that the front door was standing open. It scared him. There was something ominous and final about a dark house with its door open. He stepped up onto the threshold and called her name. Getting no reply, he felt about for the switch, found it, and got the outside and hall lights on before calling out again.

He was certain each room he entered would contain her corpse, but she was nowhere downstairs. He ran up the stairs two at a time to the master bedroom. Nothing. The rest of the bedrooms were also empty. Where was she? It had only been forty minutes since her telephone call, and her car was in the driveway.

"Hadleigh?" he called. "Haddy?"

The sound of her voice nearby caused his heart to jolt so shudderingly he thought he might have a heart attack.

"How nice of you to come," she said softly.

"Where are you?" he asked, looking around.

"Here, at the top of the stairs. You may come up if you like, but please don't turn on the light."

"What're you doing up here?" he asked, making his way up the attic stairs, only just able to distinguish her form on the top step.

"I've been thinking. Do sit down."

He sat gazing up at her, trying to adjust his eyes, but the dark was too complete.

"How did you happen to stop by, Elmo?" she asked. "It doesn't matter, really. I'm always pleased to see you. I've thought for ages now what a great pity it was we had that unpleasant falling-out. Augusta's been coming. The two of you quarrelled, didn't you?"

"That's right. We did."

"Ever so many disagreements," she said wonderingly. "I can't imagine how it all came to this. I'm afraid I've done some very foolish things. I expect everyone's going to be dreadfully upset with me."

"What foolish things have you done?"

"Christopher's taken the children. He's also pirated my trust funds and bank accounts. He's taken everything. I must say he's been very thorough." Her soft, almost otherworldly tone remained on one note, uninflected. It made the hair on the back of his neck rise. "He wants the house to be sold, but since my father made the down payment, and I kept up the mortgage payments, he'll allow me half the proceeds. Magnanimous, don't you think?"

"Eminently," he said acidly, despising Chris. "You're not going to settle for that, are you?"

"How old are you, Elmo?"

"Almost thirty-one. Why?"

"Do you know my age?"

"I think so. You're what? Twenty-seven?"

"Twenty-six, actually. Did you know I had a brother who died during the war?"

"I remember hearing something about that."

"It's extraordinary, you know, but I think of him often. He was such a lovely little boy. He had a splendid collection of model soldiers. I wonder what happened to them. It's not important. He was only six when he died. I was ten. It seems such a very long time ago, and yet I still miss him. Every so often I see a little boy who reminds me of him and I feel a terrible sort of ache inside. Sometimes, I imagine him with my father. You knew my father, didn't you? I'd forgotten that. I am glad you knew him. He was so very kind. I have a secret, Elmo. Shall I tell you?"

"Sure, if you want to."

"I have something Chris doesn't know about. No one knows about it. My father gave me some land. I also have a will, something else Chris doesn't know about. My children will have that land. It's on the near side of the Merritt Parkway, not very far from here. I drive by every so often to look at it. I used to plan I'd build a house there, one day. But that will never happen now."

Was he mistaken, or was her voice starting to fade? He sat up straighter, as if that might improve his hearing, deciding he'd get her to bed, then leave. "It could still happen." He tried to sound encouraging.

"No, it never will. A great pity, really."

"Look, why don't we go downstairs?" he suggested. "I could put on some coffee, or take you out for a meal somewhere. I'll bet you haven't eaten anything."

She didn't answer. There was an odd slithering and then, heart-stoppingly, her body toppled onto him, nearly knocking him backwards down the stairs. Wrapping one arm around her inert form, he went riser by riser on his backside down the stairs with her half across his lap. Arriving at the landing, he eased her away then felt along the wall for the light switch. When it came on, he gaped at the blood all over her, the carpet, his clothes. Jerking his head around, he saw a track of splatters starting in the bedroom. She'd hacked open her wrists in the bathroom, then climbed to the top of the stairs to sit in the dark, waiting to die. For a moment, he was paralyzed, unable to think. Then he sprang into action, darting into one of the smaller bedrooms to rip the sheet from the bed, tearing strips from it as he knelt beside her. Her breathing was slow and shallow and he worked with panicky haste, tying tourniquets around her upper arms, and binding the gaping gouges at her wrists. Satisfied he'd managed to slow the flow of blood, he tore into the bedroom to call for an ambulance. Then he somehow lifted her—she was unbelievably heavy—and stumbled with her down the stairs and into the living room. Just as he'd put her down on the sofa, he heard tires on the gravel and ran to the front door thinking it was positively miraculous that the ambulance could have come so quickly.

It wasn't an ambulance, but a long black limousine from which Frances emerged, her slim legs appearing first.

Christ! he thought. He'd had everything wrong. He'd misjudged everyone. Frances had been right all along. He didn't understand one damned thing, about any of these people.

Frances saw him, saw the blood on his clothes, and came running toward him.

"She's unconscious," he told her, leading her into the living room.

"Déjà vu," she whispered. "I've been to this place before." She went at once onto her knees to press her fingers against the pulse in Hadleigh's throat. Not satisfied, she pushed her hand up under Hadleigh's breast, exclaiming, "She's going to die! Have you done anything?"

"I called for an ambulance. I didn't know what else to do. She just sat there on the stairs talking to me. It was dark. I didn't know . . ."

"You're babbling. Shut up! Get a grip on yourself! The ambulance won't get here in time."

"She's lost so much blood. I don't know how long she was

sitting there before I got here. Just sitting there in the goddamned dark. Jesus!''

''Bring your car round! If we wait, she'll die. We'll take her
to the hospital.''

''Maybe it's not such a good idea to move her.''

''Give me the keys to your car!'' She shot to her feet, her
hand outheld. ''Give them to me! I'll drive. You bring Hadleigh. *Do it now*!'' Snatching the keys from his hand, she ran
out to his car and had it reversed, ready to go the moment he
climbed into the back seat with Hadleigh.

''*You'll get us killed*!'' he cried as Frances took the elderly
De Soto over the unlit back roads at well over sixty miles an
hour. ''*Watch out*! *Jesus*! *You just went through a fucking
stop sign*!''

''Shut up, Mr. Sheffield!'' she told him. ''You're behaving
like an adolescent schoolgirl! Be still and let me concentrate on
trying to remember where the bloody hospital is!''

The ambulance was just about to leave as Frances slammed
on the brakes outside the emergency entrance. The attendants
came on the fly, flung Hadleigh onto a stretcher and shot inside with her. Leaving the motor running, Frances called,
''Take care of your car, Mr. Sheffield!'' and ran after them.

Scared and distraught, Elmo somehow got the car into gear,
parked it in a no-parking zone, then went inside, his head at
once starting to ache from the glare of the fluorescent lights.
''Where did they take her?'' he asked the nurse on duty.

''There's a waiting room down there,'' the nurse pointed.
''They'll let you know. You want to clean up,'' she said, looking at his blood-covered clothes and hands. ''There's a men's
room first left, then a right.''

''Where did Mrs. Holden go?''

''Mrs. Holden goes wherever she wants to go,'' she said
with grudging admiration. ''We've gone a few rounds with
that lady a time or two before. Don't worry. We'll keep you
posted. Are you a member of the family?''

''Uhm, no. Just a friend.''

''Who let you in?'' the resident wanted to know. ''Who let her
in? You're in the way here!'' he told Frances, unwrapping
Elmo's makeshift bandages from Hadleigh's wrists.

''I've no intention of leaving. Attend to her physical injuries
and allow me to deal with the rest of my daughter.''

"Your daughter's unconscious! Somebody get her out of here!" he said to the room at large. The two nurses, the ambulance attendants, and Frances all looked at the young doctor. No one moved. Then the attendants slipped away, and the nurses once more busied themselves with Hadleigh's blood pressure and pulse rate.

Seeing he was fighting a losing battle, the resident ordered, "Somebody get her into a sterile suit and out of that goddamned fur coat!"

"Come on." One of the nurses took Frances by the arm and directed her into the scrub room. "Chuck the coat, the shoes, the bag, and your jewelry. Put these on, then wash your hands over there. When you come back into the E.R. use your elbows, not your hands to open the door. Don't touch anything! Understand?"

"Perfectly."

By the time Frances returned, the activity in the room was frenzied.

"Stay at the head of the table!" the resident ordered. "Move one inch and I'll personally throw you out!"

Hadleigh was being transfused with whole blood through an artery in her leg while the resident finished suturing her right wrist. A nurse began to bandage that arm the instant he shifted over to work on the other.

"Her BP's going down fast. So's her pulse."

"Son of a bitch!" The resident glanced up at the nurse tracking Hadleigh's vital signs. "Adrenaline! And get Turner. We need help in here."

At the head of the table, Frances bent, put her mouth directly beside Hadleigh's ear, and began whispering. Within minutes, before the second doctor arrived, the nurse announced, "BP's climbing. Up to eighty over fifty. Pulse up to 130." There was a collective sigh.

"Cancel Turner!" the resident ordered, finishing with the sutures on the left wrist. "We're going to make it."

Frances slowly straightened, her hand still smoothing Hadleigh's forehead.

"Come with me." The resident beckoned to Frances. "We're finished in here. She's stabilized. We'll watch her through the night, but she ought to be all right."

He took her to the doctors' lounge where he poured two cups of coffee and gave her one.

She thanked him, sat down in one of the leather armchairs and drank some of the coffee.

"Who are you anyway?" he asked, perching on the arm of the adjacent chair.

"I'm your patient's mother, Dr. Street." She read his name from the tag on his chest.

"I know that. But who *are* you?"

"It's rather interesting, you know, but that's the second time tonight I've been asked that question."

"Did you answer it the first time?"

"I don't believe I did."

"Are you going to answer it this time?"

"I doubt very much I will."

He half-smiled and lifted the cup to his mouth. "Your daughter was dying. You know that, don't you?"

"Yes."

"I mean it. She was sliding right out from under our hands. The blood loss was tremendous. She shouldn't be alive, and I have no medical explanation for why she is."

"Is that right?" she asked, her head cocked to one side.

"Come on! You were there." He paused, then said, "Folks around here seem to know you."

"They do seem to, don't they?"

"Why is that?"

"I expect it's because I've been here several times before."

"And you barged right in just the way you did tonight. Right?"

"That's right."

"What did you say to her?" he asked.

"Nothing in particular."

"No. You said something very particular, something that turned her around. She was going, and you stopped it. That's some kind of swell trick. I mean, if it's something you do regularly, we could easily get you a job in the E.R. doing your voodoo."

She smiled, and for a moment he couldn't remember what they'd been talking about. He was noticing her eyes, and her mouth. Then, he remembered, and asked again, "So who are you anyway?"

"I'm Frances Holden. I am an alcoholic, supposedly manic depressive. I am fifty-six, a widow, British. My late husband was vice consul in New York. More?" Her eyebrows lifted.

"Definitely."

"You have quite a healthy appetite for details," she said. "I live on Central Park West with my housekeeper, a most amusing woman. Aside from her, I have no women friends, but several male acquaintances. I go occasionally to the ballet. I've been trying for years to gain back my former youthful skill at sight-reading, to no avail. I shop at Bonwit Teller, and sometimes at Bergdorf Goodman. I have one child, whom you've encountered. I don't believe there is any more."

"You don't look fifty-six."

"Or manic depressive, or alcoholic?"

"Sometimes hard to tell about those things. I'm only a resident, you know. I haven't come into contact yet with all forms of the human species."

"And how old are you, Dr. Street?"

"Young. Your daughter's my first suicide, almost my third fatality."

"You've experienced two deaths, have you?"

He nodded, then swallowed the last of his coffee. "They were both traffic accidents. What did you say to her, Mrs. Holden?"

"You really wish to know?"

"I really do."

"Very well. I'll tell you. It's quite simple really. I told her what she's always wanted to hear, but won't remember when she comes round. I told her I loved her."

Elmo had dozed off in the waiting room. Frances touched his shoulder, and he came awake with a start.

"She'll recover," she told him. "You did well."

He rubbed his eyes, then looked up at her. "You were unbelievable!" he said admiringly. "I didn't even know you could drive. What do we do now?"

"You go home. I'll stay here."

"I'll hang around, keep you company."

"It's kind of you, but it would be wiser for you to leave."

"Maybe you're right. Jesus! Look at me! I'm a mess."

"Rinse your clothes in cold water."

"Doesn't anything ever throw you?" he wanted to know.

"I would say I was rather thrown tonight."

"No one would know it."

She shrugged and opened her bag for a cigarette.

"I'm sorry for my assumptions earlier this evening."

"I accept your apology."

"What I just can't get over is her sitting there talking to me, and the whole time she was . . . I can't get *over* it! We must've been talking for five, ten minutes."

"You involved yourself," she said, exhaling a cloud of smoke. "I know it was in violation of all your instincts, but you did involve yourself."

"You know what I find most interesting?" he said. "You! You really do care about her. You do a great job hiding it."

"One may love one's children without liking them, Mr. Sheffield. Hadleigh has always irritated me by her refusal to rise or fall by her own decisions. Throughout her life, she's gravitated toward those who'll make the major decisions for her. I'm more than willing to try to help save her life. I am totally unwilling to help her live it. There are things I've done in my lifetime that give me nightmares and for which no pennance will ever suffice. But I've never dealt dishonestly. I think you and I have arrived at the end, Mr. Sheffield. Rather sad, but inevitable.

"I'll tell you something," she continued. "I'd adore a drink just now. Lovely amber scotch. I can almost taste it. The thing about alcohol is that it's always there, will *always* be there. Twenty times a day I'm overwhelmed by craving, then I remind myself there's no longer any point, and the craving ends." She opened her bag, brought out a tissue, touched it to her tongue to moisten it, then dabbed at a spot of dried blood on his chin. "I feel the same craving for my husband, who can't ever again be there. Say goodbye, Mr. Sheffield."

He got up, his throat choked with sudden emotion. "I'll miss you," he said inadequately.

"I know. So shall I miss you."

When he looked back, just before pushing out through the swing doors, she was still there, her hand with the cigarette rising toward her mouth.

Twenty-four

With her share of the proceeds from the sale of the Greenwich house, along with the money from the sale of her property, Hadleigh bought a small house in Darien near the New Canaan line. The place was in critical need of repair, and many of the rooms had been inexpertly, hideously partitioned, then painted in bilious shades of turquoise and green. But the property itself was beautiful, with over an acre of grounds just begging to be landscaped.

She'd been left with little in the way of furniture since, during her extended stay in the hospital, Chris had taken advantage of her absence to hire a moving van and remove whatever he wanted. What he'd wanted were mainly items of hers: eight antique chairs and a dining table that had belonged to her grandmother, a bedroom set given to her by her parents, Waterford crystal, old family silver, even paintings. What he'd left behind was minimal and damaged in some way.

She moved into the new house with two outworn armchairs, a scarred coffee table, a set of Melamine dishes she'd bought years before for the children, a pair of twin beds from the guestroom of the Greenwich house, along with a peeling, white-painted chest of drawers she'd found in the attic. There were a few other items, mostly wedding gifts Chris hadn't deemed of value, and several pairs of curtains he'd overlooked. He'd taken all the bedding, even the mattress pads, and stripped the house of every light bulb, all the brass switch-plate covers, and even the toilet paper. His meanness was so complete she found it laughable.

With the help of her lawyer, Leggett, and a financial consultant he brought in, they arranged the disposition of her funds not only to pay for the house but also to provide her with a small interest income.

"It's going to take some time," he explained, "but, eventually, you'll get back some, maybe even all, of what he's appropriated. For now, extreme caution's the keynote. This is a very tight budget. Exceed it and you'll just have to wait it out until the end of the month for your next check. The best idea would be if you could get yourself some kind of job, stay sober, and prove to the court you're responsible. We'll get a lot of his claims thrown out when we get to court, but quite a few of them're going to stand up."

Fortunately, her Meprobamate maintained her, placing a seal over the top of her emotions. She agreed to everything, and set about trying to find a job. Having no qualifications made it impossible. It was Augusta who, having finally landed an editorial job with a decent publishing house, came through, arriving unannounced one Sunday with a Bloomingdale's bag full of manuscripts. "I need a reader," she told Hadleigh. "All you have to do is read these, write me a page or two about what you think of them, and we'll pay you per book."

"I don't know anything about writing," Hadleigh said doubtfully.

"You know how to read, and you know whether or not you like something. That's all you need. Just say whether or not the stuff's any good, and a couple of sentences why. If it's good, we'll pass it along in-house, for more readings. If it's crap, say so. The more you read, the more you get paid. I'm up to my neck in 'over the transom' submissions, and somebody's got to read them. As it is we're forever getting letters from people swearing they put a hair between pages forty-seven and forty-eight and the goddamned hair was still there when they got the manuscript back. Find any hairs, do everyone a favor, and remove them. You look lousy."

"Thank you."

"You do. What did they do to you anyway?"

"All sorts of fascinating things. I have a lovely new medication. You really don't want to know."

"Maybe I don't. Boy," she said, catching hold of Hadleigh's wrists to look at them. "You sure messed yourself up."

"I have some cold cuts." Hadleigh slid away. "Would you like a sandwich?"

"Can't stay. I've got a date in the city. I knew if I phoned to discuss this with you, you'd turn me down. I figured I'm so ir-resistible in person you couldn't possibly say no."

"My concentration's not very good."

"Just try. If it works, great. I'll have a courier service pick up and deliver. All you have to do is sit here and read. Great view," she said, gazing out the window at the dense trees rim-ming the property.

"It is lovely, isn't it?"

Augusta appraised Hadleigh for a long moment, finding her slow speech and lazy movements worrying. She looked and sounded like someone walking in her sleep. Augusta was tempted to tell her that not only had Elmo called begging her to help, even Frances had telephoned to suggest, in her non-chalant fashion, that a visit might go a long way. She didn't actually have a date waiting, she just couldn't stand the house or Hadleigh's almost palpable aura of dejection. Being here, in this grim little house, with its water-stained walls and ceil-ings, its lime-green formica in the kitchen, was too depressing. But if it depressed her, she thought, it had to be a thousand times worse for Hadleigh.

"Maybe I will have something to eat," she said, her shame compounded by Hadleigh's display of enthusiasm.

"Oh good!" Hadleigh gave her a smile and then, disarm-ingly, reached for her hand. "I'm so pleased to see you."

"Don't you mind being here alone?" Augusta asked in the kitchen as Hadleigh made the sandwiches. "I mean, doesn't it scare you?"

"It's very peaceful. When I have the money, I have quite a few plans for remodelling the house. It has potential."

"What about the kids? What's happening with them?"

"He allows me to see them Saturdays. At first, they seem rather frightened, as if they've forgotten me. Especially Ben. Bonita's always been the more flexible of the two. By the time they're due to go home, they claim not to want to go. He's going to remarry, you know, directly the divorce is finalized."

"You're joking!"

"The children don't care for her. They say she tries to play mother to them. It's something in my favor, I think. Whatever he might try to convince them of about me, the effects tend to be cancelled out by their dislike of her. Her name, incredibly, is Monkey. Can you imagine anyone allowing herself to be called *Monkey*? It's too ridiculous!"

Augusta laughed. "Surely to God it's not her real name?"

"Oh, never! Her *real* name is something frightful like Zenobia, or Euthanasia." Hadleigh smiled widely. "He has deplorable taste. I mean to say, she's attractive in rather horsey fashion, and has that dreadful locked-jaw drawl the women around here have. She *rides*, my dear; belongs to the Ox Ridge Hunt Club and smells rather strongly of manure. She does, however, have exemplary thighs. I imagine that's a large part of her appeal, all those splendid muscles. I've gone from elephantine proportions to something strongly resembling a deflated balloon. Everything simply *hangs*."

"What crap! You're just skinny for a change."

"What I have, actually, is flat flab. Very misleading."

Augusta laughed explosively. "We should *all* have flat flab," she guffawed, glad now that she'd decided to stay. Oddly, she seemed to see a lot of her mother in Hadleigh. She'd acquired a grim sense of humor that showed a previously unsuspected wit. "You really need to do something about yourself, Had. Seriously. Your hair's a mess, and if that's an example of the kind of stuff in your wardrobe, you're in big trouble."

Hadleigh touched a hand to her hair, then said, "It's the weather. I've been out shifting rocks in the garden, rain or shine. I haven't any money, Augusta. And in any case, I don't especially care about clothes. I've bought one or two things in thrift shops."

"Jesus!" Augusta made a face. "How *could* you? I could *never* wear somebody else's stuff. I mean, I could if it were somebody I knew. But a total stranger? It makes me sick even to think about it."

"Everything's cleaned before it's offered for sale. They have some quite nice things. You'd be surprised."

"I sure would. There's no way I'd do it."

"You shouldn't be so inflexible," Hadleigh said softly. "One never knows what one might have to do."

Augusta thought about it. "Maybe you're right," she said. "He's not going to get away with it, is he?"

"Probably." Hadleigh set the sandwiches on two of the Melamine plates. "I can't think about it. When I do, I want to kill him. Shall we have our lunch in the garden?"

At the weekends, Elmo drove down from New Haven to help work on the house. He spent the nights either with friends locally or in motels, in order not to compromise Hadleigh's already tenuous position. They worked together to tear down the flimsy beaverboard partitioning in the upstairs bedrooms, then began applying the first of a half-dozen coats of white paint to the green- and blue-painted walls. While she took the children off for Saturday outings, he stayed, doing odd jobs like pulling up the rotting linoleum in the kitchen, or replacing the floorboards in the half-bathroom in the front hall. While he labored, he tried to make sense of what he was doing, why he was there.

They seldom discussed personal matters, although occasionally he'd look up to find her eyes on him. She'd quickly look away, but he'd be left with a strong impression both of her confusion and her need, neither of which could be dealt with because of the detectives Chris had hired to monitor her activities. Their awareness of invisible witnesses to all they did was sufficiently inhibiting to curb even their minimal conversations. On top of that, the medication kept her permanently tired so that, without warning, she'd suddenly fall asleep wherever she happened to be. It was alarming, and she was very afraid she might fall asleep behind the wheel of the car when she had the children with her. Then, too, her memory seemed to have been affected, and she sometimes broke into tears at her inability to recall how to perform some basically elementary deed like balancing her checkbook. Elmo tried to treat it all matter-of-factly and volunteered to do a number of these things for her. Once a month, he sat down with the statement and her checkbook and made everything tally. He telephoned to remind her of doctor's appointments, or that the dry-cleaning was waiting to be picked up. She accepted his reminders and his help with quiet reserve, as if physically withholding herself from any form of commitment, no matter how primary.

During the week, when he was unable to be with her, he wondered what she was doing; he imagined her alone in her narrow bed that was set into the steeply pitched dormered room at the front of the house; he pictured her sitting at the cheap chrome and formica second-hand kitchen set they'd found in a consignment store in downtown Norwalk, with manuscript pages and the ruled pad upon which she made her notes, a cup of tea cooling, forgotten, as her work-coarsened hands slowly turned the pages. He felt, at moments, as if he loved her. But they were moments that always occurred at a distance. When he was with her, what he felt most strongly was a kind of disenfranchised kinship.

She'd changed physically from someone rounded and bone-less-looking into a being that might have been shaped purely by the elements. Her hair was very long, and bleached almost white from the sun. Her face and arms were deeply tanned from her hours in the garden; and the time spent stooping and lifting, digging and planting, had tightened and firmed her muscles. He'd never before been aware of her height. Now she appeared Amazonian. He doubted she had any idea of her beauty. She gave the impression of being totally unaware of herself, except emotionally. Her physical self was something with which she had to contend: a chore that disinterested her. With her hair bundled back off her face in a hasty ponytail, and her newly emerged cheekbones reflecting light, she looked younger than she had at eighteen when he'd first seen her on the stony beach in Old Saybrook, and had wondered what on earth she'd been doing with that asshole MacDonald. It felt as if all that had happened a hundred years ago, when the whole world had been young. It was hard for him to equate the present with that distorted, sun-dappled past, when he'd taken such enormous pride in his originality and had held himself apart from the juvenile goings-on of the others. Even his affair with Frances was something from another era, although it was only six months since they'd stopped seeing each other.

He wondered about her, too, from the new perspective of the clandestine caring she'd displayed for Hadleigh the night of her second suicide attempt. If Hadleigh knew of what her mother had done, she gave no sign. They remained as diffidently polite and aloof from one another as they'd ever been, with the exception of Frances's twice-weekly check-in calls. She called on Mondays and on Fridays. And on the Fridays, when he was there, he watched, intrigued by the way Hadleigh held the receiver in almost reverentially cupped hands, while her features acquired a look of blended hope and fear that made him want, every time, to take hold of and comfort her. For fifteen or twenty minutes, he saw the child in Hadleigh, along with a naked frailty no one should have inspired, let alone her own mother. Yet the calls spurred her in some way, and by the time they were completed, she was taller, more alert, with flickers of animation in her eyes.

After months of witnessing these calls, Hadleigh turned one night, to say, "She's a force of bloody nature, that woman, like a tidal wave, or a tornado. On the one hand, she still terrifies me. But since that night, something's different, and I can't say what. It's simply different."

"What does she say?" he asked, curious.

"We begin with questions about my general well-being, then move on to the status of the children and what, if any, contemptible deeds Chris has recently enacted. Then she inquires after the effects of my medication, and the condition of my motor skills. After that, she tells me how she's spent her week, being sure to include anecdotes regarding Mrs. Walsh. She never deviates. It's not at all dissimilar from a medical check-up. She's thorough; she palpates this and that, and then inserts various shockingly cold instruments to be certain I'm reasonably sound."

"Why don't you tell her not to call if it upsets you?"

"I couldn't possibly." She looked dismayed by the thought. "In the first place, she's my mother. And in the second place, I . . ." She stopped and pressed her palms to her temples. "In the second place," she began again. "I don't know. I just don't know. Please don't grill me, Elmo." When she lowered her arms, her hands were trembling visibly.

"I'm sorry. I guess I shouldn't have said anything."

"It's just that I'm not at a point where I can do anything more than wait out this divorce. It's *hard*. I want my children back. I try not to think about it while I'm carting rocks and laying out the flower beds, while we're trying to turn this dreary hovel into something liveable; but I think of nothing else. They're my children, Elmo, and I love them more than life. It isn't right that one person should have so much power over another, that because I'm a woman and I trusted him, he felt free to strip me of absolutely everything. I'm not saying it's his fault I started drinking, but it was he who sent me to the doctor who started me on all those bloody pills. Everything's terribly tangled, and it's as much as I can do just to get from one hour into the next. You've been such a help, so good to come here and work as hard as you do. I sometimes wonder why you bother. There's nothing I can give you in return."

"I don't want anything. That's not why I'm here."

"Of course, you want something," she said, taking him off guard. "I wish I could accommodate you, but it's not just the watchdogs." She waved her hand in the direction of the windows. "It's me."

"You're all right," he said.

"No, I'm not at all all right. The only thing I do really well now is sleep. I seem to have latent skills at it. One of these days I may go to sleep and never wake up."

"That sounds like self-pity."

"I expect it does, but it isn't, really. The only reason I'm staying awake, reading the manuscripts for Augusta, doing what I can with this impossible house, is because I want my children back. If I can possibly get them, I will. If he wins, I don't know what I'll do. It's unthinkable to me that he'd win, but he might. We hate each other, but he hates more, and with a vengeance. He's turned it all around so that now it was I who trapped him into the marriage by cleverly getting myself pregnant on the one and only occasion when we made love. Then I became a drunk, solely intent on humiliating him in front of his friends. I quite literally shoved him into the arms of other women because I'm sexless and, I quote, he didn't like 'fucking dead meat.' That's attractive, don't you think?"

"This is the first time we've really talked."

"I know, and it's exhausted me. I have to go to bed. Will you be here tomorrow?"

"You know I will. I want to hold you, Haddy."

"I can't give him any more ammunition. Have you any idea how *exposed* I feel, knowing there's always someone watching?"

"I know. I'm sorry I said anything. I'll see you in the morning. I'll pick up some coffee and doughnuts on my way over."

"Yes," she said distractedly, already on her way to bed.

Her dollhouses and models were presented in court as evidence that she was doing considerably more than "cutting out pieces of paper." The judge, in an aside, told her he wouldn't mind commissioning her to make a house for his grandchildren. Encouraged, Hadleigh thought perhaps he might lean in her favor when it came to the question of custody.

Chris's lawyer presented the many affidavits attesting to her regular purchases of liquor, and the delivery man's sworn statement that she'd been too drunk on a number of occasions to write out a check for the groceries. It seemed as if there were statements from almost everyone she'd ever encountered, either professionally or casually, during her years of marriage.

In her defense, Leggett offered countermanding statements. The recitations went on and on in the all-but-empty courtroom. Periodically she looked over at Chris who steadfastly refused to meet her eyes. Leggett produced photostats of the forged withdrawal slips Chris had used to take her money. There was even one for the long-forgotten account she'd opened in New Haven as a newlywed, with the money she'd received for returning unwanted wedding gifts. The judge frowned, and declared an adjournment until the following day in order that he might peruse the substantial documentation generated by both sides.

"It's going well," Leggett assured her. "That was great, his liking the dollhouses. Keep your chin up. I think we've got a damned good chance."

On the second day, they got around to the custody suit. Again there were affidavits from both sides. Hadleigh kept close watch on the judge, trying to gauge his reactions. She thought he seemed sympathetic to her, but she couldn't be sure. Another adjournment was called. They would reconvene the following day, when the judge's decisions would be announced.

Frances arrived by limousine early that morning. "To offer moral support. If it doesn't go as you hope, just remember you can always go back to court again in the future. This isn't the final word."

Hadleigh rode to court in the limousine with her mother, feeling even more awkward than she had on the previous days, in the brown suit purchased for her court appearance. The nylon stockings felt scratchily insubstantial; the brassiere and girdle and slip each seemed to have lace edgings created from scalloped tin; the lightweight suiting fabric and the white silk shirt she wore under the jacket were like steel wool against her skin. Her entire body was chafed raw, and she longed for the well-worn blue jeans and oversized flannel shirts she customarily wore.

The judge began by ordering Chris to return the money he'd acquired fraudulently from her accounts. Stern-faced, he addressed Chris directly, accusing him of reprehensible and criminal behavior, and threatened him with prosecution should he fail to make restitution. Hadleigh was jubilant. She'd been living almost in poverty. Now she'd have back what was rightfully hers. The judge also directed him to return various items he'd taken from the "family home" which were uncontestably heirlooms belonging to Mrs. MacDonald. Hadleigh was buoyant, and held fast to her mother's hand, certain now she was going to have it all.

"Finally," the judge said, "we come to the matter of custody of twin children, Bonita and Benjamin MacDonald."

Hadleigh's grip on her mother's hand tightened.

"I've carefully studied both sides of this case and while it is my long-time personal conviction that the rightful place of children is with their mother, I cannot make that recommendation here. Mrs. MacDonald's history of drug and alcohol abuse, and repeated attempts to take her own life, indicate an unstable personality whose influence on impressionable young children is in grave doubt. I am therefore awarding custody to the father, Christopher MacDonald, with the proviso that Mrs. MacDonald have visitation rights to be mutually agreed upon, such rights not to be unreasonably withheld by Mr. MacDonald. I am further ordering that this matter come before the bench for review in no less than twelve months to ascertain that the well-being of the children has in no way been impaired by this court's decision." The judge's gavel descended deafeningly.

It was over. Leggett was saying something but Hadleigh didn't hear. She was staring at the judge as he rose from the bench and disappeared through a doorway. He'd given her children to Chris. She couldn't believe it.

"He took them away," she said aloud. "He took them."

"Only for a year," Leggett said, his hand on her arm. "Didn't you hear him? It's only for a year, then you've both got to come back and fight this again."

"I can't possibly make it through another year."

"Of course, you can!" Frances snapped. "The worst of it's over. A year's no time at all."

"It's *forever*."

"You won everything else," Leggett was saying. "To tell you the truth, I thought he'd make the custody absolute. This way, he's left the door wide open. Hang on for a year, and you'll have your children back."

Hadleigh turned to look at her mother. "How will I make it through another year? How?"

"Come along." Frances directed her out of the courthouse to where the limousine was waiting. "You'll do what you must, Hadleigh. The decision's yours entirely. If you want them, you'll find some way to get through the time."

"I want to die," Hadleigh whispered.

Frances struck her. "God above! I loathe your self-indulgence! Get in!'' she ordered, giving a stupefied Hadleigh a mighty shove that propelled her into the rear of the black Cadillac. Seething, Frances climbed in after her. ''You've come this far,'' she snapped, ''you can make it for twelve more months.''

''You don't understand.'' Hadleigh was investigating the heat of her cheek where her mother's blow had fallen.

''I understand perfectly,'' Frances shot back. ''Don't ever underestimate either my intelligence or my experience, Hadleigh. There may be parts of my brain that have the consistency of overcooked steak, but I'm still in full possession of my faculties. I have not, and never will, do your fighting for you. You've an opportunity to put everything back together. Don't waste it anointing yourself in your fulsome tears! Give in, and you prove that moronic bastard right. Here!'' She put a cigarette between Hadleigh's fingers and held out her lighter. ''Do something creative!''

As Hadleigh was leaving the car, Frances leaned over to the window to say, ''I'd like to remind you that you're free at last of detectives. You might want to think carefully about that. I'll ring you.'' Then she tapped the interior window to signal the chauffeur to drive on.

Hadleigh watched the sleek, polished car move down the rutted driveway, trying to figure out the meaning of her mother's last remark. It seemed a gratuitous suggestion. After all, what possible difference could the absence of watchers make to her life now?

Twenty-five

"It's a rough break about the kids," Elmo told her, "but a year's not such a long time."

"Why does everyone say that? It's a *very* long time."

"But you're getting your money back, your furniture. You could even move to a better place, if you want to."

"I don't think so. I'm starting to like it here."

"All right. So now you can afford to have some of the major work done, like getting a new furnace, and overhauling the kitchen, putting in a decent bathroom upstairs. That tub must've been around when George Washington went through here."

"I don't have the money yet, Elmo. That may take some time."

"But you will get it. That's the point. Now, listen! I'm taking you out to dinner. We'll celebrate."

"Celebrate what?"

"Your new status as divorcée."

"That's right," she said slowly. "I'm no longer married. My God! I'd forgotten all about that. I'm not Mrs. Mac-Donald anymore. It's over. Ten years. It's not possible I was married to that man for ten years."

"And you've got visitation rights," he added.

"Yes, I do."

"So, let me take you out to dinner. We can celebrate my finally getting tenure."

"Really?"

"A decent salary at last, and I can't be ousted from my cozy chair. Professor Sheffield has joined the ranks of the permanently employed. Furthermore, he's going to buy you seafood at Allen's Clam House in Westport. I made a reservation.''

She gave him a tentative smile. ''Do you know I've never been on a proper date?''

He'd dressed for the occasion, she saw, in a new tweed jacket, gray flannel trousers, a white button-down shirt and striped tie. ''You've bought new clothes,'' she said, impressed.

''So have you. I'd forgotten you had such good legs.''

She blushed and turned away. ''I've been longing for days to get out of this suit, but everything else needs laundering and there's been no time.''

He put his hand on her shoulder. ''Nothing's changed as far as you and I go, Hadleigh. We'll go out for dinner, then I'll drop you off here, and go to the motel. In the morning, I'll be back and we'll give these walls one last coat of paint. You'll move a few more rocks before they're all frozen into place. We'll eat lunch, then spend yet another hour trying to decide what to do about the basement. I'll go into town and pick up a pizza and some Greek salad for dinner, and you'll drink milk and watch me down a couple of beers. I'll try not to feel guilty about drinking in front of you, and you'll try not to make me feel guilty. Then, around eleven, I'll push the box from the pizza into the trash, get in the car and drive back to the motel. Sunday morning, I'll pick up some bagels from my secret source, along with some cream cheese, smoked salmon and a Bermuda onion, and we'll eat the whole mess, then breathe noxious fumes over each other for the rest of the day, while you move a few *more* rocks and I try to figure out why the goddamned outlet in the third bedroom doesn't work. We'll have tea around four because some traditions die hard, if at all, and carry our cups around the garden while we admire your gift for rock placement. By six, I'll have washed up, and you'll be concocting something delicious to tide me over through the week. By nine, I'll be in the car, humming to myself as I drive back to New Haven. All just the same as it's been for the last year and a half.''

What he'd just described sounded, to her ears, like the outlines of a marriage. ''Why have you never married, Elmo?'' she asked him.

"I don't know. It just didn't happen. I guess I didn't want to."

"Really?" She looked at him, wondering how one managed to resist the temptation.

He laughed. "I don't mind doing my own laundry, looking after myself. I didn't want to, Hadleigh. I probably never will. Let's go eat."

There occurred during dinner a delicate modification in the way they looked at and reacted to each other. Something had shifted, Hadleigh thought, and they no longer had their previous ease. He kept stealing glances at her breasts; he also studied her hands which were large and long-fingered. Her fingernails, no matter how hard she scrubbed them, always bore traces of dirt from her work in the garden. He tried to keep the conversation light, all the while responding more and more strongly to his knowledge of her new attainability.

She felt as if she were being slowly boiled in something like gelatin, a substance that, as it cooled, would congeal around her, leaving her caught in its transparent solidity. She knew by the way he watched her mouth when she talked, and the manner in which his eyes seemed drawn to her body, that he was having sexual thoughts about her. It made her curious and afraid; curious because she couldn't imagine what it was he'd find attractive about her; afraid because he was going to put their friendship in jeopardy.

On one level, she thought it might be lovely to surrender herself into his arms, to study closely the shape of his face and the brown depths of his eyes. She might run her finger over his lips, following the shallow indentation that ran from his upper lip. He had a good chin, squared, and with a cleft in it. He was good-looking. She imagined resting her cheek against his shoulder, and became daunted by her capacity for fiction. The reality would be the unbearable moment when he'd want to push himself into her parched body. Once there, completely caught up in his own unaccountable pleasure, he'd thrust and groan until it ended, and she'd be left to wonder why people found the activity so exceptional.

She was so fearful of his anticipated advances that the drive home was made in silence. She shivered with cold, too preoccupied to ask him to turn on the car heater. Anything might trigger him, and she didn't know what she'd do if he attempted to touch her. By the time he'd pulled up in her driveway, she was completely overwrought.

"What's wrong?" he asked.

"Nothing at all. It's been a long day and I'm tired. I've got the children for the day tomorrow."

"I know that, Haddy. What's wrong? Was it something I said or did?"

"No."

"It's still early. Are you going to give me a cup of coffee?"

"What time is it?"

"Nine-thirty. You're not that tired, are you?"

"It feels much later. Yes. Do come in. I'll make tea. But you mustn't stay long. I really am tired."

He followed her into the kitchen and leaned against the counter while she filled the kettle. He seemed to have grown progressively taller and broader all evening until he now had the effect of blocking out the light. He'd assumed enormous proportions, and she felt dwarfed.

"Tell me what's wrong," he encouraged her, producing his pipe from his jacket pocket.

She dropped the cups she'd been reaching for. They made a dreadful racket as they fell, smashing on the metal rim of the counter. She swore under her breath as she bent to lift a fragment of the thin porcelain.

"I'll help." He set aside the pipe to get the dustpan and broom from the cupboard under the sink. In a few quick moves, he'd swept the broken pieces into the pan and tipped them into the garbage. Rinsing his hands at the sink, he looked over at her, saying, "For some reason, I've put you on edge. Maybe I should go."

"It might be better," she said dry-mouthed, turning off the burner beneath the kettle.

He caught her hand and held it. "Tell me what's wrong. I hate to go off leaving things this way. I'll be up all night reviewing everything, trying to figure out what it was I said or did to upset you."

"You've done nothing!" she insisted, wishing he'd leave it alone and just go.

"It started at the restaurant," he said, thinking back.

"Oh, for God's sake, Elmo! I'm frightened. Can't you see that? I've seen how you've been looking at me all evening, and the way . . . It's no good."

"How do you know that?"

"I know it."

"I don't see how you can. All you've got to go by, unless I'm mistaken, is Chris. And I wouldn't peg him as God's gift to women."

"Elmo, you're forcing the situation. It can't work."

"You keep saying that, but you don't know it."

"I've thought about it," she admitted. "Tonight's forced me to think of little else. I simply couldn't do it."

"Maybe Chris was never any good and just ruined it for you."

"Elmo," she said unhappily, "you're spoiling everything."

"How? I haven't done anything. We're only talking."

"You're forcing the issue. You're changing everything. Please. You really should go now, before it's too late."

"No. Let's talk about it for a few minutes. I admit I'd like to go to bed with you. Okay? It's out in the open. What's so terrible about that? Does that make me into something different than I was before?"

"Yes, it does," she said in almost a whisper.

"How? Why? It's a compliment to you."

"*Please*! It really would be best if you left now." She felt menaced by his determination, and by her own sense of failure. Why wouldn't he accept what she was saying?

"Okay." He backed down. "I just thought maybe we could talk about it. Have a good day tomorrow with the kids. I'll be here when you get back."

"Yes. Thank you for dinner."

He left. She went quickly to lock the door, feeling distinctly as if she'd barely escaped something of immense and perilous proportions.

Throughout her day with the children, she was periodically overcome by anger and embarrassment at what had happened the night before. She tried to put it out of her mind, but she'd think of Elmo's determination, and cringe inwardly.

It was one of the very rare times when she couldn't enjoy the twins, and this served to heighten her anger. The children were full of news about their father's wedding, which was planned for a month's time, and sounded to be a very lavish do.

"She's always telling us what to do," Bonita carped, "as if

she thinks *she's* our mother. I think the whole thing is going to be awful."

"We're getting special clothes for the wedding," Ben chirped. "Everything blue. I'm getting a whole new suit, and new shoes, and a carnation to wear on my lapel."

"He can be bought," Bonita whispered to her mother. "It makes me sick!"

"He's having fun, love. There's nothing wrong with that."

As she was letting them out at the house Chris had bought in town, off Noroton Avenue, she looked at his new silver Porsche in the driveway, and grew angrier still, knowing he'd used her money to finance his present wealth. He'd made a fortune on his investments, so much so that returning her funds hadn't at all affected his new lifestyle.

She reversed out into the road and headed toward home, but after less than a mile pulled over to the side of the road and lit a cigarette, doing "something creative" as her mother would have said. The motor idling roughly in the old station wagon, she sat for twenty minutes deliberating, then put the car into gear and continued on home.

"Have a good time?" Elmo asked from the sink where he was cleaning several paintbrushes.

"I was distracted," she said, stepping out of her shoes, "thinking about what happened here last night. I do wish I could accept what you'd like to offer me, but I can't. It means too much to me. And I could never be certain it was real."

"How real does it have to be?" he wanted to know. "How real is real?"

"I need to belong, if I'm going to be involved with someone. You frighten me because I can't help feeling you think I'm some sort of a challenge. And once you'd succeeded in meeting the challenge, you'd lose interest and go on to someone else."

"And what if you're wrong? What if it is real?"

She shook her head. "I value your friendship more than I can say. I couldn't have coped these last eighteen months without you. Last night changed it. We'll never be able to go back to the kind of friendship we had. You'd be constantly thinking of finding some way to change my mind, and I'd be constantly on my guard. I think it might be best if we part friends and leave it at that. I have to get through another year, with everyone watching to make sure I'm on my best behavior. I have too much to cope with, without the additional complications you'd add to my life."

"What happened anyway," he asked, "to turn you off so completely?"

"How do you know I was ever 'turned on' in the first place?"

"I *don't* know. That's why I'm asking."

"There are people, you know, Elmo, who simply don't care for it. I'll wager there are more than you might imagine—men *and* women."

"Maybe," he allowed, "but it's not healthy."

Her anger gushed to the surface. "Who are *you* to say what is or isn't healthy? It's a judgment you make based on whether or not a woman will go to bed with you."

"I do not!"

"I think you do. It's why I'm never entirely comfortable with you, because, despite everything you say, when it comes down to it, your attachment to anyone depends on sex."

"That is categorically untrue! I've never even so much as tried to kiss you."

"You haven't. But you've thought about it."

"Of course. I'm only human. And you're a damned good-looking woman."

"No," she corrected him. "You're only *male*. I've never looked at or thought of you in that fashion."

"Maybe that's because you've got a little problem."

"What problem, Elmo?"

"You're frigid."

"Frigid?" She laughed loudly, greatly amused. "Yes, I've heard men use that term before. Chris, for one, was fond of it. A woman doesn't want you, therefore she's 'frigid.' What a wonderfully convenient way to explain someone's lack of interest! How clever men are, coining terms to damn women for failing to be responsive to them!"

"You admit yourself that you don't like sex, that you're not good at it."

"That is true. Since we're being so frank, let me make myself absolutely clear. I never wanted Chris, and I've never wanted you. We've been friends, and I very much valued your friendship. Isn't it interesting that I'm 'frigid' because I value everything about you except your sexuality? I find that terribly interesting. Don't you?"

"Sex is a natural part of friendship," he said.

"Oh, horseshit, Elmo! Next, you'll be saying the reason I have so few friends is because of my infamous 'frigidity.' "

"Come on, Hadleigh! Don't you think this is getting a little out of shape?"

"Oh, not at all! Initially, I liked you because you said that people like Chris and his cronies were superficial and frivolous. I thought, at the time, it was terribly courageous of you. But I'm not eighteen anymore, and I've given a lot of though to your attitudes. I think you stayed on the outside, Elmo, because try as you would, you couldn't figure out how to get on the inside. Also, not once in all these years have you ever taken what I've had to say at its face value. It's as if you've been convinced all along that sooner or later you'd change my mind by demonstrating your sexual prowess, showing me graphically what I've been missing. I've seen you look at women, seen the way you assess their sexual potential, and I've been uncomfortable with it. Still, since you hadn't overtly done it to me until last night, I was willing to have you as my friend. The only woman I can think of who was absolutely perfect for you is my mother. Perhaps you shouldn't have broken off with her."

He was so flabbergasted he couldn't speak.

Seeing this, she said, "Did you really think I didn't know?"

"I had no idea you did," he blustered, feeling as if he'd just been dropped blindfolded into a deep pit.

"I've known almost from the start. I don't know why it ended, but I certainly knew it was going on. You confirmed it that night you came to the house in Greenwich, when I cut my wrists. The only possible way you could've known there was something wrong was if you'd been with my mother when I rang her."

"I came because I was afraid for you."

"You came," she corrected him, "because you didn't think my mother would. It's sad, you know, but I don't think you've ever understood either one of us. My mother, however, was infinitely more suited to dealing with you. She's terribly sexual."

"You say that as if you're proud of her."

"In some ways, I am, very much. You keep looking for ab-
solutes, Elmo, where none could possibly exist. I love my
mother. I always have, and undoubtedly always will. You've
assumed that since we don't get on well that we hate each
other. You couldn't be more wrong. Mother and I are people
who think deeply and often about love, but we don't speak of
it.

"You're surprised. You shouldn't be. I may be mad, as my
mother is mad, but we're neither of us stupid. And that's
another assumption you've made over the years. I'm tired of
being considered defective in one way or another."

"I don't think that way of you," he argued.

She smiled at him. "Not consciously, perhaps."

"Jesus Christ! I can't believe any of this."

"I'm sorry it had to end this way. I truly am."

"I don't see why it has to be so final, why we can't just go
on as we have been."

"Ah, Elmo, you're really not as bright as you'd like to
believe. My children are at stake here. I have twelve months to
get through—twelve months of being sober and in control. I
need what precious little self-esteem I have to get through it. I
couldn't possibly have you here, chipping away at me, trying
to get me to do something I don't want to do. I no longer trust
you."

"Well," he said, harried. "I guess I'll be going."

"That would be best."

Thirteen months later, the judge granted a continuance of
custody to Chris, with the proviso for review the following
year.

The same afternoon of the hearing, Hadleigh set out to buy
a pack of cigarettes. As she was driving down Noroton
Avenue the station wagon, of its own accord, turned into
Chris's street and nosed into his driveway. She sat for a
minute or two looking at the shiny silver Porsche. Then, with
sudden, reckless energy and no thought but the desire to inflict
some measure of pain upon him, she reversed the car into the
road, put the shift into drive, and floored the accelerator. She
drove straight up the driveway and into the rear end of the
Porsche, which crashed through a beam supporting the front
porch as well as the garage door beyond. The porch collapsed

in a gratifying roar of dust and bricks. The Porsche looked like a large silver accordion.

Inside the house, the twins raced to the living room window to see what had happened.

Ben shouted, "*It's Mummy!*"

Bonita gaped at the damage, and at her mother who was sitting calmly behind the wheel of her car lighting a cigarette.

"I'm going to call the police!" Ben announced. "She should go to jail! What a rotten thing to do to Dad's car!"

"Don't you do anything!" Bonita warned. "She'll drive away, and we'll pretend we were in the backyard playing and didn't see who did it."

"I sure did see who did it, and I'm going to tell!"

"You do, and I'll never talk to you again as long as I live. You'll get her *in trouble!*"

Ben shoved her aside and ran to the telephone. "She deserves to get in trouble!"

"*She does not!* I'll never talk to you again! Not ever! You stinking little shithead!"

"*Mom!*" Bonita pleaded. "*Drive away* and no one will *know* it was you!"

"It's all right, Bonita. I wanted to do it."

"But they'll put you in jail or something!"

A siren announced the arrival of a police car.

"*Mom! Go on! Hurry up!*"

"Go back inside, Bonita. Everything will be all right."

"No, it won't. Please? I don't want anything to happen to you."

"Nothing will happen. You know that I love you, don't you?"

"I know," Bonita said miserably.

She was taken to police headquarters and booked for criminal mischief. While she waited for Leggett to arrange bail, the desk sergeant called Chris to ask how he wanted to handle matters. Hadleigh fully expected the worst that would happen would be a whacking great fine, and possibly a court case regarding damages to the car. But within an hour she was being escorted, in a cruiser, to the state hospital in Newtown for observation. The Darien police had arranged to have her committed for psychiatric assessment.

"You can't *do* that!" she protested.

"We sure can. You're going in for two weeks so it can be decided if you're competent."

"Of course, I'm competent. I know exactly what I did, and why."

"People don't go around doing stuff like that. It's not the way to handle problems."

"It is if your limits have been reached, and then exceeded."

"Whatever. You're riding to Fairfield Hills on a police ticket, and that's that."

A mix of outrage and despondency kept her focused throughout the fourteen days of her confinement. Riding atop this mix was a layer of disbelief and horror that she was actually incarcerated in what was tantamount to a circus sideshow, and that no one had been able to supercede the authority of the police.

Her eyes moved constantly, absorbing the details of the place and its inhabitants. She was determined to do absolutely anything to get out of there, out of the open ward filled with somnolent, drugged women who either leaned like timbers against the walls, or who curled in sleep on the wooden chairs and benches or on the floor. She was sane enough to use whatever promises, lies, or deceit were required to convince those in power that she was fit to leave, that there was no viable reason to detain her. She claimed full responsibility for her actions, expressed awareness of those actions, as well as of the repercussions, and expressed regret she didn't feel. She had to get out of there. Once she was able to walk out into the scentless winter air, she'd begin putting her final death plan into effect.

She spent her time working out how and where she'd do it. Seated cross-legged on her assigned iron bed, she savored the incidentals of her plan. No one would intervene at the eleventh hour this time. She'd be completely alone, and away from home. There'd be all the time necessary to make it good.

She was well aware of the irony of the situation. What else could one call the tenacious grip she was maintaining on her reason, just so she'd have enough time alone to put an end to her life? So ironic did she find it that she smiled often, in contemplation of the ultimate freedom that would be hers in a mere matter of days. She viewed it with immense relief: no more court appearances, no more doomed sexual challenges, no more losses.

She thought fondly of how concerned Bonita had been, and of her own foolishness in doing what she had to the house and the car. The children might have been hurt, but she'd never stopped to consider them. All she'd been able to see was that stinking ostentatious car, that mobile symbol of his money and power, and she'd had to destroy it. She wasn't sorry she'd turned his automobile into scrap metal. She only wished she could have been there to see his face when he'd viewed the remains.

She took care to do all her weeping beneath the bedclothes in the dead of night, for fear any display of strong emotion might be construed as a weakness and therefore reason to prolong her stay. She also pretended to swallow the various tablets and capsules they gave her, although it was impossible to do anything about the liquid medications. On her trips to the lavatory, she threw the accumulated pills into the toilet and flushed them away.

By the end of her stay, all that was in her system was the cup of chicory-flavored coffee she'd had in lieu of breakfast. Those few reasonably rational women with whom she'd become acquainted began whooping and cheering at the sight of the long black limousine that drew up as Hadleigh left the building. Turning back, Hadleigh smiled and waved, then climbed into the car.

PART THREE

Connecticut 1960–1962

Twenty-six

Bonita was eleven the year her mother smashed up the front of her dad's house and wrecked his new Porsche. She blamed Ben for everything that happened afterwards, and refused to speak to him, despite the pleading of her father and stepmother. She knew that if Ben had kept his mouth shut, instead of calling the police, everything probably would've been all right. But he went ahead and called, and the police came, and then there were all kinds of phone calls—from the police, and lawyers, and even from Grandma, whose end of the conversation sent Bonita's father into a red-faced, silent fury. No one would tell her what was going on, but Bonita knew it was bad. There'd be this awful, sudden silence when she tried to ask what was going on. So, finally, one afternoon, she rode her bike down to the Puritan—a store at the corner of the Post Road that sold magazines and cigarettes and stuff—and called her grandmother collect. She was a little nervous about doing it because she could never predict how her grandmother would react to things. But she liked her grandmother, even though Ben hated her and never wanted to go into the city when she invited them. She called; Mrs. Walsh answered and accepted the charge, then put her grandmother on.

"This is unprecedented," Frances said, sounding pleased. "Are you well, Bonita?"

"I'm fine, Grandma. How are you?"

"I am as always. Where are you?"

"I'm at the store down the road. I didn't want to call from the house because Ben's always spying, and he tells them everything I do. Grandma, where's my mom? What's going on? Is she in jail?"

"What day is it? It's Thursday. I'll collect you tomorrow afternoon when you come home from school. You'll come for the weekend. Tell your father and the chimp."

Bonita laughed and said, "Okay. Does Ben have to come too?"

"I think not. I'll be there at four. Please be prompt, Bonita."

"I will."

"It might be best if I ring your father this evening and suggest your spending the weekend. Otherwise, you may have some difficulty explaining."

"Thanks a lot, Grandma. I'll be ready."

Her father and Monkey and Ben always talked about how much they disliked Frances, and how awful she was. While Bonita was sometimes confused by her, her admiration for her grandmother far outweighed the confusion. She loved the apartment on Central Park West, and the guest room, and funny old Mrs. Walsh who was forever putting the kettle on for tea, then forgetting about it while she went off to do something. She and Frances argued about the constant need to replace burnt-out kettles, and about Mrs. Walsh's habit of delivering food to the table, then going to her room without bothering to come back to clear up. The two of them were very funny, and Bonita enjoyed their arguments because they were times when Frances said outrageous things, and Mrs. Walsh gave back as good as she got, threatening regularly to, " 'ave a go, you don't mind 'ow you address me, your ladyship."

Bonita loved her grandmother's clothes, and the fact that she always hired limousines to take her wherever she wanted to go. What bothered her was Frances's impatience with Bonita's mother, although she always showed up, as if by magic, if there was some problem. It was a little amazing the way her grandmother seemed to know exactly when to arrive, even though she sometimes seemed furious about it. There'd been one Saturday when she and Ben had been spending the day at their mother's house, and Grandma had decided to come, too. She'd been right in the middle of saying something to Frances when Bonita suddenly interrupted, saying, "You shouldn't talk that way to my mother. It's not nice." Her grandmother had looked down at her, and Bonita had thought she'd be angry with her now, too. But Frances had smiled approvingly, and said, "Plucky little thing, aren't you?" which had been, Bonita knew, a compliment. She'd had to look the word up in the dictionary later, just to be sure. Plucky was defined as being brave, having courage. Bonita was thrilled. Her grandmother's approval, though seldom given, made her feel unique, especially since Ben got on her nerves and she usually sent him off to watch television in her bedroom when they were there for a weekend. "That boy," Frances had confided, "has inherited the majority of his father's genes. Pity."

Bonita liked going for walks with her grandmother along Fifth Avenue. People usually looked twice at Frances, as if she were someone famous they thought they should recognize. She was tall, and held herself very straight, and sales people always rushed to serve her; so did waiters in the restaurants where they went for lunch. She could also be unkind at times, saying things that made Bonita feel as if all her bones had been crushed, things that made her feel stupid. Bonita never forgot bringing a story with pictures—she'd been in the second grade then—that her teacher had given a gold star. Frances had spent a long time looking at it before saying, "You haven't your mother's talent. It's rather a sad little effort, Bonita. I'm surprised your teacher thought so highly of it."

For the most part, however, her grandmother treated her as if she wasn't a child, but just another person. She often asked Bonita what she thought of this or that, then listened closely to the answers Bonita gave. They had real conversations, and she wasn't afraid at all to ask her grandmother questions her father and Monkey refused even to hear. It was Frances who'd told her, the year before, what "French kissing"—something she'd heard about in the schoolyard—meant.

"Kissing with one's mouth open," Frances had told her bluntly.

"That's *horrible*!" Bonita had been disgusted.

"Only because you're pre-pubescent. In due course, you'll find a great number of things you now consider quite revolting are, in fact, rather compelling."

Her grandmother told her about menstruation, and about

making babies, and about the importance of decorum. "One might," she said, "be literally falling to pieces, but one needn't reveal it to the world at large."

"How come you'll tell me all these things when nobody else will?" Bonita had asked her.

"It's a debt of conscience," her grandmother had said enigmatically. "I now consider it at least partially paid."

The limousine was parked in front of the house when Bonita arrived home. Monkey had packed her overnight case and was standing in the living room peering out at the car through a gap in the curtains.

"I'm going now," Bonita told her, grabbing her bag.

"Take your books and make sure you do your homework," Monkey reminded her.

"Sure, sure, yeah, yeah," Bonita said under her breath, going back for her bookbag.

The driver came around to open the door, and Bonita slid into the back.

By way of greeting, Frances said, "When I was a girl, we wore uniforms to school. At the time, I thought it was a tremendous nuisance. Upon reconsideration, I do believe they have a certain value. We really must get you some more attractive clothes. Does that gibbonesque woman have any taste at all?"

Bonita laughed, then went right to the point. "Did you know it was that little bastard Ben who called the police? Did you *know* that?"

Her grandmother's eyebrows lifted, and she looked most surprised. "I did *not* know that. What a loathsome child!"

"That's what I think. I don't talk to him anymore. I *told* him not to do it, but he wouldn't listen. He *wanted* her to get into trouble."

"He truly is his father's child." Frances lit a cigarette, troubled by the implications of this new knowledge.

"You don't like my father, do you?"

"Not in the least. He lacks decency, among other things. Do *you* like your father?"

"No," Bonita answered readily. "I think he's a jerk. And you're right. Ben's just like him. Monkey's not bad. At least, she tries. *Is* Mom in jail?"

Frances sighed. "It seems your local police have an extraordinary privilege, Bonita. If they wish to, they have the power to have someone who has become a public nuisance committed to an institution to test her sanity. Your mother is presently at Fairfield Hills undergoing psychiatric evaluation at the behest of the local constabulary. She will be released on Wednesday."

"Can I go see her?"

"No one is allowed to see her. I've been in contact with your mother's lawyer who assures me her behavior has been exemplary and that she will be permitted to come home next week."

"She is *not* a public nuisance! *Ben's* a public nuisance. I hate him! Now, I *really will* never speak to him again. It's *all* his fault!"

"Unfortunately, he's only indirectly responsible. It was less than wise of your mother to do what she did."

"I'm *glad* she did it! I didn't like that car anyway."

Frances laughed and patted her hand.

"I want to live with my mother," Bonita declared.

"I'm afraid the court won't allow it."

"I don't care what the court allows. If I want to live with my mother, no one can stop me. It's not such a bad house."

"It's a frightful house," Frances disagreed, "a dismal, depressing house."

"It doesn't matter. I can live there. We'll fix it up."

"I expect you could. Whether or not it comes to pass is entirely another matter."

"I don't see why I couldn't go to court and tell the judge where I want to live. Nobody ever asked me."

"Deplorable, isn't it? Of course your preferences should be taken into consideration."

"If I can't be with my mother, can I come to live with you?"

Frances took another puff on her cigarette, then put it out. "That's out of the question, I'm afraid, Bonita. You must realize that I'm best at short visits. We'd lose whatever fondness we have for one another in very short order had we to face each other daily. Whatever sense of occasion we presently experience being in each other's company would go by the boards. It simply wouldn't work. I prefer to leave things as they are, so that the time we do spend together remains special."

Bonita decided Frances was right. "I guess maybe it is better this way. But I *am* going to live with my mother.''

"Perhaps you will," Frances said, pleased by the child's tenacity. "I will hope that your determination is rewarded."

"Thanks for telling me the truth, Grandma."

"Thank you for demanding it."

Bonita tried her mother's number every half hour on Wednesday from the time she got home from school until her bedtime at ten. After a restless, fretful night, she pretended to set off for school on her bike, but as soon as she was out of sight of the house, turned and headed for her mother's place. It was a four-mile ride, and she was thoroughly winded and half-frozen by the time she got there and ran up the front steps only to find the door locked. She went around looking in all the ground floor windows, tried the back door and the basement windows, but couldn't get into the house. She threw handfuls of gravel at the front bedroom window but succeeded only in cracking the grass. After checking the garage to see that the station wagon was gone, she found a small rock, broke one of the panes in the back door, and reached inside to unlock it. She went through every room and closet in the house, even the cellar. Finally, in a panic, she dialed her grandmother's number.

"Is she with you, Grandma? Because she's not here. I played hookey and rode out here on my bike. The car's gone and I thought maybe she drove in to see you."

"How does everything look?" Frances asked.

Bonita looked around. "There's a cup and saucer in the sink, and that's about all. It could've been there for a hundred years. I'm really worried. I called for hours last night and nobody answered. It's too early for her to be out shopping. The stores don't even open until nine or ten, except for the deli."

"I thought she seemed overly cheerful," Frances said. "I'll look into it. It might be best if you went along to school."

"I don't have a note. And anyway, I want to stay here and wait. Maybe she went out for breakfast or something." She reached to open the refrigerator door. "There's nothing in the fridge, so she could've gone for breakfast. But that doesn't explain why she didn't answer the phone last night."

"I'll ring the school and make some excuse for you. It's best if you go. You have my word I'll look into it."

"Will you let me know, please, if you find her?"

"Of course I will. Go along to school now, Bonita. I'll ring them straightaway. What's the name of your school?"

Bonita told her. The call ended. She trudged out to climb back on her bike.

Everyone was looking for Hadleigh: the Connecticut and New York state police, the local police in Darien, New Canaan, Norwalk, Westport, and Stamford. Every hospital in a hundred-mile radius had been contacted. Motels and hotels in the area had been called, as had the airlines, bus depots, and railroad stations. Frances personally made dozens of inquiries. Hadleigh seemed to have vanished.

Over dinner, Chris said, "Her goddamned mother's making a fuss over nothing. Hadleigh's off on a bender somewhere, and Frances has half the world looking for her."

"She doesn't *do* things like that!" Bonita argued fiercely. "Why are you always talking about her like she's some kind of bum or something? When she comes home, I'm going to live with her. I *hate* it here, and I *hate* the way all of you gang up on her, including that little traitor." She pointed at her brother, who stuck his tongue out, then smiled.

"Go to your room!" Chris ordered.

"No! I haven't done anything. I'm staying right here."

"Go to your goddamned room!"

"No!"

"I'm going to count to three," he warned, "and if your ass isn't out of that chair and on its way up the stairs, it's going to be the sorriest day of your life."

"*I mean it!*" she said, out of her chair and backing away from the table. "I'm going to live with my mother, and *you* can't *stop* me!" She ran off up the stairs to her room, slamming her door so hard that the chandelier in the dining room began to swing.

Friday morning, after her father had left to catch the early train into the city, and while Monkey was putting the finishing touches to the lunch bags, Bonita sneaked into their bedroom to find Monkey's address book, hoping to find her father's lawyer's name and address. It wasn't in there. Returning downstairs, she snatched her lunch bag off the counter, picked up her bookbag, and left the house.

For a second time, she rode out to her mother's house, let herself in through the broken door, and went directly upstairs to the chest of drawers where she knew her mother kept her bank statements and important papers. Sitting on the floor with the drawer before her, she went through everything until she found the copy of the divorce decree in an envelope from Leggett's office. The decree had the judge's name on it. Satisfied, she went downstairs and looked up the telephone number of the judge.

A woman answered, and Bonita said, "My name is Bonita MacDonald and I'd like to talk to the judge, please."

"I see." The woman's voice held a hint of laughter. "Is there something I could help you with?"

"I don't think so, thank you very much, unless you're a judge, too. I *really* have to talk to him. It's very important."

"Have you a pencil, dear? I'll give you the number to call, although you may have some trouble getting through to him. Is it really very important?"

"It really is, honestly."

"All right. First write down this number." She recited it, and Bonita copied it down. Then she said, "When you get his secretary, tell her I told you to call, and that it's a confidential matter. I hope everything works out."

The secretary told her court was in session but that she'd make sure he got her message, and that he might be able to return her call around noon. Bonita thanked her, then hung up to wait. She found a box of corn flakes and walked through the house eating handfuls from the box. She'd never again eat anything Monkey prepared. She'd rather eat dry cereal.

While she wandered around the house, she debated calling her grandmother, but decided she wouldn't until she had something worthwhile to tell her. It did worry her a little that her grandmother might have some news and be trying to get in touch with her at school or at her father's house. She wished noon would hurry up so she could talk to the judge then get back to the house. Monkey would pitch a fit, but she didn't care. She wasn't going to have to live there much longer. She'd be living here, and once she and her mom fixed the place up, it wouldn't be that bad at all.

By twelve-thirty, when the telephone rang, she had changed

the sheets on her mother's bed and vacuumed the entire house. She'd kept checking the time every few minutes while she'd Windexed the big window in the living room that overlooked the garden. The ringing almost caused her to fall off the chair she'd been standing on. Still clutching a handful of paper towels and the pump-spray bottle, she tore to the kitchen.

"Bonita MacDonald, please."

"It's me. I'm Bonita."

"You're a *child*! Are you sure it's me you wanted to talk to?"

"I'm very sure. You judged my mother's divorce, and a couple of weeks ago you gave me and my brother back to my dad for the second time. Now my mom's missing, but when she gets home I want to live with her."

"Slow down there," he said. "Tell me your name again?"

"MacDonald. My mother and father are Christopher and Hadleigh. I'm a twin; my brother's name is Ben."

"I don't recall . . ."

"You *have* to remember her. She's very tall, blonde, and pretty."

"A lot of couples come through my courtroom, young lady . . ."

"But you *liked* her. She *told* me you did. You said you wanted her to make you one of her dollhouses for your grand-children."

"Ah!" he said. "Now I remember. But what's all this about?"

"You told her that in a year she could have us back, but when the year was up, you kept us with our father. I don't *want* to live with my father. I want to be with *her*. And how come nobody asked *us* what we wanted?"

"How old *are* you?" he asked.

"I'm eleven. Why? Does how old I am make a difference?"

"You're a very resourceful young lady, but I'm afraid I can't do anything for you. This must go through proper chan-nels."

"But you're the one who decided she couldn't have us, and she tried so hard for the whole year. It's not fair! Nobody ever asked me. I never wanted to be with my dad. He's a jerk, for Pete's sake. It's just not *fair*!"

He stifled a chuckle, then said, "I'm sorry, but there's

really not a thing I can do. Perhaps," he suggested, "you could speak to your mother's attorney. A hearing can always be arranged if circumstances have changed."

"My mother's lawyer. I've got his number. His name's Mr. Leggett."

"Call Attorney Leggett. I can only promise that if a hearing does come before me, I'll pay specially close attention."

"Okay," she said, let down. "Thanks a lot."

She put down the phone, then picked it up again to call Mr. Leggett's office, where the secretary put her through at once.

"I know who you are," he told her. "Why are you calling, Bonita?"

She told him, and he whistled softly. "This is really something. Look. Tell your mother to call me and we'll arrange a meeting, maybe go back to petition the court on your behalf. But don't get your hopes up. You actually *spoke* to him?"

"Yes, I did."

"You're a pistol, kid," he laughed. "Have your mom call me and we'll see what we can do."

Cheered, Bonita left the paper towels and the Windex on the counter, and went out to ride back to her father's house.

As far as they were able to figure out afterwards, Hadleigh drove the old station wagon to a dirt road off Route 104, and abandoned the car about a mile from the shore of the Mianus River. She took an undetermined number of a variety of pills, along with about a third of a pint of gin. Then, leaving her coat, handbag, and shoes on the riverbank, she walked into the fifty-six degree water. Since the tide was just at the point of turning, her handbag was lifted by the water, and floated along a short distance behind her. Under normal circumstances, the combination of pills and alcohol would have killed her, but the water's extreme cold lowered her body temperature sufficiently to prevent the drugs' full effects from taking hold of her system. By chance, she floated on her back some miles along the river during the night, and was discovered soon after dawn on Friday morning by two fishermen who thought at first she was dead, but felt for a pulse on the off-chance. The Bedford police were summoned, along with an ambulance, and she was rushed off as a Jane Doe to the nearest hospital. When one of their lines reeled in her handbag, the two fishermen delivered it to the Bedford police who then called the number Hadleigh had listed in her wallet in case of emergency. Some two weeks after their discovery of the woman floating in the river, the fishermen were stunned to receive separate cashier's checks, each in the amount of five thousand dollars. Sent anonymously, the checks were attached to identical notes that read simply: with gratitude.

Hadleigh hovered on the critical list for almost thirty-six hours while Frances sat in the hospital waiting room chainsmoking Nat Shermans and reporting at regular intervals to Bonita who begged to be allowed to come but who'd have been refused admittance in any case, being under fourteen years of age.

To the disbelief of the hospital staff, Frances remained wide awake and apparently quite comfortable throughout the entire thirty-four hours of her wait. They brought her cups of coffee, and trays of food from the cafeteria, and were so impressed by her that they refused to accept her offers of payment. Privately, the nurses took bets that she was a member of the British royal family incognito, and were only a little disappointed to learn that she was nothing more than the mother of the attempted suicide in the ICU.

By Saturday morning, Hadleigh regained consciousness. She remained awake long enough to be able to make out her mother's features, and to hear her say, "You're positively *hopeless* at suicide, Hadleigh! Might I suggest that you give it up as a hobby and see if you can't try remaining alive?"

Hadleigh began to close her eyes, but Frances gave her shoulder a shake. "Listen to me! I think you should know that there *are* certain people who'd prefer you to live. Your daughter, for one, has been displaying some remarkable gumption, ringing up lawyers and judges, insisting she be allowed to come live with you.

"Three times now you've tried this. In that asinine American sport of baseball, one is chucked from the game after three failed attempts to reach a base. Perhaps you should begin following the game. You may find it has some direct bearing on your life. I warn you, Hadleigh! Try this again, and I'll give up on you. Enough is enough."

"I wanted to die," Hadleigh mouthed.

"Quite obviously! Unfortunately, it's not the area of your true talent. I will allow you to go back to sleep now. But just remember what I've said. I'm going to ring Bonita to tell her you've come round." She sighed, then said, "Dear God, Hadleigh! You're such a ninny." She bent close, and Hadleigh was enveloped in the scent of roses as her mother's lips touched against her forehead. Then she was gone.

Twenty-seven

Bonita just couldn't understand why her mother had wanted to die. Even though she'd been a witness on many occasions during her childhood to her father's striking her mother, and even though she and Ben had been given to their father, she still didn't think those were good enough reasons to want to stop living. Obviously, her mother felt she had reason enough, but when Bonita tried to talk to her about it, Hadleigh would shake her head and change the subject. The most her mother would say was, "I'd had all I could take," which came nowhere near answering the question. Bonita came to believe that if she knew more of the specifics, she might, in some way, be able to make amends and turn her mother's unhappiness around.

The most hurtful aspect of life with her mother was that, after all Bonita had done in order to be able to live with her, Hadleigh seemed almost indifferent to her daughter's presence in the house. Believing this to be some sort of temporary aftermath of her suicide attempt, Bonita undertook, at age twelve, to become the unofficial guardian of her mother's well-being. She organized the household, wrote out shopping lists, bundled the laundry into a basket so that all Hadleigh had to do was put it into the washer, and even, on a regular basis, cooked the meals they ate together.

It was she who maintained they needed some decent furniture, and dragged Hadleigh out to buy a new sofa, a dining set, and some pretty dishes instead of the old Melamine stuff.

With the return, finally, of much of the furniture from Christopher, the house began to look inhabited and even inviting. But the purchase that made the largest impact on her mother was the television set. Hadleigh took to watching old movies at all hours of the day and night and, sometimes, when Bonita couldn't sleep, she'd go downstairs to see her mother sitting on the sofa in the flickering blue-gray light from the TV, staring raptly at the screen. Bonita would curl up beside her, her mother's arm would close around her—Hadleigh felt almost unnaturally warm at these times—and Bonita would go to sleep with her head on her mother's lap.

There were, of course, good times they shared: working together in the garden in warmer weather, trying out new recipes Bonita found in one magazine or another, shopping for clothes or odds and ends for the house. For the most part, though, Hadleigh just didn't seem to be there, and nothing Bonita tried worked to snap her awake. Bonita told herself that was the way things were for now, that they'd get better in time, and she was there, in case her mother needed her.

Ben refused to visit, but Hadleigh didn't seem to care. It was as if she'd resigned herself never to having more than she already had, and the absence of her second child made no visible difference to the relative sameness of her days. Bonita couldn't help wondering if it wasn't the Librium that was responsible for her mother's state of abstraction. But when, during her annual checkup with the family doctor, she asked about this possibility, he told her, "It's just a tranquilizer, not a behavior-altering drug." So what was it, then, that was keeping her mother locked away in some room to which Bonita was refused entry?

Her grandmother was no more forthcoming, saying with inadvertently alarming casualness, "It's undoubtedly hereditary. We seem to pass on manic-depressive tendencies."

"But what was *your* mother like?" Bonita asked.

"Very ordinary, actually," Frances said.

"And was your father ordinary, too?"

"He was, rather."

"So, then, you couldn't have inherited it, could you?"

"I suppose not. Perhaps it was a bizarre gift from God."

"Grandma! That's not funny!"

"I do apologize. It isn't in the least funny."

The idea that she might, upon entering adulthood, become

like her mother was very worrying, and Bonita began closely to scrutinize her own behavior, suspicious of any impulse or thought that seemed the least bit odd or unusual. She confided her fears to her good friend Tandy Holmeyer, who gave her a peculiar look and said, "Don't be silly, Bon! There's nothing nutty about you."

"Sometimes you can't always tell," Bonita said.

"You're absolutely the most normal person I know. I mean, look at Barbie Cummings, for heaven's sake! You want to talk about crazy. That girl is twelve years old, and her mother gave her a checking account. I've seen her borrow fifty cents from someone, then write them out a check, and the kids all run around, asking, 'Where am I going to cash this?' and Barbie tells them, 'Just take it to the bank.' She's got credit cards and everything, but she's always borrowing money from everybody, then writing out checks. I mean, that's really nuts. People are always stealing her stuff. D'you ever notice? I mean, honestly. That girl's *really* crazy! Compared to her, you're the sanest person I ever met."

"Well, maybe."

One afternoon, Bonita arrived home from school to find that her mother had rediscovered her old interest in dollhouses. She'd been to an art supply store and bought blades, and set- and T-squares, heavy cardboard, and paints, and was sitting at the kitchen table with a large sketching pad, making notes and drafting her ideas for a new house. Bonita was delighted, but tried not to go overboard. She went ahead and worked around her mother, getting dinner started, while Hadleigh roughed out the design.

Her mother took to spending her evenings at the kitchen table, her supplies, cigarettes, and a pot of tea at hand, constructing a Victorian house with gingerbread trim and many chimneys, French doors leading from the library, a butler's pantry, and even servants' quarters under the roof. When the model was completed, Bonita studied it, saying, "You don't even need to make it out of wood. This one's terrific."

"It's merely a model," her mother explained. "I'll make the real one on a somewhat larger scale, with good wood."

"What'll you do with it?"

"I have no idea. I'm not concerned with the end of it. I'm only interested in the process."

"I'll bet you could sell them, and for a lot of money. Remember, the judge wanted to buy one for his grandchildren. Maybe you should find out if he's still interested."

"I'm sure he was merely being kind."

"I don't think so," Bonita disagreed. "He remembered you because of the dollhouses, Mom. I'll bet anything he'd buy one."

"It's not important." Hadleigh was crafting a chimney, using small strips of balsa wood to create its lip. Later, she'd painstakingly paint it to look like brick.

"What if I found someone who was interested, would you be willing to sell?"

"I expect so. Haven't you homework to do?"

"I'm going to do it now." Bonita stalled, wanting to make some definitive comment on the rekindling of her mother's interest in the dollhouses. The best she could come up with was, "You're really good at it, Mom."

"Thank you, love. You'd better get on with your homework."

It was funny, but in some ways she actually missed the life she'd led with Monkey and her father. She wasn't at all sad at not having her brother to contend with on a daily basis, but she did occasionally think with longing of the meals Monkey had served at regular hours, and of the clothes she'd brought back from trips into New York, and of the little she herself had been required to contribute to the running of the household. Now here she was with her mother, where she'd wanted to be, and everything was backwards. She was the one in charge, the one who had to remind her mother when to put away the dollhouse supplies, or turn off the TV set, and go to bed. What she missed most was her own role as child in the house. But, she reminded herself, she'd wanted this, and she was determined, not only to see it through, but to arrive at the future hand in hand with a happy, healthy mother who had a strong desire to stay alive.

She tried having friends over to visit, but she could tell from the way they looked at her mother that they thought she was kind of strange. It angered and embarrassed her. She refused to explain her mother, and didn't think she should have to. So she stopped asking kids over, except for Tandy who loved the dollhouses and could sit for hours examining them, asking

Hadleigh all kinds of questions about how she made the mouldings, and how she painted areas to look like real brick. Hadleigh liked the chubby little girl, and didn't mind responding to her endless questions.

"They're absolutely amazing!" Tandy told Bonita repeatedly. "I'd give *anything* to have one of my own."

"Maybe you could ask your parents to buy you one, for Christmas, or your birthday, or something."

"D'you think she'd make one for me?" Tandy could hardly contain her excitement at the prospect.

"She probably would. They're pretty expensive though."

"Like how much?" Tandy asked, mentally reviewing how much she had saved up.

"Well, one of the big ones would be about three hundred dollars." Bonita offhandedly gave a sum she thought well beyond the means of ordinary people.

"Wow! That is kind of a lot." Still, Tandy looked longingly at the most recently completed house—a neo-Gothic colonial with pillars and even bits of what looked like Spanish moss draped over the porch rails. "I'm going to ask them anyway," she decided. "Usually, if I beg hard enough, they give in. They like," she confided, "to spoil me. It's okay, being an only child, you know. I'm not one bit sorry I haven't got any brothers or sisters."

Bonita thought nothing would come of it, but one evening the telephone rang and it was Mrs. Holmeyer, asking to speak to her mom.

"She's busy right now," Bonita lied. "In the shower. I could give her a message."

"Tandy's told us about your mother's dollhouses, and we thought we'd get her one, for her birthday."

"Okay," Bonita improvised. "I can take the order."

"Could you?" Mrs. Holmeyer sounded doubtful.

"Oh, sure. I handle all the orders, write up the bills and stuff, so my mom can concentrate on getting the dollhouses ready in time. She's pretty backed up right now. When would you want it for?"

"We were hoping to give it to Tandy for her birthday in May. Will that be enough time?"

"Oh, I think so. I'll check with Mom, to be sure, but it should be all right."

"You'll want a deposit, of course."

"Right. For the supplies. Seventy-five dollars. You could give Tandy a check to bring to school."

"All right. Tandy says you know which house she likes best."

"Oh, sure. The Victorian one."

"Wonderful! Tandy will bring the check tomorrow. Made out to whom?"

"Hadleigh MacDonald." Bonita spelled it out. Then, the call concluded, she ran to tell her mother.

"We've got an order for a Victorian house!" she laughed. "Tandy's mom's going to buy her one for her birthday. *Three hundred dollars*."

"*Bonita*! That's exorbitant!"

"She didn't even blink at the price, Mom. Can you do it?"

"I suppose so. When is to be ready?"

"May."

"I'd better start on it at once."

Bonita was wild with excitement. "You could make this into a real business," she said eagerly. "And if you did one house a month, that would be three hundred dollars every month. Or you could do bigger ones and charge more."

"Don't get carried away," Hadleigh cautioned. "They take a lot of time, and it's not possible to do them that quickly."

"But you know what?" Bonita cried, more and more excited. "If you just cut out all the pieces, you could sell them that way and people could put them together themselves. We'd put in instructions, and glue and nails and stuff, and they'd have the fun of assembling the houses. They'd be kits; we'd put everything in a big box with 'Hadleigh's Houses' printed on the front, and you'd be able to make more of them. Instead of cutting out the pieces for one house at a time, we could get some kind of electric saw and cut out five or six at a time. And you know what else? We could fix up the basement and make it into a workshop. I could help you after school and on the weekends. We'd have a whole *business*! It'd be terrific, don't you think?"

Her enthusiasm was contagious, and Hadleigh felt herself becoming infected by it. "I think," she said, "I'll go down and have a look at the basement, see if I'd care to work down there."

Bonita threw her arms around her mother. "It's going to be great, Mom! I just know it. And before I forget, I'm going to call up the judge and ask him if he still wants one for his grandchildren." She released her mother and started toward the telephone, saying, "I think I'll charge him four hundred. He's a judge. He must have lots of money."

Listening to her daughter's avid outpouring of ideas, and watching her impassioned face, something seemed to slip into place inside her head and Hadleigh knew she'd just reconnected with her life. It simply wasn't possible to remain wherever it was she'd been when here was someone who, so filled with hope and determination, was insisting she share in the excitement of the unknown. She'd have preferred to stay entombed within the walls of her numbness, but Bonita wouldn't allow it, and her obstinacy finally overcame Hadleigh's longtime lethargy. She was going to have to relocate all the internal wires, make good the circuitry linking her to the outside world, because here was someone bent on seeing her do it. And how, she wondered, could she possibly let this child down? Here was this tall, skinny kid, about to enter her teenage years, joyfully bearing a burden of optimism that could cause the impossible to happen simply because she willed it.

In that moment of illumination, dozens of electric thoughts criss-crossed through her brain. Unaccustomed to the activity, Hadleigh tried and failed to track them all. There were things she knew, but she didn't know; there were ideas she recognized, yet couldn't define. Valuable information was logged somewhere beyond the burnt-out areas of her consciousness, and she had a new and sudden longing to traverse beyond the wasted regions in order to examine and put to use that information. With Bonita's help, she thought it just might be possible to get to it. And the first step would be getting rid of the tranquilizers that made her feel as if her feet were encased in cement.

She opened her arms to Bonita, saying, "I don't deserve you."

"What does that mean?" Bonita wanted to know, basking in her mother's embrace.

"It means I haven't been paying enough attention to you."

"Sure you have. I don't need that much attention, anyway."

"Everyone does," Hadleigh disagreed, holding her away to look at her. "You're going to be a beautiful woman," she said wonderingly.

Bonita made a face. "Are you kidding? My nose is too wide and I have a funny mouth."

"It's not a funny mouth. It's beautiful. You've got my mother's mouth." God! Hadleigh thought. It was true. Bonita bore a closer resemblance to Frances than she herself did to her mother. "Shall we go look at the basement?"

"Sure." Bonita's vitality seemed disproportionate to her size, something that spilled over, causing the air around her to fill with vibrations. What an amazing girl! Hadleigh thought. And how wrong she'd been, in her self-indulgent trance, to ignore her as she had.

"I think we'll make some changes," Hadleigh said as, hand in hand, they went down the misshapen wood stairs to the basement.

Misinterpreting, Bonita ran ahead to study the gloomy area, saying, "I think we'll have to. It's so dark and icky down here. Maybe it'd be a better idea to enclose the porch and make you a workshop there. You wouldn't want to be down here all day."

"You're quite right. I wouldn't."

"If we enclosed the porch and put in an electric heater, then you'd be able to stop sometimes and look out at the garden. That'd be a lot better."

How did Bonita know these things? Hadleigh wondered.

As they were returning upstairs, Bonita asked, "How come we don't see Augusta anymore?"

"I don't know. I think perhaps she's given up on me."

"Why would she do that?"

"Bonita," Hadleigh said slowly, "not everyone can deal with someone who attempts repeatedly to take her life. People find it upsetting, and they become concerned that you're going to do it again, perhaps while they're with you. It's not an attractive thought. I don't in the least blame Augusta for staying away. And in any case, she has stayed in touch with Mother. It isn't as if she's broken with us completely."

"Maybe I'll call her up," Bonita began.

"No. Please don't do that. We mustn't inflict ourselves on people, Bonita. Perhaps, in time, she'll visit again."

"But don't you miss her?"

"Very much."

"Then why don't *you* call her up?"

"Perhaps I will. For now, let's go one step at a time."

*   *   *

Bonita got her first period the following week. Tandy was impressed and jealous. "You're so lucky," she told Bonita. "I'll probably never get mine."

"Of course you will," Bonita said, having herself been prepared for this event for months, with a box of sanitary napkins and a belt at the ready in her closet. "Everybody does."

"I guess. It's just so sort of official," Tandy said wistfully. "Like you're really, finally, growing up."

"It's not all that great," Bonita played it down, despite being mightily impressed herself with the evidence of her move into womanhood. "As a matter of fact, I feel kind of strange." It was the truth. She couldn't possibly have described the odd things that began to happen, almost from the minute her period started.

Several times a day, it seemed as if she fell asleep while being completely wide awake. She'd see and hear things for a second or two, and it was as if she were somewhere else entirely. Then, it'd be over and she'd be back in the classroom, blinking, trying to catch up with what the teacher had been saying, or with some dangling thought of her own. The really odd part of it was that, for that second or two, she felt as if she'd become her grandmother, and was seeing and hearing things with her grandmother's eyes and ears. She told herself she was being dumb, and refused to think about it.

Since Hadleigh's last effort to take her own life, the amount of sleep Frances got seemed to diminish by a few minutes each night until she was getting no more than two or three hours' rest. As they always had, her nights continued to throb with the noisy dynamics of her disordered dreams, but on top of that, peculiar things seemed to have started happening. Sudden-shifting shadows, unexpected noises, a clouding of her vision: all set off minor adrenal rushes within her. Usually, it was Mrs. Walsh, dropping a glass in the kitchen, or shambling along the hallway to her room. But, occasionally, things happened for which Mrs. Walsh couldn't possibly have been responsible because she was off spending the night with friends.

There was the instance of the light that seemed to be shining directly outside her bedroom window. Yet that was impossible, since the apartment was eight stories above the ground.

And when she went to the window, all she could see was the darkened, lamp-dotted mass of Central Park below.

There was the thump at the front door which, when Frances flung it open to investigate, seemed to have had no cause. She told herself some child or prankish teenager had gone along the corridor toward the elevator, giving each door along the way a whack for good measure. It was the sort of thing a young person would do, and so she ignored it.

She spent ten alarming minutes one afternoon trying, with all her might, to get the storm window in the kitchen to close— something normally accomplished with a minimal push. The window seemed to be fighting her, and refused to catch, pushing back from the connection with the metal frame so that, in the end, she had to kneel on the counter and, using both hands, got the window shut through a mammoth effort that left her breathless and perspiring.

There was the very distinct feeling she had of not being alone in the apartment. Yet, most peculiar of all, rather than feeling distressed by any of the things that happened, she had the unshakable sense that some benevolent force had come to her aid. She wasn't completely alone, and yet she was in no danger whatsoever.

What was distressing was the return of Edwin to her dreams, and she found herself locked into ongoing argument with him, restating her case and insisting he see where his responsibility lay in all that had transpired. He'd brought it on himself, with his hedonistic determination to "have fun" and remain detached. He could, at the very beginning, have discouraged her from devoting her energies to his cause. It would have been infinitely kinder than the manner in which he'd led her on simply by his calculated omissions.

She spent angry hours of sleep battling a man who could not be made to see his culpability. It so outraged her that she returned to killing him, nightly, in her dreams. Blood splashed on the walls, on her, on the carpet. Strands of his hair adhered to the abandoned poker, held in place by rapidly clotting blood. When she looked down at herself, it was to see rivulets of bright red blood streaming down her thighs. She tried to run; she could hear the air-raid beginning, but she was rooted in place, her feet cemented to the Indian carpet, refusing to heed her brain's command to move. She screamed as the bombs whistled through the air; the ceiling above her exploded outward briefly, then collapsed down upon her. She could not outrun the dark, could not get past her own body, and so lay slowly suffocating beneath the rubble of her dream's creating.

As the air was slowly pressed from her lungs, she saw something important, and just at the moment when she was about to identify it, she was dragged upward out of sleep, to sit gulping air and listening to the muted, ceaseless flow of traffic on the streets below.

Bonita awakened, very frightened, and crept downstairs to the telephone. She knew it was a ridiculous thing to do, but she just had to call her grandmother. When Frances answered, sounding wide awake, Bonita said, "It's me, Grandma. I know it's three o'clock in the morning, and I'm really sorry, but I had this awful dream and I had to call and make sure you were all right."

"What did you dream?" Frances asked.

"It was really spooky," Bonita whispered, fearful of waking her mother. "There was this big, kind of fat guy with a moustache. I kept trying to talk to him and he wouldn't listen and it drove me crazy, so I hit him with this metal thing."

Frances drew in her breath in an audible gasp. "Bonita," she said, shaken, "I will collect you Friday. It's very important that we talk. I'll ring your mother tomorrow to explain."

"What does it *mean*, Grandma?"

"I'm not sure," Frances admitted. "I think you and I must compare notes."

"Okay. I'm sorry about calling so late. You weren't sleeping, though, were you?"

"No, I wasn't."

"That's okay, then. I'll see you on Friday."

The two of them sat in the master bedroom with the door closed, so Mrs. Walsh couldn't, on some pretext, listen in on their conversation. Frances encouraged Bonita to tell about everything that had been happening over the past month, and Bonita was more than happy to obiige.

"Sometimes it happens at school. It's almost as if I go away somewhere, just for a second or two, and I'll be in your kitchen looking into the refrigerator, or I'll be walking down the street. And when I look down, expecting to see my shoes and socks, I see your black high heels. You know? The ones with the little bows? Or the brown ones with the gold band. It's as if I'm you, Grandma, and I'm seeing everything with your eyes.

"It doesn't happen all the time," she went on, "and it hardly lasts for any time at all. But the dream the other night was really scary."

"Is there more?" Frances asked. "I want you to think very carefully. Try to remember specific details."

"Well," Bonita said, "sometimes I'm not seeing and hearing things as you, but as myself. A couple of weeks ago, just before I was going to bed, it happened. It was really weird, but I was standing outside, on the window ledge, looking into your bedroom. And last week, I was trying to open the apartment door, but it was locked and I couldn't get in."

"I see." Frances lit a cigarette, trying to find some logical explanation for all this. She kept coming back to one, seemingly inescapable, conclusion. "Tomorrow," she told Bonita, "we're going to have a little experiment. When it's done, we'll discuss this further."

The next morning when Bonita awakened, Frances was dressed and ready to go out. "I want you to stay here, and do whatever it is you do first thing in the morning. I'll be back in precisely one hour. When I return, we'll have our discussion."

"Okay," Bonita agreed.

Frances walked south to Fifty-seventh Street, then east to Fifth Avenue. Along the way, she stopped several times to look in shop windows before continuing. Turning north, she stopped two more times, to make purchases, then returned to the apartment.

Bonita had made a pot of tea and had a cup ready for her grandmother.

Frances sat down with the girl at the dining table, added milk to her tea, then looked expectantly at Bonita.

"Where are the packages?" Bonita asked.

"Do you know what I bought?"

"Not exactly," Bonita answered. "But I'm really glad you decided not to get the red purse."

"My God!" Frances exclaimed. "Tell me what you saw!"

"I saw a store window with all kinds of luggage and handbags, and the red purse. The only other thing I saw, and I didn't see it really, was I kind of felt myself carrying two small packages that were sort of heavy."

"It happens only occasionally, you say?"

"Sometimes it's stronger than other times. It was pretty strong while you were gone."

"I can't be certain this is working both ways," Frances said, taking a sip of the tea. "It's rather alarming, in any case. Am I the only one, or do you have experiences of this sort with your mother, for example?"

"Nope. Only you." Bonita poured herself a fresh cup of tea, asking, "What d'you think it means?"

"I'm almost afraid to say. There should be some very simple, highly logical explanation, but I don't have one. All I can think is that somehow you've become linked to me."

Bonita slowly put down her cup. "You mean you think it's really real?"

"Yes, I do. The dream you described is a dream I've had for many many years. There's *no one* to whom I've ever confided the details."

"Oh, wow!" Bonita paled, frightened. "I'm getting scared."

"I don't think," Frances said consideringly, "it's something either of us needs to fear. I couldn't tell you why, but I don't think we do. I am, however, going to have to take certain steps to see if I can't spare you the dreams."

"What're you going to do?"

"I don't know, but I'll think of something. I want your promise that you'll keep this our secret."

"I promise."

"You are a very special child," Frances said softly. "Very special."

She hit upon the idea of using the TV set to set up a barrier of interference. Not only did it prove successful, it actually worked to place a block between her and the dreams. Leaving the set going all night allowed Frances six or seven hours of utterly peaceful sleep.

When next they met, Bonita confirmed that she no longer dreamed of the large man with the moustache. "It still happens every so often during the day," she told Frances. "I was at lunch in school the other day and all of a sudden I could see a very nice-looking man with kind of silvery hair and glasses."

Frances laughed, flushing, and asked, "Was there anything more?"

"Nope. It was just a second or two, and that was it."

"Thank God for something!" Frances exclaimed, relieved by the knowledge that Bonita's gift was neither predictable, nor maintained for extended periods of time. "I should hate having to go about with a transistor radio appended in some fashion to my person."

"What?" Bonita was confused.

"It's nothing," Frances laughed. "Simply a joke."

Twenty-eight

Bonita had no idea what her grandmother had meant until one evening, while doing her homework in the bedroom, she went off again on one of her brief excursions to find herself looking, at very close range, into the eyes of the nice-looking, silver-haired man. It was only a moment or two, but Bonita had a very clear picture of what was happening, and forced herself away. A little shocked, she sat chewing on her pencil. She'd never thought of her grandmother as a woman, as someone who could do the sort of things she very obviously did. She had to smile, and then laugh, deciding she'd keep this new bit of knowledge secret. It just wouldn't be fair, she thought, to admit to having invaded Frances's privacy.

It did, though, cause her to reevaluate completely her assessment of her grandmother. It also raised a lot of questions in her mind about being a woman, and especially being a woman with men.

Frances said, in response to Bonita's circumspect questioning, "Women are women throughout their lives, Bonita. There's no reason for one to be less than fully functional. I'm sure, once you discover boys, you'll have no intention of giving them up simply because you happen to become sixteen, or twenty, or even sixty. Men," she declared profoundly, "can be most addictive. Just so long as you never for a moment forget that they're all no more than cleverly disguised children. The majority of them—with some notable exceptions, your grandfather, for instance—are incapable of logical thought or of any appreciable degree of sensitivity. There are some who make fine husbands and parents, but for the most part, they're purely temporary creatures. Remember that, and you'll never be disappointed in your dealings with them.''

"If they're all so rotten," Bonita said, "why do women make such a fuss over them, anyway?''

"Aahh!" Frances smiled. "For all their failings, men are delicious creatures. Even their faulty logic has its endearing moments. You *will* see, in time, Bonita. I promise you you will.''

"What's his name, the man with the nice face and the silver hair?''

Frances eyed her closely, then said, "Mr. Webster.''

"Is he nice?''

"Yes, very.''

"Are you in love with him?''

Frances laughed quite uncontrollably.

"Is it that funny?" Bonita asked, smiling.

"Very definitely," Frances said. "I can assure you that love has nothing to do with my dealings with Mr. Webster.''

"Oh!''

"Are you disappointed?" Frances asked.

"Kind of.''

"Why?''

"Because. I thought maybe you'd like to be married again, have someone to keep you from getting lonely.''

"I am never lonely.''

"Well, then, I guess it's all right.''

Hadleigh wanted the houses to be perfect in every detail. If her first two clients, the judge and Mrs. Holmeyer, were pleased, she might well be able to start up a bona fide business. But more important than that was the satisfaction she'd have of knowing that something she'd conceived of and executed entirely by herself would garner praise and even admiration.

While she worked, her thoughts ranged over a number of topics but came repeatedly back to the area of her mother. Slowly, she began to realize that she had, throughout her life, participated actively in what she'd always viewed as her mother's dislike of her. Suddenly, she was no longer doing that. Perhaps it was due to Bonita's closeness to her grandmother, and the amount of time they spent together. And perhaps, she reasoned, it was due to her own gently burgeoning sense of self-worth. Yet that, too, was as a direct result of Bonita's influence. She had always thought of herself as a large empty bowl, and had simply waited for others to fill her. Because of Bonita's refusal to accept defeat, she was now making the first concerted effort ever to fill her own needs.

She thought back to her friendship with Elmo, trying to decide if that, too, had been an example of her ineffectuality. Perhaps it had been, she thought; but at least she'd had the courage to speak the truth at the end, and to take a stand. She was actually proud of having sent him away, instead of simply giving in.

As she glued perfectly symmetrical walls together, she considered her mother, for the first time with no accompanying surge of anger. She no longer had the exaggerated awareness of and hypersensitivity she'd once had to her mother's every word, deed, and gesture. And the loss of all that was due, again, to Bonita.

Bonita was such a powerfully sane and sensible girl it would have been positively impossible for her to care as much as she did for someone who didn't both reciprocate that caring and didn't offer something substantial in return.

What was it about Bonita? Hadleigh wondered. She was changing all of them, working a kind of practical magic that seemed to elevate the lives of the people she chose to love. And how very lucky one was to be chosen by her!

It came to her that she'd like to do something special for her daughter, to share in an extraordinary event with her. And since recently she'd been thinking more and more about her childhood, she thought perhaps she'd take Bonita on a trip.

"I'd *love* to go to England!" Bonita said passionately. "We could see where you grew up, and the house you lived in with your grandmother, all of it."

"It's only a thought," Hadleigh said. "If we were to go, it wouldn't be for a few months yet, until school ends. And it would depend, too, on how much the porch will cost. There may not be enough money." The funds she'd at long last received back through the courts had been greatly devalued due to their loss of interest. The bulk of it had been promptly invested in high-yield securities to increase their monthly income. "Let me think a bit more about it. We'll see."

"Parents always say that," Bonita observed good-naturedly.

"At least we're consistent."

The very next day after they had this conversation, Frances arrived in a limousine to spend the weekend.

"I've decided," she told Hadleigh, "to take a trip abroad. I thought, if you had no strenuous objections, I'd like to take Bonita. We'd go by ship, of course. I couldn't possibly fly. I prefer the Cunard line. You won't refuse permission, I hope."

"Well, no. I had hoped to take her myself, but I'd have no objections to her going with you. I'll have to discuss it with her, of course. It really wouldn't be fair of me to make this decision for her. What made you think of this?" she asked.

"I honestly couldn't say," Frances admitted. "I was having dinner last evening when it suddenly occurred to me I hadn't been back in fifteen years. And then I thought we might make it something of a celebration, a belated birthday gift."

"Of rather epic proportions," Hadleigh said.

"Oh, well," Frances smiled. "Why not?"

"Why not, indeed!" Hadleigh suddenly laughed. "All that filthy money sitting in bank accounts growing dusty. One might just as well use it for something totally frivolous."

"My thoughts precisely. You could, you know, come with us."

"No," Hadleigh said prudently. "Your original plan is best. It wouldn't be quite the same, were I to tag along. Let me have a word with Bonita, and we'll discuss it further at dinner. And please," she added, lifting one of her mother's bags to carry it upstairs, "try not to hate the guest room. I never actually thought you'd spend a night here."

"Neither did I," Frances said. "But one never knows when one will change one's mind."

"One doesn't, does one?" Hadleigh quipped.

Frances paused in the act of lighting a cigarette to say, "I perceive certain changes in you, Hadleigh."

"And I in you. I'm glad you decided to come."

Bonita pretended to swoon. Then, seeing the disappointment

on her mother's face, said, "I'd rather wait and go with you."

Hadleigh sat down beside her on Bonita's bed, and took hold of her hand. "I had hoped to share this experience with you," she said, "but it's not a good enough reason for me to spoil what will, without question, be the opportunity of a lifetime for you. I think you should go. Your grandmother will lay it all on first class. You'll stay in the best hotels, dine at the best restaurants, do it all up in style."

"But I really did want to go with you."

"You and I will go another time."

"I'm starting to feel bad. I can tell you're disappointed."

"I'll admit that I am. But I think you should go."

"Are you sure?"

"Yes, I am."

"I don't know, Mom. Maybe I shouldn't."

"The final decision's yours, Bonita. It's healthy to make decisions, and whatever you do decide will be the right decision, because you'll have made it for yourself."

"I know that. But deciding always means somebody has to be disappointed, and that's the part I don't like."

"It's not possible to satisfy everyone. That's one of the sad facts of life."

"You won't be mad if I go with Grandma?"

"I promise you I will not be mad."

"I really did want to go with you."

"I know. And we will, another time. Why don't you go along now and talk to Mother. She's waiting for you."

Bonita hesitated, then asked, "Are you two friends again?"

Hadleigh appreciatively lifted a handful of her daughter's thick golden-brown hair. "We were never not friends, Bonita. We simply failed to understand each other for a time."

"And you do now?"

"Not completely, but we're making somewhat more sense to each other."

"I'm glad!" Bonita declared. "I love you both."

"And we both love you."

Suddenly, having made the decision and set the wheels in motion, Frances was fearful of returning to England. There was no real reason for her to be afraid, she told herself; yet Amanda was still there, as far as Frances knew. The woman could have died, but she didn't believe that for a moment. Somehow Amanda's death would have made itself known to her. She laughed, imagining typhoons and tornadoes shaping themselves as a result of Amanda's passing.

"You're goin' nutty again," Mrs. Walsh said, seeing Frances sitting alone and laughing. "I don't know 'ow I've put up with you all these years. You're the biggest bloody nutcase I've ever met up with, and that's the God's 'onest truth."

"Only second to you, Emma," Frances replied. "Your habits and eccentricities are becoming legendary in New York. Half a dozen times a day, people ring me up to verify the truth of the latest rumors regarding you."

"You see what I mean!" Mrs. Walsh stated. "People ringing you up," she scoffed. "The only one what rings you is that fat faggot Webster."

"I assure you Mr. Webster is not a faggot," Frances said smoothly. "Although he is rather on the hefty side."

"You ought to be ashamed of yourself," Mrs. Walsh said. "At your age 'n' all."

"I am not quite in my dotage yet. Please don't hurry me along."

"And what'm I supposed to do while you're off gallivantin' 'ere there and everywhere?"

"You'll have a lovely long paid vacation, won't you?" Frances told her. "More money to add to the first sixpence you ever laid hands on."

Mrs. Walsh snorted and shuffled off to put on the kettle.

It was agreed that Bonita would spend a week with Frances in New York before they were to sail.

"She simply must have new clothes," Frances told Hadleigh on the telephone.

"Of course, Mother," Hadleigh responded easily. "I'll drive her in, and leave her in your capable hands."

"Are you cracking wise with me, Hadleigh?"

"Not at all. I trust your judgment implicitly. I'm sure Hadleigh will come home with a spectacular wardrobe."

"You know," Frances said, secretly pleased at Hadleigh's demonstrably increasing feistiness, "I'm not sure I didn't prefer you as a vegetable. You were a good deal more malleable."

"But so boring."

"True."

Hadleigh laughed. "Please, just don't go overboard. I have to live with her afterwards."

"You have my promise I will not establish precedents."

Suffering silently, Bonita allowed herself to be rigged out in what Frances called "charming little shifts," and Anne Fogarty cotton shirtwaist dresses, and ballet flats from Capezio. Frances even went so far as to buy her a straw boater bedecked with silk flowers which Bonita would only carry in her hand. Nothing on earth could have moved her actually to wear the thing. It made her feel like a complete jerk, and while she was anxious to go on this trip, there was no way she was going to go wearing that hat.

The ship sailed on the last day of June. While Frances was in the stateroom getting settled in, Bonita moved slowly around the promenade deck to watch Manhattan recede, and to see the Statue of Liberty, and to breathe in the almost chewable pungency of the air hovering over the Hudson River.

She remained on deck for more than two hours, long after everyone else had gone in for afternoon tea, either in the cabin- or first-class lounges. Strains of music drifted up from the lounges while Bonita leaned on the rail, wondering if it hadn't been a mistake agreeing to come on this trip. It all felt funny, as if she was watching a movie in broad daylight that nobody else seemed to know was playing. She'd have given anything to make one more phone call home, even though she'd spoken to her mother an hour before the limousine had come to take them to the pier.

She was reluctant to go along to the stateroom adjoining her grandmother's, where her luggage was waiting to be unpacked and where Frances would undoubtedly be waiting, wanting to know what she'd been doing all this time.

In the past few weeks she'd started experiencing her visioning excursions with increasing frequency. And the whole week she'd spent shopping with her grandmother she'd felt as if she had two brains instead of one. She'd known in advance every single store they were going to go to, and even the things they were going to buy. Periodically, she'd almost been able to hear Frances thinking, and had automatically put a move on at one point because Frances was growing restless. And on their last day of shopping, when they'd stopped for lunch in a small

French restaurant on Fifty-third Street, Bonita had given the waiter her own order and then gone ahead to give her grandmother's, too, without their having discussed it. Frances had given her a wide-eyed look, and then laughed. Confused, Bonita had looked up at the waiter, but he couldn't possibly have known that what had occurred was anything more serious than a young girl being allowed to order a meal for her grandmother.

After he'd left the table, Frances had said quietly, "If you're going to begin reading my mind, I don't know what I shall do. Perhaps," she'd said confusingly, "I'll have to buy a transistor radio. It would be too absurd for me to go about with an earplug. People would assume I'm deaf."

"What're you talking about?" Bonita asked despairingly.

"Setting up electronic interference," Frances answered in tones of utmost reasonableness. "You don't seriously believe I'm going to allow you to read my mind, do you?"

"Oh, wow!" Bonita swallowed hard, and looked down at her hands. "It's getting really confusing, Grandma. I don't understand why it only happens with you and nobody else. Tandy and I experimented and nothing happened."

"You haven't told her, have you?"

"Oh, no. I just said wouldn't it be fun to try, you know, and she thought it was hilarious. It didn't work, anyway."

Frances, who ordinarily was not given to physical demonstrations, had reached across the table to take hold of Bonita's hand. "Whatever it is," she'd said, "and God knows I don't understand it myself, I don't think it's necessarily a bad thing, and you're not to be afraid. I should hate to think I was responsible, in any way, for making you unhappy."

"I know that, Grandma. I feel the same way. It's just scary sometimes, that's all."

"If it's any consolation, it scares me a little, too. But my overall feeling is that this 'connection' we have isn't a bad thing."

"I guess," Bonita said philosophically, "it must be happening for a reason."

"And we may never know what that reason might be," Frances had added. "Some things simply have to be accepted on faith alone."

New York was gone now. Only shadows indicated land, and

the sea-smell was cleaner, less redolent of garbage than the river-smell had been. Bonita leaned on the rail, the stupid straw hat still in her hand and, in a moment of rebellion, she allowed the wind to take it. It sailed away, riding on the air for close to a minute before landing, finally, on the crest of a churning green wave. When she could no longer see it, she pushed away from the rail and stepped inside the enclosed deck where rows of empty chairs sat facing the windows. She listened again to the music before making her way along to her stateroom.

Twenty-nine

With Bonita gone, the house seemed very empty. The voices of Jerry Lee Lewis, the Supremes, Sam Cooke, and dozens of others, no longer penetrated the kitchen ceiling to smother Hadleigh in indecipherable lyrics accompanied by throbbing basses and the phlegmy cry of saxophones. The telephone never rang, and the absence of Bonita's footsteps overhead was a constant reminder that she would be away for weeks on end. Hadleigh missed her far more than she'd thought she would, and the nights especially seemed long and silent. Yet she enjoyed having time entirely to herself, and spent the majority of her evenings working on the dollhouses, getting up every so often to stretch her cramped muscles and have a cigarette and a cup of tea. She'd take her tea and sit on the top step at the back door, breathing in the fragrance of summer in the garden as fireflies flickered in the shrubbery and a bold family of raccoons traipsed across the grass to sniff out the possibilities of the bin where the trashcans were kept.

On the weekends, she could sometimes hear laughter and voices from the neighboring houses, but they were merely interesting wisps of night-sounds, like the sudden rustling in the pachysandra or the all-but-inaudible fall of dead petals from the flowering beds. The sky was wonderful, luring her into an ongoing contemplation of the possible true meaning of infinity, and of how marvellous it might be to inspect those other worlds sparking at unimaginable distances.

During the second week of Bonita's absence, a heat wave

descended, making Hadleigh's work in the kitchen impossible, even with the large fan going full blast. She sat in a tub of cold water several times a day, feeling her blood cool sufficiently to enable her to climb into the baked interior of the old station wagon to drive to the supermarket, or to Ring's End for more wood. Even the slightest effort was exhausting and, finally, she temporarily relocated her workroom down to the basement where it was a good ten degrees cooler.

While moving her supplies, she imagined what her mother and Bonita might be doing, picturing them going here and there in London, or having afternoon tea at Brown's Hotel, where they'd be staying. Thoughts of various landmarks led, almost naturally, to thoughts of Amanda and the flat in Portman Square.

It had been years since she'd lost contact with Amanda, but she remembered her very vividly, and wondered if she was still there. It was inconceivable that Frances would look her up, but not impossible that she might check to find out whether Amanda was alive or dead. The woman had been a closed topic of conversation since that January in 1941 when her father had taken Hadleigh back to Leamington to live again with her mother. She'd made a concerted effort to keep in touch with Amanda, at first writing letters regularly. But when Amanda's replies started to come less and less often, Hadleigh pulled back, restricting herself to birthday greetings and cards at Christmas. By the war's end, they'd fallen out of touch altogether. Hadleigh had taken it as a sign that Amanda no longer cared for or about her and had, one afternoon before leaving England, carefully drawn thick lines through Amanda's listing in her address book.

The heat didn't let up, and by evening the house was unbearable. Abandoning her work, she set the sprinkler out on the back lawn and sat on the steps watching the spotlight fixed to the rear wall of the house turn the rotating spray of water into miniature fireworks. Feeling as good about herself as she did, she was prompted to ring up and try to talk to Ben. Her ongoing guilt about him was relieved in large part by his complete absence of effort to communicate with her. He never telephoned, never asked to visit, never showed the slightest bit of interest either in her or in Bonita. The truth seemed to be that he was Chris's child. It hardly seemed possible that Ben and

Bonita had once been halves of the same seed. Bonita was open, loving, involved, and very alive; Ben was closed, unheeding, detached, and rather inert. He wasn't comprehensible to her on the level that Bonita was, but she did think she could have made more of an effort with him. She dreaded the idea that Ben might feel about her as she, as a child, had felt about Frances.

Even Chris, however, admitted to being confused by Ben's disinterest. Now that the worst of their battles was well behind them, 'she and Chris were able to have short talks on the telephone—to discuss some matter or other having to do with the children—and she felt this to be further evidence of her rationality, and his acceptance of that.

"I've told him to call," Chris said, "but he just won't. I've offered to drop him off, but he's always got something else to do. I just want you to know I haven't put him up to any of this. If anything, I've tried to force him to see you, or at least call, but he won't."

"It's probably best not to push it. He'll come round on his own time."

"Don't count on it," Chris said. "He's been acting up like crazy the last six months or so, being rude as hell to Monkey, and refusing to clean up his room. He doesn't pull himself together over the summer, I'm shipping him off to a military academy in Virginia. They'll whip him into shape there, soon enough."

"A military academy?"

"Damned right! I don't want him around here if he's going to act up all the time. Police brought him home in a cruiser last week. They nailed him and another kid blowing up goddamned mailboxes with cherry bombs. Just what I need." Winding down, he said, "And anyway, his goddamned rock and roll music keeps the baby up half the night. I don't get some sleep soon, I don't know what I'll do."

They rang off with Chris saying he'd let her know if Ben would be going off to the military academy, and Hadleigh returned to the rear steps to watch the sprinkler.

Bonita loved life aboard the *Sylvania*. She loved the huge meals served in the dining room and watching people fill the deck chairs mid-morning while the stewards offered bouillon or juice; she loved the lounge where a trio played music nightly and the passengers got up to dance; she loved exploring the public rooms on the other decks, and standing at the stern to watch the ship's wake. The ceaseless rocking nightly lulled her into the most wonderful sleep so that, in the mornings, she had to fight her way out of it in order to check the activities scheduled for that day, and get to the shuffleboard court on time for her regular date with a charming old Englishman she'd made friends with the second afternoon out.

Frances made it clear she was free to roam as she wished but, "Please be punctual at mealtimes. I dislike dining alone, so do allow yourself sufficient time to bathe and change your clothes, especially before dinner."

It seemed to Bonita little enough to ask, and once they'd settled on the times at which they'd go to the dining room, they went their separate ways. Frances had discovered two pairs of fellow first-class passengers with a passion for poker, and they were quick to invite her to join them nightly in the games room where a discreet steward had a table at the ready, and stayed close by to take their orders for drinks. Every so often, Bonita would wander in, draw up a chair just behind and to one side of her grandmother, and watch them play. The games were a nightly test of nerves they all seemed to thrive on, with high stakes, explosive laughter at the conclusion of especially exciting hands, and her grandmother's slow and steady accumulation of winnings. For three or four hours, she'd sit drinking mineral water, chainsmoking her long, brown Nat Shermans, and, deadpan, win consistently. The others had joined together in their determination to see her out a few dollars or pounds at least once, and moaned over the full houses, royal flushes, and ace-high straights she produced with awesome regularity.

They changed to five-card stud with no better luck, then to wild-card games where her winnings proliferated. When they began talking about switching to bridge, Frances collected her latest winnings, returned her Nat Shermans and gold Dunhill lighter to her bag, stood up from the table, and said, "It's been lovely, but bridge bores me silly. If you decide again to play poker, do let me know." She bade them goodnight, linked her arm through Bonita's and left the bewildered foursome wondering if they hadn't been taken by a very cunning card-sharp.

"I didn't even know you could play poker," Bonita said.

"I haven't played in more than thirty years," Frances informed her. "Fortunately, one never loses one's card sense. And having a granddaughter conveniently situated where she was able to study the others' hands helped inestimably. Here." She gave Bonita a fistful of British and American notes. "I'm sure you'll find things to buy in the gift shop. I'd say you'd more than earned it."

"Grandma!" Bonita laughed giddily. "*You cheated*!"

"No," Frances corrected her. "*You* cheated. I didn't do nearly so well the evenings you didn't come."

"Oh, wow!" Bonita guiltily looked around, but the passageway was uninhabited. "I never even *thought* about it. I mean about the 'connection.' Boy! If they *knew* . . ."

"They'll never know," Frances said with certainty. "I'll tell you a secret. My winnings more than pay for this entire trip. They were atrocious card players, betting on the most ridiculous hands." She laughed jubilantly. "Shall we look in on the lounge?"

"They're going to have a talent contest in tourist class. We could go down and watch."

"A talent contest. That should be amusing. All right. Lead the way."

Frances laughed so hard, and tried so hard not to be heard, that Bonita thought she might have a heart attack or something. When the fat lady with the terrible voice got up to sing "The White Cliffs of Dover" Frances had to rush to the loo. Chasing after her, Bonita exclaimed, "God! You're awful! She wasn't that bad."

"She was an abomination!" Frances roared, mopping her eyes with a handkerchief. "My father used to say, 'The show's not over until the fat lady sings.' I never dreamed it was true. I came closer just then to disgracing myself than I've ever done in my life. If I'd stayed one more second, I'd have wet my knickers."

This revelation, and the way Frances expressed it, sent Bonita into spasms of laughter which, in turn, set Frances off again. It was ten minutes before they'd regained control to the point where they were able to return to the lounge.

The contest had ended, having been won by a thin young man with unfortunately protuberant ears who'd sung "Londonderry Air" in a piercingly sweet, true tenor. Accepting his prize to thunderous applause, he left the stage and the band at once swung into dance music.

"It's far livelier down here, isn't it?" Frances said. "They're such a dreary lot in first class. It just proves that money doesn't necessarily make one interesting." She tapped out the rhythm of the music on the tabletop with her long, clear-lacquered fingernails and sent Bonita off to dance with her approval when the purser stopped at the table to invite her. She lit a fresh cigarette and watched the distinguished young man in his white uniform dance with the tall, too-thin youngster who moved within the circle of his arm with natural grace and confidence.

When the young man escorted Bonita back to the table, Frances said, "I'm off to bed. Do stay on and enjoy yourself."

"I'll walk you back," Bonita offered. "Do you feel all right?"

"I am in the best of health," Frances replied airily, "for someone approaching her sixty-third birthday."

"You sure don't look that old," Bonita said, watching the slightly scuffed toes of her new white Capezios move her along. "My friends' grandmothers are all kind of pudgy, with their hair dyed blue. Not one of them looks as terrific as you do."

"I have no intention of allowing myself to decline. You dance very well, Bonita."

"Thank you."

Frances turned the key in the lock of her stateroom door, then said, "Go back and enjoy yourself. There are several young men, I noticed, who appeared keen to dance with you. They looked positively crestfallen when you came away with me."

"They did? Who? Where were they?"

"I'm sure they'll make themselves known to you upon your return."

"I don't like boys, you know," Bonita said to cover her interest. "I just like dancing."

"As long as you know your priorities." Frances got the door open, then said, "Have a lovely time. I'll see you in the morning."

Bonita gave her a quick kiss on the cheek then flew off down the passageway, pausing to turn back and wave before rounding the corner and going out of sight.

Frances stepped inside, locked the door, then sat down to count her night's winnings before adding them to those of the previous nights. She sealed the money in an envelope which she then tucked into the side pocket of her overnight case. That done, she sighed, and began her preparations for bed.

Undressed, she creamed off her makeup while the tub filled. Then she slid into the perfumed water, sighing again. She felt pleasantly tired and took her time bathing, shaking her head in amusement over the poker games and the fat lady.

In her nightgown, she switched off the bathroom light then turned to make her way to the bed.

Edwin sat with blood leaking from his battered head, his hands draped limply over the arms of the stateroom chair. She couldn't gather enough air into her lungs to scream and was glad of the sudden blackness that engulfed her.

Bonita was having a wonderful time, dancing nonstop. Every time a number ended and one of the young men thanked her for the dance, another one stepped up to say, "May I?" and off she went again. She'd danced so far with four of the young men and was waltzing beautifully with the purser when suddenly there was no music, no air. She was gazing in terror at a dead man with blood running down the side of his face. No more than two seconds and she'd broken away from the startled purser and was pushing through the dancers, shoving people out of her way with frantic strength as she ran out of the lounge and toward the staircase to the upper deck.

She ran, hearing the rasping wheeze of her own breath in her ears, up the stairs, and along the passage toward her grandmother's stateroom. The door was locked. She banged at it, calling to her grandmother, then whirled around and raced to the little room where the stewards sat when on night duty. There was no one there. She looked up and down the passageway, then set off to find him. At last, she saw him emerging with a tray from one of the staterooms.

"Hurry!" she panted. "You've got to let me into my grandmother's room! Please!"

Mercifully, he didn't ask any questions but set the tray down and began to run with her back to the stateroom where he opened Frances's door with the master key.

"Will you be needing assistance, Miss?" he asked.

"I'll ring for you, okay? I'll let you know if we need you." She slammed shut the door, and flew to kneel beside Frances, praying she wasn't dead. "Grandma? Grandma?"

When Frances failed to respond, Bonita did the only thing she could think of, the thing they always did in movies when people fainted: She got a glass of cold water from the bathroom, came back and threw it in her grandmother's face. To her astonishment, it worked. Frances stirred. She wasn't dead. Bonita went back to the bathroom for a towel, then knelt again beside Frances, gently mopping her face.

"Are you all right?" Bonita kept asking, as Frances finally opened her eyes.

"Well," Frances replied, licking her lips, "I'm not dead. Tell me you didn't actually throw water on me!"

"I didn't know what else to do," Bonita wailed.

"*Did you see it*?" Frances asked suddenly, clutching at Bonita's arm.

"I saw it," Bonita whispered. "There's a funny smell in here."

"You *smell* that?"

"Sure I do. It smells awful, sort of the way the garbage used to, when Mom would forget to take it out."

Frances sat up and took the towel from Bonita's hand. She began blotting her face, hair, and throat, then stopped and looked at her granddaughter. They gazed at each other in silence for almost a minute before Bonita asked, "Who is that man? Why do you dream about him?"

"I can't tell you that," Frances answered thickly. Again her hand closed around Bonita's arm. "It would change everything, Bonita. You must understand. I simply can't tell you."

"Do you know who he is?"

"I'll tell you this much: He's someone I knew a very long time ago."

"But he's *dead*!" Bonita whispered. "That's what the smell is."

"Yes."

"But if he's dead, then how could he be here? How could it smell like that?"

"I'm beginning to think that somehow one's worst fears may have a capacity to render themselves real."

"What does that *mean*? I don't understand."

"Neither do I," Frances said, getting to her feet, then turning to look at the chair. Following the direction of her eyes, Bonita also looked, then let out a small cry and knee-walked over to examine closely a small dark stain on the carpet. Touching it delicately with her finger, she raised her hand and turned, open-mouthed, holding out the evidence for Frances to see.

"It's blood, Grandma."

Frances sat very abruptly on the end of the bed, saying, "This is not possible. It is simply not possible."

"Please tell me who that man is," Bonita begged.

Frances closed her eyes. "There *is* no man. There cannot be a man. He's been dead for more than twenty years."

"But I saw him! You saw him!"

"I don't know *what* we saw. Perhaps we're suffering a common delusion. There are such things."

"I'm not deluded," Bonita said, going to the bathroom to wash her hands, and returning with a handful of wet tissues with which she cleaned the carpet. "You're not deluded, either."

"Perhaps I am, finally."

"No, you're not! You are not!" Bonita flung herself down beside Frances and put her arms around her tightly. "I don't want anything bad to happen to you."

"Nothing bad is going to happen to me," Frances said, not at all sure of that.

"Well, I'm staying here tonight, sleeping in that bed"—she pointed at the second bed in the stateroom—"just to make sure nothing does."

Bonita knew it was really serious then, because her grandmother did something she'd never done before. Frances held her very carefully in her arms and said, "I love you, Bonita."

Thirty

Frances was dressed as always, in perfect taste: a pair of cocoa-colored draped trousers, creamy silk shirt open at the throat, low-heeled glove-leather shoes; her hair was coiled into its usual chignon with not a hair out of place; her makeup was the same as on every other day, but it seemed to sit upon her features like something that had been applied all in one piece and didn't quite fit at the edges. There was an altered light to her eyes, so that when Bonita looked at her she had the peculiar sensation she wasn't actually being seen.

"Are you sure you're all right, Grandma?"

"I'm rather tired," was the most Frances would admit to.

But in the dining room at breakfast, she drank only a cup of tea and puffed away at her brown cigarettes one after another so that their table was enwrapped in smoke. While the cigarettes were an integral part of her grandmother's image, Bonita nevertheless found it hard to eat when it seemed as if she was trying to chew her way through the gray cloud to clear air. She said nothing, concentrating instead on trying to force the "connection" in the hope she might gain some insight into her grandmother's thoughts. Of course it wouldn't come, and she wished their link was more dependable, less erratic.

Immediately after breakfast—having patiently watched Bonita work her way through two glasses of juice, cold cereal, two eggs, bacon, sausage, and grilled tomato, as well as three pieces of toast—Frances went up on deck, selected a chair completely removed from the others, brought out a book and began to read. Seeing that Bonita was lingering, Frances laid the book face-down in her lap, saying, "You'll be late for the shuffle-board."

Bonita came over to perch on the edge of the deck chair. "I wish you'd tell me," she said. "Maybe I could help or something."

With a quirky smile that made her look more like herself, Frances said, "The truth is you're a journalist. Isn't that it? Working for some filthy rag like *Confidential*. That's it, isn't it? You're after the sensational story that'll make your career."

"Come on." Bonita smiled and gave Frances's knee a little push. "Why won't you tell me?"

"Because you have a tendency to be overimaginative, and because I can't involve you. It's bad enough as it is, what with having my private visions subject to your inspection at random intervals. Go along to your game with that feckless old fool you've taken up with. Should I find myself suddenly incapacitated, you have my word, I will, with all due haste, telegraph an urgent message."

"God, you're awful! He's very nice, and very polite."

"Then its frightful of you to keep him waiting."

"Oh, all right." Bonita got up and went on her way.

Frances watched her go, witnessing the effect she had on the people she smiled at in greeting. Although many people claimed not to like children, Bonita had a most attractive ease and lack of precocity. She was also in that stage between child and adult that rendered her less offensive simply by dint of her height and good manners. Whatever else Hadleigh might be, she'd done a fine job with Bonita.

Retrieving her book, she again attempted to read but ended by staring at the pages, unable to follow the narrative. She felt exhausted, despite the fact that she'd managed to sleep in the aftermath of last night's occurrence. Allowing her eyes to close, she saw again that monstrous image of Edwin in her stateroom, and immediately opened her eyes for fear of once more transmitting the image to Bonita.

She'd sat up in bed for quite some time after Bonita had gone to sleep, trying to think what that noisome apparition could possibly signify. She'd tried to convince herself her guilt was responsible for the three-dimensional representation of Edwin, but that didn't explain the rank odor of decaying meat they'd both smelled, or the terrifying realness of that drop of blood on the carpet. Was she finally, after so long, losing her reason? Surely, she'd long-since atoned for something she'd never intended to happen. All those stays in institutions, the periodic falls into unrelenting terror from which the only source of comfort came in bottles. Yet alcohol had never done more than distance her by distorting what she viewed, thereby reducing its fear quotient. It was her belief that she'd paid dearly for what she'd done; her ongoing abstinence from drink was proof of that.

She knew all about herself, what she was now, what she'd been in the past, and why. The nightmares over the years had been quite enough to cope with without now having to fear entering some room to discover a very real-looking corpse in an advanced state of decay occupying space there. The unfairness of it made her seethe, and her anger overcame the fear. When she ventured once more to close her eyes, all she could see and feel was the whiteness of fatigue and the welcoming gift of sleep.

When Bonita came by after her match, she saw that Frances had fallen asleep, and was glad. She'd known for ages that her grandmother didn't sleep well or for very long each night, and sometimes when she stayed with her in the city she'd hear Frances moving about, or know from the remote and tinny sounds of dialogue that she was using the TV to help her sleep. So it was good to see her resting now in the deck chair, a pillow one of the stewards had thoughtfully positioned cushioning her head and a blanket folded discreetly over her legs.

After dragging over another chair, Bonita looked again at her grandmother, thinking how serene she looked. It was a rare opportunity to study this woman openly, and she did, for quite some time, deciding her grandmother really was beautiful. People for ages had been telling her how much she looked like Frances. She wished now she could believe it was true. Frances had terrific large eyes and, to Bonita's mind, perfect cheekbones. She herself didn't seem to have any bones at all in her face. Everything was just kind of stuck on her face, the features all in the right places and everything, but not one bit special.

Reviewing what had happened the night before, she experienced a spasm of fierce protectiveness toward her grandmother. It had to be just terrible to have the awful dreams she did, and to walk out of the bathroom and see a dead man sitting there in your room. I'll look after you, she thought, filled with purpose. I won't let anything bad happen to you. Satisfied with this decision, she reached over and eased the book from Frances's lap to have a look at it. *The Spy Who Came in From the Cold.* After reading the flap copy, she decided it sounded pretty good, so, keeping her grandmother's page marked, she turned back to the beginning. A deck steward came by a short time later to ask if she cared for anything, and Bonita shook her head, mouthed, "No, thank you," and kept on reading. It was terrific stuff, all moody and sad sort of. She looked over every so often to see that Frances was still sleeping, then dived back into the book.

When, just over an hour later, Frances woke up, Bonita was so engrossed in the story, she wasn't immediately aware of Frances's eyes on her, and was startled when Frances said, "Good, isn't it?"

"It really is. Did you have a nice nap?"

"It would seem so." Frances stretched so that her bones cracked, then at once opened her bag for a cigarette. "I'm hungry," she announced, as if her need for food came as something of a rude surprise.

"Okay. Let's go eat," Bonita said readily.

"If I consumed the amount of food you do," Frances said, "I'd have to be moved from place to place by a crane."

Bonita laughed. "If I ate the amount you do," she countered, "I'd be dying of malnutrition."

"Nonsense! You're thirteen and still growing. I, on the other hand, stopped growing when Disraeli was an infant." She swung her legs over the side of the chair and sat for a moment with one arm folded on her knees, smoking her cigarette. She didn't look, Bonita thought, like someone who had the kinds of nightmares she did.

"Do you mind if I ask you something, Grandma!"

"I'll know whether or not I mind when I've heard the question."

"Do you wish we hadn't come on this trip?"

Frances took her time answering. As she was about to speak, Bonita said, "You do, don't you? I can tell. If you want to go home, I'll understand."

"We're not going home," Frances said. She would *not* be put off by ghosts!

"Are you sure? Because I honestly won't mind."

"I'm quite sure."

"Okay, then. Would it be all right if I stayed in your cabin until we land?"

"Yes, that would be all right."

"Maybe," Bonita said, "we could stay together the whole trip. I'd rather be with you than on my own, anyway."

"I'll see to altering the accommodations."

"Great!" Bonita said, folding inward first one side of the dust cover, and then the other, to mark both their places in the book.

"Snore just once and you're out!"

Bonita groaned disgustedly. "You *know* I don't snore!"

"Just don't start."

Mrs. Holmeyer came to the house to order another dollhouse. "I've been trying to get hold of you on the phone with no luck, so I thought I'd come by. I was planning to leave a note in your mailbox if you weren't here. My daughter's so crazy about the house you made her it's all she's talked about. Now my sister's girl in Hartford wants one, exactly the same. I've got a check made out for the deposit, and we were wondering if you could have it ready by the end of August."

"I think so," Hadleigh told her, elated at the thought of another project to keep her occupied. The judge's dollhouse had been completed and delivered to his home in Greenwich the week before. Since then, she'd been stalking the finally finished porch, trying to convince herself to go ahead and do more houses in the hope word of mouth would bring more customers.

"That's wonderful," Mrs. Holmeyer said. "I was a little worried your schedule might be too full."

"No. I'll be able to do it."

"They're terribly clever," Mrs. Holmeyer said, glancing around the living room. "I suppose you must be getting a lot of orders."

"Quite a few."

"Well." Mrs. Holmeyer reeled in her wandering attention. "I'd better be going. You'll call me when the house is ready?"

"I certainly will, and thank you for stopping by."

Mrs. Holmeyer went toward the door, unable to stop looking around. She gave the impression she'd never seen any place quite like it, and Hadleigh, too, looked around, trying to

see the house as she imagined this woman might. It seemed
perfectly ordinary, but perhaps by this woman's standards it
was only a notch above a hovel.

After Mrs. Holmeyer had driven off in her bronze Mer-
cedes, Hadleigh went through each room, gradually arriving
at the conclusion that she'd allowed herself to be blind to the
house. The bedrooms on the second floor had been enlarged
through the removal of the partitions, painted white, and
nothing more had been done to them. The ground floor rooms
had also been painted white. The living room looked very temporary with its grouping of new furniture and a few antiques
placed without thought. The old second-hand Formica table
was still the focal point of the kitchen, and Hadleigh looked at
it with dismay. She knew all at once that it wasn't the house
Mrs. Holmeyer had taken exception to—there'd been the
slightest wrinkling of her nose—but the lack of interest the
owner had taken in it.

The Greenwich house had received the full impact of her attention, every last detail of every room attended to. Leaving
that house had been so painful that she'd simply never
bothered to try to highlight the best this dwelling had to offer.
But it was by no means too late. She could begin with Bonita's
room, as a surprise for her return, and go on from there. Now
that the heat wave had ended and the days and nights were
cooler, it would be something to do when she wasn't busy with
the new dollhouse.

On her next trip into town, she ordered twelve rolls of
wallpaper with tiny clusters of yellow flowers on a white
ground, along with fifteen yards of matching fabric for curtains and a comforter cover for Bonita's room. She took with
her two quarts of a coordinating yellow enamel so that she
could paint the woodwork before starting with the paper.

Suddenly her days and nights were full. When she wasn't
cutting the pieces for the dollhouse, and painstakingly joining
them together, she was upstairs at work on Bonita's room, or
rearranging the furniture in the living room, or out looking for
a new set of table and chairs for the kitchen. She worked each
night until after midnight, then was up again by seven, feeling
fully productive and alive. Catching sight of the telephone on
her way through the kitchen, or upon rising in the morning to
see the extension on the bedside table, she thought of Augusta
and told herself to reestablish contact, but never managed to

get around to it. So it came as a complete surprise when the phone rang one morning to hear Augusta say, "Before you start telling me what a rotten rat I've been, how are you?"

"I'm absolutely wonderful. I've been intending to call you every day for the last fortnight, but I've been so busy I simply haven't managed to get round to it. How are you?"

"Well, basically, okay. Do you hate me, and should I hang up, or can we talk?"

"Why would I hate you, Augusta? Do let's talk."

"You sound cheery as all get out. What's going on in your life?"

"Just work. At the moment, I'm in the process of fixing up this place, and I've started accepting commissions for the dollhouses. I'd adore to see you. It's been such a long time."

"I'd like to see you, too. How about this weekend? I'm dying to get out of the city."

"Lovely. I haven't done over the guest room yet, but it's certainly habitable. When would you like to come?"

"Right now," Augusta laughed, "but I'll force myself to wait until Friday. Is that okay?"

"It's fine. We could eat here, or go out to dinner, whichever you'd prefer."

"I'll bring food. We've got loads to talk about and it'll be easier without the distraction of a restaurant. Would you mind picking me up at the station? I don't have a car these days."

"Not at all. What time?"

"I just happened to pick up a schedule on the chance you wouldn't throw the phone down in my ear. I'll get the five fifty-three. Okay?"

"I'll be waiting for you."

Augusta arrived with a hamper of food from Charles & Co., and they sat down at the new birch table in the kitchen to eat the paté and cheese and salads and baguette she'd brought.

"You want to know where I've been and why I haven't been in touch," Augusta said, after a healthy swallow of Beaujolais. "You won't believe it. I'm not sure I do myself. But here goes: You and Sheffie had a fight a couple of years ago, and guess who he called!"

"You're not serious!"

"Oh, yes indeed. He's such a goddamned vampire, but the city was starting to get to me, and he seemed kind of refreshing after the guys I'd been dating, so I let him fall into the habit of showing up every Friday night, regular as clockwork, for the weekend. I was so *stupid*!" she moaned. "I mean, the man's a moral degenerate and a complete opportunist. How could I *do* that?"

"I know very well how it could happen," Hadleigh said.

"You do? Well, anyway this went on for a whole year, until I found out I was pregnant. Goddamned diaphragms! I'll bet you anything they weren't invented by a woman. Soooo, where was I? Right. It's not as if I wanted him to marry me or anything, because there's no way on God's earth I'd get married, and certainly not to a pretentious asshole like Sheffie. But I did think he'd offer to help pay for my trip to Puerto Rico for the abortion. Forget it! He just looked at me like I'd put ground glass in his hamburger, and took off for the hills. I wound up having to go through the whole thing by myself. And you know the worst part of it? I mean, aside from hating myself the entire time I was with him, the absolutely worst part was knowing he'd turned me into the bad guy in his own mind, that getting pregnant was something I'd done to trap him into marriage. Je-sus Christ! He doesn't even smell all that good because he never remembers to do his goddamned laundry.

"Anyway," she raced on, "I could hardly call you up while all this was going on and make idle chit-chat with him listening to every word; especially since he's always had this mile-wide letch for you. And if I'd said I was coming to see you, he'd have wanted to tag along, and I didn't want you to know what a fool I was, taking up with a guy I've thought for years had no redeeming qualities whatsoever. The whole thing was an unqualified disaster. The abortion was the most horrendous experience I've ever had. It's taken me months to get over all of it, including having to move because he'd polluted my place. And finding an apartment in the city is only slightly easier than trying to walk on water. I finally heard about a place through a friend of a friend and had to fork over six hundred bucks key money to get it. Mind you, it's rent-controlled, and I love the neighborhood. You've got to come see it: an entire floor-through on Nineteenth Street. I've even got a working fireplace, and it's only one-seventy a month. God! This is great paté."

Hadleigh agreed, then said, "It's all very interesting. I think you'll quite like the story I want to tell you." She went on to relate the details of Elmo's attempted seduction, and their final argument. Augusta listened with a look almost of rapture and, at the end, pounded her fist on the table, declaring, "Jesus! That's great! I'm so proud of you! I didn't have the guts to tell him what I thought of him. I kept thinking of your mother and the way she's always been able to say exactly the right thing. All I did was tell him to get the fuck out of my face before I took an axe to his head. He ran around collecting his smelly shirts and dog-eared books—don't you hate people who do that?—looking over his shoulder as if he thought I'd really do it." She calmed herself down, cut another wedge of the Jarlsberg, and said, "Little boys should be drowned at birth, I swear."

"I think," Hadleigh said, "that what most distressed him was that I knew about his affair with my mother."

"He had an *affair* with your *mother*! Are you *serious*?"

"Oh, very. It went on for ages."

Augusta jumped up, walked across the room and pounded her fists on the wall, then dropped back into her chair. "I don't *believe* it! He's even worse than I thought. I don't know why, but that makes me angrier than any of the other stuff he's done, and I haven't told you *half* of it. God! You were so smart to get rid of him. He'd have installed himself in here like a case of termites, and you'd never have been able to get him out. What really *kills* me is he feels so goddamned *justified*. He's the injured party. But he didn't have to have his insides scraped by some squatty little guy I'm still not convinced was a doctor."

"It must have been dreadful," Hadleigh sympathized. "I was so afraid I'd get pregnant again after the twins. Every month I went through terrible anxiety, praying my period was going to come on so I wouldn't have to go through any of what you did."

"I never knew that," Augusta said sadly. "What were we talking about all those years, when we should've been talking about the important things?"

"You tried very hard, Augusta, to say important things to me. I just wasn't able to listen."

"Did I?" Augusta asked tearfully. "Were we real to each other, the way I remember it? I was such a smart-aleck, know-it-all."

"No, you weren't. You were wonderful. I could never have got through any of it without you."

"Really? I've felt like such a shit for staying away. I figured you had to hate me for backing out when things got heavy for you."

"I would never think badly of you, Augusta."

"Oh, bless your heart! I've really missed you. Jesus!" she said suddenly. "Wouldn't you just *love* to find out what your mother has to say about the son of a bitch?"

"It boggles the mind. I told him his major mistake was in losing her. She's the only woman I could imagine capable of making him toe the mark. And he would have with her, too, because he's always been highly respectful of money, despite his claims of how unimportant it was to him."

"Unimportant, my ass! He cost me a fortune. I'm still paying off the bills he ran up. I had to take out a loan to pay for the trip to Puerto Rico. Oh, was that good!" She rolled her eyes. "There was one heavenly moment when the loan officer wanted to know the purpose of my application and I had this awful temptation to tell him I was financing an abortion. Can you *imagine*!" She laughed uproariously, then fell silent. "It's been a hundred years," she said, with melancholy. "And yet a couple of days ago I was seventeen and you were eighteen, and we were buying you a trousseau. Let's never lose touch again."

"We won't," Hadleigh promised.

Thirty-one

London was familiar in the way an old dress found crumpled on the floor at the back of a closet might have been. Frances remembered it, but was puzzled by its curious styling, its texture and fabric. The city was the same, yet very different, with a flavor altered by blocks of flats and offices constructed in her absence, and somehow casual new landmarks that might have seemed appropriate in New York, but not here. The new Festival Hall sat on the far side of the Thames like an image she'd unwittingly transported with her, so nouveau was its appearance. Oxford Street, while home to the majority of all the old stores, had countless new ones, too. The American influence seemed to be everywhere, from the Wimpy Bars that sold what purported to be hamburgers but which Bonita described as "fried dog meat," to the window displays of the larger stores with angular mannequins in rather menacing poses. There was too much neon, too many people, and far too much noise.

What most upset her was their trip on the number 22 bus to Chelsea. Frances had thought to point out the Cheyne Walk flat to Bonita, but the block was gone. In its place stood a modern block constructed of concrete. On top of that, she kept losing her way, because the cinemas and shops that had been her signposts were all gone.

Bonita had never seen her grandmother other than supremely confident, and to see her now, day after day, gazing about with an expression of bewilderment was very unsettling.

She was starting to look old and unwell, and Bonita wanted to rescue her from the ravages of this experience.

"Let's get a taxi and go back to the hotel," Bonita said, taking hold of Frances's hand. "I'm kind of tired after days of walking all over, and you must be, too."

Frances latched onto this suggestion as to a lifeline, encouraging Bonita to step out into the roadway and flag down the next passing taxi. Once inside and on their way back to Brown's, Frances applied a handkerchief to her overheated cheeks, trying to concentrate on slowing the tattoo beating in her chest.

"I guess it's all really different now," Bonita said generously.

"Unrecognizably so, obviously. And this heat is unbearable. It's supposed to be raining. The sun *never* shines here, for God's sake."

"We'll be back in time for tea," Bonita said, then added, "I know you're not enjoying this. We don't have to stay. If we both can't have a good time, we should go. It's not fair to you."

"Children have an enormous investment in fairness," Frances thought aloud. "I can't, for the life of me, think why most of them grow up to be adults with no sense of it whatever."

"They just forget what it's like to be young. My mom's very fair."

"Is she?" Frances asked interestedly. "Tell me about her."

Bonita laughed. "You already know all about her. She's *your* daughter."

"I'd like to know about her from your perspective. Of course I already have my own."

"Oh! Okay. Well, she's very fair. And, in lots of ways, she's not like other mothers. I'll give you an example. We go to the movies together, and she loves it just the same way I do: not the grown-up sitting back saying what stupid kid-stuff it is, but like another kid who gets scared at the scary parts and laughs at all the funny stuff. She never gets mad if I play my radio too loud. All kids," she explained, "play music loud."

"You don't say!"

Bonita nodded. "They do. I think we grow out of it, though. Let's see. What else? We cook together and she doesn't have a fit if I mess up the kitchen. I mean, she makes me clean up after, but she's not like Tandy's mother who won't let her near the kitchen because she'll make a mess. Most of my friends don't even know how to cook. Let me think. Another thing: She's always great if I don't feel well. She takes care of me, reads me stories and stuff. She's very . . . gentle. I really like her. The only thing that scares me is that something might happen to her, or to you. When she used to drink, it scared me, because I was always afraid she'd hurt herself, or she'd get in the car and have an accident. The only other thing that scares me, and not so much anymore, but it used to, is that I might start drinking, too, when I grow up. I mean, not that I'd want to or anything, but it seemed like something she really didn't know how to stop. And I used to think sometimes it was like chicken pox or mumps, and I could get it. I've been reading about Alcoholics Anonymous."

"Have you? Why?"

"I don't know. Just to be prepared, I guess, in case anything happens."

"I don't think anything of that sort is going to happen. Here we are!"

The driver came around to open the door, and Frances gave him some notes without bothering to look at the meter. The man thanked her profusely, but she was already on her way past the doorman, telling Bonita, "Let's have tea, and continue our conversation."

The lounge was Bonita's favorite part of the hotel, with its wood panelling and bevelled glass inserts, its elaborately ornamented ceilings with the brass chandeliers. She loved the fireplaces and the groupings of chintz-covered sofas and armchairs, and the stained glass window in the main part of the lounge. She loved the enclosed display case at the rear of the inner lounge, with its pieces of oriental pottery; she loved the wall sconces, the three-tiered silver cake trays, the flowered teacups and plates, and the silver tea service.

After the waiter had served their tea and left the scones and jam and clotted cream, Frances poured for them both, then recrossed her legs to sit squarely facing Bonita.

"Tell me about me," she invited.

"Grandma, I couldn't do that."

"Why ever not?"

"I don't know. Because."

"Go on," Frances said softly.

Bonita looked at the scone on her plate, then carefully
wiped her fingers on her serviette. "All right," she said. "I'll
tell you what I think about you now, how you are now. You're
scared, but you don't want me to know how much because
you don't want me to be upset. What really upsets me, more
than anything, is that you won't let me help, because I could,
you know. I really could. I've got this feeling"—she looked
around the room, then up at the ceiling—"this feeling that I
know, but I don't know. Sometimes, I'm you." She returned
her eyes to Frances. "I read somewhere, I forget where, but I
read that ghosts can't harm people. They're just lost, or trying
to tell you something, but they won't hurt you. Grandma."
She put her hand on Frances's arm. "He's trying to tell you
something, not to scare you. He won't hurt you. And, anyway, I wouldn't let him. Why won't you tell me who he is?"

Frances merely shook her head.

"I know you loved him," Bonita said. "And I know that
lady my mom sometimes talks about has something to do with
it. What's her name? Amanda, that's it. We shouldn't have
come here," she said somberly. "I knew it that night on the
ship. Let's go home, or go on to Paris early, instead of staying
here. It's making you unhappy. I can feel it."

"I'm sorry," Frances said, lighting a cigarette. "It's
frightful that you have to share my feelings in this fashion."

"No, it isn't. I don't mind. I really don't, not one bit."

Frances was deeply moved, so much so she had to take a
hard drag on the cigarette in order not to give in to her emotions.

"Sometimes," Bonita's soft voice said, "I really am you.
At first it was very confusing, but now I'm kind of used to it.
When I was little, you used to scare me sometimes, because
you seemed so . . . impatient, I guess. And angry. Now I know
you use those things, in a way, when you don't want people to
know how you really feel. And that's okay. I like the way you
are."

"If anything should happen," Frances said, "there's
something I want you to do for me. There are two letters in my
desk. You'll know them when you find them. You're to give
them to your mother. I think you'll know what to say and
do."

"Nothing's going to . . ."

"If anything does," Frances cut her off, "give the letters to
your mother." She put out her cigarette, saying, "I'm going

to take a walk. I'd like a bit of time alone."

"Okay," Bonita said, staring without appetite at their untouched tea.

"I won't be long," Frances told her, closing her handbag with a snap.

"Okay," Bonita said again, and watched her go. Everything that was happening had a strange tinge to it, as if events had been decided a long, long time ago and nothing she could possibly do would alter what was to take place. She saw Frances go past the window up Albermarle Street and considered trailing her, but decided not to and went, instead, up to their suite.

She lay down on the bed, folded her arms under her head, and stared at the ceiling, waiting.

Frances walked up Albermarle, then cut over, working her way up to Oxford Street. Once across Oxford Street, nearing Portman Street, she began to feel a little ill, and told herself it was the heat. But the heat couldn't have been responsible for the interior quickening she felt, or the steady acceleration of her heartbeat. At the bottom of Portman Square, her vision started to cloud over and she had to stop.

Bonita silently warned, "Don't go any farther! Just stay there! Don't go on! Stay there and wait for me!"

Bonita checked to make sure she had her English money, grabbed the key, then ran out, along the corridor and down the stairs. A taxi was just discharging a fare in front of the hotel and she darted into the back, saying, "Just start driving. I don't know the names of the streets. I'll have to tell you as we go."

He shrugged and put his foot on the accelerator. At the top of Albermarle she said, "We have to go that way, over there." She pointed to the left. "Now, we go up this street across the big road at the top. It's not very far. Go slowly, okay?"

She spotted Frances leaning against a fence, and cried out, "Pull over! Right there! Stop!" She got the door open and ran up to Frances, took hold of her arm and started towing her over to the taxi. "You shouldn't have come here, Grandma! Are you all right?"

Frances wanted to toss off a quip, make some light remark, but she couldn't seem to speak.

"We're going back to the hotel," Bonita told the driver

who'd come round to help her get Frances into the taxi.

"Right you are, luv." He skipped in front of the cab and climbed back behind the wheel.

"I'm going to take you home," Bonita announced. "Are you starting to feel better?"

"Somewhat," Frances was finally able to speak. "She's still there, Bonita."

"I knew that," Bonita admitted. "I looked her up in the phone book when we got here. Amanda Adams in Portman Square. There's something very wrong about that lady."

"Yes, something very wrong, indeed."

"I'll call Mom when we get back to the hotel, let her know we're coming."

By the time they got to the airport, Frances had regained herself, but refused to discuss why she'd gone to Portman Square or what she'd thought she might accomplish there.

They arrived at the Central Park West apartment to find Mrs. Walsh had gone. She'd left a note saying she was moving in with a friend who had a house in Brooklyn Heights.

Frances was furious, and went slamming through the apartment to verify that Mrs. Walsh had cleared out her room as well as every last bit of food. There wasn't so much as a soda cracker in the kitchen.

"I'll go out and get a few things," Hadleigh offered, and left before her mother could comment.

"You could come stay with us for a while," Bonita said, "until you get a new housekeeper."

"I'd have rather a hard time of it conducting interviews from there," Frances snapped. "No, I'll be fine."

When Hadleigh returned with the groceries, Frances stopped her from putting them away, saying, "The two of you go along now. It's getting late."

Bonita could see her mother was getting ready to say something, and so went to take her arm, saying, "Come on, Mom. I'll call you tomorrow, Grandma," and hustled her mother out of there and down to the car.

"What's going on?" Hadleigh asked, once they were in the car. "What happened?"

"Nothing was the way it used to be," Bonita gave her prepared answer. "It upset her, and it wasn't fair to stay on if she wasn't having a good time."

"Well, I'm simply astonished she was willing to return by air. She's terrified of flying."

Bonita thought privately that there were other things Frances feared more, but said only, "She was fine."

"I don't know what to think," Hadleigh said. "I certainly don't care for the idea of her being on her own. I don't believe Mother's ever lived alone."

"No, I know." Bonita yawned hugely.

"I think we'll put you straight to bed and unpack in the morning."

"Okay." Bonita yawned again and, in moments, was asleep with her head on her mother's shoulder.

She managed to wake up enough to notice the changes as they went through the house, exclaiming, "You've got new kitchen stuff, and you fixed up the living room!"

"You'll look at everything in the morning. Come along now." Hadleigh held out her hand and Bonita went with her up the stairs, to stop cold in the doorway to her room. "*Mom!* It's fabulous! I love it! Oh, wow! Wait until Tandy sees this! It's *way* nicer than *her* room. She'll be so jealous. I just love it," she repeated, hugging her mother hard. "Is there more? Have you done over everything?"

"You'll see in the morning. Get yourself to bed. You're falling asleep on your feet."

With careful premeditation Frances set up the electronic barriers—the TV set in the living room, the radios in the kitchen and bedroom. Then, in her nightgown and robe, she sat down on the sofa. Her eyes watered with the need for sleep, yet every time she was on the verge of dozing off, some sound brought her wide awake, her heart thrumming. She stretched out on the sofa and, again, began to succumb to exhaustion. There was the sound of footsteps approaching. She jumped and whirled around. Nothing there.

She got up and went into the kitchen, hungry. Hadleigh had bought yogurt. She took one of the containers from the refrigerator, got a spoon from the drawer and was about to push the spoon into the yogurt when it began squirming in her hand. She looked down to see a small, silvery snake coiling itself around her fingers. With a cry, she flung the thing from her, and it fell, clanging to the floor. Just a spoon once again. She picked it up, threw it into the sink, got a fresh spoon and doggedly consumed the yogurt. Returning to the sofa, she sat down and lit a cigarette. When she looked up, a fully dressed Edwin was sodomizing a stark-naked Amanda over the side of the armchair. Rather than suffering, Amanda seemed in an advanced state of passion. Frances watched, trying to interpret the scene. It was all too real. She could even see the flush spreading across Amanda's breasts, and tiny pearls of perspiration collecting in the hair at her temples. Although she couldn't see his face, it was unquestionably Edwin. Wasn't it bad enough he had to pop up here and there, without deciding to copulate in her bloody living room? She was growing very angry with all these tricks and mirages, and stabbed out her cigarette, determined to see an end to this. But when she turned back, their images were already dissolving, blending with the smoke from her cigarette.

Sleep was a sneak thief that came unexpectedly to rob her of consciousness. She craved and feared it because it had gone completely beyond her control. Most often it crept upon her when she'd given up hoping. There were no preliminaries; she simply fell into it and awakened, unrested, four or five or six hours later.

She refused to believe it was anything more than exhaustion and another ectoplasmic trick that was responsible for the way the walls seemed to bell gently outward when she gazed at them, and for the uneven, sloping appearance of the floor. Sheer fatigue put the thought in her mind that, as she sat down on the toilet, an arm was going to shoot upwards from the bowl.

In defiance of the countless absurdities occurring within her home, she bathed and dressed each morning, but couldn't get beyond the front door. And so she began ordering food in from the Gristede's nearby, and closely scrutinized the face of the young Puerto Rican delivery boy through the peephole before opening the door to accept the groceries and hand him a check and his tip. When a boy she failed to recognize came with her order, she refused to open the door.

Food was a necessary nuisance. She had to have it in order to keep up her strength, and so she ordered it, stored the ingredients in the appropriate places, and at regular intervals went to the kitchen to prepare it. She took from the refrigerator a package of extra-lean ground sirloin, opened it, set it down on the counter, then turned back to the refrigerator for two eggs. Eggs in hand, she looked over to see that the brown package contained not sirloin but a shifting, glistening mound of writhing pink-grey worms. For a few seconds she could do no more than gape as several of the worms separated themselves from the mass and began to slide across the countertop toward her. Then seized by anger, she exclaimed, "Bloody hell!" pounding her hands down on the counter. The eggshells shattered, their contents oozing between her fingers. Automatically, she moved to the sink, her eyes still on the blind, squirming mass spreading itself across the Formica. Her soiled hand under the faucet, she reached with the other to turn on the water. When she finally looked, she saw not raw egg but a blackly viscid substance that refused to be washed away. It had life, this inky organism, and it climbed upward over her wrist, streaky tentacles reaching to her forearm. Again, for an instant, she watched the upward progress—her flesh contracting in instinctive disgust—then she remembered and laughed. "Oh, really! You'll have to do better than this. I'm utterly unimpressed. Honestly! What nonsense!"

At once the substance began to dissolve, washing away. Hands dripping, she snatched up a teatowel. "I intend to eat," she announced. "If it's to be sautéed earthworms, so be it. I've probably been eating them for years, given the standards of Manhattan butchers. You really will have to do better than this!"

With that, she laughed again, steeled herself, and scooped up a handful of the slimy worms to begin shaping a flat patty. "Worms indeed!" she scoffed, telling herself not to be squeamish, not to respond. And the meat became meat once more.

As if her declarations had been duly heard and noted, there were no further culinary incidents, although she continued to expect them. But while the kitchen now seemed a noneventful area, every other square inch of the apartment became potentially treacherous territory.

While she sat drowsily watching the evening news, something snagged her peripheral vision. At once very awake, she turned to see an enormous brown rat, its whiskers visibly vibrating as it fixed its small red-pearl eyes on hers. Its mouth opened, revealing dripping yellow fangs; its sharply pointed ears seemed to tilt slightly towards her as it dropped back onto its rear legs and a piercing squeal—like broken glass drawn across a blackboard—split the air. Then, its head still turned toward her, it fell back on all four legs and darted from the room, its long snaky tail leaving a faint impression on the carpet. Frightened and repelled, her throat pulsing achingly, she tried to decide if this was another trick or if it was in any way conceivable that the rat was real. A trick, she concluded, but looked about for a weapon just in case, and followed after clutching her umbrella, scanning the carpet for some indication of where the rat, real or not, might have gone.

It seemed to have vanished. She examined each room, coming at last to the dressing room where she stood slowly turning when again she heard the high-pitched squeal, felt the air surge violently, and the rat leaped through the air, landing with its claws embedded in her shoulders. She screamed, shaking herself wildly to dislodge the creature and, turning, saw her overnight case lying on the floor. Her heart slamming against her breast, she gazed at the small case as she investigated the several small tears on the shoulders of her blouse. The games being played here were turning dangerous. She was going to have to exercise all the rational power she possessed in order not to be sent right over the edge. Her breathing still irregular, hands trembling, she returned the bag to the shelf.

Bonita or Hadleigh or both of them telephoned daily to ask if she'd started interviewing yet for a new housekeeper, to ask about the state of her health, and to invite her to come to Connecticut. She replied that she was in touch with various agencies, that her health had never been better, and that she was far too busy to leave the city at the moment.

Bonita asked sadly, "Why are you blocking me, Grandma? I know you are. I can't see or hear anything. Even when I try as hard as I can, all I get is a kind of static."

"There is nothing, Bonita, to be seen or heard."

"I *know* there is, Grandma! Can I at least come and stay with you?"

"Not now. I'm really very busy."

"You've got all the radios and the TV going," Bonita accused.

"Listen to me," Frances said firmly but not unkindly. "I'm very close to remembering something of simply tremendous importance. I cannot allow you a part in this. Not yet. It would be too . . . You're too young, too susceptible to be involved at this juncture. It's out of the question. You must trust my judgment.''

"All right," Bonita sighed resolutely. "Will you call me if you need anything?"

"I will call you," Frances said, and put down the receiver.

Just as she was descending into sleep that evening, something touched against her knee. Shifting, she settled again for sleep, and felt another touch against her ankle. Tiredly, she scratched her ankle, and something scurried over her wrist. All in one motion she threw back the bedclothes and switched on the bedside lamp. Dozens of cockroaches fled from the onslaught of the light, dropping to the floor to go rushing away across the carpet.

She had the foresight to check her slippers before putting them on. Taking them by the toes she held them upside down and gave them a shake. Half a dozen more cockroaches fell to the floor. In disgust, she hurled the slippers across the room, snatched up her robe and marched off to the guest-room. Having installed herself in the bed, she found herself completely unable to get to sleep, and after an hour of turning from one side to the other, she got up, pulled on her robe and went to sit on the sofa in the living room. Near dawn, her eyes fell closed and she slept.

As she sat with a cup of tea late the next morning she allowed herself to give in, briefly, to her upset. Her giving in took the form of grief; she thought longingly of Arthur, recalling his generosity and tolerance. Then, coming away from an activity she'd always considered unforgivably self-indulgent, she wondered if she wasn't after all going through some form of breakdown. Perhaps the things that were happening here were delusions caused by her withdrawal from her medication. She'd stopped taking her pills temporarily, planning to resume their consumption when this showdown, or whatever it was, ended. She'd wanted her concentration completely unimpaired, and so she'd set aside the medication. Had it been a mistake? Was her body's new independence responsible for the worms and the rat, the legions of roaches? No! she decided. None of this had anything to do with whether or not she took her pills. This had to do with events long past,

and with her determination to fit together every last piece of
the total picture. She could only hope that it wouldn't take
very much longer. She was feeling the strain of nights without
sleep, of being constantly on her guard.

As she approached the bathroom that evening she was enveloped by the sudden knowledge that she was about to enter the
newly selected arena for the next stage of the battle. The air
seemed to shiver; it was thick with the motion of invisible pres-
ences. She put on the light and at once the air was less encum-
bered, less menacing. Still, she could feel eyes watching her,
charting her every movement. Whatever was in here had great
strength and density. She'd have to be very careful.

Each time she entered the bathroom now it was to discover
there'd been some slight alteration. The towels were not as
she'd left them, but lay heaped on the floor. The soap dish was
not beside the sink but on the lid of the toilet. Two distinct
sooty-looking handprints appeared on the white-tiled wall at
ceiling height. Mentally she gauged the size of her own hand
against the one that had left the prints. Hers was considerably
smaller.

As she brushed her teeth the following evening the lights
dimmed, then brightened, then dimmed again. The tumbler on
the vanity rumbled and danced, then steadied itself. The toilet
seat flew up to hit the porcelain rim with a crash. One of the
towel rails disengaged itself from the wall and flew straight
across the room. There was the thunder of feet pounding
across the room, up the wall, over the ceiling, down the far
wall. The door slammed, failed to catch, and bounced open.
She stood, toothbrush in hand, waiting for more.

"If you're quite finished," she addressed the room, "I'll get
on with what I'm doing."

As if responding to her words, the bathtub faucets spun and
water gushed from the nozzle.

"I'll bathe elsewhere," she said calmly. "You needn't
bother filling the tub. I've never been fond of bathing in a
crowd."

The water slowed, then stopped.

She shook her head, rinsed her mouth and put down the
toothbrush. "I thought we'd gone beyond adolescent pranks,"
she said, and went off to the guest bathroom to fill the tub
there.

Before trying to sleep in the guest-room bed she once more approached her bathroom, sensing as she did a tremendous disturbance in the darkness. It was precisely as if an exceedingly rowdy party was taking place within the confines of the room: a party where the guests had had far too much to drink, and a violent outbreak was imminent. She hung back, awed by the volatility of the atmosphere. It was late at night; she was terribly tired. Quietly, she pulled the door closed.

Oddly, she had no difficulty falling asleep. It struck her as suspicious and she tried to pull herself back, but it was too late. Her grasp on conscious lucidity had eased and she was powerless. Her limbs twitched into relaxation; her body seemed weighted, held down.

At some point in the night, pressure on her bladder moved her out of bed, and along the corridor to her bathroom. At the threshold she realized her error and tried to back away but it was too late. Her nightgown torn away, she was thrust naked into the room where she was pushed and pummelled, examined by harsh damp hands. The door was just there, she thought, just behind her. If she could provide some sort of distraction to turn the attention of the raucous unseen crowd away from her for only a moment, she'd be able to escape. But she couldn't think. She was too shocked by the outrageous ongoing inspection of her body, too preoccupied by her efforts to protect herself.

The room had swollen to immense proportions; it had become a vast, dank cave, filled with the stink of diseased, rotting flesh; alive with the stench of unclean bodies whirling around her in the darkness. There was no sound but the varying cadences of noisy, somehow gratified, breathing.

The exploration of her body was growing bolder, more hurtful, and she tried to curve in on herself, at the same time drawing away toward where she thought the light switch must be. Her efforts seemed to enflame the crowd. Countless hands clutched at her, squeezing hard at her arms and legs; long, ragged fingernails dragged down the length of her spine. She gasped. The pain was immediate and searing, as if red-hot knives had been thrust into her skin.

This was too real, she thought, suddenly very afraid. Dreams and tricks didn't contain pain like this, or odors so foul her lungs and throat were contaminated. She struggled, groping for the light switch, but her flailing arms and hands connected with an enclosing wall of oily, scabrous flesh, and while she couldn't hear it she was able to sense the roar of laughter her struggles provoked.

Hands wound themselves into her hair and yanked her head backwards. Instinctively her own hands rose in a blind effort to ease her tortured scalp but bony knuckles simply dug harder into her head and she was forced down until she had no alternative but to bend. The floor was shockingly cold beneath her as fists pounded into her belly, jagged fingernails pinched into her arms. Unseen pairs of hands fastened around her ankles and knees and her legs were wrenched apart as something chopped against her windpipe. There was a subtle menacing change in the air, a seeming hush of expectation as she lay gagging, trying to breathe, uselessly attempting to twist away from what she knew was about to happen.

Her eyes bulged, her teeth bared themselves in an agonized rictus; her flesh ripped. An immense object was driven into the core of her body and pulsed within her, growing. From somewhere above came the sound of a woman's laughter and for just a moment she was caught by the familiarity of the tone. Then, her attention was forced back to the monstrous parody of intercourse that was occurring. She could feel the blood gushing from her ravaged interior and closed her eyes tightly, praying for this to end. The pain was unbearable. Was this how she'd die? It felt that way. There was a pause, and then the object was savagely withdrawn, the pain of its departure surpassing that of its entry. Her body was released. It was over. She wanted to move, but was unable. She told herself she *must* move, and somehow managed to get to her knees. She sobbed, shaken by tremors and nausea, gripped by pain.

She crawled on her hands and knees out of the bathroom, the nap of the carpet further abrading her bruised limbs. With the dregs of her strength she cried, "To hell with you! You won't kill me!" and then everything gave way and she collapsed, able to go no further.

Sunlight assaulted her eyelids. Cautiously, she opened her eyes to orient herself. She was in bed, in the guest-room. Innocent air moved gently around her as she sat up. No pain, no visible evidence. It had been another trick, after all. Pushing aside the blanket, she got up and went into the master suite.

Whatever had been in the bathroom was now gone. She stepped inside and turned on the light, then clapped her hand over her mouth in horror. It was morning. She was wide awake. This was indisputably real. She gazed, sickened, at the blood splattered on the floor. She was standing barefoot at the edge of a puddle of it. Dizzy, she leaned against the wall, mentally examining herself. There was no pain, but the memory of it was intact. It had happened.

Stepping past the soiled areas she stripped off her nightgown then looked at herself in the mirror. Blue-black bruises covered her upper arms, her breasts, and torso. Her throat was circled by livid discolorations. Four enflamed vertical lines ran the length of her spine. For a few seconds she was swallowed by pain, consumed by it; it bent her double and had her retching into the sink. And then it was gone. She blinked, straightening to study again her mirror image. The pain was gone but the physical evidence remained. Looking over her shoulder, her hands braced on the sink, she saw that the floor was no longer soiled. "Bastards!" she whispered. "It's all endless games and trickery."

The marks might have been cosmetically applied so readily did they disappear beneath an application of soap and water. She scrubbed herself, then paused, remembering a woman's laughter. Could it be that there were two sources of power here, two distinctly different energies battling for her attention? Yes. That was it. Of course.

She glanced out through the shower curtain she'd kept drawn halfway back in order to keep watch on the doorway, then returned her attention to the knowledge she'd just acquired. Think back! she told herself. Concentrate! Narrowing her eyes, her jaw tight, she opened her mind, and the final piece at last slotted into place. "My God!" she exclaimed, studying the picture with fascination. "I knew it!"

She turned off the water and, reaching for a towel, slipped on the water-slick tiles and fell, catching her elbow on the rim of the tub as she landed heavily on her knees. The pain was all too real. She had to sit on the wet floor with her back against the tub and her head lowered to her knees, waiting for the nausea to pass. Her body hummed, pulsing miserably, but she would not give in and lose consciousness. She would not surrender her life without a fight.

The result of sitting for close to thirty minutes on the cold wet tiles as the air-conditioned air swept over her from the bedroom was a raging cold that filled her lungs and impaired

her hearing. The bruises on her knees made it difficult for her
to walk, and the slightest movement of her left arm was
agonizing. She bundled herself into a pair of wool slacks, a
shirt, and sweater, took four aspirin tablets every few hours
with cups of hot tea, and sat huddled on the sofa beneath a
heap of blankets, periodically sliding into a semi-wakeful state
wherein, amazed, she examined the complete picture. The
siege had ended, and she'd been victorious.

Thirty-two

Frances was seated in the middle of a long sofa in an otherwise unfurnished room of epic proportions. Wearing a black dress with loose sleeves, her legs crossed, she sat with her arms spread to either side along the back of the sofa. Bonita thought she looked very beautiful, studying her grandmother's features with more than usual curiosity. Frances seemed to be pinned to Bonita's inspection; she was compelled to remain motionless for as long as Bonita demonstrated interest. Intuitively, Bonita knew that the moment her attention wavered, even the slightest bit, Frances would regain her mobility. She inched nearer, absorbing details, noting them. It was vital to keep her eyes fixed, and to move with extreme caution. She wanted to sustain this, to prolong it perhaps indefinitely, but something flirted at the perimeters of her attention and her eyes shifted fractionally, attempting to spot what it was so that she might dismiss it. The movement of her eyes broke the air. It shattered like an immense sheet of glass; it even made a noise falling.

Looking up from the debris of the fractured air, she saw Frances at the far end of the room flinging open a door. Her grandmother glanced over her shoulder—as if to make sure Bonita would follow—before rushing out. Bonita started after her, striving to make her leaden limbs traverse the thickly carpeted expanse of floor separating her from Frances. Her lungs hurt from the effort of running, but she managed to get across the room only to see Frances disappearing through another door which began to swing closed, but not before

Bonita had a glimpse of what lay beyond: more rooms, and doors leading to still more rooms. It was impossible. She could pursue her grandmother forever, but she'd never be able to span the distance between them.

Breathless, she halted, feeling a numbing despair. "*Why are you doing this?*" she shouted into the empty room, knowing Frances could hear her. "*You don't have to do this!*"

There was no answer, but the breeze carried the scent of roses, and that, in itself, was a message. She inhaled deeply, but without satisfaction, and had to shout again, "*I don't know what it means!*"

Again she waited for some reply but all she heard was the distant sound of another slamming door. Defeated, she turned back the way she'd come, thinking to retrace her steps, only to find herself at home in the living room. She was eased by the sight of the windows overlooking the garden, and the furniture grouped by the fireplace where flames embraced a nest of logs and cast strange shadows across the walls.

Her eyes adjusting to the dimness, she became aware of figures occupying the sofa and chairs. Her father and Ben were side by side on the sofa, and her mother and Augusta sat in the armchairs flanking the fireplace. Everyone was gazing at Hadleigh, who had demarcated the boundaries of her territory with bricks and bottles of gin. Augusta had a rifle. It lay across her lap like a dozing pet, and she stroked its butt as if it were the fur-covered flank of a large cat.

"Where's Grandma?" Bonita asked them.

All the heads turned slowly toward her, and she screamed, her heart exploding with the horror of what her brain insisted couldn't be. They had no faces. Where their faces should have been were ovals filled with shifting images too small for her to see.

"Come!" a voice ordered as a hand fell upon her shoulder. "Just come straightaway!"

"Grandma!" she cried on the crest of a terrified sob. "What's *wrong* with them?"

The front door stood open. The incoming night air was scented with woodsmoke, and she sniffed appreciatively, stepping outside to see her grandmother climbing into the rear of a limousine. The woodsmoke was acquiring an acrid taste; it fogged her vision. She waved her hands in an attempt to see more clearly, hearing as she did the muffled thunder that meant the car was accelerating, going.

Suddenly, a dreadful clarity penetrated the fog of her thoughts, and she began to struggle away from the provocative puzzle of the dream. The dream clung, wanting to keep her, and she fought, kicking with her arms and legs, and came awake in billowing darkness. The house was on fire. Leaping from her bed, she groped her way to the door, got it open and staggered backwards from the blast of heat that swept in at her.

"FIRE!" she screamed. "EVERYBODY WAKE UP! THERE'S A FIRE!"

She pushed out into the hallway and burst into her mother's room, shouting at the top of her lungs.

"My God!" Hadleigh gasped.

"GET AUGUSTA! I'LL GET GRANDMA!"

Choking now and with tears streaming from her eyes, Bonita bent low in an effort to get beneath the smoke, and hurried to the guest-room. The knob seemed to be pulled from her hand as the fire sucked the door inward. The room was bright with flames surrounding the bed. Bonita took a few steps, knew she couldn't possibly get through, turned instead and ran to the bathroom where she soaked the bathtowels in cold water, and then soaked herself. Back in the guest-room she draped one of the towels over her head and shoulders, and used the other to fan away the flames.

"GRANDMA! WAKE UP!" She threw one of the wet towels over Frances, hoping she was merely asleep and not unconscious. "GET UP!" The floor was very hot, and she danced from one foot to the other, trying to take only small inhalations of the thick air, as she tugged at her grandmother's arm, unable to get her to move. "I CAN'T WAKE HER UP!" she yelled, hoping Augusta or her mother would hear her and come to help, but no one did. Certain they'd both die if she remained here any longer, she began to pull her off the bed. Frances fell to the floor with a painful-sounding thump that made Bonita grimace but didn't stop her from throwing the second wet towel over Frances and then, using every ounce of her strength, Bonita started to drag her feet-first across the room.

They were never going to make it. She could hardly breathe and had to keep ducking down to the floor in order to get a little fresh air into her lungs. She'd never have believed her

grandmother could be so heavy. She couldn't find the door.
Calm down, she told herself. It's just over there, where you
came from. Just a few more feet. Her arms felt as if they were
going to separate from her shoulders, and her wet hands kept
slipping. She'd never be able to do it. Once out of the room,
there were the stairs and then the downstairs hall. She couldn't
possibly get Frances all the way down there, and then out of
the house. Goddamnit! she cursed silently, inch by inch towing Frances across the carpet. It was taking forever. And
where was her mom, and Augusta?

She heard the sound of sirens approaching and thought,
Hurry up! Come on! Hurry up! They were clear of the room,
on the landing now, but the stairs were all the way over there
and her throat felt scorched. Her eyes were stinging. She
wanted to lie down, to get to the air that lay under the smoke,
but knew if she did she'd never get up again. Frances was too
heavy. She was exhausted, her lungs growing less and less effective as the smoke grew thicker, darker. It was no good. She
couldn't go any farther. Sinking down, she arrived at the
purer air just above the floor and filled her lungs as she drew
the wet towels up over herself and her grandmother. They
were going to die together. Maybe Grandma was already dead.
Reaching out, she lifted the edge of the towel to have one last
look, and saw the face of a complete stranger, a woman she'd
never seen before in her life.

"Wake up!" Hadleigh was saying. "Wake up!"

Bonita opened her eyes and looked wildly around her, dazed
by the ordinariness of the room and the brightness of the bedside light.

"Mom, we've got to drive into the city right now. Something's wrong with Grandma!"

"Bonita! You've had a bad dream, that's . . ."

"*Mom*! You've got to listen to me! We've got to go right
now. If we waste any time, we might be too late."

"Oh, look," Hadleigh began.

Bonita was running around the room, gathering up her
clothes. "*Listen to me*!" she begged, pulling her nightgown
off over her head. "We've got to go right now, this very
minute. You *have* to *believe* me!"

"I'll go ring her. You'll talk to her and see that everything's
perfectly all right, although I doubt she'll thank us for ringing
up in the middle of the night."

"You won't get any answer," Bonita called after her. "Just get dressed. I'll go get the car started."

"Don't you dare!"

"I'll be waiting in the car!" Bonita called, stepping barefoot into her loafers.

The doorman said he hadn't seen Mrs. Holden go in or out since she'd arrived back more than a week before. "Matter of fact, the day man was just saying to me when I came on tonight it was funny he hadn't seen her."

"You'd better come up and let us in with the passkey," Hadleigh told him.

He unlocked the door but lingered in the hallway as Hadleigh pushed it open. After the briefest glance inside, she turned to say, "You needn't wait. Thank you very much." She kept the door open a crack until he'd entered the elevator, then allowed it to swing open.

"I'll phone for an ambulance," Bonita said. "We'll take her to Greenwich."

Augusta came into the waiting room with two paper cups of coffee. She gave one to Hadleigh before sinking into the chair beside her, asking, "Where's Bonita?"

"I'm not sure." Hadleigh looked at the coffee, then placed it on the table next to her.

"How did she know?" Augusta wondered. "I mean, has it occurred to you that if she hadn't made you drive into the city your mother might have been dead by this morning?"

She turned to look directly at Augusta, confiding, "Sometimes, I can't imagine who Bonita is or how she came to be part of my life. She doesn't operate on my pragmatic level; she's on another plane entirely. I don't think it's bad. It's simply incomprehensible to me."

"In a way," Augusta said, "I kind of know what you mean." She glanced at her watch. "I'm sorry, Had, but I'm either going to have to call the office to say I won't be in, or go back to the house in a cab, grab my things and catch the next train."

"Why don't you go ahead?" Hadleigh said. "I think there's going to be a great deal of waiting."

"If you need me, I'll stay."

Hadleigh opened her bag and got out her keys. "Here. Take

the car. You can leave it at the station. We'll collect it later."

"What about the keys?"

"Just leave them under the seat. I'm sure it'll be perfectly
safe. Thieves aren't especially interested in twelve-year-old
station wagons that don't even have radios."

"Are you sure?"

"Quite sure."

"Okay, maybe I will." She leaned over to give Hadleigh a
kiss. "I'll check in tonight, see how things are going."

"I care very much for you, Augusta. Thank you for
everything."

"I know that, and same here. Call you tonight." At the
door, she turned back to add, "Give my love to Bonita.
Okay?"

Bonita was keeping watch through the observation panel in
the emergency operating room door. Her thoughts kept returning to the scene she and her mother had encountered upon
entering Frances's apartment, and to how they'd stood in the
foyer, staring in disbelief into the living room.

All the furniture had been pushed into the center of the
room to surround the sofa and the television set. Lamps had
been positioned at angles to illuminate every corner. Cold air
blasted from the air conditioning units; music blared from the
two radios, as did the sound track from a film playing on the
TV set. Beneath a heap of coats and blankets, only one very
thin arm and her face visible, they'd found Frances unconscious. The breath had entered and left her lips with a thin,
wheezing sound that had been more frightening than her free-
hanging, somehow clotted hair and terribly pallid face.

Now, Bonita had an unobstructed view of the tracheotomy
being performed on her grandmother, and she watched the
procedure with the fingers of one hand placed protectively
over her own throat, biting her lip as efficient hands hastily
erased the blood flow down Frances's too-white flesh.

Inside the room they handled Frances as if she were weightless, reviving for Bonita the memory of how heavy her grandmother had been in her dream. Yet it hadn't been Frances at
all, but some other woman, with heavy blonde hair and very
red lipstick.

She shivered and pressed closer to the door, trying to deter-
mine, from the various activities inside, what was happening.
Needles were going into Frances's arms. Some were with-

drawn with blood; some stayed and were smartly taped into place. She studied the mouths of the doctor and nurses, trying to read their lips. It was like some monstrous ballet, with blood. There was no apparent urgency. Everyone flowed languidly, as if to preordained positions, where they checked gauges, and lifted back her grandmother's eyelids, and used sterilized instruments to do this, and then that. It went on for close to an hour. Then many hands slid beneath and lifted Frances onto a waiting bed. Bonita had to jump aside as the door flung open and two nurses pushed the bed away down the corridor.

"Where are they taking her?" Bonita asked the doctor, stepping into the room.

"To intensive care. What're you doing in here? You're not supposed to be in here."

"That's my grandmother," she said somewhat indignantly. "Sure I'm supposed to be here."

"What's your name?" he asked, taking her by the arm. "Come with me." He led her in the opposite direction in which they'd taken Frances, and she twisted her head around, trying to see.

"Bonita. Why?"

"Ronald Colman's wife was named Bonita. Still is, for all I know. Have to check on that."

"Who's Ronald Colman?"

"An actor. I've met your grandmother before, you know."

"You have?"

"Yup. C'mon in here." He pushed open a door and held it while Bonita went in ahead of him. "Want some coffee?"

"Don't you think I'm too young?"

"Do you think you are?"

"Well, no."

"Okay." He poured two cups from a pot on a hotplate, came back and handed her one. "Sit down."

"No, thanks. I'll stand, if that's okay. I can't sit down right now. Too much is happening."

"Suit yourself." He perched on the arm of the sofa and drank some of the coffee.

"Why did you bring me here?" she asked, holding her cup with both hands. "What's wrong with my grandmother?"

"That's why I brought you here: to talk. Your mother's waiting, right?"

"That's right."

"Last time around it was your grandmother doing the waiting. D'you know about that?"

"Yes."

"Okay. That's how I know your grandmother." He smiled. "She's not someone you forget."

"No, she isn't. What's wrong with her?"

"Pneumonia, for starters."

"Is that why you put that thing in her throat?"

"You've got a strong stomach for a little kid," he said admiringly. "Planning on going into medicine?"

"I'm almost thirteen. That's not little. And I don't have a strong stomach at all. It made me feel sick."

"But you watched anyway, didn't you? Why?"

"I had to. If I didn't watch, something might have gone wrong."

He laughed. "I'm that way about flying. Have to keep my eyes on the runway during takeoff to help out the pilot. Anyone distracted me, we'd crash for sure."

She smiled. "We flew back from London. It was my first time, and I really liked it."

"My hat's off to you. I'd rather walk. Anyway, your grandmother's pretty run down. We'll be doing a lot of tests in the next couple of days to see what else, if anything's, wrong with her. But in her present condition, pneumonia's pretty serious business."

"Could I see her?"

"In a little while."

"Is she going to die?"

"I can't answer that. I hope not."

She decided she liked him. He had a nice, open face, and eyes that met hers directly. "Are you going to keep on being her doctor, or will the hospital give her somebody else?"

"I'll keep on." He watched her take a sip of the coffee. "Lousy, isn't it?"

"It's bitter."

"Don't drink it. You don't have to." He held out his hand for the cup, while at the same time downing the last of the contents of his own. "Come on, Bonita. We'll go talk to your mom."

As they were going down the corridor, he said, "My name's Vern, by the way. But don't let the nurses hear you call me that. Okay?"

"Okay."

"For public consumption, it's Doctor Street. Right?"

"Right."

"Anyone ever tell you you look like your grandmother?" he asked.

"Yes."

"Don't worry," he said. "I like her. I'll do my best for her."

"You can look in on her if you want, but I can't tell you when she's going to regain consciousness. My suggestion is that you go home now, get some rest, and come back this evening."

"If you think so," Hadleigh said doubtfully.

"We can't do anything here, Mom." Bonita was trying to be sensible, despite her mounting apprehension.

"She's right, Mrs. MacDonald," Dr. Street confirmed. "If there's any change at all in her condition, I'll call you."

"You'll be off duty this evening, won't you?" Hadleigh asked.

"Make you a deal," he said affably. "Tell me what time you plan to come back and I'll stop by to check her chart and bring you up to date."

"Why would you do that?" Hadleigh asked, thrown.

"As I explained to Bonita here, I've met your mother before. Let's say I have a personal interest."

"But, I . . ."

"We'll talk about it this evening. What time?"

Hadleigh looked at Bonita, unable to think.

"We'll be back at seven," Bonita told him.

"Fine. I'll meet you at the nurse's station."

Perhaps it was some trick of the light filtering through the oxygen tent, Hadleigh thought, or the result of her own fatigue, but Frances seemed to have shed years in the dozen or so hours since they'd brought her to the hospital. And, ignoring the various monitors and tubes which connected her to them, she looked peaceful, as if, in her altered state of consciousness she was viewing immensely gratifying scenes.

"She doesn't even look sick," Bonita said in hushed tones, "except for the tubes and everything."

"Her color's wrong," Hadleigh said, pulling a chair close to the bed. "I thought she'd have come round by now."

"He didn't promise that. He just said she might." Bonita walked to the far side of the bed and experimentally touched her hand to the plastic tent.

"*Don't!*" Hadleigh said sharply, causing Bonita to jerk back her hand. "You mustn't touch anything."

Because she couldn't possibly have explained herself, Bonita said nothing, and went to pull the second chair up beside her mother's. They sat looking at the woman in the tent until Hadleigh said, "We're only allowed fifteen minutes. It's nowhere near enough time."

Bonita looked around. There were three other beds in the unit. Two were unoccupied. The last, in the far corner, was enclosed by curtains.

"She's never been physically ill," Hadleigh said. "This isn't Mother."

"Yes, it is," Bonita whispered.

"No, no. You misunderstand. I mean, it isn't like her to be taken ill. Somehow, it's out of character." Hadleigh felt extremely nervous, with the sense that she was spying. Yet she also couldn't rid herself of the notion that her mother could hear them. She looked at her mother's hand and arm, discolored from the many blood samples that had been drawn, and at the thick, jagged white ridge of scar tissue on her inner arm. It took her a moment to realize what was missing: the heavy gold bracelet, and her diamond and platinum wedding and engagement rings. Without the jewelry, her hands looked vulnerable, even innocent. How odd it was to think that those items could so alter the impression given, even of one's hands! She had to fight down her inclination to grip her mother's hand, and through that contact, gain some deeper knowledge of the woman. She was inhibited by Bonita's presence, although it was her firm conviction that Bonita had more right to be there than she. She felt somewhat of a hypocrite, and fairly emotionless. Her mother was dangerously ill, but she couldn't summon up any fear, or sadness. All her emotions seemed suspended.

"It's been twenty minutes, Mom," Bonita said gently. "The nurse just gave me one of those looks."

Hadleigh's sudden curiosity extended itself to include Bonita, whose solicitousness she found inexplicable.

"What?" Bonita asked in response to her mother's puzzling expression.

"Nothing. Things are striking me oddly just now."

"I know," Bonita said, which further confused matters in her mother's mind.

Dr. Street was still at the nurse's station, and straightened when he saw them coming.

"I thought I'd hang around, in case you had any more questions."

"I can't think of anything at the moment," Hadleigh said, "although I'm certain I will the moment we arrive home."

"How about a cup of coffee?" he asked, including Bonita in the invitation.

"Not that awful stuff from before?" Bonita asked, making a face.

"Howard Johnson's?"

Hadleigh looked from the doctor to Bonita. Catching this, Street said, "Bonita and I had a visit this morning, over some of the battery acid they keep in the doctors' lounge."

"Hah!" Bonita laughed appreciatively, liking him more and more.

"Come on," he coaxed Hadleigh. "You've got to tell me about your secret life with Ronald Colman. I've always wanted to know what he's really like."

Hadleigh looked at him, a sudden illumination in her eyes. "You're a film fan?"

"You, too?"

"I've always adored films," she confessed.

"Come on," he said more positively. "You can follow me over in your car."

"All right," Hadleigh agreed.

His car was a 1948 black Buick in mint condition.

"Mom!" Bonita exclaimed. "Look at his car!"

"It's an old car."

"Oh, Mom, it's way more than an old car. It's beautiful. I wonder if he'd take me for a ride in it sometime."

"Bonita, don't be forward with him. He's merely being kind."

"No, he isn't. He likes you."

"Don't be absurd. Undoubtedly he's married with several children. You do have the most extraordinary imagination."

"You wait, you'll see. He'll ask you out to the movies. Bet you anything. I can just see the two of you, with your popcorn. And you'll get to ride in that terrific car."

"How do you manage to come up with the things you do?"

"Oh, Mom," Bonita gave a little laugh. "Sometimes, you're such a kid. I'm not 'coming up' with anything. Vern waited around. He wanted to."

"Vern?"

"He told me to call him that."

"What am I letting myself in for?" Hadleigh wondered aloud.

"Coffee, or maybe some ice cream. Don't you know anything about guys?"

"I probably know a good deal less than you do."

"Well, just relax. You'll have coffee, and you'll talk, and he'll ask you out, probably to the movies. And you'll go. There's nothing to it."

Bonita had a hot fudge sundae with chocolate chip ice cream, and used the wafer that came on the side to eat the whipped cream off the top. Hadleigh had coffee. Vern had a hot turkey sandwich, explaining, "I know it's all ersatz, including the gravy, but at least I'm not the one who has to preheat the oven and then stand around for forty-five minutes waiting for the stuff to thaw out."

"Divorced?" Bonita asked, licking hot fudge from the back of her spoon.

"Uh huh."

"Long?"

"A few years."

"Mom's divorced, too. Aren't you, Mom?"

"I apologize for her," Hadleigh told him.

"It's okay," he said easily. "I'm kind of used to your family. Don't forget I've gone fifteen rounds with your mother."

"So you intimated. When was that?"

In answer, he took hold of her hand, turned it over, and tapped his forefinger against her wrist. "I was doing my residency at the time. She barged into the O.R. and wouldn't leave, so we suited her up and let her stay."

"I had no idea," Hadleigh said, almost in a whisper.

"Oh, sure." He speared the last of the bread with his fork, dragged it around the plate to sop up the glutinous gravy, then popped it into his mouth. "The famous Mrs. Holden"—he paused to swallow—"had one of the student nurses in hysterics; two of the candy-stripers quit on the spot; and one of the RNs requested an immediate transfer out of the E.R.''

"Is that true?" Bonita asked skeptically.

"Almost." He smiled at her. "The part about her being in the O.R. is. She was really something, I'll tell you."

"Will she recover?" Hadleigh asked.

"I don't know," he said, becoming serious. "The test results won't all be in for another day or so. It really depends on whether it's just the pneumonia we're dealing with. Her white cell count's elevated, but that, in itself, isn't significant. I can't figure out the coma," he admitted. "That's the part that doesn't make sense."

It did to Bonita, but she couldn't possibly have told them what she knew. They wouldn't have believed her anyway. She continued eating her sundae, watching and listening as Vern worked on her mother. She thought the two of them were kind of cute, not a whole lot different from the kids at school in the way they were sizing each other up. The only thing missing was the small punch in the arm that the boys gave the girls to show they liked them.

She tuned out, to begin working on the details of her plan. She was going to need Tandy's help. It wouldn't work without her. But Tandy was okay; she'd go along.

"It's late," Hadleigh was saying when Bonita reconnected herself with the conversation. "We really must be going. Thank you for the coffee."

"My pleasure."

"Don't you want our phone number?" Bonita asked him.

"I've already got it," he laughed. "It's in the file."

Hadleigh looked as if she'd taken fire, so embarrassed was she. "Come along, Bonita," she said sternly.

They slid out of the booth, and Vern got up, still holding his napkin, to say, "Don't get mad at her. She's just one step ahead of everybody, that's all. I'll see you tomorrow at the hospital."

"Yes, thank you," Hadleigh said, and hurried after Bonita who was already at the door.

As they walked to the parking lot, Hadleigh demanded, "How *could* you?"

"It's nothing, Mom. He's going to call you up later and ask you out."

"You really must stop all this! I'm not looking for romance."

"You're almost out of dollhouses; and our house looks great. There's not a rock in ten miles you haven't moved. What else're you going to do?"

"I'm not interested in becoming involved with anyone, Bonita."

"He's very nice. And he likes movies as much as you do. He's pretty funny too. I loved that line about the battery acid."

"Some people," Hadleigh argued, "are better off on their own."

"You're not," Bonita stated. "It'd be good for you to have someone to go to the movies with. He'd probably die of gratitude if you cooked him dinner."

"Please stop now."

"Okay, but I know I'm right."

Thirty-three

"I know this is a pretty rough time for you right now, and maybe a break would do you good. I thought, if you were interested, we could catch an early movie Friday night. Or Saturday, if that's better for you. I hate going by myself around here. It's not bad in the city, but it's such a family thing in the suburbs. The whole gang piles into the station wagon to go off to the movies. I went a couple of times on my own, you know, when there were flicks I really wanted to see. Felt like a total misfit, sitting there with my popcorn, trying to be nonchalant while all these families were settling in like they were on a visit to the Lincoln Memorial. Mom and Dad eager as hell, shushing up the kids and getting them arranged with their Junior Mints and Twizzlers." He gave a dispirited little laugh.

Hadleigh listened, thinking Bonita had been right. How could she have known Vern would call? And why was a thirteen-year-old able to pick up on things that escaped her entirely? It might be a good idea, she thought, to start paying closer attention to what Bonita had to say. Obviously, she was aware of all sorts of things Hadleigh wasn't.

"Are you still there?" he was asking, "or have I put you to sleep?"

"I'm still here. I'm not asleep."

"It might take your mind off things for a couple of hours."

"Dr. Street . . ."

"Vern."

"Dr. Street, I appreciate the invitation, but I really don't think it's possible just now. Perhaps, at some other time, but with Mother ill . . ." She had to stop, unsure of what she was trying to tell him.

"Your mother would be the first person to tell you to take a breather for a couple of hours. So, why don't we make it Saturday? You'll probably be ready for a movie after the week you've been having."

"Are you always so persistent?"

"Nope. Only when I meet someone I want to know better. Give in, Hadleigh. You know you're going to go with me. Can't you hear that little voice in your head saying, 'Go on'?"

She laughed in response to his enviable self-confidence, then thought for a moment of the way he'd taken hold of her hand, tapping the scar on her wrist.

"Unless," he continued, "you can't stand the sight of me. In which case, you're off the hook."

"I'm not very good at this."

"Good at what?"

"It's rather like a game I never had an opportunity to learn. I find it mystifying, to be perfectly honest."

"I'll teach you," he said, so that, for no reason, she shivered. It was as if he'd made some utterly unanticipated sexual remark.

"I don't know that I wish to learn."

"Sure you do. We all do."

"Look, there's simply no way I could go off with you to see a film without feeling guilty that I was, in some oblique fashion, neglecting my mother. If you like, though, you're welcome to come for dinner on Saturday."

"You've got a TV, right?"

"Yes."

"Okay, it's a deal. *Wuthering Heights* is on at nine o'clock. Merle Oberon, Olivier. Perfect. I'll bring the popcorn."

"All right."

"What time?"

"Six-thirty."

"Six-thirty, with popcorn. Maybe I'll spring for some Junior Mints, too, for Bonita."

*　　　*　　　*

"You don't want me hanging around," Bonita said. "I'll just get in the way. I thought I'd sleep over at Tandy's, spend the weekend with her." Things were going to work out perfectly, she thought, pleased Vern had called, as she'd predicted. If she left Friday night, she could be back by Sunday evening. She still had to go over the details with Tandy, but she knew Tandy would go along.

"He's expecting you to be here," Hadleigh said apprehensively. "I was rather counting on you, actually."

"Mom, you don't need me here. Nobody has a date with a kid around to watch. You won't be able to talk."

"It's dinner, not a date. And it was your idea to offer him a meal."

"Mom," Bonita said, as if addressing a young child, "you're so hopeless. It's a date. He's a really nice man, and he's even kind of not-bad looking. He thinks you're gorgeous, for Pete's sake. It'll be fine. You'll have dinner, and he'll think it's terrific because all he ever eats is frozen stuff or garbage from restaurants. You'll see. It'll be easy."

I need a drink, Hadleigh thought. It would be Elmo all over again; another man attempting to foist his desires on her without any regard for what she might want. "I hate having to cope with . . . situations," she admitted.

"But there isn't any 'situation,' " Bonita argued. "He's coming for dinner. He likes you. What's wrong with that?"

"What's wrong is that I'm not interested in having a man about the place, Bonita, and I can't think why I've consented to this."

"Then call him back and tell him it's off. Something came up, and you can't do it."

"How could I possibly do that?"

"It's easy. You look up his number in the phone book, you call him and say you've thought it over and decided it's a lousy idea, you can't imagine what you were thinking of, and forget it, chum. Maybe some other time."

"How do you *know* these things?"

"God, Mom! Everybody knows that stuff. Didn't you ever have boyfriends when you were my age?"

"No."

"That's right. I forgot. You want *me* to call him?"

"I think not."

"Okay, I'll stay home. I just thought you'd be more comfortable without me. I wasn't thinking. I'm sorry." She put her arms around her mother.

"This is dreadful," Hadleigh said, appalled by the weakness she was displaying. "You're quite right. I did extend the invitation, and it's wrong of me to force you to be here when you should be with your friends. *I'm* sorry, Bonita. There's no reason why you should have to spend the evening playing chaperone to me. Ring up Tandy and make your arrangements for the weekend."

"I don't have to go, Mom. I just wasn't thinking."

The longer this debate continued, the more guilty Hadleigh felt, and the more convinced she became that she'd long ago abdicated her place as parent, allowing far too much to fall on Bonita's shoulders. Everything seemed to be peaking suddenly, and her mother's illness was in some way responsible.

"He really is a nice man," she told Bonita, smoothing the girl's heavy hair. "And I do like him. I'm rather distraught over Mother's being unwell, but it's not a good enough reason for me to be going on as I have been. It's simply ludicrous to make such a fuss over having someone to dinner. And I haven't the right to make you feel obligated." She hugged her, then released her. "Go ring up Tandy and make your plans."

Bonita didn't move. "Everything's changed. You feel it, don't you?"

"I feel something," Hadleigh acknowledged.

Bonita wanted to tell her everything would be all right, but if she said anything, she'd have to explain too many things. "Make him the chicken with champagne sauce," she said. "He'll love it. He'll be grateful to you for the rest of his life for giving him real food made by human hands."

Tandy said, "I'm going with you."

"Are you *nuts*? There's no way we can *both* go."

"Oh, yes there is. I've got it all worked out."

"What? What've you got worked out? I swear, if you've said anything . . ."

"Hold your horses! Now, you've told *your* mom you're spending the weekend with me. Right?"

"Right."

"And I've told *my* mom we've been invited to go to Vermont for the weekend with Cindy Carmichael. I've already checked with Cindy and she'll cover for us. So, all you've got to do is tell your mom you're going with me and Cindy to Vermont. It's perfect!" Tandy said happily. "There's no way anybody will be able to check on us."

"I don't know," Bonita said doubtfully. "I've got to think about this."

"There's no *time* for you to think about it!" Tandy bellowed into the telephone.

"But I've got to go food-shopping tomorrow with my mother. And then we have to go to the hospital, to see my grandmother."

"So what? First of all, going to the supermarket doesn't take all day. Second of all, get your mom to go to the hospital in the morning. Then, you can go shopping from there. Tell her you've been invited, and you really want to go. She'll understand. I mean, nothing's changed with your grandmother. Right? She's still in the coma. She might be in it for ages. I don't mean to be unkind or anything, but your mom's going to let you go. You already told me that."

"Okay. But how are we supposed to be getting to Cindy's place?"

"That part's easy. I've already told my mother that Cindy's mother's picking us up at the Darien Sports Shop. Because Cindy and her mom have to get Cindy's tennis racket. Right? So all you have to do is meet me there. It's perfect! Didn't I tell you?"

"It is close enough to the station."

"Of course it is!" Tandy said, losing her patience. "I'm not stupid, you know. I've worked this out very carefully."

"We'll have to make it no later than three-fifteen."

"I'll meet you at the side entrance, on the parking lot side."

"If you're late, Tand, I'm going without you."

"I won't be late! Why would I be late? I'm the one who's set up this whole thing."

"Don't worry, Grandma," Bonita whispered through the plastic. "I'm going to take care of everything. I have to take Tandy with me. I don't want to, but it's the only way I could work it out. I think she'll be okay. I mean, she's good at keeping secrets, and I think she'll understand." She paused and looked as closely as she was able at her grandmother's face, waiting, hoping for some reaction, however minimal. Frances lay unmoving, her face a pale, perfect heart shape. "Don't worry," Bonita whispered again. "I love you, Grandma."

"Did you remember your passport?"

"Right here!" Tandy patted the side of her shoulder bag.

"Okay! We're going to have to run to make the three forty-five. Let's go."

The train was already at the platform as they came bounding into the station. Bonita cursed under her breath, positive they'd get to the platform just as the train started pulling out. But the conductor must have seen them because nothing moved. The train sat and waited, as if holding its breath. The girls came huffing up the stairs to the platform, threw themselves into the nearest car, and fell gasping into a seat as the doors slid closed and the train surged forward.

"*I'm going to die!*" Tandy panted, red-faced and perspiring. "My mother'll be happy, though. I probably lost five pounds back there. I'll have the thinnest body at the funeral parlor."

"Boy! I hope I've got everything." Bonita was going through the contents of her purse, checking items off a mental list, and trying, at the same time, to keep one segment of her mind perfectly clear, in order to receive instructions.

"God! Your lips are moving," Tandy said. "Are you *talking* to yourself? It's so creepy when people do that."

"I'm trying to *think*!" Bonita snapped. "Everything depends on something else. Now, the first thing we'll do is get a taxi to my grandmother's apartment. You'll stay in the cab and go around the block, so I can tell the doorman my mother's waiting for me, but couldn't find a place to park, so she's driving around. It happens all the time, so he won't think there's anything strange about it. You'll get the cab to stop at the corner, and wait there for me. I've got the keys. I'll go up, get the money, call the airlines and book our seats. Then we'll go right to the airport, pay for the tickets, and be on our way by eight o'clock. *If* we're lucky, and the plane's not full. If we miss the BOAC flight, there's another one at ten o'clock on TWA, but I'd rather catch the earlier flight. That way, we'll be able to get into London, get a hotel room for the night, leave our stuff, and go do what has to be done."

"What're you going to do, anyway?" Tandy asked, for perhaps the tenth time.

"We're going to see someone. That's all I'll tell you."

"But why? What're you going to do there?"

"Tandy, stop asking questions. It was your idea to come along, but I'm not going to tell you anything. You'll find out when I do."

"You mean you *don't know*?"

"Something like that. I'll know when we get there."

"Boy!" Tandy's eyebrows shot up and down. "Maybe we'll have time to see something," she said. "I've never been *anywhere*, you know. This is so exciting!"

"We won't have time to fool around sight-seeing. I've already told you that. My grandmother's sick, and my mother thinks we're on our way to Vermont. We'll just do what we're there for, turn around and come straight back."

"I wasn't talking about fooling around. But if you get to see this woman tomorrow, we'll have the whole rest of the day and evening before we have to fly back on Sunday morning. We could do loads of stuff."

"If we get to see her right away, then we'll get the next plane back."

The conductor came to collect the fares and Bonita automatically asked for, "Two singles to Manhattan," and held out a ten-dollar bill.

"I have money," Tandy said, her change-purse in hand.

"It's okay, Tand. Save it in case you find something to buy in London. Although, if you buy anything, I don't know how you're going to explain it."

Tandy looked crestfallen. "I hadn't even thought of that," she said, returning the change-purse to her bag.

"I never knew you could run so fast," Bonita congratulated her. "That was really something."

"I never knew either." Tandy looked down at herself. "Did your mom think it was funny, your wearing dress-up clothes to go shopping? I had to make up this whole story about how we were going to be stopping on the way to Vermont to have dinner with Cindy's grandmother, so we had to wear skirts and everything. And my mom kept trying to look at what kind of stuff I was packing, so I had to bring my bathing suit. I've never told so many lies in my entire life. I just hope I remember them all."

"You will. You've got a terrific memory. You always remember all those dates in history. I don't know how you do it."

"I do have a good memory." Tandy was pleased by the compliment and her round face creased into a smile. "I even remember our phone number from the old house and I was only four when we moved from there."

"I'm glad you're coming with me," Bonita told her. "It kind of makes it easier."

The doorman greeted her, accepted her explanation that she'd come to pick up her grandmother's medication, and returned to his racing form. The elevator operator asked after Mrs. Holden, and Bonita explained, "She's in the hospital. That's why we had to come in, to pick up her medication. Her doctor needs to know what she's been taking."

"Oh!"

"I might be a few minutes," she said. "You don't have to wait. I'll ring when I'm ready to come down."

She let herself in with her grandmother's key and carefully closed the front door, then went directly through to the master suite. The overnight case was on the shelf in the dressing room and she lifted it down. Her hands were sweaty and she wiped them on the sides of her skirt before opening the case. The envelope was tucked into the side pocket. She pulled it out and peeled back the flap to verify that it contained a thick wad of English and American notes. The dollars she put into her wallet, the pound notes she left in the envelope, sliding it and the wallet into her purse. Then she went to the telephone in the living room.

Pitching her voice low, she duplicated her grandmother's accent exactly as she spoke to the ticketing agent on the other end of the line.

"I would like to book two first-class tickets for your eight o'clock flight this evening to London. My granddaughter and her companion will be coming to collect the tickets. They'll pay in cash. Since they'll be travelling unaccompanied, I'd be most grateful if you'd see to it that your special-services people are notified to give them assistance should they require it."

The ticketing agent confirmed that seats were available, noted the names and ages of the two girls, then said, "They're over twelve, Mrs. Holden. You do realize they'll have to pay full fare?"

"I am aware of that. I'm sending them along with sufficient funds."

"Right. Well, they're all set. Just make sure they get here an hour ahead of flight time."

Bonita thanked her and hung up.

Arriving downstairs she couldn't see the cab and at once became panicky. God! What if the driver was some kind of pervert and had kidnapped Tandy? Or what if Tandy had decided to change the plan for some reason? Where the hell was the taxi? She looked up and down the street, then at her watch. It was five-forty, still rush hour, and they had to get all the way out to Idlewild and pick up the tickets. When she looked up again, the cab was pulling in to the curb. She exhaled painfully, yanked open the door, jumped into the back beside Tandy and told the driver, "We're going to Idlewild, and we're late. So go as fast as you can. Okay?"

"You're running up quite a tab here, you kids. You sure you've got the money to pay?"

"For heaven's sake!" Bonita cried, exasperated. "Do we look like we're fooling around?"

"How would I know?" he drawled, one arm hooked over the back of the seat.

"Okay!" she fumed, opening her bag. "I'll give you ten dollars on account. The rest you get when you get us to BOAC *on time.*"

"You got it, kid." He whisked the bill from her fingers, turned forward and floored the accelerator, throwing both girls back against the seat.

"*Don't kill us!*" Bonita yelled. "Just get us there in time!"

"You were gone for ages," Tandy complained in an undertone. "I was beginning to think you were never coming out."

"I told you I had to get the money and then make our reservations. I could hardly go charging in there, could I? I mean, they'd have thought it was a little strange."

"I guess. But he"—she pointed her chin at the driver—"was asking me all kinds of questions about what was taking you so long."

"What did you tell him?"

"I said you probably had to go to the bathroom."

"*What*?"

"Well, it was all I could think of."

"*The bathroom*, for Pete's sake."

"Pardon me, okay? I'm not used to all this."

"It's okay," Bonita said, calming down. "So far, it's going perfectly. You're sure you've got your passport?"

"I told you. It's right here."

"Show me."

Tandy rolled her eyes and opened her bag.

"Okay? Satisfied?"

"Can I look at it?" Bonita asked.

"Sure. Just don't lose it."

"Where am I going to lose it?"

"You know what I mean."

"Sure. I thought I'd have a look then toss it out the window."

"If you're going to be so mean, maybe I won't go with you."

"I'm sorry. I'm not being mean. I've just got to make sure nothing goes wrong. This is *very* important, Tand. I can't tell you how important it is."

"I *know* it's important, and I know you're nervous, but you don't have to take it out on me. I'm only trying to help."

"I know you are, and I really appreciate it." Bonita gave back the passport and turned to look out the window. "I'll feel a lot better once we're actually on the plane. The traffic's really heavy. Boy!" She went quiet, her fists clenched in agitation.

They got to the terminal at five after seven. Bonita was sweating so heavily she was sure people would pass out from the smell of her. Tandy looked grim as she marched along at Bonita's side, carrying her little overnight case in one hand and holding her shoulder bag secure with the other.

"Look at the lineups!" Bonita exclaimed. "There must be a zillion people waiting." She looked up, spotted the first-class check-in counter, and dragged Bonita toward it.

"Excuse me," she said to the man behind the counter. "We have tickets on the eight o'clock flight."

"What name?"

"MacDonald and Holmeyer. My grandmother . . ."

"Just a moment, please."

He began fiddling with a computer terminal below the counter and Bonita turned to look at Tandy, offering her an encouraging smile. "Don't worry," she said.

"I'm not worried," Tandy lied, imagining the various punishments her family would dole out if they ever found out what she was doing.

"Here we are," the man said. "How do you wish to pay?"

"Cash." Bonita got out her wallet.

The man stared at her for a moment, then closed his eyes and gave his head a little shake, as if to clear it, before telling her the amount. He watched in complete disbelief as she counted out the bills.

"You both have passports?"

"Yup. You want to see them?"

He extended his hand and the girls presented their passports, which he studied for what felt like hours.

"What's the matter?" Bonita asked finally.

"Just checking your ages. Children under twelve must be accompanied to the gate by an adult . . ."

"We're both over twelve," she cut in. "And anyway, my grandmother called and was told the special-services people would see to boarding us."

"Since you're both over twelve," he said with a little smile, "I don't think that'll be necessary, do you? Here are your boarding passes and your tickets. It's gate six. They'll start boarding in about twenty minutes. Enjoy your flight, ladies."

"Just one moment!" Bonita's voice thundered, sounding to Tandy's ears very like Mrs. Holden's. "I don't think I like the way you're hustling us. In the first place, my grandmother specifically requested special services. And in the second place, you didn't even bother to tell us where the first class lounge is. Just because we're kids doesn't mean we're stupid. I don't like your attitude one little bit and I think I'm going to write your name down. I'm sure my grandmother will want to lodge a complaint about the way you're treating us."

Tandy was thunderstruck and watched with amazement as the man behind the counter underwent a complete transformation into someone suddenly most concerned with the girls' well-being and comfort. "I'll call them right away," he told Bonita, fumbling with the telephone and nearly dropping it.

"Never mind that!" she barked. "Just tell us where the first-class lounge is!"

"Certainly." He gave them directions, and without bothering to thank him, Bonita pulled Tandy away.

Out of sight of the ticketing counter, Tandy looked back over her shoulder, then at Bonita and said, "First, I thought for one horrible moment he was going to stop us. And then, the way you let him have it, God! I thought he was going to have a heart attack when you started saying all that stuff about reporting him."

"Some people just love to give kids a hard time," Bonita said angrily. "He was such a jerk. Listen, we don't have to go to the lounge if you don't want to. It just made me mad that he wasn't even going to say anything about it. If you'd rather, we can head for the gate. They're going to start boarding pretty soon."

"We've got time," Tandy said. "Let's get some magazines and chocolate bars to eat on the plane."

"They'll be serving dinner."

"How do you know that?"

"Because I just flew on this airline a couple of weeks ago, and because they told me when I made the reservations."

"Oh!"

"And anyway, you eat way too much chocolate. I'll bet if you gave up candy for a month you'd be skinny as anything."

"You think so? I'd love to be skinny like you."

"I'm not so skinny. It's just my height."

"I'd love to be tall, too. You're so lucky."

"You'll probably get a lot taller," Bonita said charitably. "Your dad's pretty tall."

"But my mom's practically a *dwarf*. And what if I take after her?"

"Your mother is *not* a dwarf. God! She's just not very tall."

"*Your* mother's *so* tall. I'd give anything to be that tall. Or not fat."

"So eat Lifesavers instead of chocolate bars."

"That wouldn't work. I can eat a whole roll in five minutes. Drives my mom nuts. She hates the way I crunch them. I'm starving."

"We'll eat on the plane."

"How about a bag of potato chips?" Tandy looked longingly at the gift shop as they went past.

"They're even worse then chocolate bars."

"How d'you know all this stuff?"

"My grandmother told me."

In a small voice, Tandy said, "I forgot all about your grandmother."

"*I* didn't. That's why we're doing this."

"Bonita, what if she dies anyway? I mean, I don't want to upset you or anything, but what if she does? Have you thought about that?"

"Sure I've thought about it. But I *have* to do this."

"But if she dies, how will it be important?"

They'd arrived at the gate and showed their boarding passes to the ground attendant who told them, "Have a seat, girls. We'll start boarding shortly, and we'll get you on before the crowd."

The waiting area was jammed. "We could sit on the floor, I guess," Tandy said.

"We can't get our clothes dirty. I didn't bring anything else. We'll just have to stand."

"I'm tired," Tandy carped, then seeing Bonita's expression, added, "but I don't mind."

They set down their small bags and stood looking out at the planes on the tarmac.

"What if she does die?" Tandy picked up the thread. "What will all this mean then?"

"Tandy, I'm doing this for my grandmother. It's something she wants me to do. It'll make a difference."

"What if that woman's not there? What if she's gone away, or she's on vacation or something?"

"Please! She'll be there. She's waiting."

"Waiting? I don't get it. Boy oh boy! My stomach's rumbling."

"Well, tell it to stop. It'll have something to eat soon."

Tandy stared at her, then began to laugh.

"What's so funny?" Bonita asked with a smile.

"This is. I bet if I go home and tell my mother I flew to England for the weekend she'll threaten to wash my mouth out with soap for lying."

"She doesn't actually *do* that, does she?" Bonita was revolted by the notion.

"She only threatens. Can you *imagine*? God! It'd be disgusting, foam and stuff all over your mouth."

"Who'd *do* a thing like that?"

"I don't know. The worst punishment I ever get is being grounded. And that's no big deal. What's your worst?"

"My mother doesn't punish me."

"Are you kidding? You mean when you get in trouble she just lets you get away with it?"

"I don't get into trouble. Well, not until now, anyway. And I'm going to have to tell her about this eventually."

"You've *never* been grounded?"

"Nope."

"God!" Tandy was so impressed she was briefly speechless.

Thirty-four

"I have the feeling, from moment to moment, that you're hiding away, but you're able to hear every word I speak. Then I wonder if you haven't decided to go away once and for all, the way I thought you had, so often years ago, when you vanished for days and sometimes weeks, and we didn't know where you were. Eventually, there was always a telephone call, someone ringing up to say where you were and would we please collect you. Did you ever think how afraid we were, how much we feared you wouldn't return? I hope to God this isn't what you're about now, although it feels much the same, and I'm afraid in exactly the way I was then.

"I'm beginning to hate the sound of my own voice, and the way I keep on sitting here, trying to tell you what I think. Even unconscious you frighten me, and I can't help wondering if I gave you that power; if, somewhere, a very long time ago, I agreed to enter into this with you. You'd be as alarming as possible, and I'd respond with appropriate fear. It makes a certain, rather dreadful sense.

"I've always believed that in some remote part of yourself, you cared for me. Now, I think there had to be a point in your life when caring became, to your mind, a sign of weakness, and so you stopped revealing it. I don't know. It's mad, rambling on this way, wanting you to hear me. There's always the chance, though, that if I hit on something, you'll open your eyes, fix me with one of those notorious *looks* of yours, and say something bitingly witty. Why does so much of what you say have such a razor edge to it? It's clever, but hurtful, too, and I've cringed inwardly most of my life at the things you've managed to get away with; outrageous behavior and endless forgiveness.

"Quite likely, I'll never know now what you think and feel, but I am grateful for how good you've been to Bonita. At first, when the children were small and they went off with you, I'd feel this dreadful jealousy, because you were demonstrating an interest in them you never displayed in me. I stopped after a time, and was glad, really, that Bonita seemed to fill a special place for you, and you for her. She loves you very much, you know. I've often wondered what the two of you talk about, how you communicate. Bonita's essentially my opposite, and undoubtedly it's that that appeals to you. She doesn't endlessly question everything before taking a single step. She just takes her steps and asks her questions as she goes along. I very much admire that quality in her. Sometimes, looking at her, it doesn't seem possible she was formed from any part of me. I don't see myself in her. Perhaps that's just as well. Oddly enough, it's you I see in Bonita. She even resembles you, rather strongly."

She wet her lips and drew back her shoulders to ease the muscles, never taking her eyes from her mother. She fully expected Frances to awaken at any second, and she didn't want to miss that moment when it came.

Vern had reviewed the test results with her upon her arrival at the hospital an hour earlier. "Her white cell count's improving," he'd told her. "And all the other tests are negative. I'm sorry I can't tell you more. We'll move her out of here and into a private room."

"When?"

"Now, if you like. There's a room available."

"Does this mean she's getting better?"

"Seems to be. It all depends on whether or not the medication can knock out the pneumonia. Her temperature's still elevated, but that's nothing unusual. I wish I could tell you more, but there's nothing to tell right now. We're just going to have to wait it out. Where's Bonita?"

"Gone to Vermont for the weekend with friends. I didn't see any point to keeping her here. She left yesterday afternoon."

"She's a great kid," he said. "I mean that. I'm not saying it to score points."

"No, I didn't think you were."

"Well, are we still on for tonight?" he asked.

"Has something come up?" she asked.

"Not for me. Is the invitation still good?"

"Well, yes."

"Great. So, I'll see you later."

She'd already shopped for the meal, and planned to take her time preparing it this afternoon before returning here to the hospital for another brief visit with her mother. She glanced at her wristwatch. Just after nine. She'd have plenty of time to get everything ready. She couldn't understand, though, why this man appeared so eager to spend time with her. She'd started gaining weight this past week, eating in order not to drink. She couldn't be bothered with clothes, or makeup, or pretending an interest in anyone or anything that didn't genuinely draw her. He'd grow bored with her soon enough, and go on his way. She just wished it wasn't necessary to have to *prove* how boring a person she was, before anyone would believe it.

"Why the hell doesn't anyone ever help?" she angrily asked the inert form on the bed. "Why is it we've got to get through every bloody thing all alone? I'm so sick of it. If one plays by the rules, they change them to throw one off, to force one to stay on one's own. I *do* hate being alone, but why should I have to give myself away in order not to be alone? It isn't fair. I loathe the unfairness of it all. And look at you! Neither dead nor alive, and I've got to sit here and hope you choose to stay alive so you might answer a question or two. It'd be just like you to spite me and die. God! Sometimes you infuriate me! I'd like to know why, for example, you decided one day to make my life a positive hell and then, on another day, decided to take up my daughter. Nothing you've ever done has made sense to anyone but you, and yet even unconscious you command more respect than anyone will ever show me if I live to be a thousand years old. I don't even care anymore if I never do get answers. I really don't. It's just so damned hateful to have you lying here with your mind ticking away, keeping all of it to yourself. I'd prefer to have you awake, and caustic as ever, than in this condition.

"I've never wanted you to die, but I think you wished *I* would. I do think that. Have you any idea what a truly dreadful mother you've been? Yes, yes. You've had a knack for arriving in the hour of crisis. But you've never been there for the day-to-day little things that matter most. I've tried so hard to be what I thought you wanted that I've never taken the time to be whoever it is I was intended to be. The only one of the lot of us who's been herself from the start is Bonita, and she's the only one you've evidenced any abiding love for. If you've doted on her as you have because she's been so much her own person, I want you to know she's that way because she's been allowed to be, because she's had a mother who's never made a secret of her love. I don't even think you like yourself especially, so why do we all care so goddamned much whether or not you live or die? If you were conscious, I swear to God, I'd hit you.

"I'm so tired of being angry with you. Please wake up, and I'll stop. If you die, I may never be able to let it go, and I don't want to find myself a cheap copy of you in another thirty years. I don't want to be polished and clever, and filled with pain underneath. I merely want to *be*, and I want you alive. And do you know what else? This will amuse you, I'm sure. For all your vanity, and your sometime cruelty, and your self-concern, we all love you. Father loved you. Bonita does. And so do I, with all my heart. I'll go to my grave wondering why and how I could love someone like you as much as I do, but there you are. Perhaps it has something to do with the way you've always spit in life's eye, and your damnable defiance of other people's rules. *Wake up*! Four or five days and nights of sleep should be more than enough for anyone. You've made up for years of insomnia. It's time to open your eyes."

There was a sound and she whirled around to see a nurse in the doorway.

"Get out! I don't care what your reason is for being here. Just get out!"

The nurse moved off, and Hadleigh turned to look back at Frances.

"Oh, God!" she whispered and went closer to the bed.

Beneath her closed lids, Frances's eyes were moving rapidly, as if she were watching something intensely important.

Both girls fell asleep after dinner. Bonita awakened to a terri-

ble guilt at having abandoned her mother at such a critical
time. But she *had* to do this. Choice wasn't involved. Still, she
was halfway over the Atlantic, and her mother didn't know
where she was. What if the plane crashed? And what about
Tandy?

She looked at her friend who was asleep with her head at an
awkward angle against the arm of the seat. She shouldn't have
allowed Tandy to get involved in this. If anything went wrong
. . . Nothing was going to go wrong. Tandy was being a very
good sport about the whole thing. And she'd been very clever
in setting up their weekend-in-Vermont alibi. If there was
enough money left, maybe she'd buy Tandy a special present.

The overhead lights had been turned off, and most of the
other passengers were sleeping. It gave her a strange feeling to
think that there were over a hundred people floating up here in
the air, in the dark. She rearranged herself, and wondered how
her grandmother was. So far, there'd been mostly silence, and
a kind of static. Probably, by Sunday night, Frances would be
unhooked from all the machines and needles, and she'd be
sending the nurses for mineral water and Nat Shermans. They
probably wouldn't let her smoke. That would make Frances
furious.

Tandy was snoring softly and Bonita suppressed her sudden
giggles. Sometimes when she slept over, Tandy talked in her
sleep, and woke Bonita up. She'd have entire conversations in
her sleep, and when Bonita would tell her about it the next
morning, Tandy would go all red and laugh, wide-eyed, as if
she couldn't believe it. This was the first time she'd ever
snored. Bonita couldn't wait to tell her about it.

Because of the heavy morning traffic heading into the city,
they didn't arrive at Brown's until almost nine-thirty. The
reception clerk seemed dubious about allowing two thirteen-
year-olds to book a room.

"My grandmother, Mrs. Holden, and I stayed here a few
weeks ago," Bonita said. "And I've got cash. I'll be happy to
pay for the night in advance. Maybe I should talk to the
manager."

"Uhm, no. I'm sure that won't be necessary. One moment
please." The young woman got up from the desk and went
through the doorway to an inner office.

"I hope we're not going to have a problem," Bonita told
Tandy who was looking around the small reception room, fas-

cinated. "I don't want to have to start trying to find another hotel."

"It's very old-fashioned, isn't it?" Tandy said, trying not to reveal her disappointment. The place looked very drab and unspecial, not at all as exciting as Bonita had made it sound.

"If we have time, and everything goes right, we could have afternoon tea. You'd love it, Tand. You sit in the lounge on one of the sofas, or in the armchairs, and they bring a little table, with a tablecloth, and a whole tea service, and plates of cakes and scones. Maybe we'll have lunch here too. They have this duck paté with Madeira sauce that's the best thing ever. The rooms are really nice, you'll see."

The clerk returned and asked Bonita to fill out a registration card. "Just for the one night, is it?" she asked.

"That's right, although we may have to leave this afternoon. But we'll pay for tonight." Bonita finished printing the information, then signed her name with a flourish.

"We hope you enjoy your stay," the woman said pleasantly, handing Bonita a card with the room number, and a key.

"Aren't you supposed to take us up to the room?" Bonita asked, in that same tone she'd used on the ticketing agent at the airport.

Smarting at having been told how to do her job by a child, the young woman stood up from behind the desk, smoothed down the skirt of her brown suit, and asked, "Have you luggage?"

"We've got it," Tandy said, holding out her little overnight case.

"Very good. If you'd like to follow." She set off toward the Dover Street side of the hotel, and the two girls exchanged a glance before going after her.

Bonita looked at the key. It was the same room she'd shared with her grandmother. "I hope it's not an omen," she told Tandy, as they were climbing the stairs to the first floor. "We've got the same room Grandma and I had last time."

"Maybe they thought you liked it last time, so you'd like it this time, too."

"Maybe. Now, listen. We're going to leave our stuff and head right over there."

"Okay. Boy, does it ever feel funny, being awake when it's really the middle of the night!"

"You slept for hours. Don't tell me you're still tired."

"Aren't you?"

"I will be, but I'm not now. I'm too anxious to be tired." The static was changing, becoming an almost inaudible whispering she was certain would gain in volume.

The reception clerk took the key from Bonita, opened the door, looked around the room, then, without a word, left them.

"Boy! Wasn't she a bitch?" Tandy said, mocking the way the young woman had flounced across the room. Then, turning, she looked around. "This is nice, isn't it?" she said doubtfully, gazing at the cabbage roses on the wallpaper.

"It's not the Holiday Inn, you know," Bonita defended the place. "This hotel is *old*. It has a history. Important people have stayed here."

"It's a little like my granny's house in Boston. Even smells a little like it."

"D'you have to go to the bathroom or anything?" Bonita asked.

"Maybe I better."

"Okay. It's just over there."

Tandy closed herself into the W.C. then through the door, asked, "How come the water thing's up on the wall? What's the chain for? Is that what makes it flush?"

"Just pull it when you're finished," Bonita told her, going into the bathroom to verify that there were sachets of French's shampoo, vials of bath oil, and individually boxed bars of soap. She loved these little touches, as well as the heated towel rail, and the immense tub. Maybe she'd have time for a bubble bath. She paused, her hands on the rim of the sink. The whispers were gaining in volume. They'd have to hurry.

The toilet flushed noisily, and Tandy appeared saying, "How come they have everything in separate rooms?"

"I don't know. Maybe so one person doesn't tie up the whole works. I could be having a bath while you were in the john."

"That makes sense. I'll just wash my hands and then I'm ready."

Bonita sat on the side of the tub to wait, watching Tandy open one of the boxes and shake out the soap. Tandy was so cute, with her long, blonde braid, and her stocky little body. She had a really cute face, too.

"Your lips are moving again!" Tandy accused. "Boy, you better not be going all weird on me!"

"I'm not going weird. I was just thinking."

"That's what you said before."

Once they were in the taxi on their way to Portman Square, Bonita had a moment of undiluted terror. "God, Tand! What if the woman's really a witch!"

"*What*? What're you *talking* about? We're going to see a *witch*? *I'm* not going, that's for sure."

"I'm being silly. There's no such thing as witches," Bonita said halfheartedly. "Not really."

"You're really making me nervous, you know that?" Tandy cried angrily.

"I'm sorry. I'm scared, all of a sudden."

"So let's not go."

"I have to. I just have to."

"Well, just don't leave me alone with her."

"Don't *you* leave *me* alone with her!"

"Who is this lady anyway?"

"You'll see."

There was a panel of polished brass mailboxes in the foyer. Bonita went down the row, saw A. Adams, and felt a sizzling along her nerve-endings, as if she'd received an electric shock. The air was humming gently.

"Second floor," she told Tandy, and started toward the stairs. "Over here they call the first floor the ground floor."

"Listen! What if she's not home? What do we do then?"

"She's home," Bonita answered in a whisper as they approached the door. "Here it is." Her knees were suddenly weak and she had to swallow twice before putting her finger to the bell. The girls looked at each other. The whispers were a voice inside her head now.

The door opened and there was a long moment of silence as the girls gazed at the woman who stood there and she, in turn, looked inquiringly at them. Bonita was sure her heartbeat must be audible, along with the insistent voice inside her head, cautioning her not to be misled by the ordinariness of this woman's appearance.

"Are you Amanda?" Bonita found it difficult to speak. "I mean, Mrs. Adams?"

"Yes?"

Bonita tried to smile. "I'm Bonita MacDonald. You know

my mother, Hadleigh. She used to be Holden. I'm her daughter," she said redundantly.

"You are Hadleigh's daughter?" the woman half-smiled.

"That's right. And this is my friend, Tandy Holmeyer."

"How do you do." Amanda glanced at Tandy, then returned her eyes to Bonita. "Is your mother with you?" she asked Bonita.

"No, she isn't."

"Oh, dear," Amanda said, with a sudden full smile. "How very rude of me. Do come in." She stepped away from the door expectantly. Again the girls looked at each other, then moved inside, to wait while Amanda closed the door. "Please," she said, extending her hand, "come in and sit down." She turned to lead the way into the lounge. The girls followed. Bonita was gathering impressions; they seemed to be printing themselves on small discs that slotted into place in her brain: the woman was not very tall, and rather plump, although not fat. She was wearing a blue silk dress patterned with geometric lines. Her hair was an unreal shade of golden blonde, cut short and curled forward against her face. Her ankles were slim and her legs looked good in surprisingly high-heeled shoes. Bonita was accustomed to seeing her grandmother in shoes like that, but she'd never thought other women her age might also wear them. Unlike Frances, though, this woman looked old. With the curtains still drawn, and the lamplight catching her face fully, it was possible to see the wrinkles underneath her makeup.

"Do sit down," Amanda invited. "Perhaps you'd care for some tea?"

"Oh, no thanks," Bonita said quickly. "You're going out. I mean, we don't want to make you late or anything."

"Not at all," Amanda said pleasantly, with a smile that showed her teeth. "There's nothing that won't wait. Tell me. How is your mother?"

"Oh, she's fine."

"It's been a very long time since I last saw her."

"I know that. She's been talking about coming to visit, and she probably will." The voice said, *She'll never come to this place*! "Tandy and I just flew over for the weekend, you see."

"For the weekend? The two of you, on your own?" Amanda's eyebrows arched, her face acquiring a look of suspicion.

"That's right." *Watch her closely! Don't take your eyes from her for a moment!*

"Is that the sort of thing youngsters do these days?"

"Not exactly," Bonita explained. *Keep it vague! She'll tip her hand. She'll create the opening.* "We left last night and just got here this morning."

"You've come directly from the airport?" Amanda glanced over at the foyer as if she'd neglected to see their luggage.

"We stopped at the hotel first." *Don't say which hotel! Don't give any more information than you must!* "I guess maybe I should've phoned before we came, but I thought it'd be better to come right over." She expected the woman to ask why, but she didn't.

"You've flown over for the weekend, and you've booked into a hotel. You didn't stop to have breakfast?"

"No," Tandy interjected with a defiant look at Bonita.

"You must be hungry," Amanda said. "I'll put on the kettle."

"That would be nice," Tandy declared on a triumphant note. "Thank you."

"And some toast, perhaps?"

"That would be nice, too," Tandy told her.

"Of course." Amanda's eyes rested briefly on Tandy before she turned and went to the kitchen.

The moment she was out of earshot, Tandy leaned over to whisper, "She's no witch. She's very nice. And why did you say no? I'm *starving*, and she *offered*."

"It's a mistake," Bonita hissed, angry. "Don't do or say anything else! Just listen to me, and when I tell you to do something, do it. Don't ask any questions; don't argue, just do it!"

Rebuked, Tandy sat back and looked around. Her impression was that nothing here had been changed in years and years. The place was spotlessly clean, yet in the corners, at ceiling height, faint streamers of dust wafted gently to and fro. "This kind of looks like my grandmother's house, too," she murmured.

Bonita was looking at a collection of paperweights on the coffee table. While Tandy was busy studying the place, Bonita's hand shot out to snatch the smallest of the glass weights and deftly deposited it in her purse. "I'll bet," she said, "it's exactly the same as it was when my mother was a little girl and lived here."

"Your mother lived here?"

"During the war, when my grandmother got sick, my mom lived here for six months." As she spoke, she got up and went over to the kitchen doorway to see Amanda placing slices of bread in an old-fashioned drop-front toaster. "I could help," she offered, visibly startling the woman who turned, frowning for a moment, before recapturing her smile.

"Not necessary," Amanda said. "It won't take a moment."

Bonita backed off and turned to face the room, her eye caught by a grouping of photographs in ornate silver frames on a mahogany table. Going closer, she saw that one of the pictures was of her mother as a little girl. And another, she was sure, was of her grandfather. She wanted to inspect the pictures more closely but didn't dare. While at first sight of Amanda her instincts had argued there'd been some mistake, the voice was reminding her to keep her guard up. *She only seems ordinary. Remember that*!

"That is indeed your mother," Amanda said, placing a tray on the coffee table. "There's a photograph there of your grandfather, as well." She came to stand close to Bonita, lifting one of the portraits to stare at it for several seconds with rapt attention. Her proximity had a threatening aspect. Bonita had the feeling that the woman's soft body was capable of absorbing her, should she get too close. She'd be sucked through the blue silk and trapped inside all that soft, swelling flesh. "This is your grandfather," Amanda was saying, her eyes glittering as she held out the picture for Bonita's inspection, then stood waiting for some response.

"I thought it was," Bonita said, taking a cautious step backwards. "I don't remember him very well. I was only four when he died."

"Yes, I know." Amanda retrieved the photograph and returned it to the group on the table. Her hands were small and soft-looking, her long nails polished a deep pink shade. The sight of those small hands was almost as alarming as the weight of Amanda's arm suddenly descending across her shoulders. "Come have some tea."

Obediently, Bonita allowed herself to be directed back to the sofa, although the skin across the tops of her shoulders felt singed. Resuming her seat, with Amanda once again at a safe distance, she said, "My grandmother and I were here a few weeks ago. Did you know that?"

Amanda didn't answer, but busied herself pouring a splash of milk into each of three fragile flowered cups before adding the tea. She looked up and with another smile that revealed her teeth, asked, "Sugar?"

"Yes, please," Tandy said. "Four."

Again Amanda fixed Tandy with her eyes. This time Tandy distinctly felt heat, as if the sofa had suddenly begun smoldering beneath her. She couldn't understand what was happening here and, from moment to moment, had the sensation she was dreaming. Amanda lowered her eyes and, with a small set of silver tongs, dropped, one after the other, four cubes of sugar into the tea before handing Tandy the cup.

Tandy reminds her of your mother, the voice said. *Watch closely! She can't hide how she feels. In this light, she's starting to become confused. She's beginning to think you are me, and that Tandy is Hadleigh.*

"Did my grandmother come to visit you?" Bonita asked, accepting her cup of tea from the woman.

Amanda sat back and lit a cigarette, her eyes on Tandy, who was trying not to wolf down the several pieces of toast she'd taken from the tray. It's true! Bonita thought, studying the slight downturning of the corners of Amanda's mouth. She doesn't like Tandy! She's looking at her as if she's tired of having to watch her eat.

"Why," Amanda asked slowly, "would Frances have come to see me? We haven't been close in many years." Her expression had gone flat, as had her voice. "Frances," she said, as if the name in her mouth had a bitter taste, "would never come here."

"But you were such good friends," Bonita fed out the lie.

Amanda laughed unpleasantly. Tandy stopped chewing and stared at the woman. It didn't seem possible she could have made a sound like that. Tandy's appetite was gone suddenly and, trying not to draw attention to herself, she returned her half-full plate to the tray.

"What nonsense!" Amanda declared, crushing out her cigarette in a small crystal ashtray. "Frances couldn't possibly have spoken of the two of us as friends. Let me ask you something. Why have you come here?"

"I have something to tell you."

"Oh, yes?"

Tandy stared now at Bonita, startled by the change in her voice, and in the way she looked. Tandy blinked, confused and frightened. Bonita was beginning to sound older, her voice deeper. And she looked different. It was probably the light, but her hair was darker, her features sharper, more defined.

"My grandmother is ill."

"Ah!" Amanda nodded. "I'm sorry to hear that." Despite the words, she appeared satisfied, as if some vague knowledge had been made concrete.

"Are you?" Bonita challenged.

Tandy moved surreptitiously closer to Bonita.

"Of course," Amanda answered smoothly. "A very long time ago we were best friends. We knew each other as young girls. Did you know that?" Amanda's eyes were acquiring an uncertainty, as if she wasn't quite sure to whom she was speaking.

"I thought we were friends," Bonita said, and Tandy's head shot around at the utterly altered voice that had emerged from her friend's mouth. "I did think that, Amanda. I was wrong, though, wasn't I?"

"I . . . Of course we were friends."

"No. I was your friend, but you were never mine. I simply couldn't see it." Bonita was moving, getting up from the sofa to stand on the far side of the coffee table.

"I haven't the faintest notion . . ." Amanda again emitted the glacial laugh and reached, with a faintly trembling hand, for another cigarette. She lit it, inhaled, and smoke curled from her nostrils, winding upward into her hair. With the lamplight behind her it seemed as if her entire head was enveloped in gray smoke. Tandy's hands had gone sweaty and she wiped them down the sides of her skirt.

"You know precisely what I'm saying," Bonita's deep, cultured voice insisted. "It's taken me all this time, but I know now what you did."

"This is absurd! Just what is it you're trying to say?"

"You know!" Bonita insisted.

"I assure you . . ."

"*You know*! Such a simple thing. Ridiculous, really. A glove on the floor, but I couldn't see it. A bloody glove, just on the far side of those floor pillows. You were there!"

Suddenly, to Tandy's horror, everything went crazy.

"You had everything, always!" Amanda cried, the upper half of her body straining forward. "It wasn't enough you had Arthur and the children and the swank flat in Chelsea. Not enough you had the best of everything, you had to decide you wanted Edwin, too! He was *my* friend. It was *I* who introduced you; *I* who rang you up to let you know he'd returned. That was my mistake, of course, letting you know. I watched you mooning over him before they left for America. I saw the way your great calf's eyes followed him. And I was *glad* when they left! You couldn't have him! So you married Arthur. You didn't deserve him! You'd never done anything, *ever*, to warrant the attention everyone paid you!"

"Now it all comes," Bonita breathed. "Now. How did you do it? What happened after I left?"

"*I saw what you did!*" Amanda laughed bitterly. "You were pathetic, absolutely pathetic, throwing yourself at him. And he wouldn't have you. He couldn't have had you! I *warned* you, but you wouldn't listen! Neither of you would listen! *Of course I was there!* I had to tell him, had to make him see what was happening. But would he take it seriously? No. Not until you arrived, and then when he was fixing the drinks, my God, it was too sad! Taking off your clothes, throwing yourself at his head! I saw it all! Oh, yes. I saw all of it!"

"What did you do, Amanda?"

"*I couldn't do anything for him!*" she shrieked. "The raid had started. He was sitting there, dazed, with all that blood. I had to get out of there! Bombs were falling!"

"He asked you to help him and you refused, didn't you? It didn't occur to you to get help from one of the wardens, did it? No. You were too angry, even to want to help him. Isn't that right?"

"I HATED YOU!" Amanda screamed. "You were supposed to get caught, and be hanged! You were supposed to *die* for what you'd done!"

"You finished it, didn't you? You picked up the poker and you hit him, and kept on hitting him until he was dead. Then you ran, fully believing he'd be found and I'd be blamed for his death."

"*It didn't happen*! The bloody building was demolished and you got away with it!"

Tandy could feel her eyes gaping and her mouth hanging open as her head swivelled back and forth.

"You wanted to ruin my life, Amanda. And you did your damnedest, didn't you? First you took my daughter, and then you tried to take Arthur. But neither of them wanted you, did they? Poor Hadleigh drove you wild with her questions and her dreadful hunger. And Arthur couldn't be had."

"*I could have had him*! *I could have*!"

"You tried, and you lost. You let me suffer for twenty-two years for something *you* did!"

"When they took you away that day I could barely contain my happiness!" Amanda smiled. "You played right into my hands, and they took you!"

"Aaaah!" Bonita sighed. "Come here, Tandy!"

Equally frightened by both these people, Tandy hesitated. She wished she could wake up.

"Come here, Tandy!" Bonita said again, holding her hand out. It was beginning to fade quickly. There was a deep sighing inside her head. Reluctantly, Tandy approached her, and Bonita grasped her hand. When Tandy looked back at Amanda, she seemed very old, as if the bones beneath her face were slowly collapsing inward.

"You tried, with everything in your power, to destroy me, Amanda. And yet here you are, alone, with nothing more than a handful of photographs. I pity you!"

"*How dare you offer me your pity*! You always thought you were *so* clever, with your acerbic remarks and cryptic comments! I nearly had you. I nearly did. If it hadn't been for that raid, you'd have hanged! And I'd have been there to watch it."

Again, Bonita emitted a deep, rattling sigh. And then there was silence, followed by a sudden breeze gusting through the room that lifted Bonita's hair as she began pulling Tandy toward the door, then stopped.

"If my grandmother dies," Bonita said, "so will you! I have the power to make things happen. You'd better pray nothing happens to her; you'd better start right now. Because *if my grandmother dies, you will too*!"

Then the door was open and she and Tandy were running as

fast as they were able, along the hallway, down the stairs, out through the front entryway, into the street, and along the square. Just before they got to Oxford Street, Bonita staggered to a standstill, collapsing in tears against the wall of a building.

There was nothing left, nothing at all. There was only a whiteness inside her head.

"What's the matter?" Tandy cried, clutching her friend's hand. "What is it?"

"There's nothing left!" Bonita sobbed. "It's over; it's over!"

Somehow, Tandy knew, and stood stroking Bonita's hand, crying too, in fear and disbelief and sorrow.

Thirty-five

Hadleigh returned home, briefly confronted the empty rooms, then went to the kitchen to unwrap the bottle of Tanqueray she'd stopped to buy after leaving the hospital. There was no tonic water, but there was a pitcher of orange juice. She used it to dilute the gin to a pale yellow, then stood for some time gazing at the glass before carrying it out to the back steps where she sat, feeling the cooling end-of-day air gentle on her skin.

The garden was darkly green, and almost perfect. Several of the rocks rimming the beds might have been better placed, but she dismissed the impulse to shift them. She wanted to savor the moment as she lifted the glass to her lips and then took the first swallow. It was good, sharp-edged and punishing.

She'd spoken to Chris earlier, having called to talk to Ben. But they'd taken Ben down to the military academy early, without bothering to inform her. She'd wanted to be angry but she had no anger left. And, besides, what was the point? Ben hadn't belonged to her in years, if ever. He was Chris's child, but without his father's commitment to playing by the established rules. Ben was defiant, and something of a bully, and a coward, as most bullies were. In her thoughts of him, he was forever a toddler, rather sweet but with a tendency to whine. His actuality always came as a shock. He was such an angry, enflamed boy, and had acquired the habit of talking to Chris in a loud, grating voice, as if Chris were feeble-minded. Hadleigh couldn't understand why Chris tolerated his son's rudeness, why he approached Ben repeatedly with a kind of optimistic mistrust, as if he thought, 'This time, he'll respond as I'd like him to.' Ben never did. Ben was tall, and overweight, and had a permanent curl to his upper lip. And when he spoke to any adult, he seemed to be suffering under the massive weight of his gigantic intolerance. It further shocked her to recognize her intense dislike of her own child.

The light in the trees was incredibly rich, painfully full; it made everything look edible. If she opened her mouth she could bite chunks out of the fanning leaves, the springy grass, the top-heavy mums defying gravity; she could chew on the clouds, and touch her tongue to the wafers of bark shed by the cord-wood she'd cut in preparation for the winter. She'd had one of the dying elms taken down in late spring, and the trunk had been left in four-foot lengths she'd split with a wedge and an axe, hacking away, creating echoes that had seemed to shake the foliage as she'd proved her strength over a period of five days. Using bricks to keep the wood elevated above the ground, she'd stacked each piece, and finally covered it all over with heavy-gauge plastic sheeting she'd bought at Ring's End. She thought now that perhaps she'd been happy that week. Her body had labored while her mind had floated unencumbered; she'd reviewed her best memories the way her mother had, once upon a time, selected chocolates: tasting each one and rejecting those that didn't suit her palate.

She got up to refill her glass, noticing that the kitchen was starting to lose its light. She switched on the bulb in the range-hood, then went back to the rear top step. After the initial, highly pleasurable burr created by the first drink, she now consumed the liquid automatically. There was a thirst to be slaked, and there appeared to be no reason why she shouldn't meet the internal demand.

It was odd, she thought, talking these days to Chris. She had no anger left for him. Its loss deprived their conversations of impetus. She had to make lists in order to keep words in the air, to give him something concrete to which he could respond. They were old, tired warriors who'd long-since forgotten what it was they'd gone to battle over. There still existed a need for periodic communication, so they did it with hollow efficiency, even with a degree of affection. Now that they were no longer married, they were able, within limits, to be friends. She asked each time after Monkey and the baby; he asked after Bonita and Frances. It was all polite, sanitized, dehumanized.

Vern Street was not exactly impolite, but for him social niceties were a waste of time; and he was alarmingly human. Her eyes were drawn repeatedly to his hands, which were large and not as she imagined the hands of a surgeon would look. They were too broad, and didn't look capable of placing delicate sutures in incisions, or of holding slim, potentially lethal instruments. The sight of his hands made the backs of her knees hurt, as if her tendons had suddenly drawn too tight. When he talked, she found herself watching his mouth instead of his eyes. She missed much of what he said, and was disgusted with herself for being lured by the shape of his lips and the frequency of his laughter.

He was offhandedly solicitous, yet more sincerely caring than the majority of people she'd met in her life who'd made a pretense of concern for purely social reasons. And he smelled clean. Elmo's clothes had always had a musty smell; so had his car. And Chris had taken fastidiousness all the way to fetishism. She'd come to despise him, at the end, for his leap from her body and his ensuing rush to the shower. She wondered if he did the same thing to Monkey. It was likely, in view of the amount of time Monkey spent fondling horses. She laughed aloud, and raised her glass only to discover it empty.

"Time for a refill," she said aloud, pushing inside through the screen door.

The drink poured, she stared into space, wondering what Bonita might be doing at that moment in Vermont. Her throat muscles clenched at the thought of her daughter, and she was caught in the vise-like grip of welling emotion. Snatching up the glass, she went outdoors again, swallowing against the tightness in her throat, anesthetizing her emotions with gin-flavored orange juice.

The ringing of the doorbell jarred her and, instinctively, she began to rise, then thought she'd stay where she was and whoever was at the door could just bugger off. She waited, listening. After a minute, the doorbell went again. "*Piss off!*" she whispered fiercely, and took a gulp of her drink. The silence was holding. Good. She began counting silently, A thousand and one, a thousand and two, and was up to a thousand and twenty-three when a figure appeared at the foot of the steps, and she jumped, startled.

"I had an invitation," Vern said. "Of course, under the circumstances, I didn't think it would still be good. But I thought I'd come over, see if you wanted to talk. Sorry if I scared you."

"You scared bloody hell out of me! Hasn't anyone ever told you not to do things like that!"

"Often," he answered, putting one foot tentatively on the bottom step. "I drum up business going around giving unsuspecting women heart-attacks."

"I believe it."

"You've got a whole new sound tonight," he said. "It's different."

"Oh, really?"

"Yeah. In the dark, listening to you, you sound like your mother."

"Excuse me!" She abruptly pushed upright and opened the door. "I need another drink. Would you care for one?"

"Have you eaten?"

"I have not. Would you care for a drink?"

"Maybe you should have something to eat."

"I am not remotely interested in food. A drink?"

"What are we having?" he asked.

"Gin and orange juice. Filthy, but effective."

"Okay, sure. I'll have one."

"Wait here!" she commanded. The screen door slammed after her.

From the foot of the steps, he watched her get another glass from the cupboard. Her movements lacked coordination, and he could tell she was well on her way to being drunk.

"There you are!" She gave him his drink, then managed to sit down without toppling off the step.

"Mind if I sit with you?"

"I don't mind." She moved to one side to make room, and at once felt crowded as he sat on the step beside her.

"So," he said, clinking glasses with her. "What d'you think?"

"About what?"

"About anything. Cheers."

"Cheers. I'm thinking right now of the positively blissful potency of alcohol. There is most definitely a reason why such a lot of people find it so compelling."

"I take it you're planning to go on until you're completely blitzed."

"I was in the Blitz, you know."

"Were you?"

"I was. I slept through the better part of it, beneath a dining table."

"You didn't go to a shelter or anything?"

"I did not. Stayed under the table."

"You're drunk," he said quietly.

"Not quite." She was glad it was beginning to get dark. She couldn't see his hands or mouth too well.

"You'll make yourself sick," he said reasonably. "You're not used to that stuff. It'll go off like a bomb inside you."

"Have you come here to administer a lecture?"

"Not me, kid. I'm just pointing out the obvious. It's a talent I have. That, and remembering trivia. D'you ever wonder what became of Grady Sutton, or Zasu Pitts?"

"I cannot say that I've stayed awake nights wondering."

"So, who are your favorites?"

"Film stars? Let me think. Melvyn Douglas. He was lovely in 'Anthony Adverse.' And William Powell and Myrna Loy. Super, they were, as the Thin Man and his wife. Or were they Nick and Nora Charles? No matter. Judy Holliday, Clark Gable."

"Don't forget Ronald Colman," he prompted.

"Shangri-La. Leslie Howard, Olivia de Haviland. Chris, you know, discovered very early on that films were a much more successful aphrodisiac for me than alcohol. He used to take me often. It's the only part of our marriage I actually miss. Not what came after. The films."

"Maybe I'll check out the kitchen, see what I can put together in the way of some food."

"I thought you were limited exclusively to frozen dinners."

"I can handle eggs, too. I'm not entirely handicapped."

"I have no appetite. But you're welcome to forage for yourself."

He stared at her, not moving. "What's the point, Hadleigh? You're going to have one hell of a hangover in the morning. Then you'll have to have a little hair of the old dog to ease the pain, and the next thing you know, you'll be in Silver Hill, popping Antabuse and vomiting at the thought of a drink. Where'll that leave Bonita?"

"You know all about me, do you?"

"I'm the guy with the repair kit, remember?" He took

hold of her wrist and traced the scar with his finger. "I did a damned good job, too, but it was your mother who worked the real magic."

"My mother? What had she to do with it?"

"She was there in the O.R. We talked about it the other night."

"I recall some reference."

"She was really something," he said proudly. "Wouldn't leave, so we got her suited up and let her stay."

"In the operating room?"

"We were losing you. It was the damnedest thing. She never told you about it?"

"Not a word." She'd turned and was paying full attention. "What happened?"

"We were going nuts. All your systems were starting to shut down, and she knew it. She started whispering in your ear, and the next thing we knew, you were turning around, stabilizing." He was seeing it again. "I remember looking up, for a second or two, and thinking, 'What the hell's going on here?' Afterwards, we talked. She didn't want to tell me what it was she'd said, but I wouldn't turn it loose and, finally, she told me."

"What? What was it she said?"

"She told me all sorts of things about herself, where she shopped, and that she had just one child; all kinds of stuff. I kept asking her to tell me, and she said, 'I told her what she's always wanted to hear, but won't remember when she comes round. I told her I loved her.'"

"She *said* that?"

"An exact quote."

"Oh, God!" She was going to begin weeping, and tried to forestall it by downing the rest of her drink. "Oh, God! God, God, goddamn! I need another one!" She lurched upright and fell against the screen door. When he moved to help her, she cried, "Just stay where you are! *Stay*! This will *not* undo me!" She reeled into the kitchen and grabbed the near-empty Tanqueray bottle, left her glass on the counter and went dizzily back out. She was about to tilt the bottle to her mouth, but his hand forced her arm down.

"You really don't want to do that," he told her. "It's just punishment for uncommitted crimes."

"How the hell would you know?" she demanded.

"I'd know," he said levelly. "I patch up drunks every day of the year, and their victims. They're the guiltiest bunch of bastards I've ever met." He took the bottle from her and poured the last of the gin over the side of the steps.

"Mr. . . . Doctor Street . . . Vern, what you just did constitutes a serious breach of etiquette."

He laughed. "You're one very proprietous drunk."

"In my family, style is of the essence."

"I don't know about style, but I'd say sobering you up and getting some food into you would be essential."

"I worked very hard to get into this condition. I have no desire to be sober. Nor is it your responsibility to oversee my actions."

"When's Bonita coming home?"

"Tomorrow. What has that to do with this?"

"Don't do it to her, to yourself, or to me."

"You are nothing to me. Less than nothing."

"I could be something to you."

"Oh! You'd like to go to bed with me. Is that what we're to do now?"

"I don't think so."

"You're lying!"

"Nope. I'm telling the God's honest truth."

"You mean to say you've no interest in removing my clothes and putting me down on my back? No interest in satisfying all your male urges?"

"Oh, I admit I've got a little interest in that." He smiled and folded his arms over his knees. "I like tall, long-legged women. *Sober*, tall, long-legged women."

"Isn't it handy to know one's requirements! Have you always known them?"

"Only recently."

"Did she truly say that?" she asked, feeling herself starting to fold inward.

"She truly did. Does it help or hurt?"

"Both. It all helps; it all hurts." She wound her arms around herself and looked up at the sky. "I thought it would be better, being anest . . . anesth . . . drunk. It's actually worse. I'm terribly sorry, but I'm afraid I'm going to be sick."

"Come on." He took hold of her arm, drawing her up and inside to the bathroom.

"Please don't stay!" she begged.

"Shut up and keep your head down!"

When she'd finished, he bathed her face with a cold wash-cloth and made her drink a glass of water.

"I don't know if I'll be able to forgive you for witnessing that," she said, tasting the residual bitterness in her mouth.

"You'll be able to," he said confidently, pushing her into one of the kitchen chairs before going over to study the contents of the refrigerator. "It's going to have to be eggs. I can't handle anything else." He took out one of the packages of chicken breasts and stood looking at it. "Was this going to be for my dinner?"

"In another century," she answered, testing with her fingers the soreness in her abdomen.

"Too bad." He returned the chicken to the shelf and brought out the eggs.

"There's a frying pan in the cupboard beside the stove," she directed.

"Thank you. Why don't you put on some coffee?"

"Yes, all right."

"Aside from showing up unexpectedly at twilight, I'm not basically a scary person. Shit! I always get the goddamned shells in with the eggs." He picked out several pieces of broken shell and dropped them into the sink. "Broke the damned yolks, too! I hope to Christ you *can* cook. Nope!" He shoved her gently away. "This time, I'm doing it. But next time, it's your turn. What're you so frightened of, anyway?"

"Men don't listen. They simply pretend to in order to get you to do the things they want you to do."

"Such as?"

"Taking off one's clothes and opening one's legs."

"There are worse things."

"No, there are not," she said firmly. "I'm tired of wasting words and thoughts on people who have no genuine interest in hearing them."

"Come on! I've got all kinds of genuine interest."

"So you say. In the end, though, you'll show yourself to be like the others."

"I resent that. There's only one of me. Ask my mother! She'll tell you."

"That's different. You haven't any desire to bed your mother, have you?"

"That's grotesque! She's sixty-seven years old. It's pretty

rotten of you to suggest I harbor Oedipal attitudes.''

She reached past him to put the coffee pot on the burner, then rested against the sink, saying, ''Listen, I'm tired of games. It seems I've had to play them all my life, and I refuse to go on with it. I've never liked sex; never liked the feeling I get afterward of having been used for purposes that haven't anything to do with me, or my well-being. I do like you. I cannot imagine why you'd want to linger here, doctoring me, if not for some reward you have in mind. I'm nowhere near sober, although I'm not, unfortunately, as drunk as I was a short while ago. Like most men, you'd like to think you'll turn me around, influence me, use your charms to arouse the responses you're convinced are there, just below the surface, simply awaiting the attentions of the right man.''

''Now, just hold the phone a minute there!'' he told her. ''This is you talking, not me. You're the one who started all that stuff about taking off clothes. I never said a word. How the hell would I know what kind of responses you have or haven't got? And how the hell do you know I'm all that confident of my own whatevers? I've never maneuvered anyone in my life, and I'm not about to start now. I could get pretty resentful, you know, being lumped in with a bunch of other guys without even being given half a chance to state my case.''

''No,'' she said, throwing him. ''You're quite right. I'm the one, aren't I? Because I like the look of your hands, and I find myself watching your mouth when you speak, and I have the utterly arbitrary idea that you might just influence me.''

''And that's what scares you. Right?''

''Yes. Those eggs will burn if you don't do something.''

He turned off the burner while she automatically got the plates.

''You're gorgeous,'' he said, ''in a kind of unkempt, country-girl way, but you're nuts as a fucking bedbug.''

''Do you always swear such a lot?''

''Not in front of my patients. How d'you get them out of the pan without them coming all apart?''

''Give it to me.'' She moved him aside, grabbed the spatula from his hand and efficiently served up the eggs. ''Here!'' She gave him a plate and carried her own to the table. ''The coffee will only be a few minutes more.''

''Got any bread?''

"In the second drawer there."

He found the bread and brought it and the butter to the table. Busy with the food, he didn't look at her for a minute or two. When he did finally, he felt terrible. She was sitting, her hands in her lap, gazing at her plate, in tears.

"Hey!" He put his hand on her shoulder. "I didn't mean to upset you."

"You haven't. I've upset myself. I don't know anymore what I want. I've seen you every day this week, sometimes several times in one day, and I've felt something I've never felt before. I don't even know why, or what it is. I thought I'd come home tonight and drink myself into oblivion, just drink until I couldn't think anymore, about anything. But here you are! Here you are! You've saved my life once and now you're behaving as if you'd like to save it again. I don't want to care. Caring's too dangerous. It's all wrong!" She covered her face with her hands.

"What's all wrong?"

"Oh, God!" she exclaimed, revealing her wet face. "It's all just talk, nothing more than talk; talk to protect me, talk to cover everything up. My mother died today, and I want you to make love with me."

"C'mere." He pulled her over onto his lap and brought her head down on his shoulder. "It's okay, Hadleigh. I understand."

"She actually said that, that she loved me?"

"She said it."

"She loved me. I knew she did. I did. Do you like me at all, or are you simply being kind?"

"Hey!" he chided. "I'm here, aren't I?"

"How am I going to tell Bonita?" she cried.

"You'll tell her. You'll be all right."

"You think so?" she asked hopefully.

"I know so."

Thirty-six

"Is it real, your tolerance? I've always wondered that about men."

"What've you always wondered?" he asked, at sea.

"Men say they don't mind, that they're just as happy, but all the while they're simply biding time, determined to have the outcome precisely as they wish it."

"Look, Hadleigh. Everybody wants the ending of his or her choice. It's not dishonest to hope for things. And I think the majority of people mean the things they say when they say them. I do, anyway."

"I want to believe you."

"How'd you get to be so skeptical?"

"I started at an early age. How did you come to be so open-minded?"

"Same reason."

"It's maddening! The one time when I truly want something, it won't work. I suppose it doesn't matter. It's as if I've always been tethered in some fashion. All at once, I've been cut free, and I don't know how, or what, I'm to do. It's absurd, but I feel orphaned."

"That's not absurd. What you feel is what you feel. Feelings are real."

"You don't seem angry or put out."

"I don't feel angry or put out. Want to try a few other things? Maybe I'll find something on the list that fits."

"I'm not used to being teased."

433

"Hate it?"

"No. It makes me feel young, as if you know the joke, but I don't. It's the adults who always know the jokes. They hold the knowledge over their children's heads with horrid superiority."

"You're not like that," he said. "And I'm no joker."

She looked at him. "You're not, are you? Why did she die?"

"Her lungs filled, she couldn't get enough oxygen, and finally her heart gave out."

"It was terribly odd, you know. Her eyes started moving very quickly, as if she was watching something. And then, all at once, she sighed, very contentedly. She sighed once more, and then she was perfectly still. I've never seen her look so . . . happy. Her features smoothed out and she looked as if she'd seen something that gave her immense pleasure. I saw it happen, but I can't absorb it properly. I can't believe there'll be no more special cigarettes and mineral water and limousines; no more Frances. I can't believe the telephone won't ring, that I won't hear her voice. It's as if a great part of me is gone. I have to keep looking down at myself, to be sure my legs and feet are still there."

"It's hard," he explained. "I know."

"This can't possibly be what you hoped for," she said sadly. "All this self-pitying preoccupation."

"Hey! You loved your mother, and she died. You're supposed to feel badly. It'd be a little bizarre if you felt like going out dancing."

"I wish Bonita were home." Her voice sounded small. "I can't think why I say that, knowing how upset she'll be. She adored her grandmother."

"The two of you will comfort each other."

"I lean far too much on her as it is. I feel guilty about it. But she's so competent and self-controlled, and I've never been."

"Maybe it makes her feel good to be able to be leaned on. Have you ever thought of it that way?"

"I never have. How is it you understand these things?"

"I'm on the outside. It's easier, when you're looking in, to see how all the pieces fit."

"What time is it?"

He lifted his watch from the bedside table. "Almost two."

"It's very late. You must be getting bored with me."

"Why're you so hard on yourself? I'm not bored. You're not boring."

"But we haven't . . . I mean, I couldn't . . ."

"Oh, look. It doesn't matter. You're going to have to take my word for that." He yawned, then excused himself. "That's fatigue, not boredom," he hastened to explain. "And anyway, talking's the best part of it. Sure, when I was about eighteen and always ready, I used to think it never lasted long enough. Eighteen-year-old boys are on a par with rabbits." He chuckled. "The thing is, I'm not eighteen anymore. Thank God. All the naked, potentially embarrassing stuff is out of the way, and neither one of us has died from it, so it's easier to talk."

"I would like to. It's just that I'm afraid, and I don't know why."

"You worry too much. I have to admit that knowing you worry about it makes me kind of self-conscious. I mean, it's a little unfair that I can hear and understand you, but the body's deaf. Tends to be kind of a contradictory situation, but men are like that. You have to learn to believe the part that talks, not the part that stands up and salutes."

"If I had a drink or two, I could do it."

"I'd rather take my chances on you sober."

"Why do men *want* women anyway?"

"Are you kidding? All this gorgeous warm flesh. Even blind, deaf, and with my hands amputated, I'd want to touch you. Did it ever occur to you that to a guy like me you might just be a miracle? I don't get to be with lovely looking women every day. I don't know why you'd even consider sleeping with me. I'm not that good-looking. I don't have any hot lines. I don't have the wardrobe, or the car, or even the right attitude."

"Perhaps that's what I'm attracted to."

"Really?"

"Yes, really. I was married to the man with the wardrobe and the car and the money. I couldn't comment on his attitude. I've never been quite sure what it was."

"I'll bet a hundred bucks you don't know how gorgeous you are."

"I'm not," she argued.

"See! I win. You want to know something? I bet you've never once stopped to think what kind of a thrill it would be for me just being seen having coffee with you in Howard Johnson's.''

She smiled. "Honestly?"

"Where've you been all your life, Hadleigh? I'm just Joe Ordinary from Lowell, Mass., who thought the best he'd ever get was someone who thought he wasn't totally revolting. I mean, I think I'm a pretty decent person and all that. But to meet someone like you is sheer stupid luck. I can't even believe I'm *here*, if you want to know the whole truth. I mean, Jesus Christ! We're naked and in bed, and we're talking. If somebody tried to take this dream away, I'd kill them. I only came over this evening because I knew you'd be feeling rotten, and I didn't want you to be alone, knowing you were feeling that way.''

"You're telling the truth, aren't you?" she said, with the sense she was being given something very special. "You are. I can tell.''

"Sure, I am. I mean, if there's a chance in a million that I could spend time with you, I'd take it. You're a great big delicious pink and white cake and I'd like to swallow you whole. I'd like to squeeze you so hard your bones'd crack. I'd like to nibble on you until there was nothing left but a tiny little pile of nice white bones. I'm *crazy* about you. So what're you doing here with me?"

"I think I'd like to be squeezed and nibbled.''

"God! You're going to get it.''

He made it possible for her to accept him, and she experienced a very real sadness when it ended. She felt altered by their intensely orchestrated motions together, as if she'd managed to leave behind the more fearful segments of herself.

"As first times go, it wasn't all that bad, was it?" he asked with a smile.

"Not at all. I only wish I weren't so hopeless at it.''

"Stop worrying, will you! Everything's just dandy. You feel good; you taste good; you smell good. You're just not all that experienced.''

"You can tell?" How mortifying! she thought.

"I'm tickled pink by it. I get to be the one to display the whole bag of tricks.''

"The day of my father's funeral my mother made love to a young friend of my husband's and mine in her dressing room. I don't think she was ever aware that I knew.''

"That makes sense, in a way."

"Does it?"

"Sure. It was her way of proving to herself that she didn't die, too."

"Do you suppose that's what I'm doing now?"

"Maybe. Probably."

"It does make sense," she saw. "Perhaps it's why I never felt angry with her for it. But viewing it that way, it shows how much she did love my father. It does. Vernon, she's beginning to make sense to me. Why does it have to be now, when it's too late?"

"Why is it too late? This way, when you think of her, it'll be with fondness."

"You're most perceptive. I like you very much. I have done from the start."

"I like you very much, too." He kissed her cheek, running his hand through her hair. "Would you like me to be here tomorrow when Bonita gets back?"

"What a kind man you are!"

"Nope. Just an offer of moral support, if you need it."

"But you *are* kind. I think, though, it might be best if I handle this on my own."

"You know something? You're not the coward you like to think you are. You're pretty ballsy, if you want to know."

"Ballsy?" she laughed. "I'm a terrible coward. I get sick at my stomach thinking of how I'll tell her, what I'll say."

"Just tell her the truth, that her grandmother's heart simply stopped beating."

"Simply stopped," she repeated. "Vernon, I want to make love again. I've never said or done such things in my life."

"Maybe it's time you did."

"I'm not afraid of you. I trust you."

The silvery touch of his exceptional caress took her into another realm of existence, into an immense watery cavern where the water sent shimmering sheets of color to pierce and dazzle her.

"I keep feeling," she told him later, "as if I love you."

"You don't want to confuse this with something else," he warned.

"I'm not confused. And there's no need for you to think you must respond in kind. When the children were little and I told them I loved them, I used to feel dreadful when they didn't at once parrot the sentiment. I'm no longer as young or as naive as I once was. I'm simply telling you the truth. There may be no value whatever in my love."

"Every goddamned thing about you has value. We're going to break you of the habit of downgrading yourself."

"If you choose to be with me, I'll be very happy."

"Maybe I'm so crazy about you because you're not very bright. Can't you tell when somebody's fallen for you?"

"No, I can't. Is that how you feel?"

"Yes, ma'am, it is."

"And we'll see one another again?"

"I'll come tomorrow when I finish up at the hospital. And the day after that, and the day after that, too."

She gave him a lovely smile he thought he'd remember his whole life long.

Bonita had the cab stop at the Central Park West apartment on the way to Grand Central.

"There's something I have to get," she told Tandy. "I'll only be five minutes."

The letters were under a box of unopened stationery at the back of Frances's desk, where she'd known they'd be. Without reading them, she put them into her purse and started for the door, stopping halfway there to breathe in deeply the sudden, strong scent of roses. There wasn't a sound, within or without, and after a moment, she continued on her way to the door.

Tandy said, "I don't care if I get in trouble. I'm glad I went with you. Will you call me tomorrow?"

Bonita said she would, then climbed into the first of the cabs waiting at the Darien train station.

Everything was confirmed by the silence of the house. Dropping her overnight bag and purse on the sofa, she went to the window, spotting her mother standing at the bottom of the garden.

Hadleigh saw her and held out her arms. Bonita went directly into the embrace, saying, "I'm sorry, Mom. I'm really sorry, but I didn't have any choice. I had to go. I really didn't think it would be this way."

"But how did you know?" Hadleigh asked. "Who told you?"

"Mom, can we go inside? There's some stuff I have to tell

you, some things I have to give you.''

Hadleigh frowned, confused, but allowed Bonita to lead her into the house.

"Sit down, okay?"

"Yes, all right."

Bonita got her purse and came to sit beside her mother on the sofa. "Grandma wanted me to, so I went to London. Don't interrupt, okay? Let me just tell you the whole thing."

Hadleigh listened to the whole story from start to finish with her mouth open, and looked horrified when Bonita got to the part about their visit to Amanda. For the sake of preserving her credibility, Bonita left out any references to the "connection," and simply narrated all she'd learned.

"I knew you wouldn't believe me, so I brought you something to prove it really happened." She opened her bag and gave her mother the paperweight.

"Oh, no!" Hadleigh breathed, holding the weight on the palm of her hand. "You *were* there! But whatever possessed you . . ."

"Grandma made me promise. And there's one thing more. She also asked me to give you these letters. She said to tell you she'd written them to Grandpa, but she wanted you to have them because there'd be a time when you'd want to share them. Could I go see her, Mom? Will you take me?"

"Of course, if it's what you want."

"Now?"

"Yes, all right."

Bonita got up to go change her clothes, leaving her mother with the letters in one hand and the paperweight in the other, and a head filled with the details of a story she wouldn't have believed, had Bonita not placed the proof in both her hands.

Hadleigh tactfully elected to wait outside while Bonita approached her grandmother's casket.

They'd put weird makeup on her and done her hair all wrong, Bonita thought. She was glad no one would see Frances looking this way, that the coffin would be sealed before she was buried on Long Island next to Grandpa.

"I did it, Grandma," she whispered. "I guess you know that, though. I hope you can still hear me, even though I can't hear you anymore. I knew it was over, but I thought maybe you'd still be here when I got back. There's one part of it you don't know about: I put a curse on her. She's not going to get away with what she did. I promise. I wanted you to know that. Okay?'' She straightened, her hands gripping the satin-lined sides of the coffin. "Boy! You'd really be mad. They did your makeup all wrong." Quickly, she looked around to make sure no one was there. Then she reached into her pocket, pulled out a tissue and carefully wiped away the excesses of eyebrow pencil, rouge and lipstick. "That's better," she said. "Well, I guess I'd better go now. I'll never forget you, Grandma." She kissed her grandmother's forehead, whispered, "Goodbye," and then backed away.

As they were driving home, Bonita asked, "What happened to her rings and bracelet?"

"I have them," Hadleigh told her. "I thought you'd like to have her jewelry."

"I would. Thanks a lot. How did your date go?"

'My . . . ? Oh, Vernon. He's coming round later. I thought you wouldn't mind.'

"Why would I mind? You like him, don't you?"

"Yes, I do."

"Good. I'm glad."

Hadleigh pulled the car to a stop in the driveway and switched off the ignition. "I've been thinking about what you told me, and about what sort of mother she was. I did love her, Bonita."

"I know that. And she loved you, too, Mom."

"I thought perhaps we could take a trip to England next summer. We could visit all the places you never got to see."

"Poor Tandy was really disappointed because we didn't see or do anything. We just flew over and flew back. I made sure she had tea at Brown's, though."

"Perhaps we could take her with us."

"Mom! That'd be so great! I know she'd just love it, and so would I. Could I call her and tell her?"

"Of course, if you'd like. And if her parents will give permission."

"Thanks, Mom. I know they will." Bonita flew out of the car and started running toward the house.

Hadleigh took her time, climbing slowly from behind the wheel to stand looking up at the cloudless sky. She had the sudden whimsical notion that her mother had become inextricably part of the ether and was somewhere up there, highly amused as she surveyed the scene. Hadleigh extended her hand to the sky, allowing her fingers to curl into the air. There you are, she thought, smiling, up there in the back of a bloody limousine, admiring the view with a glass of mineral water in one hand and a Nat Sherman in the other. She laughed, pleased by the image, knowing Frances would have loved it.

EPILOGUE

A registered package arrived for Hadleigh in early September. Enclosed was a letter from a firm of London solicitors that stated they were, in compliance with their client's last will and testament, sending her a bequest.

"What is it, Mom?" Bonita asked.

Hadleigh parted the wrappings, pushing aside layers of straw to reveal the paperweights resting like the eggs of some eerie creature in a bed of matted straw.

"I loved those paperweights as a child," Hadleigh said quietly. "I used to study them for hours on end."

"Are you going to keep them?" Bonita asked worriedly.

Hadleigh looked up at her. "I think not," she said levelly.

Bonita wandered over to the window as her mother replaced the letter in the box, collected some of the spilled straw, then carried the package out to the kitchen.

Gazing at the leaves fluttering down from the trees, Bonita thought, I did it, Grandma. I actually did it.

On New Year's Eve, which they spent quietly at home, Hadleigh gave Vern the letters she'd painstakingly copied onto her own stationery. The originals she'd put away for safekeeping.

"What's this?" Vern asked.

"I didn't compose them," she explained, "but that doesn't matter. They're self-explanatory; they say everything."

"Do you want me to read them now?"

"If you like."

"I'll read them now." He kissed the tip of her nose.

"As you like. I'll just go make a cup of tea."

"Ah!" he said. "They're *that* kind of letters."

She paused in the doorway to smile at him. "Yes, they are," she said, then drifted away.

He sat gazing into the space where she'd been, then tore open the envelope.

THE LETTERS

If I give you this letter, it will be because I've admitted to you that I've fallen, that for long hours at a stretch I can't stop thinking of you; images form and reshape themselves endlessly in my mind; I simply can't stop. It's frightening; it makes perfect sense; it's frightening nevertheless.

It would seem that I've travelled through time and so many experiences, so many broken moments when regaining my feet seemed to require more of an effort, more strength than I had left, only to arrive at this point somehow still intact, somehow even better able to understand the nature of caring, somehow able to care. That it's the audible track of your thoughts and outrageous laughter and compatible insights that pin me painlessly in place defies my comprehension. The last thing I ever expected was to find myself staring blankly at walls, reviewing events long past, and recent conversations, studying it all in an effort to see why and how this has happened.

The truth of life, regardless of the self-protecting day-to-day commentary we offer up to others, is that we all need and want very much to be valued. Some of us require particular appraising; I'm so delighted by the thoughts, therefore, you've chosen to share, so far, with me. You make me laugh; you make me pause to consider new thoughts; you have the selflessness to be complimentary.

My daydream scenarios have a common quotient: They all involve time, and the ripening of mutual appreciation. I've lived a hundred years; I've been old all my life. I want simply to be allowed to care, to be cared for in return, and not be judged, or vied with. It could just be, you know, that the reward for all the days survived isn't an uneventful and serene old age, but the discovery of someone who likes the sound of your voice, the pleasurable inquisitiveness of eyes and hands and heart.

I've had to write this in part to try to ease the not-unpleasant internal spasm that occurs coincidentally with my circular thoughts of you. This is new, and tremendous; I have enormous uncertainty and a dreadful, aching certainty. I would fear more than anything else falling in love by myself. I'm too old; it's too late. I don't want to be too old, or to discover it is indeed too late. All those years of hoping, where would they go? I suspect they'd collapse, ultimately, and suffocate me. How sad that would be, when all along all I really craved was to be with the one person capable of reciprocating the craving, the one who—along a parallel course—had also survived the flux of the years in order to arrive at this momentous time.

It's close to impossible to write about emotion without being maudlin, or overly sentimental, or simply cloying. The truth, I know, is huge; the love is there. It exists in an immense quantity, withheld for a lifetime—small doubts invariably prompt the withholding of certain vital elements of one's self from transitional situations—in the optimistic belief that somewhere there is one person whose emotional life has remained as successfully secret as one's own. It's you. If you are willing to be unafraid, to allow it to happen, to step into a state of trusting vulnerability, I am here. You've always known me, now that you think of it. It's simply taken the slow dissolving of all those others' faces layered upon mine; it's required the refining of your desires; it's needed all these years for the image, finally, to come clear: reality imposed upon reality.

My God! I love you. It's terrifying, but I'm willing to take the risks and stand revealed. I will trust you; I will value you; I will not seek to change any of those qualities that here, at the turn of life's road, I find most lovable. I will begin at your feet and paint you in the colors of my affection. I will be wherever it is necessary to be, and I will hope only that you choose to find me necessary.

I am already real; I exist in my own right. Now I dream of the perfect, respectful alliance of amiable minds. I could compact time for you, or make it elastic. I could, with my touch, renew your long-ago dreams: dreams spun on youthful, idealistic afternoons when everything seemed possible, in that time before life placed doubts upon your tongue. We have to go on feeding the dreams, you know, feeding on them while nurturing the secret, insulated by the unshakable knowledge that we are loved absolutely, as we dreamed we would one day be. Will you allow it, for both our sakes, to happen? The moment is here, now; a flutter of the eyelids, the briefest hesitation, and the wounded will vanish instantly, flying into retreat. It will be the last time. It's simply too dangerous to stand alone on the wire; too perilous balancing naked on the wire. I love you. Shall I meet you on the safe, other side, or shall I step out into the air and plummet from your view? I love you. It's always been there, an infant sleeping. Will you whisper, and tip-toe past it? Or will you scoop the giddy child into your arms, being brave, and risk the contagion of the giddiness?

You could, you might, throw out a barricade of words; the self-protectiveness may, by now, have grown stronger than your desire to be found lovable. In that event, I shall be defeated utterly.

My blood halts, shunts sporadically along fearful veins and arteries. There is everything at stake; there is nothing to lose. Help me and I will help you. I love you.

All of your life you've been looking for fire, seeking the heat of an involvement that would be the perfect compliment, the element of warmth that would thaw the incisive coolness of an overtime intellect. In the beginning, you believed absolutely that the quest would be of finite duration. Within a limited number of years, you believed, once you had attained your majority along with a certain insight into the hazards of the quest, the embodiment of the fire would present itself to you at the appropriate moment. Of course, this woman's potential for combustibility would be visible only to you, or to the rare few others like you, who were gifted with the ability to discern the flinty edges upon which you might make fire.

Time, though, offered other alternatives, challenges to which the clear, unfettered intellect responded. The heat-seeker subsided, sinking deeper within, to wait. Decisions made had to be honored; and perhaps the yearning to be singed, harmlessly but electrifyingly, was, after all, nothing more than a young man's delusionary dreaming.

In the intervening years, the pursuit of success and the love of tangible rewards were allowed to overshadow that still-living need. But at moments when in the company of others—especially in the company of others—your eyes turned opaque and the hidden hunger rose tenuously to the surface, scanning the round-edged horizons with a mounting sadness and an itching fear that, although you still sought to believe she existed somewhere, it was perhaps only within the boundaries of your own, increasingly hazy, imaginings.

Nevertheless, despite the vagueness of her features, her completeness remained clear. She was the one in whom you might immerse yourself without fear of being lost entirely; she was the one whose mind and body beckoned you ceaselessly, yet who had the wisdom not to attempt entrapment, but left you free to return again and again to investigate the dimensions of her thoughts and her flesh. She was the one whose eyes and limbs summoned you constantly so that, even when apart, your mind held her in its palm and you peered, with wanting and appreciation, at the glinting miracle of the single living soul who could not only contain your searching passions but could also turn, at passion's end and, with a knowledgeable smile, make you laugh, and then provoke your rested mind into galvanic thought.

She was the one who satisfied your sense of aesthetics but also the perennially acquisitive hunger of your brain. She had the skill to love you in elegant lust, and the thoughts to surprise you with their eloquent simplicity. She was the one with innate good taste, who would never perform embarrassingly in public or private. She was the one with whom the occasion was always perfectly met. Her sense of time and place and person was impeccable. And you'd given up hoping she might exist; you'd given up acknowledging even that that hope had once lived in you. It had become, with time, simpler to deny the need because too many gaudy dancers had flirted too close, only to reveal themselves deficient in body or mind. She could not exist, you had come to believe, because your need had reached a point of unseemliness. After all, what man, after so many years of living, could hope to have credibility if he admitted to himself, or to others, that he still sought the perfect other half of himself? No. The fear of ridicule, either one's own, or that of others, had grown stronger than that stubborn, shrunken need to give of one's self fearlessly, safe in the deeply rooted knowledge that there was sanctity in the giving. Go on! you scoffed at yourself. Don't be a complete fool! Admit that you're looking and every hungry woman within a hundred miles will come banging at your door in the dead of night claiming to be the one. No. Better to go below ground instead and cloak the last vestiges of your need with conversational philosophy having to do with the techniques of living alone, not to mention the rewards of living free of all responsibility.

In time, we all come to be of an age when we commence publicly prevaricating in order to hold harmless the dreams that have refused to die, no matter how experience and daily life have battered them. We lie. We've enshrouded ourselves in the trappings of routine, yet all the while, inside, a thin voice is whispering messages about your dreams. And you wonder why the damned things won't finally die and leave you in peace.

Then, one day, at that very instant when you've prepared yourself to relinquish your final hold on that all-but-dead need, she presents herself to you. A door swings open, and your startled eyes fill greedily with the sight of all you'd given up hoping you'd find.

The thing to be remembered is this: She was tracking a similar course. The only difference between the two of you is that she was slightly more quick to perceive your advent into her world. And now, here it is. This is it. Here you are, the two of you, together, striking sparks.